AI for Understanding Subtext in Film and Drama

AI for Understanding Subtext in Film and Drama offers a novel, rigorous, and deeply reflective approach to one of the most elusive problems in aesthetics and interpretation: how meaning emerges when it is not explicitly stated.

Drawing on film and drama case studies—from *Pulp Fiction* and Bergman to Pinter and Mamet—Prof. Yair Neuman develops a structured methodology for uncovering subtext through a disciplined tri-alogue between the human reader, the text, and artificial intelligence. This book introduces third-mind hermeneutics: a theoretically grounded, pedagogically applicable framework that uses large language models as tools for attentive observation rather than mechanical explanation. The result is a work that enriches aesthetic experience, sharpens interpretive skill, and extends the analysis of subtext beyond art to everyday human interaction.

This book will be of strong interest to researchers and advanced students, scholars in human–AI interaction and AI for the humanities, and educators teaching interpretation, subtext, and critical reading. It is suitable for graduate-level courses, advanced undergraduate seminars, and interdisciplinary programs that bridge the humanities, social sciences, and AI studies.

Yair Neuman is a leading figure in applying AI for the humanities. He is the author of numerous peer-reviewed papers and academic manuscripts, and was a visiting Professor at MIT, the University of Oxford, the University of Toronto, and the Weizmann Institute of Science.

AI for Understanding Subtext in Film and Drama

Yair Neuman

Routledge
Taylor & Francis Group
NEW YORK AND LONDON

First edition published 2027
by Routledge
605 Third Avenue, New York, NY 10158

and by Routledge
4 Park Square, Milton Park, Abingdon, Oxon, OX14 4RN

Routledge is an imprint of the Taylor & Francis Group, an informa business

Library of Congress Cataloging-in-Publication Data
Names: Neuman, Yair, 1968- author
Title: AI for understanding subtext in film and drama / Yair Neuman.
Description: New York, NY : Routledge, 2027. | Includes bibliographical references and index.
Identifiers: LCCN 2026022009 (print) | LCCN 2026022010 (ebook) | ISBN 9781041367864 hardback | ISBN 9781041367857 paperback | ISBN 9781042004485 ebook
Subjects: LCSH: Subtext (Drama, novel, etc.) | Film criticism--Data processing | Criticism--Data processing | Artificial intelligence | Motion pictures--History | Drama--History and criticism | LCGFT: Film criticism | Literary criticism
Classification: LCC PN1995 .N3878 2027 (print) | LCC PN1995 (ebook)
LC record available at https://lccn.loc.gov/2026022009
LC ebook record available at https://lccn.loc.gov/2026022010

ISBN: 978-1-041-36786-4 (hbk)
ISBN: 978-1-041-36785-7 (pbk)
ISBN: 978-1-042-00448-5 (ebk)

DOI: 10.1201/9781042004485

Typeset in Times
by KnowledgeWorks Global Ltd.

Contents

Preface

In life, drama, and film, we face "scenes" whose meaning is implied rather than explicitly stated. To understand a scene, we must therefore turn to the *subtext*, which is the implicit meaning of the text. However, understanding the subtext is a challenge. The challenge is particularly interesting in the context of film or drama, where scenes are intended to possess some aesthetic value or evoke a dramatic effect. It is not always clear, though, what the "inward significance" of a scene is.

This book aims to present a new approach for understanding subtext and the dramatic effect it generates in scenes. The approach uses AI, specifically Large Language Models (LLMs). In contrast to some attempts to use AI in the current social sciences and humanities, this book proposes a well-structured approach for understanding subtext *in concert with* AI. This approach appears to have several key advantages over traditional methods of text interpretation, as well as over naive attempts to apply AI to the humanities, psychology, and the social sciences. These advantages will be fully discussed. In a nutshell, what I consider to be the main benefits of the proposed approach can be defined both negatively and positively. Negatively, the benefit lies in avoiding overinterpretation of the subtext due to a subjective or ideologically/theoretically biased reading. Positively, it lies in a clear, structured understanding of the subtext, while respecting the text and its complexity.

This book is structured as follows. The first part presents the theoretical background and the AI-based approach for reading between the lines of a scene. Regardless of the academic tradition that compels us to cite our theoretical ancestors, my references are motivated not by the obligation of citation, but only by the relevance of the references to the main justification of this book, which is the use of AI for reading between the lines. Chapter 1 is a general theoretical introduction, and Chapter 2 presents the importance of reading a text through *attentive observation*. Chapter 3, "On terrible coffee, two embarrassed men, and an angry woman," presents a "functional" approach to understanding the subtext. This approach guides the analysis of case studies in Part II. This part comprises three main case studies (Chapters 4–6) that involve a structured analysis of subtext in film and drama. Whenever analyzing the subtext of a scene, I present the detailed instructions fed into the AI model and the detailed output it generated. Both the instructions and the outputs may seem tedious and cognitively overloading for some readers. Indeed, they are tedious and cognitively overloading. However, this is a book about using AI for reading between the lines, and the devil is in the details. To fully grasp the power of AI, it is best to pay close attention to how we talk to the machine, the specific instructions we provide it, and the outcomes that result from its thinking process.

Part III of this book presents a slightly different approach to subtext, described as reading *in-between* the lines. This approach focuses on identifying more complex patterns of subtext by examining absence, transitions, border zones, and silence. Then, in Part IV, I analyze several cases using the guidelines for reading in-between the lines. In this context, Chapter 8 analyzes the milkshake scene from *Pulp Fiction*. In Chapter 9, patterns of misaligned emotional intensity are revealed in *The Vortex*, a 1930s English drama. In Chapter 10, I analyze a scene from Bergman's tantalizing TV series *Scenes from a Marriage*. Chapter 11 aims to expose the subtext of an enigmatic scene that appears in Harold Pinter's play *The Homecoming*. In Chapter 12, I analyze the dating scene from the romantic comedy *Enough Said,* featuring the late James Gandolfini, best known for his iconic role in *The Sopranos*. Chapter 13, presenting the last case study, exposes the evil of righteousness in David Mamet's play-based film *Oleana*.

Each chapter opens with an abstract and concludes with a summary of the chapter's main points. In between, intensive efforts are devoted to understanding the subtext in dialogue with the AI. This process would be better described as a "trialogue," as it takes place between the human mind, the text, and the artificial mind of the language model.

It is my hope that, as a reader, you will benefit from this book, which presents a novel approach to studying subtext in film, drama, and real life.

Prof. Yair Neuman, Israel

DISCLAIMERS

This book contains analytical content generated with the assistance of artificial intelligence. The analysis is intended for academic, educational, and critical purposes only. All movie titles and characters are trademarks of their respective owners.

This book presents outputs from Large Language Models (LLMs) to demonstrate how AI can analyze subtext. The following tools have been used:

- OpenAI ChatGPT, GPT-5-mini model
- Anthropic Claude, Claude Sonnet model 4.6
- Google Gemini, Gemini model 1.5 pro (Google DeepMind)

These tools were used to analyze the subtext of films and dramas.

While the AI provides the initial subtextual analysis, the final interpretations and academic framework are curated and structured by the author, and their use is the responsibility of the reader.

Finally, this book includes very brief extracts from various film and drama sources for scholarly/academic analysis. These citations consist of limited portions of the original works (significantly fewer than 300 words per instance) and are reproduced here under the principles of *Fair Use* as provided for in copyright law. No copyright is claimed in these original materials, and all rights remain with their respective owners. The inclusion of these extracts is intended solely to illustrate the academic methodology presented in this book and is not intended to negatively impact the market for the original works.

Part I

Reading Between the Lines

1 Royale with Cheese
Subtext and the Inward Significance of Art

ABSTRACT This chapter introduces the concept of *inward significance* as the core of aesthetic experience and examines how subtext operates as its primary vehicle. Through a close reading of a scene from *Pulp Fiction*, the chapter demonstrates how apparent triviality, atmospheric cues, and misplaced emotional intensity generate a disharmony that invites interpretation. Drawing on Bateson, Berger, Peirce, and Aristotle, it argues that meaning in art emerges at the unstable boundary between the text, subtext, and the subject's mind, and that inward significance can be experienced but never fully articulated. In addition, the chapter proposes a novel methodological framework in which large language models function as tools for *third-mind hermeneutics*: not to replace interpretation, but to expose implicit patterns through structured dialogue with the human. Three central benefits of the proposed approach are presented: interpretive joy in dialogue with the machine, pedagogical applicability, and the extension of subtext analysis to everyday life.

TWO CRIMINALS IN AN OLD CHEVY

In *Pulp Fiction* (dir. Quentin Tarantino 1994), there is a scene[1] where Jules (played by Samuel L. Jackson) picks up Vincent (played by John Travolta), who has just returned from Europe. Jules and Vincent are criminals working for their crime lord, the notorious Marsellus Wallace. They are not young street punks, but professional and cruel hitmen doing the dirty work for their boss. Driving an "old gas-guzzling, dirty, white 1974 Chevy Nova" in a "homeless-ridden street in Hollywood," they discuss Vincent's experiences in Europe and the differences between there and "here." The physical setting of their conversation creates a certain *ambiance* that seems to influence our understanding of the scene, or at least sets the stage or scenery for the dialogue. What is this scenery? Can we describe it clearly in words? It is no easy matter to answer these questions. The *Set design* or *Stage scenery* serves as a background to the conversation and is not the focus of our attention. I used the approach presented in Neuman (2024),

DOI: 10.1201/9781042004485-2

provided ChatGPT with the description of the scene, and used the following prompt[2]:

PROMPT 1.1

Ambiance refers to the mood, character, quality, tone, atmosphere, and other elements, particularly of an environment or milieu.

##

Describe the ambiance expressed in the following scene: [SCENE HERE]

##

Output is in the form of bullet points with one word for each bullet point (e.g., SERENE, WARM).

ChatGPT described the ambiance in the scene as:

MODEL'S OUTPUT 1.1

[Model Output—Begin]

- GRITTY
- SEEDY
- MENACING
- RETRO
- URBAN
- RESTLESS
- DIRTY
- TENSE
- NIHILISTIC
- PREDATORY
- COOL
- CYNICAL

[Model Output—End]

When asking the model to use a single word to describe the ambiance, it used the word GRITTY and explained it as follows:

MODEL'S OUTPUT 1.2

Gritty means:

Rough, raw, realistic, and unsanitized—often showing the harsh or dirty side of life.

It's used to describe:

- Settings that feel dirty, rundown, or urban
- Stories that are violent, bleak, or morally tough
- Characters who are hardened, streetwise, or damaged

In your scene, the word "*gritty*" well describes the setting, given the dirty car, homeless-filled street, and tense, predatory vibe.

The model describes the scene as unconsciously communicating a gritty atmosphere. This atmosphere exists in the back of our mind, and it is important to understand it, as will be shortly illustrated. Note also that, while watching the scene, we are *unconsciously* exposed to the ambiance functioning as *stage scenery*. When asked to explain the meaning of a scene, you may want to recall this ambiance. Now, let us return to the conversation taking place in this gritty ambiance.

At a certain point in their conversation, Vincent asks Jules: "... you know what they put on French fries in Holland instead of ketchup?" and answers "Mayonnaise," to which Jules responds with astonishment "Goddamn!" and disgust "Uuccch!". This scene, like others in Tarantino's films, involves a kind of small talk in which nothing of substance seems to happen. The scene lacks powerful dramatic elements, such as shooting, plot twists, or moments of high tension. In fact, and from a critical perspective, one may even ask why one should bother learning about what the French call a Quarter Pounder with cheese ("Royale with cheese"), or what they call a Big Mac ("le Big Mac"), or indeed why it would be of interest to anyone that the characters discuss the way they serve fries with mayonnaise in Holland instead of ketchup. For those who watched the film and enjoyed it, these may sound like nonsensical questions, but for the curious and reflective observer, they may initiate an interesting discussion about the subtext underlying the above-mentioned scene in particular and the subtext of scenes in general.

THE QUEST FOR MEANING

What I would like you to notice is that the quest for meaning arises only when there is some kind of anomaly, difficulty, misalignment, or some other kind of "disharmony" that we experience when reading a text, whether the text is the script that we read or the visual scene we watch in a film. Let me emphasize that I use the word "read" in a general sense that is applied to all kinds of texts, from drama scripts to visual scenes.

We can elaborate on this point of anomaly by drawing on Bateson's idea of information as "a difference that makes a difference" (Bateson, 2000). In the above scene, there is a difference between the emotional intensity with which Jules responds (e.g., "Goddamn!") and the factual, neutral knowledge presented by Vincent (i.e., that in Holland they put mayonnaise on French fries). Moreover, Jules' response seems to be misaligned with the ambiance we previously identified. In the context of a "harsh or dirty side of life," such emotional excitement over the topping used on fries appears misplaced, an idea that will be fully discussed in Chapter 9.

These differences call for a resolution, and the place to find it is in the subtext. In all the cases we discuss in this book, a *difference arises that necessitates the use of subtext as an explanatory device*. It can be the difference between the emotional intensity assigned to minor issues and the emotional diminution assigned to important ones, or it can be the difference between the expected response to an utterance and the actual response. In all these cases, there is some kind of difference that invites us to dig deeper, because we experience it as a difference that makes a difference. In other cases, where the meaning of the scene is clear, there is no need to dig deeper into the subtext. Do you know the iconic scene "Anybody seen Richie?" from Steven Segal's action film "Out for Justice"? (dir. John Flynnis, 1991). Not much subtext is needed in order to understand the scene. However, even in this case, this scene, which I personally find hilarious, has its own depth; otherwise, it would not have become iconic.

Let me return to the scene from *Pulp Fiction*. If this scene had been a realistic representation of small talk, such as those we encounter in our daily lives, its aesthetic value within the general plot would probably have been negligible. It could have been a "filler" in-between the important scenes. However, this scene is not a representation of real small talk. It is *artistically imagined* small talk contextualized in a film, and as such, it should be experienced first-hand and analyzed.

To understand the meaning of this small talk, we should recall Edgar Degas, the 19th-century painter, who said, "Drawing is not what you see but what you must *make others see*" (my emphasis). If a film director is like a painter, then what does he make us see through this small talk? From a naïve perspective, this looks like a silly question because what we see seems clear. We observe two characters, and the script presents them in the context of time (morning) and place (inside a driving Chevy on a Hollywood, homeless-ridden street). The characters are two young men, one white, one black. Both are wearing "cheap black suits with thin black ties under long green dusters." The fries conversation is contextualized when Vincent asks, "But you know what the funniest thing about Europe is?" and answers, "the little differences." The differences he considers "funny" are the name of the Quarter Pounder and the topping used on French fries. Apparently, this is what we see: small talk between two criminals about funny little differences in food culture. This "text" lies in front of our eyes and is easy enough to read. However, art is not about copying reality, and the scene does not seem to realistically represent an idle discussion about differences in food culture. There is clearly more to it than the Quarter Pound and the topping.

THE INWARD SIGNIFICANCE OF ART

Long ago, it was Aristotle, as interpreted by Durant (1926/1922, p. 66), who realized that art is not (only) about "outward appearances." As interpreted by Durant, the aim of art is to represent not the outward appearance of things but their *inward significance*. (my emphasis). So, here we have a director making us see the "inward significance" of a piece of small talk. But how is it that we cannot simply "see" it in the sense of being able to articulate this inward significance? To answer this question, we can use the term "subtext," defined as the "underlying or implicit meaning that, while not explicitly stated, is understood by an audience" (Wikipedia). The scene is a "text" whose inward significance is in its subtext. While the director does not directly expose the inward significance, he manipulates us to experience it *through the text.*

This explanation appears to shift the center of gravity to the "subtext," the meaning that lies hidden beneath the surface of the text. It does not really resolve the question of what is truly happening in the drama and what its inner significance may be. It just pushes the explanation one level deeper, from the text into the subtext. This explanatory move raises the question of what this "inward significance" could be, why we cannot easily articulate it, and how the director manipulates us to sense this inward meaning. Moreover, it begs the question of where the inward significance is located. Is it somehow "underneath" the text? Only in our mind?

Identifying the inward significance of art is a challenge, first because it is not quite clear what is meant by "inward significance." Therefore, it is not clear what we are looking for. For instance, does inward significance refer to the *theme* of the film? This is an interpretation I would like to reject at this early stage in the book. *The inward significance is not the same as a theme.* It is not *the abstract idea underlying a work of art.* For example, by observing *The Conformist* (dir. Bernardo Bertolucci 1970), it is easy to identify the theme of conformity versus nonconformity in this masterpiece. However, the film's inner significance cannot be reduced to the abstract theme of conformity versus nonconformity.

Here is another problem associated with the idea of inward significance. Is there a single universal inward significance to a work of art? The answer is trivially negative. For my late grandfather (my father's father), who was born in 1894 and raised in Poland before World War I, there would have been no "inward significance" in this movie scene concerning differences between the two food cultures he was not familiar with. For a man of such a different historical and cultural background, there would have been no "inward significance" in Tarantino's scene or even in the film as a whole. Therefore, there seems to be no universal inward significance, whatever it is. It is therefore implied that, to understand the inward significance of art, we must decipher the *specific cultural code/s* through which a movie scene, for instance, results in "inward significance."

Let us assume that the above-mentioned scene has a culturally coded significance. Why can't we just "see" it? As explained by John Berger in his seminal work (Berger, 1972), "Seeing comes before words. The child looks and recognizes before it can speak." Berger points to the phenomenology of seeing and its precedence over words. From both a developmental and an experiential perspective, we first experience, then "talk" about it. As we think and reason *through the mediation of language*, understanding the inward significance of a scene must be secondary to the act of seeing it. There is the experience of seeing, and our understanding of it is only an after-the-fact analysis of or reflection on the experience itself, the latter being a primary experience that, to a large extent, remains inaccessible to us. When you read the opening of *The Waves* by Virginia Woolf (1931), you can sense her "primitive" experience of observing the sea. *The Waves*, however, is not this experience, but an *interpretation* and representation of it.

Seeing is not an innocent or simple process, and, as C.S. Peirce explains, there is no way to avoid some form of *mediation* whenever we cogitate. It means that the primacy of seeing is "viciously" entrapped in a cycle of seeing-mediating, and we already see through schemes we impose on what we see: "The relation between what we see and what we know is never settled" (Berger, 1972). Returning to Virginia Woolf and the opening of *The Waves*, it is clear that her rich poetic description somehow echoes the phenomenology of seeing. It somehow reflects the pre-reflective experience. Nevertheless, it is an interpretation of her experience rather than an unfiltered image of the image per se. For instance, describing the sea as "indistinguishable from the sky" is not pure perception but an artistic interpretation of it. Understanding the "inward significance" of the scene in *Pulp Fiction* presents a challenge due to the primacy of seeing and its mediated nature. Articulating the inward significance of the scene turns out to be far more difficult than might be naively assumed.

ART AS A MANIPULATION

Art is a form of manipulation grounded in a variety of techniques, some of which express universal aesthetic values, as identified by the architect Christopher Alexander (2002), while others involve specific codes of the medium and cultural codes at different levels of resolution. Being members of a certain culture prepares us to understand the inner significance of Tarantino's scene. However, this is an intuitive form of understanding that should be better described as experiencing. Intuitively *experiencing* the artistic value of Tarantino's small talk is different from *understanding* its meaning (i.e., inward significance). The overwhelming majority of those who saw *Pulp Fiction* and enjoyed it would have no idea how to explain the subtext of the scene, nor would they have been able to identify its "inward significance" and how it contributes to the aesthetic pleasure of watching the film.

In general, there is an inherent, unbridgeable gap between experience (e.g., seeing) and its interpretation. In art, this gap has a unique and specific aspect, and there is a good reason for this gap between the intuitive experiencing of art and its understanding. Art works like magic. Knowing the trick destroys magic, and therefore art, as a form of manipulation by the artist, hides its tricks. Here, I would like to speculate about one possible dimension of this manipulation. My speculation is based on the concept of *mentalizing*: "Mentalizing is the activity of holding in mind, appraising, and reappraising the mental states (e.g., thoughts and feelings) of others and the self." It is a basic "psychological capacity and activity" (Hawksdale et al., 2025). This paper speaks of a "structure of mentalizing consisting of four dimensions, each with two polarities." One dimension is automatic vs. controlled processing. It concerns the way we respond to events, whether impulsively or consciously and deliberately.

The theory of mentalizing emerged in the context of mental health, and it is clear why a preference is given to being controlled and reflective. However, when observing *Pulp Fiction*, our minds are powerfully drawn into a world in which they are *automatically* and *unreflectively* guided by artistic manipulations. *Artistic manipulations are possible only by intentionally loosening up and allowing ourselves to move deliberately into an automatic, unconscious mode of processing, which is far beyond the scope of conscious articulation.* However, and in sharp contrast to an individual who lacks control over his mental states, the participant in the artistic experience *willfully* and *deliberately* agrees to relinquish control over his mental states. He is like a participant in hypnosis who steps on stage and willfully accepts entering into the illusion. This self-determined positioning is unique to the experience of art. Here, the inward significance, whatever it is, is introduced subconsciously and in a way that cannot be simply articulated by reading the surface structure of the drama. This means that scenes, like the small talk previously discussed, have underlying, implied, and complex forms that are not directly and simply accessible to the observer. However, it also means that the observer of *Pulp Fiction agrees* to participate in an experience in which they are well aware that they will be manipulated, and that this manipulation somehow involves an underlying, hidden structure/pattern, which is experienced as the movie's inward significance.

Through the text, the director invites us to discover the subtext/s, which, in turn, may lead to the inward significance of the scene. Let me clarify. What we see is the "text." Through a variety of techniques, the text directs us to the implicit subtext, which, in turn, results in the aesthetic effect that we, as observers, may experience as inward significance:

Text → Subtext → Inward significance

Does this mean that the "surface structure" of the text does not count? The answer is negative. The magic cannot happen *unless* the manipulation occurs at the *boundary* between the text and the subtext. This is a crucial point, and missing it is one of the key, often-overlooked failures of "overinterpretation" (see Eco, 1992), in which the text is dismissed in favor of the subtext. There is no easier way to destroy the joy of reading *Peter Pan* than "exposing" it as a colonial novel, or the pleasure of watching Noël Coward's *The Vortex* (Coward, 1924) by interpreting it as some kind of queer melodrama grounded in Coward's personal sexual preferences. If there is a lesson to be learned from ideologically motivated art in the current West and *Socialist realism*, it is that subordinating art to ideology results in failure because a subtext is imposed on the text, rendering it the primary focus and overshadowing the original architecture of the artwork, where the subtext is implied rather than stated. The problem is even more acute because, in some cases, the primary focus is given to the reader and the reflective reading. The reflective critical stance that defines post-modernism has gained autonomy and superiority over what was previously considered the ultimate focus of art …

ART AS A BOUNDARY PHENOMENON

Art is a *boundary phenomenon*, and the magic happens "*in-between*" the text and the subtext, in-between the real and the imagined, and in-between the text, the subtext, and the reader. Like the *Borromean rings*, losing one element inevitably results in the collapse of the structure. Here, we may define the inward significance as *the aesthetic experience of the observer, which is located at the junction of text-subtext-reader.* This aesthetic experience is not about "beauty" There is nothing beautiful about the scene from Pulp Fiction. When using the idea of the aesthetic experience,

I use it synonymously with the inward significance of experiencing art. Art is a dynamic process unfolding in a mental space that Winnicott described as the *potential space* (Winnicott, 2018). Later, I will devote significant effort to explaining the difference between reading "between the lines" and "*in-between* the lines." For now, it is sufficient to understand that the inward significance of a painting, drama, or movie scene cannot be simply reduced to a single hidden factor we call the subtext, nor can it be trivially deduced from the text. The artist employs a multitude of techniques that manipulate our minds to expect, infer, guess, be surprised, wonder, and, above all, to effectively experience art in its deep complexity through its inherent ambiguity, which leaves enough space for interpretation.

In fact, there is a good reason to argue that the inward significance of art can be identified as that which *cannot be fully articulated or reduced.* This is an important point. The inward significance can only be experienced, but it cannot be *fully* articulated. The aesthetic experience, whether of a piece of drama or music, is like a high-dimensional space that we cannot visualize. Following this analogy, the inward significance of art cannot be seen, just as a high-dimensional space cannot be visualized. However, while a high-dimensional space cannot be visualized, it can be mathematically represented, used, and projected into a lower dimensionality to gain a more intuitive understanding. Following this analogy, we can think of the complex inward significance as something that cannot be *fully reconstructed* or articulated from the perspective of experiencing it, yet can be approached through the subtext. Like the observers in *Plato's cave*, we are left only with the shadows, while the real show happens elsewhere, beyond our reach.

In this context, reading between the lines is akin to a post-mortem analysis of the experience, where we ask ourselves: How did we get tricked by the movie? This form of analysis does not aim to replace the artistic experience with a cold, analytical approach, but rather to approach it from a reflective perspective. Reading between the lines may be considered an artistic form in itself, where, through careful analysis, the reader may find a different kind of joy in peeling away deeper layers of the drama and recognizing/creating hidden, previously unknown patterns. One should not confuse this reflective activity with professional criticism, which serious artists usually dismiss. The great film director Andrei Tarkovsky described professional critics as people who "categorically do not understand anything" (Tarkovsky, 2019, 46:40). This hostility, expressed by a great film director who was also a highly educated intellectual, can be interpreted as a response to interpretations that seek to reduce the inward significance of art to theoretically grounded clichés that justify the critique's status and can be communicated to readers seeking to decipher the mystery of a film.

AI FOR UNDERSTANDING THE SUBTEXT

So far, the challenge is rather clear, but what does AI have to do with it? One of my primary lines of research focuses on how artificial intelligence can serve as a tool for interpreting, rather than merely replicating, human meaning-making processes. In this context, I approach AI not as an engineering project, but as *augmented intelligence*—a platform for enhancing our understanding, a new way of probing the way humans construct, share, and transform significance across language, art, and social life. By combining *"attentive observation," deep theoretical orientation, AI tools*, and *human interpretation*, I aim to develop what may be described as *third-mind hermeneutics*: the application of AI and formal models to reveal patterns of thought, affect, and culture that are otherwise invisible (or difficult to recognize) using traditional methods, be they "qualitative" or "quantitative". In this context, my aim is not to replace the joy of the intuitive experience of art but to complement it through the joy of reading in-between the lines, through the mediation of AI.

Choosing AI as a tool and *partner* for the hermeneutic reading of a text is far from a trivial move in the current academic world. However, Large Language Models (LLMs) are a revolutionary platform for addressing the grand challenge of understanding human beings and their artifacts (see, e.g., Neuman, 2025). While LLMs introduce a revolutionary platform, one should not approach this tool in messianic terms, only to be later disappointed by the fact that current AI is too human to be fully trusted. AI is a powerful tool and of a kind unknown to human beings in the past. However, it is just a tool, and without mastering its use, we are liable to disappointments. I am always surprised to learn about people's disappointment with the tool. They are like adults trying to play the cello without taking a single lesson, then "surprised" to find that they do not play like Rostropovich. The problem is not with the cello, but with how we use it.

In this book, as in my previous works (e.g., Neuman, 2025), I advocate a modest and reflective approach to the use of AI, in the sense of *augmented intelligence*, that aims to empower rather than replace human intelligence. All insights presented in this book were generated *in dialogue* with the AI rather than as a simple output of the machine. It is in dialogue that the LLM should be used for a literature review, research of texts, and reflection. While the study of subtext has a long tradition (e.g., Laurent, 2021), the novelty of the current book lies in its approach to understanding subtext, which leverages the human mind in concert with AI to better comprehend the inner significance of movie or drama scenes.

Three clear benefits of the approach presented in this book are as follows. First, one may find joy in reading between the lines of a drama *in dialogue* with AI. This is, of course, a totally different kind of experience than the primary experience of art. By this joy of working with the AI, I do not mean the patronizing, smirking attitude of some academics who believe that, when they interpret, they are shining the light of Christianity upon ignorant natives. The joy I'm discussing here is like a child's feeling of revelation upon discovering, through the use of a powerful tool, something that had escaped their notice. Take the example of a child peering into a microscope and uncovering the inner structure of a leaf through the microscope's mediation. For some, seeing the patterns that connect (Bateson, 1979) may be a source of joy, and this is the first benefit of the approach proposed in the book. Here, the joy involves working *in concert* with AI to identify these patterns. One must realize the unique contribution of AI to this joy. The LLM is not only a powerful and efficient tool for analyzing text but also a tool for thinking with. We can use it to reflect on our ideas and even on the model's outcomes. Working with an LLM means working in concert with an artificial mind capable of dialogue, reflection, and unsurprisingly misunderstandings and errors. At this point, creativity must be discussed. I don't consider the process of identifying subtext a simple matter of finding pre-existing patterns lying passively beneath the surface. At a more advanced stage of the process, we can work in concert with the LLM's artificial mind to creatively "identify" the subtext. This process is difficult to understand but easy to recognize. Whenever a novel interpretation is generated, one which is firmly grounded in the text, we know that creativity has been involved.

A second benefit of the proposed approach is the ability to teach subtext *with AI*. It is a *pedagogical* benefit. The current qualitative approaches to interpretation suffer from well-known problems, including overinterpretation, ideological biases, and imposed schemes. Personally, I find no interest in reading a drama through ready-made spectacles, whether neo-Marxist, psychoanalytic, or post-colonial. The problem with these ready-made spectacles is that, in too many cases, they close rather than open the interpretive process. By that, I mean that, when we adopt one of these schemes, we might discover nothing new, only what we already knew in advance. For instance, many years ago, I realized that, for the neo-Marxist, each and every social experience can be reduced to the holy triad: (1) The rich and powerful who (2) exploit the poor and weak, and (3) the process in which this dominance is practically and symbolically maintained. Walking in the world with neo-Marxist spectacles, like any other ideological spectacles, blinds one to the multitude of meaning-making processes characterizing human beings. Indeed, the world includes many instances that illustrate the neo-Marxist holy trinity in action, but its use to understand the aesthetic experience of art is of extremely limited scope. Just try to explain the inward significance of Andrei Tarkovsky's films, such as *The Mirror* or *Stalker*, through a neo-Marxist perspective, or to decipher Noël Coward's brilliance using Lacanian psychoanalysis, and you will find yourself facing a dead end. There are, of course, sophisticated wizards, such as Žižek, who can greatly amuse us with their ideologically guided reading. His Lacanian analysis of popular culture (e.g., Žižek, 1992) is a masterpiece in the genre. However, once the charm has worn off, one could easily feel that reading Žižek is more akin to attending an intellectual circus than embarking on a scientific expedition, returning home from the jungle with some precious items that can be classified scientifically to teach us something valid and rigorous about the natural world.

One of the main differences between an ideologically guided approach, such as the one used by Žižek, and the one proposed in this book is that I aim here to expose the subtext through well-structured analysis of micro-moves in the text, rather than to reveal the "inward significance" directly using a guiding theory. A rigorous exposure of the layers of subtext is used to point to the inward meaning, and there is no claiming to grasp it directly.

Let me further clarify this. The approach used in this book does not aim to show, in a top-down manner, how theory is instantiated in the expression of popular culture (e.g., *Pulp Fiction*). It is a *theoretically oriented approach rather than the use of a theory for* interpretation. In Chapter 2, I emphasize the importance of attentive observation, which always begins with a respectful hearing of the text. Instead of rushing to explain it, we first listen to it. Next, we carefully observe it, and only then do we start applying our AI-based methodology, guided by theoretical concepts rather than the interpretive dominance of a single theory. Therefore, what I would like to propose is basically a *methodological* framework, in the broadest sense of the term, for analyzing the subtext of a scene, rather than an imposed theory, and I shall not assume that there is necessarily only a single subtext. Using this approach through a complementary process of top-down and bottom-up analysis, we can benefit from the deep insights gained by some theories without fully committing to them. For instance, we may utilize important concepts they introduce, such as the concept of *potential space*, while remaining flexible, free, and independent from religious or ideological dogmas that have been imposed on the text.

In summary, the proposed approach has a clear pedagogical application: making implicit meaning explicit through a structured methodological process, enabling students and researchers to develop interpretive skills while maintaining the necessary balance between exploration and exploitation, between use and discovery.

The third benefit of the approach presented in this book could have the title "Beyond Fiction: Subtext in Everyday Life." It is the benefit of applying the approach and methods introduced in this book to understanding subtext in everyday life. One of my colleagues, a psychologist by qualification, is always bothered by my research into literature, film, and drama as a source of understanding real human beings. She repeatedly reminds me that the characters in a novel are not real human beings and questions the validity of my analysis, asking whether it can be generalized to a population of real individuals. Writing this book has further strengthened my opinion that the analysis of film and drama is relevant to real-life situations. Understanding movie scenes involves grasping the inner significance of the interactions portrayed there. A scene cannot have inner significance unless it resonates with something that exists deep within our minds. This resonance is not only about the drama unfolding on the screen but also about ourselves as human observers. I could provide many more justifications for studying film and drama to understand real-life situations. However, I shall refrain from being too apologetic.

The bottom line is that watching films and drama has value beyond the aesthetic pleasure, per se. Drama evokes, and can then be used to understand, certain human dynamics in real-life situations. For instance, in one of the chapters, I present an analysis of *The Vortex* by Noël Coward (Coward, 1924). When I first watched the film, which is based on the play, I had entirely different intentions. However, upon careful reading of the play, I observed something interesting: misplaced emotional intensity. For instance, one of the characters, an elderly, gay, upper-class Englishman by the name of Pawnie, repeatedly uses emotionally exaggerated language (e.g., divine) to discuss unimportant objects such as his bathroom tiles. When I watched the play, I was not initially aware of this "behavior." This sparked my interest, and I began developing a structured approach to studying it, working *in concert* with an LLM to expose hidden patterns of misplaced emotional intensity. The analysis uncovered interesting patterns, the most important of which is that misplaced intensity is complemented by the diminished importance of other issues. The lesson for real-life situations is straightforward: whenever exposed to misplaced intensity, it may be interesting to look for whatever has been set aside and asymmetrically silenced. The methodology developed for analyzing *The Vortex* can be applied to a variety of social situations where misplaced intensity is evident, helping us expose the underlying significance of real-life scenes.

The approach presented in this book always starts with the "naked" experience of the drama. Some anomalies are then pointed out, and we turn to the subtext in order to resolve them. The analysis continues with a careful and attentive examination, through which certain details of the drama are revealed. These are details that are suspected to be cues for understanding what is happening between the lines. The process then proceeds through cycles of work with an LLM to methodically and systematically examine the details and expose the underlying subtext. In this context, the design of the prompts involves cycles in which, through dialogue with the AI, we carry out a structural analysis of the behavior of interest in the drama or film.

DISCUSSION

I define a structured LLM-based approach to analysis as:

> A theoretically guided and well-structured set of step-by-step instructions that can be used in silico by a large language model to (1) identify and analyze behavior and (2) uncover meaningful patterns.

The final step in such a process is the integration of the identified patterns with the original aim of narrating the inward significance of the text. It is in this last phase that we may say the proof of the pudding is in the eating. This proof primarily provides a novel understanding grounded in recognized patterns. The process is completed when we examine its outcomes reflectively in light of the potential benefits previously mentioned. First, readers should ask themselves whether they have found a benefit in working with an AI to read between the lines of a drama they have already watched. How is this process different from working alone or with a human colleague? Did they learn something new? Did they recognize layers they had not been aware of? Were they enriched by interesting interpretations?

Second, readers should ask themselves whether they have learned a *structured approach* for *exposing the subtext*. Can they replicate the approach with others and use it to expose the subtext in other films and dramas? In other words, do they find a clear pedagogical application in making implicit meaning explicit for students and for developing interpretive skills?

The third benefit, previously titled "Beyond Fiction: Subtext in Everyday Life," is that the approach and methods introduced here can be applied to understand subtext in everyday life. Each case I analyze includes such an example, and the reader may wonder whether they can apply the approach to better understand other real-life interactions. In this context, I will demonstrate how misplaced emotional intensity in *The Vortex* serves as an artistic distraction that, quite paradoxically, reveals the dark aspect of the characters' dynamics. I will show you how the use of AI to analyze gestures and facial expressions can help us read a scene from Tarantino's *Pulp Fiction*, this time concerning the price of a milkshake, and I will show you how to explain the anxiety experienced by Marianne in Bergman's seminal drama *Scenes from a Marriage*.

The main points of the chapter are:

- Art is about inward significance.
- The inward significance is not explicit and can never be fully restored.
- Subtext is the implicit meaning of the text.

- To understand the inward significance of a scene, we should identify the subtext.
- The motivation for understanding the subtext emerges from some kind of disharmony in reading the text.
- The challenge of understanding the subtext involves all the challenges of interpretation, including ideological bias and overinterpretation.
- LLMs are revolutionary technologies that can be extremely helpful in exposing and analyzing the underlying meaning, or subtext.
- Through the subtext, we may understand the inward significance of the drama.
- The main benefits of the approach proposed in the book are: the joy of exposing hidden patterns by working in concert with AI, a structured way of interpreting that can be shared, taught, and applied, and relevance for analyzing real-world situations beyond drama and film.

NOTES

1. In a film or drama, a movie scene is "a complete unit of storytelling, usually consisting of a sequence of events and dialogue taking place in a specific location and time" https://www.studiobinder.com/blog/what-is-a-scene-definition/
2. From now on, each prompt/output will be marked. Whenever one of my comments is inserted in the model's output, it will be marked with a right arrow.

REFERENCES

Alexander, C. (2002). *The nature of order: An essay on the art of building and the nature of the universe, Book 1: The phenomenon of life*. Center for Environmental Structure.

Bateson, G. (1979). *Mind and nature: A necessary unity*. E. P. Dutton.

Bateson, G. (2000). *Steps to an ecology of mind*. University of Chicago Press.

Berger, J. (1972). *Ways of seeing*. Penguin Books.

Coward, N. (1924). *The Vortex: A play in three acts*. Harper & Brothers.

Durant, W. (1926/2022). *The story of philosophy*. Dover Publications.

Eco, U. (1992). *Interpretation and overinterpretation*. Cambridge University Press.

Hawksdale, H., Meng, B., Feigenbaum, J., Fonagy, P., & Nolte, T. (2025). Measurement of mentalizing: A systematic review and development of a construct validity framework. *Clinical Psychology Review*, 102657.

Laurent, P. (2021). *The subtle subtext*. Penn State University Press.

Neuman, Y. (2024). *AI for understanding context*. Springer.

Neuman, Y. (2025). *AI for understanding human conversations*. Routledge.

Tarkovsky, A. A. (Director). (2019). *Andrey Tarkovsky: A cinema prayer* [Documentary film].

Winnicott, D.W. (2018). *The maturational process and the facilitating environment*. Routledge.

Woolf, V. (1931). *The waves* (https://gutenberg.net.au/ebooks02/0201091.txt).

Žižek, S. (1992). *Looking awry: An introduction to Jacques Lacan through popular culture*. MIT Press.

2 The Cat as a Looking Glass

Attentive Observation for Uncovering the Subtext

ABSTRACT In the previous chapter, I emphasized the methodology for using AI to understand a scene's subtext. This chapter takes a step back to discuss the attitude that should guide us. More specifically, I suggest that reading between the lines does not primarily depend on interpretive theory or technical methods, but on a cultivated capacity for attentive observation. Through three personal anecdotes drawn from art education, agriculture, and police detective work, the chapter illustrates how perception is often distorted by blindness, expectation, habit, and theoretical fixation. Drawing on John Burroughs's concept of "the art of seeing," the chapter emphasizes that deep observation arises from interest, patience, and emotional investment rather than from formal protocols. In this context, attentive observation involves a disciplined suspension of judgment and an openness to subtle, often imperceptible cues—the "faintest signs" that guide discovery. Literary examples from Hebe Uhart further illustrate how sensitivity to mundane details may direct us to hidden patterns of meaning.

THE ART OF SEEING

In *The Homecoming* (dir. Peter Hall, 1965), a scene occurs where the characters eat their lunch (approximately at minute 56). Please watch the scene. The full movie is available on YouTube. Now answer the question: Did you notice something interesting about the way they *hold their spoons*? Can you recall the specific details? Now, return to the scene and note carefully the different ways in which different characters hold their spoons. Have you noticed a pattern? Can you speculate about the meaning of this pattern? This brief exercise in observation aims to prompt a discussion on attentive observation and how it may prepare us for a more nuanced and demanding exposition of the subtext.

Understanding what is between the lines requires us to be good observers; otherwise, we may fall into the everlasting pitfalls of clichés, over-interpretation, or under-interpretation. In contrast to interpretive theories that are easily learned and applied (e.g., neo-Marxism), the art of seeing is a challenging and ongoing endeavor. To get a sense of the challenge, and as a second appetizer, I would like you to recall or watch the scene from *Pulp Fiction* where Vincent takes Mia to Jackrabbit Slim's, and they order their hamburgers and drinks. This scene is available on YouTube as well.

 DOI: 10.1201/9781042004485-3

Carefully observe the scene in the film from their arrival at their destination until they start smoking. Write down what you see. Next, try to explain the "inward significance" of their discussion over the price of Mia's milkshake. After completing this task, we can start discussing the art of seeing and its importance for reading between the lines. Keep the scene in mind. In the third part of the book, we will analyze it as the first case study.

Instead of defining the art of seeing, I would like to start with three personal anecdotes. The first concerns my experience in teaching painting to children. As was common at the time, I taught the children to paint still life by placing some objects on a stand in the center of the room. In one of the lessons, I put an apple on the stand. Almost all the children painted a nice apple with a stem (pedicel) and a leaf. There was one problem: the apple had no stem or leaves! The children did not paint what they saw, but what they thought an apple should look like. Almost 40 years have passed since this lesson, but I still remember my surprise. I tried to question the children about the gap between what they saw and what they painted, but I got no explanation. All of them noticed that the apple on the stand lacked a stem and a leaf. However, the overwhelming majority of the children painted the apple with a stem and a leaf. In fact, they were quite surprised to realize that what they painted was different from the real apple on the stand.

Many years later, as a professor in the department of cognitive and brain sciences, I interviewed a painter who was an expert in hyper-realistic painting. He told me that what he teaches his students is 90% observation and 10% technique. The imagined apple immediately popped into my mind. This anecdote highlights the importance of seeing and teaches us something interesting about how blindness and distortions are built into our cognitive system. This has nothing to do with "intelligence" or "education." Some of the most extreme examples of blindness and distortion are found among people considered to be intelligent. Therefore, the art of seeing involves a unique and complex sensitivity, more than intelligence or education.

A second anecdote concerns a totally different field: agriculture. My brother-in-law is a farmer who grows sunflowers for their seeds. The seeds are a popular snack in many parts of the world, particularly in Eastern Europe, the Mediterranean, and Asia. They are often sold roasted and salted. I have consumed these seeds occasionally since I was a child, and when he challenged me about their quality, I was taken aback.

The question arose in the context of greedy merchants who try to sell old sunflower seeds as fresh ones. "When you look at a seed," he asked me, "do you know how to identify an old, bad seed being passed off as a fresh one?" Up to this point, I had probably held hundreds or even thousands of seeds in my hand, but I had never taken the time to carefully examine one. His answer surprised me. He told me that greedy merchants polish the seeds in a machine to create the impression of a recent seed with a fresh, new appearance. It is an industrial procedure analogous to injecting Botox into an old, wrinkled face. Whenever you are interested in buying sunflower seeds in the market, he advised me, check their surface to see if they look or feel polished. If this is the case, they are surely fake. This idea had never occurred to me, as I had never carefully observed a sunflower seed or expressed any interest in the properties of sunflower seeds, nor in whether they were fresh or old. We are attentive when we have skin in the game. Otherwise, why should we care about fake sunflower seeds or fake honey, where the bees are fed with sugar rather than allowed to consume natural pollen from flowers?

The third example concerns detective work. Many years ago, I volunteered as a police detective. Once a week, I would take a gun and handcuffs and join a detective team for a night shift. Most of my shifts were with a tough Russian-born detective named Oleg. Occasionally, we passed a car that raised Oleg's suspicion: "Let us check the driver," he would tell me, "this guy must have a criminal record." "How do you know?" I would ask. His answer was always: "Experience." In the overwhelming majority of cases, he was right, and I was extremely curious to understand what he saw that I missed. Both of us patrolled together. Both of us observed cars with some people sitting inside or near them, but we did not see the same thing. "Experience" was certainly the magic word, but I never got an answer in the form of a protocol that told me how to see the same things as Oleg. The art of seeing existed as implicit knowledge gained through experience.

After working with Oleg for a couple of months, I started seeing things, incriminating signs that were not evident at first sight; the way people looked at you, the way they held their cigarettes, and certain features of their cars. Finally, I even succeeded in merging my academic background with the detective work. On one occasion, we received information from an informant that two groups of teenagers were planning to fight in a certain public park. When we arrived at the scene, we were looking for the leader, but we did not know who he was. Numerous teenagers were swirling around the park, and there was an urgent need to identify the leader before all hell broke loose. The detectives were nervous, and their threatening behavior injected stress into the crowd. I carefully observed the teenagers and noticed that their gazes were all turned toward one guy who looked very ordinary. He was a rather "gray figure" who blended into the crowd, with no special features that might catch our attention. I hypothesized that, under stress, the youths would turn their gaze to the leader to gain confidence and protection. My guess was that this gray man was the leader, a guess confirmed after we busted him and sent the testosterone-pumped teenagers to look for some more constructive activity. From a blind academic, I had finally turned into an attentive and effective observer.

ATTENTIVE OBSERVATION FOR READING BETWEEN THE LINES

What is the common denominator of these anecdotes taken from totally different fields? The first is that "seeing" is far from trivial. On too many occasions, we are either blind to the "faintest signs" or simply impose our predispositions upon the object (the apple anecdote). These are not children's fallacies, but pitfalls that also threaten adults when they need to make sense of themselves and their environment. In fact, adults and academics are highly prone to failures in observation and interpretation, given factors such as ego involvement, a lack of genuine interest in what is observed, religious devotion to certain theories, functional fixedness, and so on. However, there are other lessons, and to learn them, let us turn to an insightful essay by the American "naturalist" John Burroughs.

In what he calls the "art of seeing," Burroughs (1908) observed that what we love to do, we do well. This shows that a strong motivational factor underlies attentive observation. This motivational factor is powerfully expressed by Dillard (1974) in her *Pilgrim at Tinker Creek*. She was an attentive observer and lover of nature: "I learned to recognize," she writes, "slowing down, the difference in texture of the light reflected from mudbank, water, grass, or frog" (Dillard, 1974, p. 5). Her sensitivity to differences in texture indicates her great sensitivity and her talent for mediating, through writing, her unique perspective on things. In fact, Dillard teaches us that observation is not just the ability to notice minor details. She shows us that attentive observation is an *active and creative art*. When describing clouds as like a "tablecloth whipped off a table" (Dillard, 1974, p. 10), she actively and creatively directs us to look at clouds in a way we have never thought of before.

It is only possible to teach people to read between the lines of a drama if they love drama and have a genuine interest in it. *This is something AI cannot do for us.* In the previous chapter, I focused mainly on the methodological aspects of using AI to expose the subtext. However, there is a preliminary condition for applying the methodology: passion. The passion and the stakes should be yours. This attitude is crucial, and it must be accompanied by the suspension of automatic judgment and by an *openness* and *flexibility* to see what is not already preconceived in the mind. Let me repeat that. Reading between the lines of the text is no different from conducting good detective work. You must have a deep interest in the text, and you must approach the text with openness and suspend automatic judgment; otherwise, you may see a leaf when there is only an apple.

In this context, an important aspect of seeing, or what I would like to call "*attentive observation*," is to suspend immediate judgment, which is based on the surface structure of what is observed or on one's predispositions, and to carefully and openly *listen* to the text with both respect and interest. This attitude involves silence and observation rather than imposing oneself on the subject. When teaching my students, I find myself repeatedly asking them to suspend their judgment, a request which is sometimes interpreted as an attempt to silence their voices. However, for attentive observation, at least for the first phase, your own voice must not be heard; just shut up and listen, truly listen.

As Burroughs points out, attentive observation is about discovery, where the mind, like the detective eye, "reads the faintest signs" (Burroughs, 1908, p. 149). Observing with interest and reading almost imperceptible signs to discover something new is the art of seeing. "Power of attention and a mind sensitive to outward objects, in these lies the secret of seeing things" (Burroughs, 1908, pp. 151–152). Unless you attend to the faintest signs with great sensitivity, you can discover nothing, and the proof of the pudding will be in the discovery. If you are an attentive observer, you will be able to see things that a surface structure reading of the text misses. To understand the subtext of a film or drama, you must be sensitive to the "faintest signs." These cues point to the underlying subtext.

The Argentinian author Hebe Uhart was a great observer. In *A Question of Belonging* (Uhart, 2024, p. 191), she noticed that women swallow pills in a different way than men: "women grab the little morsel with their fingers" while men "gulp the pill from their open palm." I never paid attention to the difference between men and women in this mundane activity. After reading Uhart, I found myself amused to realize that she was right. This wonderful observation requires a deep interest in human beings and the ability to evacuate some inner space through silence and listening. It is what Bion, following Keats, referred to as *negative capability*. Reading Uhart, you can sense negative capability in action. She observed a minor and mundane behavior, such as swallowing a pill, and identified a pattern differentiating between men and women. Her attentive observation also extends to animals and herself. She observed (Uhart, 2021, p. 179) that whenever she was confused, she looked at how her cat perceived her to understand "what was happening" to her. She realized that her cat served as a mirror for her. Observing your cat and realizing that it mirrors your mental state is indicative of great sensitivity and a high level of attentive observation, both to cats and to oneself.

DISCUSSION

What can we learn so far, and why did I devote time to discussing attentive observation? The aim of the book is to introduce a structured approach to reading between the lines of film and drama using AI. What I would like to emphasize is that, to work in concert with the AI, it is not enough to feed it with prompts. To read deeply into the text and expose its hidden layers requires, first and foremost, a state of mind, described in this chapter as attentive observation. This state of mind is particularly relevant when we transition from reading between the lines to reading in-between the lines.

The idiomatic expression "to read between the lines" denotes the act of inferring meanings that are implied rather than explicitly stated. In conventional usage, it refers to interpretation guided by subtle cues such as tone, omissions, or contradictions within a text. By contrast, the form "in-between the lines" is not a standard idiom in English and, when taken literally, typically designates the physical *space* separating printed lines. However, when employed in a poetic or literary context, "in-between" acquires a distinct meaning. It evokes liminality, ambiguity, absence, border zones, and transitional states, transforming the phrase "in-between the lines" into a metaphor for the indeterminate zones where meaning is suspended, emerges, or dissolves. Thus, while "between the lines" signifies a culturally coded interpretive practice for identifying implied meaning, I use the phrase "in-between the lines" to emphasize a specific and more demanding approach to the subtext. To read in-between the lines, through the assistance of AI, requires us to approach the text with sensitivity to identify subtle cues and guide the AI in reading in-between the lines. The art of seeing is a prerequisite for guiding AI in reading between the lines, and more specifically, in-between the lines.

In summary, this brief chapter encourages us to adopt a particular mindset before utilizing the AI's perspective. The use of an LLM to read between the lines of a scene can be significantly improved if we understand our role in this process. Our role is not that of an ignorant subject asking the oracle for an answer. Working in concert with AI requires the appropriate state of mind, and our human intelligence, limited and partial as it is. In the following chapters, I demonstrate how to use AI to reveal a scene's subtext. The proposed approach is then illustrated through three case studies: a British play from the 1930s and two films.

The main points of the chapter are:

- Seeing is not trivial or naïve. Genuine observation is challenging and is easily distorted by ego, clichés, expectations, and theoretical biases.
- Predisposition overrides perception. The "imagined apple" anecdote illustrates how people often perceive what they think they see rather than what they actually see.
- Expert observation is experiential: the farmer and detective anecdotes demonstrate that skilled seeing emerges from lived, attentive practice—not explicit rules.
- Motivation and love drive perception: as John Burroughs observed, attentive observation depends on desire, interest, and emotional investment.
- Attentive observation requires suspended judgment: one must silence premature interpretation and ego-driven reactions if one is to truly observe.
- Sensitivity to "faintest signs" enables subtext reading: subtext depends on noticing minimal, often overlooked cues.
- Reading "in-between" the lines is a liminal practice: it goes beyond standard inference into ambiguity, transition, and indeterminacy—requiring a distinct epistemic stance to guide the AI.

REFERENCES

Burroughs, J. (1908). *Leaf and tendril* (Vol. 8). Mifflin Company.
Dillard, A. (1974). *Pilgrim at Tinker Creek*. Harper's Magazine Press.
Uhart, H. (2021). *Animals*. Archipelago Books.
Uhart, H. (2024). *A question of belonging*. Archipelago Books.

3 On Terrible Coffee, Two Embarrassed Men, and an Angry Woman

The Pragmatics of Subtext

ABSTRACT Subtext is the underlying meaning of the text. However, in itself, the concept of meaning requires clarification and "operationalization." This chapter presents a pragmatics approach to meaning. Building on the premise that meaning emerges through interaction rather than intention alone, this chapter introduces the idea of *meaning-as-a-response* as a dialogic model for studying subtext. Through illustrative cases—including the "terrible coffee" example and a grotesque sketch—the chapter demonstrates how a misalignment between the expected response to an utterance and the actual response may direct us to the subtext. A detailed, theory-driven prompting protocol is presented to operationalize this process using large language models. The prompts involve a systematic identification of speech act deflection and relational shifts. The chapter also provides a pedagogical adaptation of the prompts for student use and outlines their applications to real-life conflict analysis in intimate relationships. Together, these elements establish misalignment as a central diagnostic engine for computational subtext analysis.

WHERE IS MEANING HIDDEN?

In the previous chapters, I explained that understanding the inward significance of a scene involves reading between the lines, but I didn't define the idiom. The Oxford Dictionary defines "to read between the lines" as "to look for or discover a *meaning* that is hidden or implied rather than explicitly stated" (my emphasis). This definition describes reading between the lines as the process of uncovering the hidden, *implied meaning* of a text. The Cambridge Dictionary explains this idiom in a similar way: "to find *meanings* that are intended but that are not directly expressed in something said or written" (my emphasis). Both definitions use the word "meaning," which, from a pragmatics perspective, may be generally described as that which is communicated. It still begs the question of what is communicated. To explain this point, let us try to explain what is communicated by the following line:

> "Ride with me to get somethin' to eat, dog."

This is a line from a rap song, "Gin and Juice" by Snoop Dogg (1994). Here, the word "dog" does not refer to a canine animal but is used in a connotative sense

 DOI: 10.1201/9781042004485-4

(Danesi, 2003) as slang for "friend" or "homie." Understanding the meaning of the specific words, we can read the line as follows:

> "Ride with me" - come along in the car with me
> "to get somethin' to eat" - to pick up food
> "dog" - slang term for friend, buddy, or homie (like "dude" or "bro")

The literal meaning of this line is that Snoop Dogg is inviting someone to join him for food. Now that we understand the text, we may ask ourselves what it means. If we adopt the functional approach to language, then the question is: what is communicated by this line or even by the whole song? Asking what the song communicates is an expression of a functional approach to language. However, a song is not a representation of human interaction; therefore, to understand its meaning, it may be better to use a different theoretical framework. This is an important point. To expose the subtext, we should look for the implicit meaning. The perspective provided by pragmatics is only *one* possible way to approach the meaning of meaning.

The pragmatics approach is relevant when analyzing an utterance, which is the basic unit of communication. If we consider something as an "utterance," we assume that it is a unit of communication conveying a specific *action* through language. The pragmatic approach is highly constructive in certain contexts, while limited or totally irrelevant in others. For example, the "action" communicated by the above line is probably an invitation. However, the communicated meaning of the song cannot be expressed solely by the aggregate of the speech acts that appear in it. The meaning of the song cannot, therefore, be reduced to its speech acts or revealed through a functional analysis. As I repeatedly emphasize, theory should not be considered in dogmatic religious terms. It is just a tool, and tools may be functionally relevant in some contexts while irrelevant and potentially misleading in others. Moreover, analyzing the song reveals the importance of seeking meaning within the appropriate unit of analysis. A scene involves an evolving event that is multidimensional and multisensorial. We observe a scene where humans interact with each other. We see and listen to them, while simultaneously processing other contextual information that arrives, for instance, through the ambiance. When asked to identify the meaning of the scene, we cannot reduce it to a single unit of analysis, whether an utterance, a slice of the visual image, or any other constituent element. Meaning emerges as a holistic experience. However, when we are interested in understanding the subtext, we must analyze a well-defined and relevant unit of analysis. Here, I focus on the utterance, but it is only a partial and limited pragmatic choice.

To inquire about a subtext requires us to adopt a *meta-perspective* on the concept of meaning and to ask ourselves which theoretical framework and which concept of meaning may be relevant to address the challenge we seek to address. In certain contexts, meaning can be understood as a communicated action. This approach is relevant for analyzing human interaction at the utterance level. In another context, we may need to use a different sense of meaning. Here, I would like to start with the pragmatics approach, as it is extremely simple and powerful when applied with an LLM to understand the subtext of utterances in interpersonal interactions, such as those in drama and film. By reading between the lines, I employ this approach to expose the subtext through a *microanalysis of the interaction, as expressed in* the utterances. This approach, given its reliance on language, is irrelevant to understanding other aspects of a drama, such as the visual scenery. For example, the opening scene of Tarkovsky's *The Mirror* features a beautiful woman sitting on a wooden fence, her back to the viewer, gazing out at the countryside. Tarkovsky is a director who "paints" the scenes, with similar aesthetic sensitivity to Fellini, another painter-director. The scene portrayed by Tarkovsky can be frozen and presented as a stand-alone frame, retaining its inherent aesthetic value.

When we look at the scene, we intuitively sense that it is laden with inward significance. It invites us to ask whether the woman is waiting for someone. It invites us to speculate about the identity of the figure approaching the woman from afar. However, the inward significance of this scene cannot be understood through the lens of linguistic pragmatics. It requires us to adopt a totally different approach.

It is important to recognize that understanding the inward significance of a drama is a challenge that requires more than one tool and one modality. As explained in the book's concluding chapter, the best we can achieve is limited, partial access to this inward significance. Therefore, whenever I present a methodology for understanding the subtext of a scene, I will never claim to offer a silver bullet for deciphering the scene's meaning and inward significance. I consciously and explicitly adopt a limited and modest approach that can never lead to a complete understanding of the subtext. Here, and for the sake of simplicity, I begin with a specific approach that focuses on language and text. In the following chapters, I will add a visual analysis of facial expressions and body language. No one learns to play cello by starting with the prelude from Bach's Cello Suite No. 1, so I will start with the basics, acknowledging that they have no pretension of covering the complexity and depth of a scene's inward significance.

THE PRAGMATICS OF HUMAN COMMUNICATION

From the perspective of pragmatics, people communicate *functionally.* When someone says to his sweetheart, "I love you," he does not utter the words for nothing. His communication is functionally *expressive.* One of the clear benefits of the pragmatics approach is that it enables us to identify different types of speech acts, which are utterances that perform an action. What action is performed by the utterance "I love you"? The answer is complex, as expected, because it is context-dependent, but today, we have powerful tools for exposing the context (Neuman, 2024). The above utterance can function declaratively to announce a transition in relationships. It may be the first time the guy expresses his love, marking a transition in the relationship or resolving ambiguity over his feelings. However, there are many other possible actions that can be performed by the same utterance, such as expressing one's feelings and ensuring commitment to a long-term partner. Regardless of this complexity, the pragmatics approach tells us to map and understand the *actions* performed through language in a given *context.* To a large extent, this approach shifts the burden of explanation to the context, but it is nevertheless helpful in mapping the various types of speech acts and in directing us to look for the actions. LLMs are a promising platform for understanding context in pragmatics analysis (Neuman, in press), as will be explained shortly.

Sometimes, meaning is explicitly communicated in a way that, within a given context, requires no further clarification. In this context, the meaning of the communicated action is readily identifiable through the speech act. For example, when one arrives at a restaurant, and the waiter asks, "Would you like something to drink, sir?" he is using the *speech act* of *questioning*. What action is performed through the question? It is an invitation to answer. His utterance is functional as it seeks an answer. Notice that this utterance is inherently *dialogic* as it *expects a response*. This dialogic aspect is highly important, and it will be fully discussed later.

If we reply positively to the waiter's question, he may ask for clarification, depending on the level of detail in our answer, and we are supposed to specify the drink we would like. In this context, the meaning of the utterance "Would you like something to drink, sir?" is the communicated function or action performed by the utterance. For people well-immersed in the context, the meaning of this utterance is explicit and requires no intensive processing of additional information. No meaning is fully explicit, but in some cases, it is relatively easy to understand with no explicit reliance on a subtext. While context is *always necessary for understanding* (Neuman, 2024), there are situations where it is processed automatically and with minimal effort.

In other cases, an utterance can have an implicit meaning different from its explicit appearance. For example, phrases like "You are such an asshole" can serve as an insult or a critique. However, this utterance can also convey, through intonation, facial expression, and other contextual cues, a very different meaning, such as the pleasure a woman expresses at her husband's recent prank. The need to read between the lines appears when the communicated speech act of the speaker diverges from the apparent speech act of the utterance (e.g., criticizing). In the above example, "You are such an asshole" may be an *expressive compliment* delivered through *ironic assertion*, where the literal insult is pragmatically reinterpreted as affectionate praise due to the incongruity between semantic content and contextual appropriateness.

THE PRIMACY OF THE SUBTEXT

The more one examines human communication, the more one realizes that implicitness is not the exception, but rather the default state of communication. But why is this so? Why can't we simply talk "explicitly" and avoid all the trouble associated with implied meaning? There are several causes of implicit meaning, primarily rooted in the fundamental nature of language and the inherent difficulty of reading (Ortega y Gasset, 1959). Here are several possible sources of ambiguity in an utterance.

1. Structural-linguistic causes
   (Properties inherent in language systems)
   Polysemy and lexical ambiguity: Words carry multiple meanings, and context must be used to disambiguate them. "Bank" could refer to either a financial institution or a riverbank. A dog in a rap song means "friend." Selection of the intended meaning remains implicit in the word itself.

2. Cognitive-processing causes
   (Limitations and features of human cognition)
   Attentional focus: Speakers can only attend to a limited amount of information at once. What remains in peripheral awareness may influence meaning without being explicitly articulated. Background assumptions operate implicitly by cognitive necessity.
3. Pragmatic-functional causes
   (Communication efficiency and cooperative principles)
   Common ground and shared knowledge: Rational speakers omit information already mutually known. "Remember Prague?" relies on shared experience. The common ground itself cannot be made explicit within each utterance—it forms the background against which utterances make sense.
4. Social-interactional causes
   (Face management and relationship maintenance)
   Politeness and face-saving: Indirect speech acts protect both the speaker and the hearer. "Could you possibly…?" as a request allows refusal without direct confrontation.
5. Strategic-intentional causes
   (Speaker goals and rhetorical choices)
   Plausible deniability: Speakers may intentionally leave meaning implicit to avoid accountability. Veiled threats, sexual harassment, and bribery offers often rely on deniability: "Nice business you have—shame if something happened to it."
6. Rhetorical-aesthetic causes
   (Artistic and persuasive effects)
   Poetic compression: Poetic language achieves density of meaning through radical implicitness—multiple interpretive layers coexist. The ambiguity is the point, not a bug that needs to be fixed.
7. Psychological-emotional causes
   (Internal barriers to explicitness)
   Repression and psychological defense: Unconscious conflicts, traumatic content, or threatening material may emerge only indirectly through slips, symptoms, or displaced expression. The implicitness isn't chosen, but it is psychologically necessary.
8. Situational-contextual causes
   (Features of the communicative situation)
   Multimodal communication: Gesture, facial expression, prosody, timing, and physical context carry meaning that doesn't require verbal encoding. A raised eyebrow can negate explicit verbal content.
9. Power and ideological causes
   (Structural inequalities and dominant discourses)
   Hierarchical communication: Subordinates cannot always speak explicitly to superiors. Suggestions, hints, and hedging protect against the consequences of direct statements. "Perhaps the boss might consider…" instead of "You're wrong."
10. Unintentional or emergent causes
    (Meaning that arises without deliberate encoding)
    Unintended implicatures: Speakers may communicate meaning implicitly without being aware of or intending to convey it. Freudian slips, unintended

presuppositions, or accidental tone convey meaning that the speaker didn't consciously encode.

Let me summarize what we have learned so far. First, reading between the lines involves implied meaning, where, from the perspective of pragmatics, meaning is the intended or implied action (i.e., speech act) communicated by the utterance. Second, reading between the lines is the norm rather than the exception because human communication inherently requires inference for various reasons, including linguistic, pragmatic, and socio-cultural factors. Finally, it is no trivial matter to understand the communicated meaning of an utterance as it requires us to go beyond the utterance itself. Here, I would like to introduce a twist to the narrative so far presented. I would like to argue that, in order to understand the subtext of a scene, it is not enough to identify the communicated meaning of a speech act. The functional aspect of language, as expressed through speech acts, can serve as a first step in revealing the hidden subtext that carries a different meaning from that presented so far. To present a structured approach to going beyond the utterance, I would like to first introduce the idea of meaning as a response.

MEANING AS A RESPONSE

Previously, I presented the dialogic aspect of the utterance. An utterance is an action performed through language. It is a functional action in an interpersonal context and expects some response. Here, I would like to elaborate on this highly important aspect of meaning, starting with the work of an engineering professor in the late 1970s. The idea of meaning as a response was originally elaborated and presented by Neuman (2025a).

In 1979, Roger Conant, a professor of information engineering and a pioneer in cybernetics and information theory, published an insightful paper (Conant, 1979) that received little attention. To date, the paper has only had a few citations. This lack of recognition is comparable to the reaction to Conant's most-cited paper, which, to date, has earned almost 2,000 citations.

Conant's central thesis resonates surprisingly with the idea of meaning as a response, a pragmatic theory of meaning associated with the work of Bakhtin, as interpreted by Holquist (1983). We will need to look carefully at Conant's argument to understand this strange alliance between a Russian intellectual and an American engineering professor.

The context of Conant's argument is information theory and its success. Emerging in a narrow engineering context, Shannon's information theory gained enormous influence, well beyond its original, rather limited scope. Conant's paper first points to the limitations of Shannon's notion of information in calculating "the information carried by real messages transferred in the *real world of human conversation*" (my emphasis). Conant convincingly illustrates this point. Suppose he writes, someone is shouting, "Fire!" According to Shannon, the information of this message is reducible to the *probability* of its appearance in human interaction. If the probability of hearing "Fire!" is low, then it carries a lot of information. Let us assume that you have seldom heard the word "Fire!" and that the probability of hearing it is the same as the probability of hearing the word "mitochondria." According to Shannon, these two words carry the same amount of information. However, argues Conant, the meaning of "Fire!" is its "effect on those who hear it." It is the escape *response* that conveys the message's meaning, not its probabilistic aspect. The important thing about a *message*, whether intentional or not, is its *meaning, which is modeled by a corresponding response, whether the expected response or the actual.* As Conant suggested, information exists in the *relation* between a message and a receiver, and a message carries information if it *modifies the receiver's representation*, as will be evident from that person's response. The person shouting "Fire!" probably meant to warn other people of danger. Escaping from the theatre, the audience's response expresses the meaning of the utterance. The meaning of "Fire!" is the speech act of *warning,* expressed through the escape response of the audience. Conant further showed how to represent knowledge as a vector, similar to the one used today by LLMs, and how to model knowledge modification through transformations in a vector space. The modern expression of this approach is evident in LLMs, where all knowledge is represented in the form of dynamic, complex, and contextual numerical representations (i.e., vectors).

In sum, Conant proposed that the meaning of a "message" is expressed through its impact on our representation. From a general perspective, and through the model of deep neural networks, we can see how this idea applies to the problem of understanding the inner significance of a scene.

Imagine yourself observing a masterpiece such as *Under the Volcano* (dir. John Huston, 1984). It is your "self" observing the scene with its huge network of memories, cultural codes, associations, and sensory modalities. This network is a vast and dynamic structure that exists in the past, present, and future. It is a model already "trained," but one that responds in real time through its working memory and anticipates future moves through nonlinear interactions among the network's units.

While experiencing the film, your network responds. It changes, even if only for a short time, in a way that somehow corresponds to the film. Emotions are evoked, some guesses are made, and the network's holistic response and its temporary changes in response to the film constitute the film's inward significance, or aesthetic effect. However, let me return to Conant's idea in the limited context of human interaction.

Interestingly, Conant's theoretical approach aligns with Holquist's in his seminal work, *Dialogism* (Holquist, 1983). One of the central ideas Holquist brings out from Bakhtin's work is that meaning is fundamentally *dialogic*. Every act of speaking or writing is situated in a *dialogue*, even if the other speaker is imagined or absent. The notion of dialogue is not restricted, of course, to human beings. From the most general perspective, a dialogue is any interaction where messages are exchanged, interpreted, and responded to. In human interaction, when people communicate, they respond to an utterance (i.e., the most basic unit of communication). Therefore, *the meaning of any utterance is determined in part by how it is answered.* In this sense, meaning does not reside solely in intention or in the words themselves, but in how others respond to those words.

In Holquist's interpretation of the dialogic approach, to say "meaning is a response" is to emphasize that utterances become meaningful *only* in their social context, through the interplay of dialogue, and that the dialogic nature of language makes meaning inherently dynamic and unstable, always in a process of becoming through interaction. In other words, meaning is never fixed as in a dictionary. This is a crucial point, and one must thoroughly understand its meaning and implications. If meaning is dialogic and can be partially explained by the responses it elicits, then there is no need to decipher the mind's codes or the person's hidden intentions. To understand the meaning of an utterance, we just have to analyze the response it generates, and the meaning will appear before our very eyes. No need for neuroscience, MRI, or depth psychology, just a structured approach to analyzing utterances and responses. This is the first benefit of modeling meaning as a response.

A second benefit is that the need to expose the subtext may be signaled by differences between the utterance and the response. Therefore, when identifying a *misalignment* between an utterance and a response, we can use it as a lead to expose the subtext. The subtext is *the context supporting our understanding of meaning as a response.*

Finally, the idea of meaning as a response changes the meaning of a subtext, and this is a highly important point. The subtext is not the utterance's implied meaning but the *interaction's implied meaning, i.e., the dynamic pattern characterizing the interaction*. This understanding shifts the focus of our analysis, directing us to examine the inward significance of an interaction, including the aesthetic values derived from the text and its subtext.

Imagine you are watching a film from the 1960s. In the opening scene, the camera zooms in on an American suburb, then into a house, and finally into a typical middle-class American kitchen. Imagine it as the kind of house that appears in Richard Yates's classic *Revolutionary Road* (Yates, 1961/2008). A couple is sitting in the kitchen. The husband is reading a newspaper and addresses his wife, saying, "Honey, would you mind bringing me some more coffee?" The woman stares at him and replies, "Do it yourself, you lazy pig." This "coffee" example will be used in the current chapter with different variations. Now, given the minimal context we have so far, the wife's response comes as a surprise. The husband seems to have used the speech act of *request*. The action communicated by the utterance appears to be an honest and polite request for a cup of coffee. What is the expected response to what looks like a polite request? Maybe compliance. In such a case, the meaning of the utterance as a request would have been revealed by the wife's response. However, the wife's response involves a personal attack. It calls into question the meaning of the husband's utterance, at least as represented in her mind, and requires more context to understand whether the meaning of the husband's utterance points to a subtext to which we were unaware. To understand the gap between the husband's utterance and the wife's response, we should examine the subtext, which is the underlying meaning of the interaction.

Both Conant and Holquist focus on the process of meaning-making. They focus on the interaction between individuals, how utterances change representations, and how they are responded to. However, despite the theoretical appeal of this approach, a lacuna remains regarding how meaning-making can be studied "objectively," specifically through the mediation of AI. By "objectively," I do not intend to say that meaning exists independently of its interaction, an idea that contradicts the basic tenets of the dialogic approach; rather, I mean that the interactional and subjective *process* of meaning-making can be studied *structurally*, regardless of our own personal biases, inclinations, or theories. Moreover, I ask how the idea of meaning as a response can guide us in using LLMs to study subtext and the inward meaning of a scene. To address this challenge, I begin with several variations of the coffee example, the first of which concerns terrible coffee and a married couple.

WHAT IS TERRIBLE? THE COFFEE OR THE WIFE?

A famous question, attributed to Paul Watzlawick, is: When can couple therapy be terminated? The answer is: when the husband says to the wife, "This coffee is terrible," and they *both* know he is referring to the coffee. We can use this insight to illustrate how interactional meaning can be objectively analyzed within a specific context.

Imagine a husband and wife having their breakfast back in the 1950s. This historical context is important because the asymmetry of relations was quite different from what we observe today in the United States. In the 1950s, it was normative for the housewife to serve breakfast. Today, even discussing the idea that an American housewife would serve breakfast may be considered a justification for a lawsuit.

In our imagined scenario from the 1950s, the husband tastes the coffee and says, "The coffee is terrible." In response, the wife shouts, "You are such an ungrateful swine!" In itself, and given the limited context of the example, we do not understand the meaning of the husband's original utterance. His intention is beyond our reach. It may have been to point out that the coffee tastes terrible because it is a poor brand. Alternatively, he may have been suggesting that his wife is terrible because she does not know how to prepare a decent cup of coffee.

Deciding which of these two possible intentions the utterance expresses is not trivial for three reasons. First, we have no access to the person's mind. Second, it is not clear whether the person himself has a valid access to his own "intentions," and third, several intentions can be expressed by a single utterance. However, from the wife's response, we can infer that she interpreted the utterance as negatively loaded and likely a criticism. The idea of meaning as a response enables us to transcend mental structures and intentions, and to study objectively how meaning is formed "in-between" individuals, and how this meaning/subtext explains the clash that appears in the dialogue. It is clear from the wife's response that what she read between the lines of her husband's utterance was implied criticism. When he criticized the coffee, he was criticizing her. The subtext is evident through the wife's response. Here is a second example, this time from a dramatic sketch.

TWO EMBARRASSED MEN AND AN ANGRY WOMAN

My second example concerns a very short humorous sketch by Hanoch Levin. Levin was Israel's most important and influential playwright, known for his sharp, often provocative combination of dark humor, existential despair, and social critique. Here, I discuss a scene from *The Gigolo from the Congo and Other Characters* (Levin, 1994), a collection of short, absurdist sketches and monologues, often darkly comic and grotesque. These pieces reflect Levin's signature blend of existential despair, bodily humor, and brutal emotional honesty.

The title of the short sketch I use translates to: "Two embarrassed men and an angry woman." The context is a husband, his wife, and a guest seated at the table eating. The guest is the first to speak, asking: "Excuse me, could you please pass the salt?" This utterance echoes Searle's classic example (Searle, 1969), illustrating the illocutionary force of an utterance (i.e., what kind of act is being performed in saying something). The second utterance is by the husband, asking his wife to pass the salt:

Husband: Genia, could you please pass the salt?

This utterance implies that the wife did not respond to the guest's request. The first aspect of the subtext is that the wife did not answer the guest's request. It can be formalized as follows:

1. Analyze the given utterance
2. Decide whether it implies something that does not explicitly appear in the utterance (yes/no)
3. If your answer is "yes," then provide a short answer to the question: What is implied? What is the subtext of the utterance?

We understand that the wife did not respond to the guest's request, but the wife does not respond to her husband's utterance either, and he repeats the request:

Husband: Excuse me, Genia, could you please pass the salt?

This second utterance involves a repetition of the first, plus emphasized politeness (i.e., "excuse me"). At this point, the wife responds, and all hell breaks loose. Her reaction is explosive. She erupts with a long, furious monologue, accusing her husband of being weak, emasculated, soft, even impotent (?), attacking his masculinity in a grotesquely humiliating and darkly comedic fashion.

Here again, we have an utterance whose meaning can be naively interpreted as a request. The wife's response, though, has nothing to do with the request. She accuses her husband of "barking" and yelling at her as though she is a dog, and then blames her husband for impotence (?). Her response is misaligned with the husband's utterance. A trivial request is responded to with a humiliating personal attack and mockery.

When I was an undergraduate student, I read all the plays available at the university library at that time. I have read all of Levin's plays, and the above sketch effectively conveys well-known themes in his works, such as how a mundane domestic exchange can escalate into a grotesque, explosive, psychological confrontation. The sketch also includes humiliation, sexual frustration, power imbalance, and the raw cruelty often found in intimate relationships. Though the sketch is minimalist on stage, its emotional and rhetorical force is maximal as the wife's response shatters the facade of polite bourgeois decorum.

The misalignment between the utterance and the response is a trigger for analyzing the subtext or, at the very least, speculating intelligently about it. To address this challenge, I would like to utilize an LLM and demonstrate how the analysis can be applied to understanding the subtext of a scene from one of Noël Coward's most successful comedies, *Private Lives*. First, I present the general prompt and apply it to the coffee example. In the next chapter, I present the scene from Private Lives and analyze it to expose its subtext and the interaction's inward significance.

THE ART OF PROMPTING

LLMs require instructions to generate output. They are not inherently motivated to work. When instructing the model to do something, you are prompting it to think. Prompting can be simple. I can explicitly ask the model to expose the subtext and the inward significance of the interaction. However, as a language model, an LLM is prone to the same problems as a human being, such as the difficulty in understanding the concept of subtext when pursuing the idea of "inward significance." Prompting the model directly and explicitly may be effective to a certain extent, depending on the complexity of the task. However, the most constructive approach that I have found after many hours engaged in such projects involves working in concert with the LLM through theoretically oriented, detailed, and well-articulated prompts. For example, I guide the model to identify the subtext of an interaction by first identifying the speech acts that describe the utterance and the response. The decision to use speech acts is motivated by adopting a linguistic pragmatics approach. This is not something that the model can decide for itself. Moreover, the decision to focus on pairs of utterances and responses defines our *unit of analysis*. This is an important point because it directs the model's attention to certain units of the interaction. Next, I seek misalignment between an utterance and a response. Identifying a misalignment triggers the process of uncovering the subtext, but first, I must provide the model with an explanation of how to recognize misalignment.

Here you can see why I emphasized the methodological aspect in Chapter 1. I adopt a general theoretical *framework* (i.e., pragmatics), but avoid swearing loyalty to any particular *theory*. Understanding the difference between a framework, a theory, and a model is crucial, and my focus is on a framework that provides general guiding principles, rather than more specific details. Using the framework, I guide the model (i.e., the LLM) through well-structured, clearly articulated, stepwise instructions. By examining the LLM's output, I assess its quality, identify errors, clarify misunderstandings, and propose ways to improve the model. I also ask the model to reflect critically on its own outputs and to make improvements. This is not a single-shot prompting of the machine but a recursive process, monitored and regulated through reflection. Prompting is an art no less than it is science or engineering. The next prompt presents the general and detailed instructions (i.e., prompt) that we (i.e., Yair and the Machine) designed. I recommend that you read it carefully, regardless of the task's demanding nature.

PROMPT 3.1

PURPOSE

Use this prompt to systematically:

1. Identify when a response deflects from or misaligns with the expected speech act sequence.
2. Infer the interactional subtext of the response without speculative psychologizing.

This framework analyzes what utterances do in interaction, not what speakers "really feel" unless explicitly supported by evidence.

Required input data

Provide the following:

- Target Utterance:
- [Speaker A: …]
- Response Utterance:
- [Speaker B: …]
- Context Window (mandatory):
- If missing, explicitly write: no extra-context available.

Operational constraints

- You may analyze only what is linguistically and interactionally observable.
- You may not attribute:
  - Stable personality traits.
  - Long-term intentions.
  - Hidden psychological motivations.
- You may infer:
  - Interactional functions.
  - Relational positioning.
  - Turn-taking effects.
- All subtext claims must be:
  - Evidence-cited.
  - Structurally supported.
  - Confidence-rated.

Step 1: *Expected response mapping*

For the initial utterance, identify:

1.1 Primary speech act

Identify exactly one speech act, such as:

- Inform
- Request
- Complain
- Compliment
- Question
- Offer
- Directive
- Expressive
- Commissive

You may add up to two secondary acts if necessary.

1.2 Lexical and structural evidence

Cite the exact words or features supporting your classification.

1.3 Expected response type
What speech act would normally follow in conversational pragmatics
(e.g., acknowledgment, agreement, repair, reassurance, compliance, clarification)?
1.4 Conversational goal (interactional only)
What interpersonal move is being attempted?
(e.g., repair initiation, coordination, evaluation, solicitation, bonding)?

Step 2: *Actual response analysis*
For the response utterance, identify:
2.1 Actual speech act performed.
2.2 Typical adjacency function.
To which speech act does this response type normally reply?
2.3 Response focus
Does the response target:
- The content of the utterance?
- The speaker as a person?
- The relationship itself?
- None (non-sequitur)?

2.4 Response strategy
Classify the engagement style, for example:
- Engages
- Avoids
- Redirects
- Challenges
- Attacks

2.5 Paralinguistic/orthographic markers
List: punctuation, profanity, volume markers, timing, emoji, etc.

Step 3: Alignment Assessment
Compare expected vs. actual:
- Direct alignment: Yes/No
- Partial alignment: Yes/No
- Complete misalignment: Yes/No

3.1 Alignment score (mandatory)
Assign a 0–10 score with a one-sentence justification based on:
- Semantic continuity
- Adjacency pairing
- Topic maintenance
- Role-appropriate uptake

Step 4: *Deflection pattern identification*

If misalignment ≥ partial, classify the deflection type (select only with ≥2 supporting markers; otherwise choose "insufficient evidence"):

- Topic deflection
- Emotional deflection
- Authenticity deflection
- Responsibility deflection
- Temporal deflection
- Insufficient evidence

List the specific markers justifying the category.

Step 5: *Subtext inference*

Subtext as a bridge to inward (aesthetic) significance

(Open-Category, Evidence-Bound Version)

CONCEPTUAL PRINCIPLE

This step proceeds through two analytically distinct but sequential layers:

1. Interactional subtext—What the utterance-response pair *does and means inside the interaction itself.*
2. Inward (aesthetic) significance—What this interactional meaning *produces in the observer as an experience* (affect, tension, disturbance, irony, shock, recognition, alienation, etc.).

Rule:

You may not move to inward significance until the interactional subtext has been explicitly stabilized.

5.0 PRECONDITIONS

Step 5 may only be applied if the following have already been completed:

- Speech-act mapping (Steps 1–2)
- Alignment assessment (Step 3)
- Deflection identification (Step 4)

If any of these are missing, output:

"Subtext and inward significance cannot be inferred without stabilized interactional misalignment."

Layer 1—*Interactional subtext (non-psychological, action-level meaning)*

5.1 EVIDENCE ANCHORING (MANDATORY)

Quote only what is strictly necessary:

- Minimal textual evidence (≤12 words per quote): "…", "…"
- Structural cues observed (examples only; not exhaustive):
  - adjacency or delay
  - topic abandonment or maintenance
  - person-directed vs. content-directed targeting
  - escalation or de-escalation markers
  - interruption
  - repetition
  - non-sequitur
  - rhythmic disruption

These are examples, not a closed list. You may name other relevant structural cues if warranted.

5.2 CORE INTERACTIONAL SUBTEXT (FORMAL DEFINITION)

You must express the subtext of the interaction itself using this invariant structure:

> "Instead of [expected cooperative act], the responder performs [observable substituted act], thereby shifting the interaction from [prior interactional frame] to [new interactional frame]."

Constraints:

- No emotions
- No personality traits
- No inferred motives
- Only observable interactional moves and frame shifts

5.3 RELATIONAL CONFIGURATION (OPEN-CATEGORY DESCRIPTION)

Now describe what the interactional shift implies about the relationship-in-action, using your own analytic categories.

You may consider dimensions such as (examples only, not mandatory):

- Power redistribution
- Intimacy or distance
- Alignment or rupture
- Contestation or submission
- Exposure or concealment
- Coordination or breakdown
- Provocation or withdrawal
- Control of conversational trajectory

⚠ These are illustrative prompts, not a taxonomy.

If none apply, you must explicitly state that the relational implication is indeterminate from the available data.

All relational claims must be:

- Interactional (not psychological)
- Supported by evidence from 5.1
- Expressed as situated shifts, not traits

Layer 2—*inward (aesthetic) significance*
(Observer-Facing Meaning)
This layer answers:
What does witnessing this interaction *do* to perception, expectation, affective orientation, or moral attention?
This is not about what the characters feel.
It is about what the scene produces in the observer.

5.4 AESTHETIC ACTIVATION (OPEN-CATEGORY DESCRIPTION)

Identify the structural feature that generates inward significance.

This may include, for example:

- Disproportion
- Sudden escalation
- Norm violation
- Intimacy rupture
- Power inversion
- Ambiguity
- Cruelty without warning
- Absurdity
- Emotional dissonance
- Threat emergence

⚠ This list is open. You may specify a different activation source if needed, provided it is grounded in structure rather than psychology.

5.5 INWARD EFFECT ON THE OBSERVER (OPEN-CATEGORY DESCRIPTION)

Describe the aesthetic–phenomenological effect induced in the observer.

This may include, for example:

- Shock
- Unease
- Tension

- Irony
- Dark humor
- Moral disturbance
- Alienation
- Empathic rupture
- Suspense
- Recognition

⚠ Again, this list is not exhaustive.
You may name a different effect if it is precisely described and evidence-linked.

5.6 INWARD SIGNIFICANCE (INTEGRATED AESTHETIC FORMULATION)

Now integrate:

- The interactional subtext (5.2)
- The relational configuration (5.3)
- The aesthetic activation source (5.4)
- The observer effect (5.5)

into one coherent inward-significance paragraph, using this guiding form:

> "Because a routine interaction is reconfigured into [new interactional frame], the observer experiences [aesthetic effect], activated by [structural feature]. What initially functions as [ordinary communicative action] now reads as [experiential meaning], producing [tension/unease/irony/etc.] rather than stability or resolution."

This paragraph must:

- Remain observer-centered
- Avoid psychologizing characters
- Derive strictly from interactional structure

5.7 SCOPE CONTROL AND CONFIDENCE

You must conclude with:

- A scope statement, such as:

  > "This inward significance is confined to the observable structure of this exchange and does not rely on character backstory."

- A confidence level: High/Medium/Low

With one sentence explaining why the inference is more or less constrained.

You can see that the prompt is well-structured and detailed. Is it the only set of instructions that I could have used to address the challenge? The answer is negative. Can the prompt be improved? The answer is positive. However, given the quality of the above prompt, we may consider it good enough to test on another coffee example.

APPLYING THE PROMPT TO THE COFFEE EXAMPLE

The previous section provided detailed instructions for the AI. At this point, I used ChatGPT and ran the prompt on the following coffee example. The choice of the exact model depends on several parameters. Currently, there are several successful LLMs, and updates, revisions, and improvements appear at such a pace that I cannot recommend a single model. Therefore, I primarily use the models of ChatGPT, Gemini, and Claude to illustrate the analysis, rather than to determine the best model.

Running the above-mentioned prompt on a coffee scenario, I generated an output. Instead of presenting the raw output, this section summarizes and explains ChatGPT's output, point by point. The provided input was:

Husband: The coffee is terrible.
Wife: Fuck you!

First, the LLM identified the husband's primary speech act as a *complaint* and as "informing" (about the coffee's quality) as a secondary option. What is the expected response to this speech act? The AI suggested that it might include: acknowledgment, repair (offering to make/replace), reassurance, explanation, or agreement. The actual response, though, is different from the one expected, and the AI identified it as:

Abusive insult/personal attack (single-word imperative-style profanity directed to interlocutor).

The model argued that:

This type of response typically replies to a prior turn by attacking the speaker (person-directed) rather than the content; it often follows provocation or is used to escalate/close a sequence.

Moreover, the AI identified the response focus as:

Targeting the speaker as a person
and provided the following evidence: direct second-person target implied by "you" (person-directed), not addressing "coffee."

The identified response strategy is therefore:

Attacks/Redirects/Escalates. (It redirects from item evaluation to person-directed aggression.)

The analysis is supported by paralinguistic/orthographic markers:

- Profanity ("Fuck")—strong escalation marker.
- Direct second-person pronoun ("you")—person targeting.
- Lack of repair/mitigation (no apology, no follow-up)—abrupt.
  Confidence (for 2.1–2.5): High — markers are explicit in the text.

The next step tested the alignment between the utterance and the response and identified a complete misalignment. The model explained it as follows:

> The response shows near-complete semantic and adjacency discontinuity—the husband's complaint about an object expects content uptake/repair, but the reply attacks the speaker, abandoning topic and adjacency pairing; only a minimal conversational relation remains (the two turns are part of the same dyadic exchange).
>
> The next step analyzed the deflection pattern and first identified *topic deflection* using the following markers:
>
> - Shift of referent from "coffee" → person (content → speaker).
> - Non-sequitur adjacency (no repair/acknowledgment).
>
> It also identified *emotional deflection* through the markers of:
>
> - Strong profanity.
> - Immediate person-directed attack (escalation rather than calm redirect).

Up to this point, the model correctly analyzed the interaction. It was hypothesized that the husband's utterance was a complaint and that the wife's personal attack was misaligned with the expected response. The deflection is both *topical*, shifting from the coffee to the husband, and *emotional*, as expressed by the profanity and personal attack. At this point, the analysis provides justification for examining the subtext. The meaning of the husband's utterance as reflected by the wife's response violates our expectations and calls for an explanation. The meaning of this very short interaction between the interlocutors must be examined by turning to the subtext.

The core *interactional subtext identified by the LLM is as follows*:

> Instead of acknowledging or addressing the complaint, the responder engages in a person-directed, abusive attack, thereby shifting the interaction from a problem-report/repair-seeking frame to a confrontational frame.

This observation is rather descriptive, and what we are looking for resides in the relational configuration the model identifies as follows:

- Control of conversational trajectory transferred to the responder (the wife halts the repair sequence and reorients the topic).—Evidence: abrupt insult replaces expected uptake. Confidence: Medium–high.
- Rupture/contestation rather than coordination—the exchange foregrounds conflict rather than joint problem-solving.

- Distance or boundary-raising (the responder treats the complaint as an opportunity to attack, which can function to repulse or punish rather than collaborate).

The relational pattern invites us to reflect on the interaction's inward significance. In the case of the coffee examples, this is a low-hanging fruit. This is a toy example provided with no context. Nevertheless, the model correctly identified the aesthetic activation:

- Sudden escalation and norm violation (expected cooperative uptake is subverted by an immediate insult).

And the inward effect on the observer (phenomenological) is:

- Shock/unease at an abrupt personal attack in response to a mundane complaint.
- Tension due to unexpected power/trajectory inversion.
- Moral attention (the scene invites the observer to judge appropriateness and assess stakes).

The model further explained it as follows:

> Because a routine interaction is reconfigured into *a confrontational frame*, the observer experiences *shock and unease,* triggered by the abrupt abandonment of the topic and the *profanity-driven escalation*. What initially functions as *an ordinary evaluative complaint* now reads as *an interpersonal rupture*, producing tension and moral attention rather than coordination or problem resolution.

Following a structured approach, the model correctly analyzed our toy example. Interestingly, the same subtext appears in Levin's scene. In this case, too, the dramatic effect is generated by an abrupt personal attack misaligned with a previous utterance. This attack not only violates our expectations and social norms of conduct but also reveals the underlying relational structure between the interlocutors. A wife, politely addressed by her husband, responds in ways that indicate power relations, the externalization of conflicts, and the projection of hidden frustrations (i.e., the husband's impotence) into the shared social sphere of dining with a guest.

In a deep sense, Levin's humorous sketch is similar to the humor presented in *Borat* (dir. Larry Charles 2006). In both cases, expected social norms are violated in an embarrassing and unexpected way. Paul Watzlawick, a leading researcher of human pragmatics, communication, and mental disturbances, insightfully proposed the coffee anecdote. The inference that the implicit meaning of the husband's utterance is about the wife, regardless of any supporting evidence, is a pathological move. From the perspective of couple therapy, the micro-interaction that we analyzed is a signal that the couple's therapy cannot be terminated.

Regarding the *pedagogical* benefit, here is a one-page student version of the prompt that can be used as a chat sheet:

Speech act deflection and subtext—One-page student analysis sheet

PURPOSE

Use this tool to:

- Detect when a reply does not respond as expected.
- Describe what the exchange does interactionally.
- Identify what the scene produces in the observer (tension, shock, irony, etc.).

Rule: You may analyze only what is observable in the dialogue.
No speculation about hidden motives, personality, or emotions.

Input:

- Target Utterance: ____________________
- Response Utterance: ____________________
- Brief Context (if any): ____________________

Step 1. What was expected?

1. Primary speech act (circle one):
   Inform/Request/Complain/Compliment/Question/Offer/Directive/Expressive/Commissive
2. Evidence (quote 1–3 key words):
   "____________________"
3. Expected reply type (choose one):
   Acknowledgment/Agreement/Repair/Reassurance/Clarification/Compliance/Other: ____________________
4. Interactional goal (one phrase):
   Problem-solving/Evaluation/Coordination/Alignment/Bonding/Other: ____________________

Step 2. What actually happened?

5. Actual speech act: ____________________
6. What does the reply target? (circle one):
   Content/Speaker as person/Relationship/None (non-sequitur)
7. Response strategy (circle one or two):
   Engages/Avoids/Redirects/Challenges/Attacks
8. Markers you see (check all that apply):
   ☐ Profanity ☐ Repetition ☐ Abruptness ☐ Capitalization
   ☐ Long delay ☐ Emoji ☐ Interruption ☐ None

Step 3. Are they aligned?

9. Alignment type (circle one):
   Direct/Partial/None
10. Alignment score (0–10): ____________________
    Why (one sentence):

Step 4. Is there deflection?

If alignment is partial or none, check any that fit (must have evidence):

- Topic deflection
- Emotional deflection

- Responsibility deflection
- Temporal deflection
- Insufficient evidence

Evidence for deflection (one line):

Step 5. Subtext and inward significance

You may only continue if Steps 1–4 are complete.

Layer 1. Interactional subtext

11. Minimal evidence (2 short quotes max):
""/""
12. Core interactional subtext (fill in the structure):
Instead of [expected act], the responder performs [actual visible act], shifting the interaction from [old frame] to [new frame].
13. Relational shift (choose or describe one):
Power shift/Rupture/Distance/Contestation/Control shift/Coordination breakdown/Other: ____________________

Evidence from the lines:

Layer 2: Inward (observer) effect

14. Structural trigger (circle one):
Sudden escalation/Norm violation/Disproportion/Ambiguity/
Power inversion/Intimacy rupture/Absurdity/Other: ____________
15. Effect on the observer (circle one):
Shock/Unease/Tension/Irony/Dark humor/
Moral disturbance/Alienation/Recognition/Other: ____________
16. Inward significance (2–3 sentences)
Because the interaction shifts into ____________________,
the observer experiences ____________________,
activated by ____________________.
What began as ____________________ now feels like
____________________.
17. Scope & confidence
Scope statement:
This interpretation is based only on the visible structure of the exchange.
Confidence level (circle one):
High/Medium/Low
Why: ____________________

RELEVANCE FOR ANALYZING REAL-LIFE SCENARIOS

In Neuman and Cohen (2026), I propose an approach for identifying accepting and dismissive responses in a dialogue. In this work, I consider situations involving a conflict between members of a couple, such as:

1. Household chores: Disagreement over sharing household responsibilities.
2. Spending habits: Argument about financial decisions and budgeting.
3. Social plans: Differences in preferred social activities and frequency of outings.
4. Family dynamics: Conflict regarding in-laws or extended family interactions.

I also examine 20 escalating dialogue acts involving:

1. Blaming: Assigning fault or responsibility to the other person.
2. Personal attacks: Criticizing the other person's character or traits.
3. Sarcasm: Using mocking or ironic remarks that can provoke anger.

These dialogue acts may be useful in analyzing a marital conflict, and there may also be significant benefits for reading the subtext of a marital interaction, for instance, in a family therapy clinic, using the pragmatics approach and methodology previously presented. Imagine AI observing the interaction between husband and wife. Whenever a misalignment appears, the AI can get into action to expose the subtext. Applying a situational analysis (Neuman, 2024), the AI may identify a conflict over social preferences, in which escalating, unconstructive dialogue acts, such as personal attacks, play a major role. The AI may question the misalignment of utterances, analyze the deflection patterns, and use them to uncover the explicit meaning underlying the specific couple's painful interactions. This is a clear real-life application of the proposed methodology to the interaction patterns studied by Watzlawick and his colleagues using their revolutionary interactional perspective.

DISCUSSION

Here I will summarize the main points of this chapter, but first, I would like you to answer the following questions (yes/no):

1. Did you ever think that speech acts could be used to understand the subtext?
2. Did you ever think that misalignments and deflections between speech acts could direct us to an understanding of the subtext?
3. Have you ever been exposed to the use of LLMs to identify a subtext?

If you negatively answered these questions, there is a good chance that you learned something from this chapter.

This chapter began with a deceptively simple question: Where is meaning hidden? By trying to answer this question through pragmatics, dialogism, and concrete interactional examples, we arrived at a position that is at once both modest and demanding. Modest, because it explicitly rejects the fantasy of full access to intention, psychology, or inward life. Demanding, because it requires disciplined attention to structure, sequence, and response. The central move of the chapter was to shift the locus of meaning *from intention to interaction*, and more specifically, from utterance to response. By adopting the idea of meaning as a response, this analysis bypasses speculative mentalism and redirects analytic attention to what is observable: what was said, what was expected to follow, and what actually occurred. Misalignment between these elements is not treated as noise or error, but as a *diagnostic signal*. It is precisely at the point where interaction fails to proceed "normally" that the subtext becomes legible.

The coffee examples and Levin's grotesque sketch were not chosen for their narrative richness but for their structural clarity. In all cases, the dramatic or affective force of the exchange emerges from a disproportion between an innocent utterance and an excessive or deflective response. The insult, the eruption, or the humiliation does not merely add emotional color; it retroactively transforms the meaning of the initiating utterance. What appeared to be a request or a complaint is reconfigured as an act embedded in a power struggle, a relational rupture, or a long-standing interactional pattern. The subtext, in this sense, is not hidden behind the utterance but revealed through the response.

This shift has several important implications. First, it reframes subtext as an *interactional* phenomenon rather than a psychological one. The subtext is not what the speaker "really meant," but what the interaction does. Second, it allows us to treat subtext as something that can be analyzed systematically, without collapsing into subjective impressionism. By grounding the analysis in speech acts, expected adjacency pairs, and observable deflections, we can explain why a particular exchange invites deeper interpretation. Third, it opens a clear methodological pathway for using LLMs—not as mind-readers, but as structured observers of interaction.

The detailed prompting protocol presented in this chapter is therefore not just a technical appendix but a theoretical commitment translated into operational form. Each constraint in the prompt—prohibiting psychologizing, enforcing evidence citation, stabilizing interactional misalignment before aesthetic interpretation—reflects the chapter's core epistemological stance. The model is not asked to be clever or insightful in a literary sense; it is asked to be careful. When it succeeds, it does so by making explicit what human readers often grasp intuitively but cannot easily articulate.

Finally, the notion of inward (aesthetic) significance emerges here not as a rival to interactional analysis but as its consequence. Once the interactional subtext is revealed, we can ask what the exchange does to the observer: how it produces shock, unease, dark humor, or moral disturbance. In this framework, aesthetic experience is not mystified; it is anchored in structural features such as escalation, norm violation, and frame rupture. What we feel as viewers or readers is inseparable from the way the interaction unfolds.

In this sense, the chapter does not offer a general theory of meaning, nor does it claim to exhaust the richness of dramatic interpretation. It offers something narrower and, for that reason, more robust: a way of noticing when meaning becomes problematic, a method for articulating why it becomes problematic, and a disciplined path from interactional anomaly to subtext and inward significance. If the chapter has succeeded, it should have made ordinary exchanges feel slightly less ordinary—and moments of communicative breakdown feel newly intelligible.

The main points of the chapter are:

- Reading between the lines is looking for the subtext: the hidden or implied meaning.
- "Meaning" can be understood in several ways.
- The functional/pragmatics approach to meaning focuses on actions performed through language (i.e., speech acts).
- Meaning is usually implicit for several reasons.
- Meaning-as-a-response suggests that the subtext is the interaction's implied dialogic meaning.

- The subtext represents the *interactional* dynamics between the interlocutors.
- Misalignment between utterances directs us to the subtext.
- The chapter provides a structured prompt for identifying the subtext.
- The prompt is applied to the coffee example.
- A student's version of the prompt is provided to support learning and training.

REFERENCES

Conant, R. C. (1979). A vector theory of information. *Annals of the International Communication Association*, *3*(1), 177–194.

Danesi, M. (2003). Metaphorical "networks" and verbal communication: A semiotic perspective of human discourse. *Sign Systems Studies*, *31*(2), 341–364.

Holquist, M. (1983). *Dialogism*. Routledge.

Levin, H. (1994). *The gigolo from the Congo and other characters.* United Kibbutz Press.

Neuman, Y. (2024). *AI for understanding context.* Springer.

Neuman, Y. (2025). *AI for understanding human conversations.* Routledge.

Neuman, Y. (2025a). An AI-supported methodology for analyzing deflections and misalignments in human interactions. *Integrative Psychological and Behavioral Science*, *59*, Article 74.

Neuman, Y. (in press). Large language models for understanding context: Implications for pragmatics analysis. In N. Taguchi (Ed.), *Generative AI for pragmatics analysis and pragmatics teaching.* Cambridge University Press.

Neuman, Y., & Cohen, Y. (2026). Automated detection of acceptive and dismissive dialogue acts: A synthetic LLM-based dataset and a SetFit classification model. In *Proceedings of the International Congress on Information and Communication Technology (ICICT 2026).*

Ortega y Gasset, J. (1959). The difficulty of reading. *Diogenes*, *7*(28), 1–17.

Searle, J. R. (1969). *Speech acts: An essay in the philosophy of language.* Cambridge University Press.

Yates, R. (2008). *Revolutionary Road.* Vintage Books. (Original work published 1961)

Part II

Case Studies

4 A Honeymoon That Went Wrong

Subtext in Private Lives

ABSTRACT The previous chapter presented a functional approach for exposing subtext through the analysis of misalignment. This chapter applies this methodology to a concrete dramatic text, Noël Coward's *Private Lives*. Focusing on a brief micro-interaction from the opening honeymoon scene between Sibyl and Elyot, the chapter demonstrates how subtle deviations in speech acts, emotional reciprocity, and response structure generate diagnostically rich subtext. Using the LLM, I map emotional deflections and shifting alignments that come together to expose an asymmetrical relational pattern beneath the surface of romantic celebration. The analysis demonstrates how minimal discursive moves generate inward aesthetic significance through tension, irony, and instability.

WHAT DO YOU EXPECT OF A HONEYMOON?

Previously, I presented one possible procedure for analyzing the subtext of an interaction and understanding its inward significance. For simplicity, I focused on a decontextualized toy example, but now, I would like to test the approach on a drama. Therefore, I analyze a micro-interaction from *Private Lives*. The case study was originally presented in Neuman (2025) and is elaborated here to analyze the subtext.

Noël Coward's *Private Lives* is a highly successful romantic comedy from the 1930s. My discussion refers both to the written play (Coward, 2013) and the 1976 BBC TV version, featuring Penelope Keith as Amanda and Alec McCowen as Elyot. The comedy describes a divorced couple named Elyot and Amanda. While celebrating his honeymoon with his new wife, Sibyl, Elyot unexpectedly encounters his ex-wife, Amanda, who has also arrived at the same hotel in France to celebrate her honeymoon with her new husband, Victor. Although divorced for five years, their meeting revives their love, setting the stage for a stormy, chaotic plot. With its tantalizing ups and downs, this comedy has been intensively studied, with some interpretations wittingly described by Coward as intelligent but "absolute rubbish" (Richards, 1970).

Producing a verdict of intelligent but absolute rubbish is a danger facing the interpretation of any play, especially when one tries to expose the subtext of a scene. This danger has been discussed before, specifically in the context of shifting attention from the aesthetic-intuitive experience of the play to its analytic understanding. At the same time, while watching the play, one may intuitively grasp patterns of interaction. If such patterns do exist, then it means that some interpretations of the play are

DOI: 10.1201/9781042004485-6

more reasonable than others, and in particular, others that involve *overinterpretations*. The ability to ground our intuition in patterns is a challenge, but a challenge no different from any attempt to seriously understand the meaning of human interactions. For instance, in the play's opening scene, Sybil stands on the balcony, amazed by the view. She says (Coward, 2013, p. 10):

> "It's heavenly, look at the lights of the yacht reflected in the water. Oh dear, I'm so happy."
> Smiling, Elyot responds to this utterance, saying:
> "Are you?"

These two lines of dialogue from the opening scene illustrate the promise and difficulty of understanding the meaning of an interaction through micro-level analysis. Let me explain. Elyot's new wife appears to be excited. She has just been married and has arrived in France to celebrate her honeymoon. The context of a happy new marriage, a honeymoon in France, and a breathtaking vista merge into a sense of excitement. She shares her excitement with her new husband, who responds with the question: "Are you?"

What is the meaning of Elyot's response? To what extent does this micro-interaction represent a (mis)alignment between the interlocutors? Is it a skeptical comment? A humorous teasing? What does it teach us about how he understood his wife's utterance? Does it represent a more general pattern of interaction? Is it possible to identify the subtext of this short exchange? To answer these questions, we should read between the lines.

UNDERSTANDING THE INTERACTION

To recall from the previous chapter, an alignment exists when there is a correspondence between the conversational moves of the speakers. If Sybil shares her excitement, she probably expects Elyot to *acknowledge* her excitement rather than question her happiness. In cases of misalignment, we can identify a deflection point that may be highly informative for understanding the subtext and the interaction's inward significance. Specifically, it may help us better understand the turmoil in the play's dynamics, its romantic moments, and its interpersonal crises. Beyond the benefit of reading between the lines of this play, this understanding may be highly informative for understanding fractures and crises in real-life interpersonal relationships. To analyze this micro-interaction, I used the previously presented prompt (see Chapter 3). This time, I provided the AI with the context preceding Sybil's utterance and Elyot's response:

> The scene opens on a hotel terrace in France, on a warm evening. An orchestra can be heard playing somewhere nearby. A young woman, Sibyl Chase, steps out through the windows onto the terrace. She is blonde, pretty, and dressed smartly for travel. She walks forward, stretches her arms wide, and takes in the view with an expression of pure, unguarded happiness. It is a small, wordless moment, but it establishes the mood efficiently: we are in a world of pleasure and elegance, of continental hotels and evening orchestras, and this young woman is exactly where she wants to be. Everything, for now, feels perfectly right.

Sibyl calls for Elyot, urging him to come out and share the view with her. Her tone is warm and a little impatient, the way you speak to someone you're sure will agree with you once they see it for themselves. Elyot calls back that he'll be a minute.

It's a tiny exchange, but it already sketches the dynamic between them. She is fully present in the moment, open to it, wanting to share it. He is somewhere else, not quite there yet. She uses an intimate nickname—"Eli"—and the added "dear" has the slightly insistent tenderness of a newlywed who hasn't yet learned that her enthusiasm isn't always contagious.

After a pause, Elyot comes out. He is about thirty, quite slim and pleasant-looking, and also dressed in traveling clothes. He walks right down to the balustrade and looks thoughtfully at the view. Sibyl stands beside him and slips her arm through his.

Utterance: [Sibyl: It's heavenly. Look at the lights of that yacht reflected in the water. Oh dear, I'm so happy.]
Response: [Elyot (smiling): Are you?]

I analyzed this interaction using Gemini. Here is the analysis generated by this model:

MODEL'S OUTPUT 4.1

Title: Speech act deflection, misalignment, subtext analysis

STEP 1: EXPECTED RESPONSE MAPPING

1.1 Primary speech act
Expressive (Sibyl expresses her internal emotional state).
Secondary act: directive (she commands him to "look").
1.2 Lexical and structural evidence
Expressive: "It's heavenly," "I'm so happy."
Directive: "Look at the lights…"
1.3 Expected response type
Affiliation/Validation.
In a cooperative romantic context, the expected response to "I'm so happy" is a reciprocal declaration ("So am I") or an agreement with the evaluation ("It is beautiful").
1.4 Conversational goal (interactional only)
Bonding/Shared Attention.
Sibyl attempts to align their emotional states and visual focus to create a shared "we" moment.

→ At this point, the model validly recognized Sybil's conversational goal: Trying to align her excitement with Elyot as an expression of bonding and shared attention. This analysis invites us to examine Elyot's actual response and the extent to which it converges or diverges from the expected response.

STEP 2: ACTUAL RESPONSE ANALYSIS

2.1 Actual speech act performed
Question (Verification/Inquiry).

2.2 Typical adjacency function
Questions typically follow complex information or ambiguous statements that require clarification, rather than simple expressions of happiness.

2.3 Response focus
The speaker as a person.
Elyot ignores the content (the yacht/lights) and focuses solely on scrutinizing Sibyl's state.

2.4 Response strategy
Redirects/Challenges.
He engages with the topic but shifts the mode from sharing the feeling to examining it.

2.5 Paralinguistic/Orthographic markers
"(smiling)" (ambiguous visual cue: could be affectionate, amused, or patronizing).
"?" (Interrogative syntax).

→ In response to our question, the model understands Elyot's response as expressing a shift from *sharing* the feeling to *examining* the feeling. Instead of addressing her utterance by aligning with her object of excitement, he shifts the focus to Sybil as the object of his attention. This shift naturally leads us to assess the alignment between the two utterances.

STEP 3: ALIGNMENT ASSESSMENT

Direct alignment: No

Partial alignment: Yes

Complete misalignment: No

3.1 Alignment score: 5/10
While Elyot maintains the topic (her happiness), he violates the preferred interactional response (reciprocity) by shifting from a statement of fact to an inquiry, disrupting the "bonding" momentum.

→ As you can see, the model proposes a low to moderate alignment. This is enough to justify the following steps, identifying the deflection patterns and exposing the subtext.

STEP 4: DEFLECTION PATTERN IDENTIFICATION

Deflection type: emotional deflection and authenticity deflection.
Markers:

1. Shift in modality: Sibyl uses the declarative/absolute ("I *am* so happy"); Elyot uses the interrogative ("*Are* you?").
2. Withholding of reciprocity: He does not mirror the emotion or the gaze (he does not look at the yacht, he looks at the situation/her).
3. Ambiguous affect: The stage direction "(smiling)" combined with the question suggests a detachment from the emotion she is projecting.

→ Interestingly, the model identified *emotional* and *authenticity* deflections. These two types of deflection point to the exact nature of the divergence between Elyot's response and Sybil's utterance. At this point, the LLM is ready to expose the subtext of this micro-interaction.

STEP 5: SUBTEXT INFERENCE

Layer 1 — Interactional subtext

5.1 Evidence anchoring
Text: "I'm so happy"/"Are you?"
Structure: Adjacency pair mismatch (Declaration → Question).
Visual: "(smiling)" acts as a softener to the structural challenge.

5.2 Core interactional subtext
Instead of confirming the shared emotional reality, the responder engages in scrutiny, thereby shifting the interaction from mutual celebration to asymmetrical observation.

5.3 Relational configuration
Differentiation: Sibyl attempts to merge their experience; Elyot maintains distinctness.
Control of trajectory: By asking a question rather than agreeing, Elyot halts the momentum of the romantic cliché and forces Sibyl to justify or re-evaluate her state.
Observer/Subject dynamic: The interaction positions Sibyl as the subject experiencing the emotion and Elyot as the observer analyzing the validity of that experience.

→ The model identified an important point: the subtext, or the hidden dynamic, is the shift from celebration to asymmetrical observation with all the implied consequences of such a shift. Now, when we can clearly articulate the meaning of the subtext and ground it in the text, it is possible to move to the next phase and to speculate about the *dramatic effect* of this subtext on the observer.

Layer 2—Inward (aesthetic) significance (Observer-facing meaning)

5.4 Aesthetic activation
Ambiguity and irony.
The structural feature generating significance is the minimal response. A two-word question dismantles a paragraph of ecstatic description. The "smile" complicates the reading—while it prevents the response from being outright hostile, the question prevents it from being entirely warm.
5.5 Inward effect on the observer
Unease/Tension.
The observer anticipates a harmonious resolution to the "honeymoon" setup. Elyot's response introduces a subtle discord, suggesting that the reality of the scene is not as stable as Sibyl claims. It acts as a "check" on the sentimentality.
5.6 Inward significance (Integrated aesthetic formulation)
Because a routine romantic declaration is reconfigured into detached inquiry, the observer experiences unease, activated by the mismatch between Sibyl's absolute certainty and Elyot's skepticism. What initially functions as honeymoon bonding now reads as ironic distance, producing tension rather than stability or resolution.
5.7 Scope control and confidence
Scope: This inward significance is confined to the observable structure of this exchange and the immediate stage directions, without relying on knowledge of the play's full plot.
Confidence: High. The linguistic shift from declarative to interrogative is a hard structural fact that explicitly denies simple agreement.

HOW VALID IS THE INTERPRETATION?

I believe that, upon reading the above analysis, one may find it both valid and interesting. However, at this point, the reader may also question the validity and quality of the model's analysis. There are several methods for evaluating the quality of the output.

First, we should realize that, given the structured prompt, we can replicate the analysis. There is no black box that can serve as an interpreter. A structured process is materialized in the prompt. We can replicate the prompt and even compare the outputs from different models. Given the probabilistic nature of LLMs, we should not expect full replication of the output. However, we can still expect the model's important points, such as misalignment, to be replicated.

Beyond replicability, there is *face validity*. Here is how the AI engine of Google explains face validity:

> Face validity is the extent to which a test or measure *appears* to measure what it's supposed to measure, based on subjective, surface-level judgment by test-takers or

non-experts, making it a weak but important first step for relevance, trustworthiness, and participant buy-in, though it doesn't guarantee actual accuracy.

Reading the model's analysis, it is clear that it produced a very high face validity. Moreover, the analysis is deeply grounded in the text itself and in explicit contextual information (e.g., Elyot's smile). It is not a gut feeling but an analysis with boots on the ground. Ultimately, my judgment of the model's quality of interpretation hinges on whether it offers *a new and non-trivial understanding that is generated through a structured process and grounded in the text.* If you read the model's output, you can see that it clearly meets this criterion. While the vast literature on interpretation has traditionally struggled to define a good interpretation, and while traditional approaches to the social sciences have offered their own measures of reliability and validity, the AI era calls for fresh, innovative approaches. The general criterion I presented above is the one guiding the work done in this book, and it will be useful to articulate it:

> The quality of a model's interpretation of a scene resides in the novelty and non-trivial exposure of a subtext that is generated through a structured process and grounded in the text.

There are secondary criteria for evaluating the quality of the subtext. For instance:

> The quality of the exposed subtext of a micro-interaction can be evaluated through its predictive value for following interactions in the drama.

At this point, let me analyze the conversation to summarize our understanding and highlight the predictive value of the subtext revealed by the LLM. I start by reporting on the previous exchange and then describe what happened next.

Sybil invites Elyot to enjoy the scenery, expecting compliance/agreement. She aims to share her joy. Elyot delays compliance ("Just a minute!") and provides a judgment of the scene ("Not so bad"). He acknowledges the content (the view) but reframes the scenery as moderately appealing—nothing to be excited about. The alignment between the utterances is partial. It addresses the setting ("Not so bad") and acknowledges the utterance ("Just a minute") but does not reciprocate enthusiasm or act on the invitation. The deflection is mostly emotional, as Elyot avoids matching the enthusiasm his wife expresses. There is a misalignment between the "lovely" and "Not so bad." Ely controls the situation by moderating his wife's excitement and emotionally distancing himself from the event.

Given her husband's moderate response, Sybil repeats and amplifies her excitement ("It's heavenly!"), emphasizing her high emotional state ("I'm so happy!"), again, seeking confirmation from Elyot. However, he questions her happiness in a way that is used to address factual or exaggerated claims by asking, "Are you?" It seems that Ely is trying to *turn her off* again. A husband who consistently "turns off" his wife this way could be described as emotionally dismissive or invalidating. It is a behavior that undermines emotional intimacy. By dismissing what matters to Sybil, he creates emotional distance. The behavior also signals a lack of appreciation, rather than affirming or acknowledging her perspective; he devalues it. Finally, it can feel competitive or one-upping—implying that her experience or judgment is not good enough.

The meaning Elyot attributes to Sybil's utterance is therefore of an exaggerated claim that should be undermined and downplayed. Therefore, his response undermines Sybil's emotional statement instead of aligning with it. This response shows misalignment, as it undermines the expected support and suggests doubt or emotional detachment. Again, we observe an *emotional deflection* where Elyot avoids emotional affirmation and possibly reflects discomfort with emotional intimacy. Regarding relations, we can see that Elyot takes control of the emotional tone, possibly asserting a cooler or more distant stance. Moreover, his response may suggest disbelief, sarcasm, or disconnection, hinting at a strain or unresolved tension in their dynamic. His style leans toward coolness or ironic detachment, contrasting with his wife's effusive openness.

We may hypothesize that Elyot has an insecure character, low empathy, a need for superiority, a critical/judgmental thinking style, and defensive/dismissive coping strategies, and that he expresses possible narcissistic traits.

How valid is this understanding of the subtext? We can use the analysis of the micro-interaction as a context, and feed it into the next cycle of analysis, where we examine the next exchange characterized by misalignment. To avoid cognitive overload, I will briefly describe what happens next in the play and outline the main outcomes of the model's analysis.

HOW PREDICTIVE IS THE SUBTEXT WE EXPOSED?

To Elyot's "question," Sybil responds with the same question. Instead of affirming or explaining her feelings, Sybil redirects attention back to Ely. She interprets Ely's question as doubting and responds with emotional mirroring and deflection. She does not elaborate on her feelings, confirming she is happy, but challenges him to match them. Therefore, her response expresses partial alignment, engaging emotionally and maintaining the affective tone, but sidesteps the question of her own emotion in favor of assessing his. Therefore, Sybil's response expresses two types of deflection. Responsibility deflection, in which she shifts emotional responsibility onto her husband by returning the question, and emotional redirection, in which she seeks emotional validation or parity rather than providing self-validation. Her response is indicative of vulnerability and insecurity. She is seeking acknowledgment, and when she does not get it, she anxiously turns to Elyot, checking his stance. While Elyot seems to be a narcissist seeking power and significance, Sybil may be a woman seeking acceptance from a powerful and significant other (i.e., her husband).

Sybil is seeking an emotional connection, even if it is through indirect means. Elyot's response presents an emphatic affirmation with intensification ("Oh, of course I am! Tremendously happy!"), showing complete alignment with Sibyl. However, given the previous analysis, we may question the authenticity of his exaggerated response. He is "tremendously happy," and the gap between his previous dismissive and cynical approach and his use of the strong adjective "tremendous" calls into question the authenticity of his response. However, Sybil does not question the authenticity of his exaggerated response. The authenticity issue is resolved when Sybil says:

> "Just to think, ...here we are, you and I, married!"

Elyot responds by saying:

> "Yes, things have come to a pretty pass!"

The phrase "things have come to a pretty pass!" is an idiomatic expression meaning that circumstances have reached an unfortunate, troublesome, or undesirable state. It often expresses dismay or irony about how badly a situation has deteriorated. In this context, when Elyot says this in response to Sybil's romantic reflection about their marriage ("Just to think ... here we are, you and I, married!"), he actually hints that their marriage represents a sorry state of affairs or an unfortunate turn of events. His utterance carries a tone of resignation mixed with complaint, as if he is saying, "Well, this is what we have come to" or "Look what a mess we have gotten ourselves into." It is particularly cutting because it reframes what his wife sees as a romantic moment (celebrating their union) as something regrettable or problematic. This is the third instance so far where Elyot dismisses his wife, misaligns with her emotions, and forms an emotional point of deflection. In other words, Sybil seeks intimacy through affectionate reflection, while Elyot responds as if she were describing a rather problematic situation. His move reveals a complete misalignment, as he ignores her intimate intent and reframes the positivity of her romantic utterance as negative. He undermines her emotional vulnerability with a dismissive response and retreats from an intimate moment through sarcasm, suggesting underlying marital dissatisfaction. His defensive and deflecting communication style indicates emotional unavailability or relationship strain.

Sybil's final utterance ("Don't laugh at me! You mustn't be blasé about honeymoons, just because this is your second!") uses a defensive rebuke, accompanied by a personal accusation about Elyot's experience. Her response suggests that she perceives Elyot's utterance as a mockery and aims to address it, attributing his attitude to his marital history. Her response shows partial misalignment: she responds to the negative tone but misinterprets the target. Sybil expresses vulnerability while attacking her husband's credibility. She reveals insecurity about being his second wife and displays a high level of tension, underlying jealousy, and defensive positioning. The communicative style, accusatory and defensive, suggests deep-seated insecurities about their relationship.

Summarizing the analysis, we can gain a deeper understanding of the characters, their relational patterns, and the dynamics between them. Sybil is an expressive and emotionally involved character seeking acknowledgment from her husband. Regarding known personality types, we may hypothesize that she is a dependent personality whose most basic need is *acceptance*. Her responses are indicative of insecurity and vulnerability. In contrast, Elyot seems to be a narcissist seeking to express his superiority and power, while exposing his own vulnerability and emotional distancing.

The relational pattern is mostly asymmetrically misaligned. Even in this short interaction, Elyot is completely misaligned with Sybil, presenting mostly emotional deflection points. Among the four responses he generates, two present complete misalignments, one presents partial misalignment, and one is allegedly complete alignment (Tremendously happy!). On the whole, he presents emotional points of deflection and moderate to low expressions of intimacy. The meaning he attributes to Sybil's utterances expresses his distorted representations. Sybil's emotional expressiveness and need for acceptance and acknowledgment are often interpreted as factual statements, whose authenticity can be questioned or viewed negatively.

Regarding meaning-as-a-response, Elyot's responses to Sibyl's are highly diagnostic of his character and relational patterns. Sibyl is more moderate in her alignment, which is primarily partial, and her points of deflection mostly involve shifting the responsibility to Elyot. This move aligns with her portrayal as a dependent character. However, unlike Elyot, her meaning-making is less distorted and more realistic. When she responds, she usually aligns with Elyot's communicative aim. The allegedly happy couple arriving in France to celebrate their marriage exposes their personalities, relational patterns, and problematic dynamics.

The subtext analyzed at the beginning of this chapter meets the criterion of prediction. It provides us with an accurate diagnosis of Elyot, Sybil, and their interaction. Prediction is a limited criterion, as plot twists can alter our understanding of characters and their interactions. In this case, the subtext originally identified by the model may be used by the director/playwright to manipulate us in one direction, only to surprise us later. Regardless of plot shifts, the analysis seems to meet the main criterion for evaluating its quality.

DISCUSSION

The opening scene of *Private Lives* is misleading. A just-married couple arrives in France to celebrate their honeymoon. The first thing visible from their room is a beautiful scenic view. Up to now, our amygdala has been positively stimulated through smiles, "darling," and the expected context of a honeymoon with its wonderful ambiance. However, Coward is tricking us. It is an artistic manipulation, as underneath the surface, a subtext flows like magma. Let us repeat what the model has to say:

> Because a routine romantic declaration is reconfigured into detached inquiry, the observer experiences unease, activated by the mismatch between Sibyl's absolute certainty and Elyot's skepticism. What initially functions as honeymoon bonding now reads as ironic distance, producing tension rather than stability or resolution.

Notice that when processing the play in real-time, the observer has no time to stop and reflect on what is happening, though the impression may be registered in his mind. What he sees is a misleading scene. We have a newlywed couple celebrating their honeymoon in romantic France. They stay in a wonderful place with a beautiful view. This context primes us to expect the best. However, beneath the surface, a contrasting dynamic unconsciously signals to us that things might not be as they seem.

This subtext is indicative of a conflictual relationship, asymmetrically expressed by Elyot. Sibyl, unaware of this subtext, is truly happy. Subconsciously, our minds begin to sense the danger facing an innocent victim, but we still lack explicit and strong evidence to support our suspicions. The subtext is hidden from us through the real-time chatting and the ambiguity of the opening scene. Is Elyot just joking with his new wife, or is he really a *douchebag*? The tension between the surface and the underlying subtext, the ambiguity of the interaction, and the cognitive overload of processing the interaction in real time prevent us from explicitly understanding what is happening. It is only through the machine that we can save ourselves some cognitive effort and identify the subtext, even as a preliminary context for analyzing the subsequent moves. At a certain point, one is tempted to whisper to Sybil, "Beware of this douchebag. It is your new husband, and you love him, but remember the Titanic. There are early warning signs that you might soon hit an ice-berg." However, Sybil is a character captured within the play. Our understanding cannot be communicated to her, which is a part of what makes the drama so appealing.

The main points of the chapter are:

- The approach introduced in Chapter 3 has been applied to the opening scene of *Private Lives*.
- The AI correctly identified the misalignment between Elyot and Sibyl.
- The subtext is the shift from mutual celebration to asymmetrical observation.
- The inward significance of these scenes lies in the dramatic tension that contrasts with the context of a honeymoon.
- The subtext identified in this micro-interaction is highly diagnostic of Elyot, Sibyl, and their relationships.
- This subtext primes our understanding of the following interactions and provides context for analyzing them.

REFERENCES

Coward, N. (2013). *Private lives*. Bloomsbury.

Neuman, Y. (2025). An AI-supported methodology for analyzing deflections and misalignments in human interactions. *Integrative Psychological and Behavioral Science*, *59*, Article 74.

Richards, D. (1970). *The wit of Noël Coward*. Sphere Books.

5 The Rabbi and the Physicist

Subtext in A Serious Man

ABSTRACT This chapter extends the misalignment framework from localized utterance–response deflection to the more structurally radical form of misalignment known as the *dialogue of the deaf.* Using the Rabbi–Larry consultation scene from the Coen Brothers' *A Serious Man* as a case study, the chapter demonstrates how subtext may emerge not only from isolated conversational slips but also from *incompatible worldviews.* Through a sequence of structured AI-assisted prompts, I diagnose the scene as a dialogue of the deaf driven primarily by asymmetric reality frames, crossed agendas, and metaphor–literal disjunction. The chapter then reconstructs the scene's subtext as a displacement of concrete human suffering into spiritual abstraction and shows how this displacement generates its aesthetic effect. Methodologically, the chapter advances a typological and computational procedure for identifying dialogues of the deaf, their subtexts, and their dramatic effects, with applications to both cinematic interpretation and real-life therapeutic discourse.

THE SUFFERING OF A NICE JEWISH MAN

In the previous chapters, we learned that a misaligned utterance and response pair (U-R) points to the existence of a subtext through which this misalignment can be resolved. The misalignment has been discussed in a very specific sense. Let me explain it formally:

> There is an utterance U which, given a certain context C, primes us to expect a response R, where R belongs to a set of probable speech acts S. However, the speech act of the actual response does not belong to this set. Therefore, we hypothesize that a subtext exists, which explains the coherence of U-R.

This formal explanation suggests that a *subtext is a specific type of context.* Whenever a scene requires an explanation, we hypothesize that there is a different context that can resolve our difficulty in understanding the text.

The current chapter extends the above-mentioned formal statement (i.e., There is an utterance U …), but to a *dialogue of the deaf.* In such a dialogue, the misalignment is of a different nature, as it concerns different forms of disconnectedness between the speakers. Before explaining this point, I would like you to ask yourself the following questions:

1. Can you name at least three criteria for diagnosing a dialogue as a dialogue of the deaf?

 DOI: 10.1201/9781042004485-7

2. Are you familiar with an AI-based approach for automatically identifying and analyzing this type of dialogue?
3. Do you know of a methodology for exposing the subtext of such a dialogue and its inward significance?

If you answer these questions negatively, there is a good chance you will learn something new from this chapter.

The dialogue of the deaf is taken from the Coen Brothers' film *A Serious Man* (dirs. Joel and Ethan Coen 2000). First, I present the general plot, then focus on a dialogue that invites analysis of its subtext. I will also present a *typology of dialogue-of-the-deaf patterns* to support a structured, theoretically grounded analysis of the dialogue.

Set in 1967 suburban Minnesota, *A Serious Man* follows Larry Gopnik, a reserved and nerdy Jewish physics professor who organizes both his teaching and his private life around the belief that the world, though complex, is ultimately governed by rational principles, ethical consistency, and just causality. He teaches his students the uncertainty principle but fails to grasp the deep uncertainty of the social world he inhabits. The film systematically dismantles Larry's illusions by staging a cascade of misalignments between Larry's worldview and reality, mainly the social reality.

Larry's collapse begins when his wife, Judith, announces that she wants a divorce—not for any "justifiable" reason, but because she has supposedly achieved emotional and spiritual "clarity" with another man, Sy Ableman, a manipulative individual who uses his soft voice and sneaky language to influence others. The betrayal is framed in therapeutic and ethical language: desire is recoded as truth, abandonment as growth, and Larry's decency as emotional stagnation. Worse still, Sy is admired as kind, wise, and morally elevated, while Larry is displaced from his own home by the new happy couple, who offer "understanding," "support," and politeness. Here, the film introduces a major moral discrepancy: ethical language is used to justify ethically devastating outcomes, and moral goodness fails to secure moral standing.

At work, Larry encounters a second distortion of justice. A failing Korean student attempts to bribe him in order to pass a failed test; when Larry refuses on principled grounds, the student's father hints at legal retaliation. Larry's loyalty to rational standards and institutional norms of morality places him in danger rather than protecting him. The promise that truth and integrity will be structurally rewarded collapses under quiet coercion and procedural threat.

Seeking alignment between reason and faith, Larry turns to a series of rabbis, hoping that religious authority will help him to address his issues. Instead, he receives parables, evasive answers, and stories that defer meaning rather than clarify it. Spiritual authority mirrors the same indeterminacy as the secular world: interpretation replaces explanation, and ambiguity replaces justice. The meaning of the things that happen to us is described as something to be endured, not something to be understood or resolved. However, the gap between Larry and the rabbis is not only philosophical. The two rabbis Larry consults are portrayed as rather ridiculous figures, given their irrelevant, surreal parables and metaphors.

Parallel to these crises is Larry's conflict with his hostile, antisemitic neighbor, who aggressively contests property boundaries and weaponizes legal intimidation. The neighbor is Larry's ethical opposite: blunt, territorial, openly exclusionary. Yet while

Larry behaves cautiously and lawfully, the neighbor escalates without consequence. The legal and social systems are presented as being structurally tilted toward aggression rather than fairness. This conflict reveals another misalignment at the heart of the film: restraint weakens, while hostility operates efficiently. This is just another expression of the film's underlying theme: "The righteous suffer while the wicked thrive." This is a classic Jewish theological problem that appears in the *Babylonian Talmud* (Berakhot 7a). Why is it that the righteous suffer while the wicked thrive? In the *Book of Job*, the most direct and honest answer is given to this problem. In *A Serious Man*, the theological answer seems to be that the universe is indifferent to us and to our moral conceptions. In such a world, and surrounded by people who weaponize desire as truth, aggression as legitimacy, and ambiguity as wisdom, Larry remains faithful to a moral-rational framework that offers him no protection or comfort.

LOOK AT THE PARKING LOT!

My analysis focuses on Larry's meeting with the first rabbi. Larry is waiting in the synagogue for a meeting with Rabbi Nachtner, an experienced rabbi, but surprisingly, the one who welcomes him is Rabbi Scott, described as a shockingly young junior rabbi. The older rabbi could not make it due to another obligation, and Rabbi Scott was called in to cover for him.

Regarding the young rabbi, there appear to be two informative cues. The first concerns his appearance. The rabbi lacks facial hair. In contrast with the old rabbi in the film, who wore a long beard and had a traditional Eastern European appearance, Rabbi Scott is clean-shaven. This might signal a lack of masculinity, and indeed, Rabbi Scott's appearance is that of an immature child. Moreover, it might signal a new generation of rabbis who are clean-shaven, modern, and seek to distance themselves from traditional Judaism. Indeed, when Larry tells the rabbi that his wife is asking for a divorce, he uses the Hebrew word "Gett." At first, Rabbi Scott does not understand what Larry is saying. There is a long silence with the sound of ventilation in the background, emphasizing Rabbi Scott's hesitation. Scott eventually asks: "A what?" and immediately corrects from a question to an affirmation: "Oh, a Gett. Uh-huh, sure." There is ambiguity as to whether he didn't understand Larry's pronunciation of the Hebrew word, or whether it took him some time to recall its meaning because he was not well-versed in Jewish tradition. In any case, what we observe is a very young and probably modern-style rabbi who is expected to advise the suffering Larry.

In the rabbi's office, Larry sits "tensely hunched." Here is a description of the facial expression, as created by Gemini:

MODEL'S OUTPUT 5.1

> The person's facial expression appears serious, perhaps even concerned or uneasy. Their brow is furrowed, creating lines across their forehead, and their eyes, though partially obscured by glasses, seem to hold a focused, or perhaps slightly troubled, gaze. The set of their mouth is neutral, not smiling, which further contributes to the expression's somber or pensive mood.

Larry's facial expression communicates his deep concerns. The reason for Larry's arrival at the meeting is clearly stated. He describes his feelings metaphorically as if a carpet has been yanked out from under him; he is unsure how to react and generally feels confused and disoriented. This is a man who has experienced a shock and tries to elaborate on his trauma. It is a clear and explicit cry for help. The Rabbi's first response is not an expression of empathy, and in this sense, he is missing the point. Indeed, instead of expressing empathy, he asks for the reasons behind Larry's wife's decision. Moreover, Rabbi Scott is quick to frame the problem as a theological one: "losing track of *Hashem [The Hebrew term for God]*, which is the problem here." This is not the answer given by the Book of Job, but the rabbi was asked to consult rather than explain the suffering of the serious man.

The rabbi's almost automatic "diagnosis" results from his own personal perspective, as expressed in "I too have had the feeling," and "I too have forgotten how to see Him in the world." Rabbi Scott's automatic response supports our hypothesis that he is some kind of modern rabbi. His framing of Larry's pain as missing God's presence in his life seems to echo Christian protestant beliefs more than traditional Jewish responses to the problem that "the righteous suffer while the wicked thrive."

Here, we have a man who has been informed by his wife that she wishes to leave him. The crisis is one of personal abandonment. However, Rabbi Scott sees the problem as "losing track" of God, and he continues, explaining to Larry that it is a matter of *perspective* and that with the right perspective one can see *God.* To explain this point, he refers to the parking lot (?), which they can see from the office window but not from other perspectives. This metaphor teaches us nothing about perspectives. It is an obscure metaphor presented by the young rabbi in an exaggerated, embarrassing manner. Larry is trying to get things back on track by explaining that his wife is actually cheating on him, and this is a dialogue of the deaf as Rabbi Scott is obsessed with his own explanation: "You can't cut yourself off from the mystical, or you'll be—you'll remain—completely lost." The one who is probably lost is the Rabbi himself, because he has lost track of Larry's suffering.

The dialogue certainly looks like a dialogue of the deaf. But what do we mean by that? What are the indicators that a dialogue is a dialogue of the deaf? And is it possible to use an LLM to test the hypothesis that a dialogue is a dialogue of the deaf? Note that, in this case, I propose the hypothesis that the dialogue between Larry and Rabbi Scott is a dialogue of the deaf. First, I test whether this hypothesis is supported by the text, and only then do I seek to expose the subtext.

I began by designing a prompt that tests whether a conversation is a dialogue of the deaf:

PROMPT 5.1 CHECKING WHETHER A CONVERSATION IS A DIALOGUE OF THE DEAF

A "*dialogue of the deaf*" is a discussion in which each party is unresponsive to what the other says.

Task: Identify whether the given scene contains a "dialogue of the deaf."

→ You can see that first I define the thing I would like to inquire, and next define the exact task for the LLM. The specific instructions are then as follows:

Instructions:
Analyze the conversation in the following scene.
Use the <Multi-Layered Diagnostic Checklist for Dialogue-of-the-Deaf Scenes>.
Answer the following questions:

1. Do the characters pursue incompatible goals?
2. Do responses address previous lines or deflect?
3. Are misunderstandings accidental or strategic?

For each question, provide a yes/no judgment and a brief explanation.
Output format: Decide whether the scene presents a dialogue of the deaf.
The scene is taken from the film "A Serious Man."
Here is the scene: [INSERT SCENE HERE].

→ You can see that I directed the model to use a checklist. I don't rely on the model's understanding; I support it with the necessary definitions, instructions, and resources for the task. The prompt continues:

First, check whether the dialogue meets the standards for a dialogue of the deaf. Use the following checklist:

<Multi-Layered Diagnostic Checklist for Dialogue-of-the-Deaf Scenes>

Layer 1—*Semantic continuity* (Basic coherence test)

1. Are the lines syntactically responsive, but semantically misaligned?
   - Characters answer, but not meaningfully.
2. Does the topic appear consistent on the surface while meanings diverge?
3. Is the exchange structurally a dialogue but functionally a pair of monologues?

If yes → proceed to Layer 2.

Layer 2—*Goal alignment test* (Pragmatic mismatch)
Evaluate each speaker's conversational goal to include the following:

- Informational: seeking facts
- Emotional: seeking comfort/recognition
- Instrumental: persuading, manipulating, avoiding
- Performative: displaying identity, dominance, wit
- Narrative: constructing a self-story

Questions:

1. Are the speakers pursuing different types of goals?
2. Is there a stable mismatch (not just momentary misalignment)?
3. Do their goals make true communication structurally impossible?

If yes → proceed to Layer 3.

Layer 3—*Subtext analysis*

Identify what each character *wants but does not say.*

1. Do the characters' subtexts contradict each other?
2. Are they "talking from different emotional worlds"?
3. Does each utterance protect a wound rather than engage the other's meaning?

If yes → proceed to Layer 4.

Layer 4—*Incompatible frames/World views*

A dialogue of the deaf requires incompatible "frames" such as:

- literal vs. metaphorical
- delusional vs. grounded
- strategic vs. emotional
- fantasy vs. realism
- trauma vs. everyday logic

Questions:

1. Are the characters' interpretive frames incompatible?
2. Do they inhabit different ontologies (different "realities")?
3. Does this incompatibility persist right through the scene?

If yes → proceed to Layer 5.

Layer 5—*Structural outcome test*

1. Does the conversation fail to progress? (No new shared meaning emerges.)
2. Does frustration, confusion, or escalation occur without resolution?
3. Do the characters end the exchange exactly where they began—only more alienated?

If all layers hold → this is a true dialogue of the deaf.

You can see that I have designed a structured, detailed prompt to determine scientifically whether the dialogue constitutes a dialogue of the deaf. By scientific, I mean:

> *A structured procedure that can be fully replicated and used to test a given hypothesis.*

In this context, I emphasize that the decision about whether a given conversation is a dialogue of the deaf is not based on a gut feeling or a soft interpretive reading. The prompt involves a clear definition of what constitutes a dialogue of the deaf and detailed criteria for determining whether the analyzed dialogue is indeed a dialogue of the deaf. The prompt is also scientific in another sense. By applying the prompt, we are also ready to accept an outcome, saying the dialogue is not a dialogue of the deaf. By testing structurally whether this is a dialogue of the deaf, the prompt does not impose judgment. Moreover, the prompt has clear pedagogical benefits. We can use it to guide students and researchers in making their own informed decisions.

Here is the model's output. But before specifying its output, let me reiterate that the LLM is a tool, not the voice of God emanating from the burning bush. Therefore, the model's output is not necessarily valid, fully correct, or complete. Additionally, it does not necessarily yield interesting or non-trivial results. Whenever we examine the model's output, we should consider it both critically and constructively. By a constructive perspective, I mean one that asks us to perform *error analysis* to understand, in dialogue with the model, why it failed in certain respects, and to improve the prompt for the next round of analysis.

MODEL'S OUTPUT 5.2

1. Do the characters pursue incompatible goals?
   Yes.
   - Larry's goal is primarily emotional and existential: he seeks clarity, grounding, and implicit moral justice regarding his wife's betrayal and the collapse of his life.
   - Rabbi Scott's goal is primarily performative and theological: he aims to reframe Larry's crisis into a lesson about perception, God's presence, and spirituality.
   - These goals are not only different but operate on non-overlapping levels—Larry wants help with *what is happening to him*, while the Rabbi redirects toward *how to interpret reality spiritually*.
2. Do responses address previous lines or deflect?
   Mostly deflect.
   - The Rabbi often acknowledges Larry's words superficially but quickly redirects them into abstract spiritual generalities ("perspective," "seeing Hashem," "parking lot").
   - When Larry introduces the crucial concrete fact—his wife's affair with Sy Ableman—the Rabbi briefly reacts but immediately returns to mystical framing, avoiding Larry's concrete emotional reality.
   - This creates syntactic responsiveness with semantic misalignment.
3. Are misunderstandings accidental or strategic?
   Strategic (structural), not accidental.
   - The Rabbi is not confused; he is deliberately operating within a theological-existential interpretive frame that displaces Larry's immediate emotional and practical crisis.

    - Larry, in contrast, continues to press toward literal, relational, and moral meaning. The "misunderstanding" persists because each man is committed to a different meaning-making system, not because of confusion.

☑ Final Decision
Yes—this scene is a clear example of a dialogue of the deaf.
Why it qualifies fully:

- The conversation remains structurally intact but fails to produce shared meaning.
- Larry's emotional and moral crisis is never truly engaged by the Rabbi.
- Rabbi Scott's mystical reframing floats above Larry's suffering without touching it.
- The scene ends exactly where it began:
    - Larry is still lost and destabilized.
    - The Rabbi is still marveling at the parking lot.
- No convergence of interpretive frames occurs.

This is a textbook example of:

- Emotional realism vs. theological abstraction
- Trauma logic vs. symbolic meaning
- Human betrayal vs. cosmic justification

In short, they are speaking grammatical English to each other—but not inhabiting the same reality.

Using a structured prompt, the LLM clearly identified the dialogue as a dialogue of the deaf. As the model suggests, "The conversation remains structurally intact but fails to produce shared meaning." To deepen the analysis, I designed the next prompt to identify the specific types of misalignment characterizing the dialogue.

PROMPT 5.2 TYPOLOGICAL ANALYSIS

A dialogue of the deaf can involve different types of misalignments. Here is a typology that can help us to understand which of the types is expressed in the meeting with the Rabbi:

Typology of dialogue-of-the-deaf patterns

Type 1—*Crossed agendas*

Each character pursues a different conversational goal.

- One wants facts; the other wants emotional validation.
- One wants to end a relationship; the other wants logistical clarity.
- Effect: The words do not meet because the purposes do not meet.

Type 2 — *Topic drift/non-sequitur loops*

Each response shifts the topic instead of answering.

- A answers X, B replies to some imagined Y.
- Effect: Meaning dissolves into parallel monologues.

Type 3—*Emotional overload*

The emotional stakes prevent receptive listening.

- Anger, fear, shame, humiliation.
- Effect: Characters hear *tone*, not *content.*

Type 4—*Strategic deafness/weaponized misunderstanding*

A character *pretends* not to hear in order to dominate or evade.

- Narcissistic withholding.
- Legalistic obstruction (interrogations, depositions).
- Effect: Communication failure is used as a tactic.

Type 5—*Asymmetric reality frames*

Characters inhabit different interpretive universes.

- Estragon and Vladimir in *Godot.*
- Conspiracy theorist vs. rationalist.
- Effect: They cannot share premises, so meaning cannot be shared.

Type 6—*Metaphorical vs. literal logics*

One character speaks figuratively; the other responds literally.

- Child/adult.
- Visionary/bureaucrat.
- Effect: Subtext and text separate completely.

Type 7—*Unspoken trauma barrier*

A character's unarticulated wound blocks real listening.

Effect: Dialogue becomes displacement: they talk about anything *except* what matters.

###

Instructions:

Given the dialogue, determine whether it fits one or more types of "dialogue of the deaf" such as:

- Crossed Agendas
- Topic Drift
- Emotional Overload
- Weaponized Misunderstanding
- Asymmetric Reality Frames
- Metaphorical vs. Literal
- Trauma Barrier

Cite the textual cues that support your classification.

Running this prompt, ChatGPT produced the following output:

MODEL'S OUTPUT 5.3

Typological classification: Rabbi Scott scene

This scene exhibits not one but a cluster of dialogue-of-the-deaf types.

The dominant pattern is Asymmetric Reality Frames, supported by Crossed Agendas, Metaphorical vs. literal logics, and an unspoken trauma barrier.

There is no strong evidence of Weaponized misunderstanding.

Type 1—Crossed agendas (✓ Present)

Each character pursues a fundamentally different conversational purpose.

Larry's Agenda:

- Emotional grounding
- Moral clarity
- Practical understanding of betrayal
- Existential fairness

Textual cues [Removed to avoid copyright issues, YN]:

→ I removed other textual cues to avoid any copyright issues.

Larry is seeking recognition of injury, injustice, and destabilization.

Rabbi Scott's Agenda:

- Spiritual reframing
- Theological interpretation
- Perceptual correction

Effect: They are not negotiating the same problem.

Larry speaks from the standpoint of life-collapse, the Rabbi responds from the point of view of cosmic abstraction.

Type 2—Topic drift/non-sequitur loops (✓ Present)

Responses repeatedly veer away from the emotional core.

Key drift moment:

Larry introduces the emotional bombshell:

- *"Well, she's, she's seeing Sy Ableman."*

Rabbi replies:

- *"Oh. ... I'm sorry."* Then immediately:
- *"But—this is life... You have to see these things as expressions of God's will."*

Effect: The conversation never stabilizes on the topics of betrayal, humiliation, or rage. Each time it almost does, the Rabbi floats the discussion back upward into abstraction.

Type 3—Emotional overload (✓ Present, Asymmetrical)

Larry is clearly emotionally overwhelmed; the Rabbi is not.

Larry's nervous, halting speech ("*she's, she's seeing*") signals shock and cognitive flooding.

Effect: Larry cannot fully articulate what he needs. The Rabbi does not slow down or ground him emotionally—he accelerates into abstraction instead.

Type 5—Asymmetric reality frames (✓ Dominant Type)

This is the core structural failure of the scene.

Larry's frame:

- Social reality
- Betrayal
- Divorce
- Humiliation
- Moral causality

Rabbi's frame:

- Mystical perception
- God's will
- Symbolic references
- The parking lot as a spiritual metaphor

Effect:

They do not merely disagree—they do not share the same ontology.

Larry wants human justice; the Rabbi speaks of cosmic acceptance. This alone is sufficient to generate a classic dialogue of the deaf.

Type 6—Metaphorical vs. literal logics (✓ Present)

The Rabbi's metaphors glide past Larry's literal disaster.

Effect: The Rabbi's figurative language cannot strike home because Larry is dealing with:

- Divorce papers
- Social scandal
- Personal betrayal

Their logics never intersect.

Type 7—Unspoken trauma barrier (✓ Strongly present)
Neither character speaks directly about:

- Humiliation
- Sexual betrayal
- Anger
- Shame
- Fear of social collapse

Textual displacement:

- They speak about:
  - "perspective"
  - "Hashem"
  - "the parking lot."
- instead of:
  - rage
  - humiliation
  - despair
  - sexual jealousy

Effect: The dialogue becomes a ritual of avoidance. Both men collaborate—unconsciously—in not touching the real wound.

Type 4 — Weaponized misunderstanding (✗ Not dominant)
There is no clear evidence that:

- The Rabbi is being strategically evasive in order to dominate.
- He is legally obstructing or gaslighting.

His failure is sincere but structurally inappropriate, not manipulative.
☑ Final Typological Verdict
This scene is a compound dialogue of the deaf, structured primarily by:

1. ☑ Asymmetric reality frames *(dominant)*
2. ☑ Crossed agendas
3. ☑ Metaphorical vs. literal logics
4. ☑ Unspoken trauma barrier
5. ☑ Topic drift
6. ⚠ Emotional overload (Larry only)
7. ✗ Weaponized misunderstanding (absent)

→ The model summarized the analysis as follows:

This exchange fails not because the speakers lack empathy, but because they inhabit incompatible reality systems: Larry speaks from a place of betrayal and humiliation, while the Rabbi speaks from a realm of abstraction and cosmic meaning, making genuine contact structurally impossible.

At this point, we understand that this is a dialogue of the deaf characterized by several types of misalignments, the most salient being asymmetric reality frames. These misalignments prompt us to explore the dialogue's implicit meaning, its subtext. I used Prompt 5.3 for the subtext analysis:

PROMPT 5.3 SUBTEXT ANALYSIS

Understanding the subtext of a dialogue involves looking beyond the explicit words spoken to uncover the unspoken thoughts, emotions, motivations, and power dynamics at play. It's about discerning what the characters *really* mean, feel, or want, even if they're not saying it directly.

Task: Based on your analysis of the scene, identify the subtext of the dialogue. For the task, use the following *Guidelines for Understanding Subtext*:

1. Identify explicit goals vs. Implicit desires:
   - Explicit goals: What do the characters *say* they want or are discussing?
   - Implicit desires/needs: What do they *actually* want or need, underneath their words? This often relates to their deeper emotional or psychological state.
   - *Example in "A Serious Man": Larry explicitly wants advice from Rabbi Nachtner; implicitly, he needs understanding, validation of his pain, and practical help with his life falling apart.*
2. Analyze power dynamics:
   - Who has more power in the conversation? How do they assert it?
   - How does the less powerful character try to gain agency or express themselves?
   - Are there shifts in power?
   - *Example: Rabbi Scott clearly holds the dominant position (religious authority, calm state of mind compared to Larry's "addled" state). He uses this to steer the conversation into his preferred spiritual domain.*

3. Look for incongruence (Words vs. Actions/Tone):
    - Do a character's words match their implied feelings or actions?
    - Is there a discrepancy between what is said and how it is said (if you had tone/body language)? In text, look for stage directions or descriptions of *how* lines are to be delivered.
    - *Example: Rabbi Scott's chuckles at "no offense" might suggest a slight amusement or dismissal, despite his polite words.*
4. Pay attention to omissions and silences:
    - What *isn't* being said? Why?
    - What are the characters *avoiding* discussing?
    - What does silence communicate (e.g., discomfort, thought, strategic pause)?
    - *Example: The "long silence" after Larry says "And she wants a Gett" suggests the weight of the statement, and perhaps Rabbi Scott gathering his thoughts or initially misunderstanding.*
5. Examine character relationships and history (if known):
    - How do the characters typically interact?
    - What is their established history or social role? This influences the way they speak to each other.
    - *Example: The dynamic between a troubled congregant and a rabbi carries inherent expectations of guidance and solace, which colors the subtext of their exchange.*
6. Spot deflections, evasions, and shifts:
    - When a character avoids a direct answer, changes the subject, or rephrases something, what are they trying to achieve or avoid?
    - *Example: Rabbi Scott's consistent redirection from Larry's practical problems to spiritual interpretations is a major deflecting tactic. Larry's "Um..." is an evasion/expression of discomfort.*
7. Consider the cultural, social, or professional context:
    - How do societal norms, professional roles, or cultural expectations influence the way the characters communicate (or fail to communicate)?
    - *Example: The religious context of the dialogue is crucial. Rabbi Scott is fulfilling his role as he understands it, which might mean offering spiritual comfort, even if Larry seeks secular counsel.*
8. Analyze figurative language and metaphors:
    - When characters use metaphors, what underlying meaning are they trying to convey? Are they understood by the other party?
    - *Example: Rabbi Scott's "losing track of Hashem" and "looking at the world... through tired eyes" are metaphors for a spiritual crisis, which he frames as "the problem here," subtextually dismissing Larry's material suffering as merely a symptom.*

9. Look for emotional undercurrents:
   - What emotions are simmering beneath the surface (e.g., anger, fear, sadness, frustration, impatience, desperation)?
   - How do these emotions affect the dialogue's flow and meaning?
   - *Example: Larry's "I feel so.... addled" conveys deep confusion and distress. His later statement, "The boss isn't always right, but he's always the boss," carries a subtext of resignation and perhaps cynical weariness, which Rabbi Scott completely misinterprets as jovial agreement.*
10. Notice repetition and emphasis:
   - Why does a character repeat certain words or phrases? What are they trying to emphasize or reinforce?
   - *Example: Rabbi Scott's repeated urging to "Look at the parking lot" emphasizes his fixed spiritual perspective and his inability to shift focus.*

ChatGPT generated the following subtext analysis:

MODEL'S OUTPUT 5.4

1. Explicit goals vs. implicit desires

   Larry

   Explicit Goal:
   - To explain his situation and seek rabbinical guidance regarding the Gett and his wife's actions.
   - Implicit desire/need:
   - Larry needs:
     - Emotional validation
     - Moral clarity
     - Recognition of injustice
     - Practical guidance
     - Someone to say: *this is wrong, and your pain makes sense*

   Subtext:

   Larry is not in fact asking a legal or religious question—he is asking whether his suffering is *real, justified, and seen.*

   Rabbi Scott

   Explicit goal:
   - To offer spiritual guidance through perspective and awareness of God's presence.

     Implicit desire/need:
     - To demonstrate competence and wisdom
     - To affirm his own theological identity

    - To be meaningful in a role that quietly fails to meet real-world suffering

   Subtext:
   He is less focused on Larry than on proving that suffering can still be managed spiritually.

2. Power dynamics
   - Rabbi Scott holds institutional and symbolic power:
     - Religious authority
     - Interpretive authority (he decides *what the problem "really" is*)
   - He asserts control by:
     - Reframing Larry's problem as a failure of spiritual perception
     - Leading Larry physically to the window
     - Monopolizing interpretive meaning
   - Larry is disempowered:
     - Disoriented ("*addled*")
     - Seeking approval
     - Repeatedly redirected

   Subtext:
   Larry is structurally subordinate: his personal suffering must pass through the Rabbi's symbolic filter to be considered valid.

3. Incongruence (Words vs. tone/action)
   - Rabbi Scott speaks with polite warmth, but:
     - Chuckles at Larry's careful social gesture.
     - Launches into abstraction immediately after learning of the affair.
   - Larry speaks haltingly and tentatively, showing:
     - Shock
     - Speech collapse ("*she's, she's seeing Sy Ableman*")

   Subtext:
   - Rabbi Scott's calm confidence is emotionally incongruent with the gravity of Larry's crisis.
   - Larry's politeness masks emotional devastation.

4. Omissions and silences
   Key silences:
   - The "long silence" after:
     - *"And she wants a Gett."*
   - No one directly discusses:
     - Humiliation
     - Sexual betrayal
     - Rage

    - Jealousy
    - Fear of social annihilation

Subtext:

The silence marks the point where:

- The truth is too heavy for ritual speech.
- Language switches from *human pain* to *spiritual displacement.*

5. Character relationship and history
    - Rabbi–Congregant dynamic:
        - Larry expects care, wisdom, grounding
        - The Rabbi delivers doctrine and metaphor
    - Larry seeks the *older* Rabbi:

    Subtext:

    Larry does not trust Rabbi Scott to understand life's cruelty—only its theology.

6. Deflections, evasions, and shifts

    Major deflections:
    - Betrayal → "God's will"
    - Emotional injury → "perspective"
    - Divorce → "cosmic order."
    - Despair → "parking lot."
    - Larry's "*Um...*" is a failed attempt to resist abstraction—a soft protest he cannot articulate.

    Subtext:

    Deflection functions as:
    - A defense against emotional reality
    - A ritual containment of chaos
    - A refusal to confront injustice directly

7. Cultural, social, and professional context
    - Jewish religious authority structure:
        - Rabbis are expected to provide moral anchoring
        - A Gett has both legal and theological implications
    - Midwestern, polite, conflict-avoiding ethos

    Subtext:

    The cultural context demands meaning over protest, acceptance over confrontation, and theology over rage.

8. Metaphors and figurative language
    - "*Losing track of Hashem.*"
    - "*Seeing with tired eyes.*"
    - "*Fresh perspective.*"
    - "*Visitor in the parking lot.*"

Subtext:
These metaphors spiritualize injustice, quietly redefining:

- Betrayal as a *problem of vision*
- Suffering as *interpretive failure*
- Moral injury as an *optical illusion*

9. Emotional undercurrents
   Larry:
   - Shock
   - Shame
   - Fear
   - Humiliation
   - Loneliness
   - Existential terror

   Rabbi Scott:
   - Anxious reassurance
   - Defensive faith performance
   - Mild nervous cheerfulness (“*Ha-ha-ha!*”)

   Crucial Line:
   - “*The boss isn’t always right, but he’s always the boss.*”

   Subtext of this line:
   - Bitter surrender
   - Cynical fatalism
   - Obedience without belief
   - This is not faith—it is resigned submission

   The Rabbi hears it as affirmation; it is actually spiritual exhaustion.

10. Repetition and emphasis
    - Repeated fixation on:
      - *“Perspective”*
      - *“Seeing”*
      - *“Look at the parking lot.”*
    - The Rabbi repeats visual language because:
      - He cannot address moral injury
      - He only knows how to re-teach perception

    Subtext:
    Repetition reveals doctrinal paralysis: he keeps restarting the same spiritual loop because there is no real bridge to Larry’s reality.

☑ *Final subtext synthesis (Core meaning beneath the scene)*

Larry is asking whether his suffering is morally real and whether someone will stand with him against injustice. Rabbi Scott is answering a different, safer question: how to see God in chaos without confronting the chaos itself. This is not comfort—it is: metaphysical pacification.

Larry's pain is:

- Psychologically real
- Socially humiliating
- Morally destabilizing

But it is treated as:

- A problem of vision
- A spiritual misunderstanding
- A failure of perspective

Subtext in one sentence: The subtext of this scene is not guidance but displacement: Larry brings betrayal and terror, and the Rabbi converts it into optics and theology, leaving the core wound untouched.

Here, I propose the following prompt to identify the structure of the dramatic effect and inward significance of the scene:

PROMPT 5.4 IDENTIFYING THE DRAMATIC EFFECT AND THE INWARD SIGNIFICANCE OF THE SCENE

The subtext of a dialogue of the deaf may have a powerful dramatic effect on the audience.

Here are several explanations as to why dialogues of the deaf are dramatically powerful

1. Because the real drama happens in the *subtext*, not the words.
   When characters "listen past" each other, the spoken dialogue becomes a surface mask. Underneath, in the subtext, characters reveal:
   - fear
   - desire
   - shame
   - longing
   - domination
   - avoidance

   The gap between what they say and what they cannot say creates dramatic tension.

2. They externalize inner conflict.
   When two characters can't hear each other, the audience sees:
   - each character's private logic
   - each character's emotional wound
   - the *collision* of incompatible inner worlds

   This exposes the psychological structure more sharply than "normal" dialogue would.

3. They dramatize the tragic limitations of human communication.
   We discover something existential:
   Even when we speak the same language, we may not inhabit the same world.
   This produces irony, frustration, or poignancy.
   Dialogue-of-the-deaf scenes often function as micro-tragedies: communication fails, connection fails, and meaning collapses.

4. They reveal power relations.
   Because characters pursue different conversational goals, the audience sees:
   - who dominates
   - who evades
   - who is desperate for contact
   - who refuses vulnerability

   The *failure to hear* reveals a map of the social order.

5. They heighten the audience's involvement.
   When characters talk past each other, the audience becomes the only entity that truly understands both sides.
   This creates:
   - engagement
   - dramatic irony
   - emotional investment

   The audience becomes the hidden interpreter that the characters lack.

   ###

Instructions:

Based on your analysis so far. Use your subtext analysis of the scene to explain how the SUBTEXT of the DIALOGUE OF THE DEAF generates a dramatic aesthetic effect.

Avoid clichés and focus on the way in which the explicit dialogue and the IMPLICIT subtext generate the dramatic effect and INWARD SIGNIFICANCE of the scene.

Running this prompt, ChatGPT provided the following analysis:

MODEL'S OUTPUT 5.5

Below is a prompt analysis of how the subtext of this dialogue of the deaf produces its dramatic effect and inward significance, grounded strictly in the Rabbi Scott scene and avoiding generic formulations.

Dramatic effect and inward significance of the Rabbi Scott Scene

1. The real drama happens in the subtext, not the words

   On the surface, the scene is calm, polite, and even mildly reassuring. Nothing overtly explosive happens. Yet the subtext is saturated with collapse.

   - Larry's spoken lines are restrained, hesitant, and socially cautious.
   - Beneath them sits:
     - sexual humiliation ("*she's seeing Sy Ableman*"),
     - existential terror ("*I don't know which end is up*"),
     - and moral disorientation ("*She's usually right about these things*").

   By contrast, Rabbi Scott's words are fluent, confident, and metaphor-laden. But the subtext beneath *his* speech is not wisdom—it is avoidance masquerading as meaning.

   The dramatic tension is generated precisely here:

   - Larry speaks as if he is asking for advice.
   - Subtextually, he is asking whether reality itself has betrayed him.
   - The Rabbi responds as if the problem is epistemological ("how to see"), while Larry's wound is relational.

   The audience hears both layers simultaneously. The effect is a quiet but relentless emotional suffocation, not comfort.

2. *The Scene externalizes Larry's inner conflict by splitting it across two voices*

   Larry's psyche is effectively split across the two characters:

   - Larry's side of the split:
     - chaos
     - shock
     - humiliation
     - fear that nothing makes sense anymore
   - The Rabbi's side of the split:
     - order
     - interpretive control
     - spiritual rationalization
     - the insistence that meaning still exists *if only one looks at things in the right way*

   What Larry cannot integrate psychologically—that his life is collapsing for reasons that do not feel just—is projected outward into an interlocutor who insists the collapse is meaningful. Thus, the scene dramatizes not merely a failed consultation, but an inner conflict between:

   - a mind that experiences catastrophe,
   - and a mind that is forced to insist that catastrophe must still be intelligible.

   This is why the scene feels quietly violent: Larry is fighting against the need to keep believing.

3. *The scene stages the tragic limitations of communication without grand gestures*

   The tragedy here is not loud. It unfolds through:

   - non-answers
   - polite nods
   - metaphors that land nowhere
   - and a final image—the parking lot—that is offered as revelation and received as existential blankness.

   The audience perceives something devastating:

   Larry and the Rabbi are not disagreeing. They are not even misunderstanding each other. They are inhabiting incompatible meaning systems.

   The Rabbi's world presumes:

   - divine order
   - hidden structure
   - significance behind appearances

   Larry's lived reality offers:

   - betrayal without explanation
   - humiliation without redemption
   - loss without narrative shape

   The tragic force lies in the recognition that no amount of goodwill can bridge this gap. The result is not conflict but metaphysical loneliness.

4. *Power relations are revealed through interpretive control, not aggression*

   The Rabbi never raises his voice. He is kind, composed, and even gentle. And yet, he completely dominates the meaning of the scene.

   Power is exercised through:

   - who gets to define what the problem really is,
   - who is allowed to speak in concrete terms,
   - and who must translate their suffering into abstraction in order to be heard.

   Larry brings:

   - a wife,
   - a betrayal,
   - a rival,
   - a divorce.

   The Rabbi converts all this into:

   - "perspective,"
   - "seeing Hashem,"
   - and "God's will."

   The effect is subtle but serious:

   - Larry's specific suffering is overwritten by general metaphysics.
   - His personal catastrophe is absorbed into impersonal cosmic order.

   The power imbalance becomes visible not through coercion, but through interpretive erasure.

5. *The audience is forced into the role of the only true listener*
   Because the two characters never fully meet:
   - Larry cannot hear the Rabbi's abstractions as meaningful.
   - The Rabbi cannot hear Larry's suffering as irreducible.

   Only the audience hears both:
   - the spiritual language and its protective function,
   - the human pain and its unspeakability.

   This puts the audience in a uniquely painful position:
   - We understand why Larry is desperate.
   - We understand why the Rabbi retreats into metaphysics.
   - And we understand that this mutual failure is irreversible within the scene.

   The dramatic effect is therefore not one of resolution but one of witnessing:
   - witnessing the gap,
   - witnessing the loneliness,
   - witnessing the failure of language to express what the soul is actually undergoing.

   Inward significance of the scene (Core insight)
   At its deepest level, this scene is not about divorce, nor is it about God. It is about this inner catastrophe:

   The moment when a human being discovers that the language meant to give meaning to suffering can no longer connect with that suffering at all.
   Larry does not leave with:
   - guidance,
   - clarity,
   - or reassurance.

   He leaves with:
   - a visual metaphor he cannot use,
   - a theology he cannot identify with,
   - and a world that still feels broken.

   The parking lot becomes the final cruel image:
   - offered as revelation,
   - received as emptiness.

The dramatic power of this dialogue of the deaf lies in how Larry's moral and emotional collapse is steadily translated into spiritual abstraction, allowing the audience to feel—more acutely than either character—the brutal gap between human suffering and the meanings meant to accommodate it.

The inward significance of the scene, as identified by the model, is not about the failure of personality, nor about existential emptiness. It is about a gap. An unbridgeable gap between the suffering of a single individual and the institutional meaning systems that claim to accommodate it. As summarized by the model:

The moment when a human being discovers that the language meant to give meaning to suffering can no longer connect with that suffering at all.

As observers, we seem to sense intuitively what the participants in the interaction miss in their communication. A pleasant, polite consultation often masks a deeper, more painful miscommunication. This is not a trivial form of miscommunication but a dialogue of the deaf, signaling a deep gulf between suffering and meaning-making systems. This is not a philosophical issue per se, but an emotionally loaded personal experience that we can subconsciously identify with. Paradoxically, it is the terms used in the conversation itself that lead us to the subtext (i.e., the dialogue of the deaf), and this, in turn, leads us to the scene's inward significance. What we learn from the model's analysis is that the scene does not have just one inward significance. The dramatic aesthetic effect of the scene yields various experiences, as detailed by the model. While the subtext, in the form of interpersonal dynamics, is clearly exposed, the scene's inward significance to the observer is beyond our direct access. It is something we can only speculate about, no more.

At this point, we may ask about the relevance of this methodology for analyzing real-life interactions. One clear direction is to study therapeutic discourse addressing human suffering and ask whether it exposes the gap previously mentioned, or papers over it with clichés, parables, and abstract philosophical theories. In Neuman (2026), I discuss a scene from Dostoevsky's *The Brothers Karamazov*. A woman who has lost her young son arrives at a monastery to visit an old monk, Father Zosima, the Elder, much admired for his "holiness." The woman approaches the monk from a position of suffering, and he tries to comfort her by telling her to be happy because her baby is in the company of God's angels. These kinds of situations, as long as they require the analysis of subtext for addressing misalignments, may be analyzed structurally to expose the gap. While in *The Brothers Karamazov*, the poor woman accepts the monk's consultation with enthusiasm, there is good reason to suspect that the monk's advice is an attempt to mask the loss using clichés of ignorance, and that after leaving the monastery, the poor woman will still mourn her lost child. While misalignments may not always be explicit, they are a cue that invites us to look more deeply.

DISCUSSION

The opening scene of the film *A Serious Man* evokes a world steeped in superstition. It is the same Eastern European Jewish world that appears in the novels of Bashevis Singer. It contrasts with the modern and prosperous states in which the main plot takes place. However, what we learn through the difference is that the world is the same in terms of our explanatory schemes and their failure to comfort the suffering individual, from Job to Larry.

Let me summarize the model's analysis. First, it identified a dialogue of the deaf, characterized by several dominant types of misalignments. To explain these misalignments, I turned to subtext analysis, which revealed that the scene, despite its appearance, is not about guidance but about displacement: Larry brings betrayal and terror, and the Rabbi converts them into perspectives and theology, leaving the core wound untouched. In terms of the three benefits proposed in the introduction, you should first ask yourself whether you have learned something new by working in concert with the AI.

Through a structured and detailed approach, we learned that a meeting initially labeled as a consultation is actually about how individuals and institutions may engage with a single individual's suffering in ways that are both blind to it and irrelevant to it. Rabbi Scott, despite his politeness and goodwill, is completely blind to the needs of the person asking for his support. Subtext, though, is about a relation, and despite Rabbi Scott's dominance in this dialogue, it is Larry's avoidance that constitutes and maintains this dialogue of the deaf.

To understand the benefits of using AI, consider comparing it to intelligent human interpretations of the film, such as the one posted by Evan Puschak[1] on his YouTube channel, *The Nerdwriter, which* has 3.23 million subscribers. This intelligent analysis focuses on Larry's psychology, arguing that his "inaction" is the "cause" of so many of his problems (1:49). It identifies the "cause" of Larry's suffering in his personality. However, the core of the film, according to Puschak, is questioning "the persuasiveness of every interpretive device" (3:23). According to this philosophical existential interpretation, "There is no God, there is no objective or cosmic purpose for us" (6:34), and all forms of interpretation seeking to find meaning in this silent cosmos, from the religious to the one proposed by science, are doomed to failure.

Now compare this reading of the film to the one presented so far. In terms of the first benefit of using AI, this approach to the play allows us to start reading the text with boots on the ground. Through the structured analysis of micro-moves, we identify the various types of misalignments and, through them, the subtext of the interaction. Instead of blaming poor Larry for his unassertiveness, we focus on the dynamics that explain the misalignment between Larry and the Rabbi. Instead of reading the drama through an existential, philosophical, and top-down perspective, we ask how the dialogue leads us to the subtext, ultimately revealing its inward significance. Here, the second benefit of a pedagogical approach is clear. The chapter provides a structured prompt and guidelines for analyzing and exposing the subtext of other scenes. But what about the inward significance? Puschak ignores the dramatic effect through his philosophical spectacles, while the prompts we use expose how the dialogue of the deaf generates dramatic tension, embedding Larry's deep metaphysical loneliness.

The main points of the chapter are:

- A dialogue of the deaf provides another context of misalignment.
- This dialogue is illustrated in a scene from *A Serious Man*.
- The chapter provides prompts for identifying this type of dialogue, the specific types of misalignment it presents, the subtext, and the dramatic effect.
- The analysis offers new and nuanced insights into the scene's subtext, supported by textual evidence.

- The inward significance of the scene may involve the experience of loneliness and the realization that the language meant to give meaning to suffering can no longer connect with that suffering at all.
- The approach can be extended to other contexts where we study the subtext of similar real-life dialogues.

NOTE

1. https://www.youtube.com/watch?v=3vDmWFTvzto

REFERENCE

Neuman, Y. (2026). *Uncertainty: From probability to fiction and religion*. Brill.

6 Was It Mostly Poopy? *Subtext in* Portnoy's Complaint

ABSTRACT *Portnoy's Complaint* is a hilarious novel adapted to the screen. This chapter analyzes a scene from *Portnoy's Complaint* as a case study in identifying subtext through interactional misalignment. While the scene, on the surface, appears to be a comic depiction of maternal intrusion and an adolescent's struggle for independence, the chapter demonstrates that its deeper structure is organized around a paradoxical communication pattern in which every possible response by the son is sanctioned. Using a formally structured, AI-assisted diagnostic prompt, the chapter shows how apparent alignment between question and answer can still conceal a core interactional contradiction. The analysis further demonstrates how this unique type of interpersonal dynamics generates the scene's distinctive aesthetic effect—transforming farce into psychological suffocation—and clarifies its inward significance as a dramatization of psychic entrapment and arrested individuation. Beyond literary analysis, the chapter establishes the pedagogical and clinical relevance of the proposed diagnostic tool, illustrating its applicability to real-life family dynamics and therapeutic assessment of covert control structures.

"WAS IT MOSTLY LIQUID OR MOSTLY POOPY?"

Portnoy's Complaint is a 1972 film adaptation (dir. Ernest Lehman, 1972) of the 1969 novel by Philip Roth (Roth, 1969). The original novel is both hilarious and a profound reflection on psychology and family dynamics. The novel gained enormous popularity among readers and critics alike and is repeatedly cited as one of the greatest American novels of the 20th century.

The novel/film is grounded in the family dynamics of a Jewish American household, which is an emotional pressure cooker. The protagonist, Alex Portnoy, grows up between a father who is weak, avoidant, and chronically constipated—physically and emotionally blocked—and a mother who dominates the domestic sphere with relentless vigilance, discipline, and emotional intensity. The family dynamic is defined by imbalance: the father retreats into passivity while the mother expands into every available psychological and physical space. In this context, Alex's home becomes a site of constant supervision, moral judgment, and hysterical care, where illness, guilt, food, and cleanliness are charged with meaning.

Alex's relationship with his mother is the emotional and thematic core of the novel, oscillating between dependence, resentment, guilt, and the desire for liberation. She is fiercely protective, intensely anxious, and pathologically invasive, treating Alex as both her greatest responsibility and her primary emotional outlet. Her love is absolute

 DOI: 10.1201/9781042004485-8

but claustrophobic, generating in Alex a lifelong conflict between craving approval and needing autonomy. This bond produces his characteristic neurosis: his compulsive sexuality, his oscillation between shame and defiance, and his inability to form stable intimate relationships. Even as an adult, Alex remains psychologically entangled with his mother's voice inside his head, policing his desires and undermining his freedom. The "complaint" itself can be read as an extended struggle to separate his own identity from the maternal symbiosis that both shaped and protected him.

In one of the scenes, the teenager Alex leaves the dining table to go to the toilet, where he usually masturbates. In the movie scene, you can see a very small apartment with the toilets located near the kitchen table, where the family members dine at a small table. A moment later, the father gets up from the table with a look of pain, picks up a newspaper, and heads to the toilets. He is hurrying Alex to go out and explicitly expresses the urgency of the situation in an explicit and carnivalesque way: "I haven't come up with anything in a week!" The mother intervenes in the conversation, approaches the toilet door, and knocks on it aggressively, shouting, "Open up!" Here, a conversation develops between Alex and his intrusive mother, who expresses pathological curiosity about what is happening behind the closed door. The mother commands Alex to open the door. She asks whether he is in pain, demands to know exactly where it hurts, and warns him not to flush the toilets because she wants to see what he has done in there.

At this point, Alex gets out of the toilets, trying to avoid his mother saying that he has some homework to do. However, the mother opens an intrusive and paranoid investigation. First, she asks Alex whether he flushed the toilets, even though she had asked him not to. Alex admits that he flushed the toilets. The mother interrogates him about what was in the toilets, which he had flushed so quickly, and Alex responds, "Diarrhea." "Was it mostly liquid or mostly poopy?" the mother asks, and Alex impatiently responds, "I don't look. I didn't look. Stop saying poopy to me. I'm in high school."

Alex responds to his mother's intrusive and detailed questioning, first providing a straight answer (diarrhea) and then trying to avoid the questions, protesting against his mother's childish approach to him (I'm in high school!). However, the dialogue continues, and the mother's response reminds us of the angry woman from Levin's sketch. She is on the defensive and the offensive at the same time. She addresses him using his full name, "Alexander Portnoy," which is a classic parental move: it signals that she's serious, that this is not casual, and subtly reminds him of who he is in relation to her—a son, her son, whatever else he thinks he's become. Then, she informs him that his secret has been revealed. The final line is the emotional gut-punch. Hannah—his sister—has been reporting to her. The mother is not just angry; she is letting him know he has been watched, and that his secret has now been revealed.

At this point, there is a tension over whether Alex's secretive masturbating activity in the toilets has been exposed, but Alex's revealed secret is surprisingly different. The mother reveals that after school, he goes with his friend, Melvin Weiner, to Harold's Hot Dog Palace to eat "Hazzarai" (i.e., Pork).

The mother approaches the father for support over Alex's shameful secret, but the father is trying to avoid the fuss, arguing that he is busy moving his bowels. However, Alex's mother totally ignores his request. She "reports" to her husband with a mix of sarcasm and accusation about their son's "sin," and points out that her son, the exemplary "A student" who prides himself on being too mature for childish language, leads a private life after school that others do not see. By asking what he does when nobody is watching, she suggests that beneath the façade of maturity and achievement, there may be behaviors or desires that contradict his carefully maintained image. The father repeats his request, begging to be left alone. He is asking for peace while he is trying to release his painful bowel. However, the mother continues by threatening Alex and asking him:

Mother: Alex, answer me something. How do you think Melvin Weiner gave himself colitis? Why has that child spent half his life in hospitals?
Alex: Because he eats Hazzarai.
Mother: Don't you dare to make fun of me!
Alex: All right. How did he get colitis?
Mother: Because he eats Hazzarai! Moreover, it's not a joke!

At first glance, this scene appears straightforward in its portrayal of family dynamics. "Reading the lines," we observe a highly hysterical, neurotic, and pathologically intrusive mother spying on her son's activity in the toilets. Alex's secret is not the pleasure of masturbating, but the pleasure of eating food not cooked by his caring mother. Reading between the lines, we understand that the food symbolizes symbiosis; the mother's food is contrasted with the impure and dangerous food Alex consumes outside. It is a dangerous food, interpreted as the cause of poor Melvin Weiner's colitis.

I would like you to take a minute or two to reflect on the subtext of the scene. From the perspective presented in this book, the subtext, the underlying meaning, is about the *interactional dynamics*. First, decide whether there is a subtext to this scene, or whether the interactional meaning is fully explicit. If you think there is a subtext, then write it down in front of you, ensuring the interactional dynamics are not trivially expressed by the scene. At this point, I would like to ask whether you have used the concept of the *double bind* to describe the subtext. If the answer is negative, let me expose a hidden layer of the interaction and its deeper significance for the observer.

CAUGHT IN A DOUBLE BIND

In the previous chapters, the trigger for exposing the subtext was a misalignment, as expressed in the interaction. It was a misalignment between the expected response to an utterance and the actual response, or the misalignment expressed by a dialogue of the deaf. Is there a misalignment in the above "poopy conversation"? Try to articulate the misalignment that exists in the scene. To help you in your mission, let us identify the speech acts underlying the final part of the scene with the help of the LLM. I ran a speech act analysis, and here is the model's output:

MODEL'S OUTPUT 6.1

- Mother: "Alex, answer me something."—Directive (command)
- Mother: "How do you think Melvin Weiner gave himself colitis?"—Question (information-seeking)

- Mother: "Why has that child spent half his life in hospitals?"—Question (rhetorical/information-seeking)
- Alex: "Because he eats Hazzarai."—Answer/Assertion
- Mother: "Don't you dare to make fun of me!"—Prohibition/Reprimand
- Alex: "All right."—Compliance signal
- Alex: "How did he get colitis?"—Question (clarification request)
- Mother: "Because he eats Hazzarai!"—Answer/Assertion
- Mother: "And it's not a joke!"—Declaration/Reprimand

The mother commands Alex to answer her question regarding the cause of Melvin Weiner's colitis. Alex's answer is correct, at least as his mother expected. In this case, there is no misalignment between the utterance/question and the response/answer. However, the mother's response to Alex's answer is a prohibition/reprimand. It combines two speech-act functions in a single utterance:

Prohibition = a direct ban on a specific action
→ The speaker is saying: *"You are not allowed to do this."*
Reprimand = a scolding for behavior already performed or initiated
→ The speaker is also saying: *"What you just did is wrong and deserves correction."*

So, in "Don't you dare to make fun of me!" the mother is doing both at once:

prohibiting future mocking (*don't do this again*), and
reprimanding Alex for the mockery she believes has already occurred.

However, Alex provided *exactly the answer his mother anticipated from him.* We know it is the right answer because, when Alex asks his mother for the answer, she gives him the exact same answer that Alex provided. There is a *perfect* alignment between the expected response and the actual response generated by Alex, yet he is still criticized for his correct response. Here we can articulate the misalignment. The misalignment is not between the expected and the actual response, but between *the alignment of the utterance-response and the mother's response to this alignment*! This is a much more sophisticated form of misalignment than we have observed so far.

This misalignment, more accurately described as an anomaly, invites us to examine the interaction's underlying meaning. When presenting the book (Chapter 1), I emphasized that I use a theoretically grounded approach to guide the AI, but not in an imposed, top-down manner. I illustrated this approach in the previous chapter, where I used a prompt to diagnose a dialogue as a dialogue of the deaf. The same approach is also applied in the present chapter.

First, we noticed an anomaly that requires an explanation. Here, the explanation is guided theoretically by the hypothesis that what we observe is an example of a *double bind.* Bateson presents the concept of the double bind (Bateson, 2000) as a communication dilemma in which a person receives two or more conflicting messages, making it impossible to respond to one without failing to respond to the other. The mother commands Alex to provide her with an answer. Alex has two options. It is clear that he does not believe Melvin's colitis was caused by eating hot dogs made out of the ultimate Jewish taboo animal—pork. However, misaligning with his mother's "medical theory" is impossible, as that would have negative consequences. Nevertheless, when he provides the "correct" and expected answer, he is attacked and threatened by his mother! There is no way of avoiding the painful experience of the dilemma. Whatever he chooses will mean paying a price.

My hypothesis is that this anomaly can be explained by appealing to the subtext. As explained in Chapter 3, the subtext concerns the dynamics of interpersonal relations, and here I hypothesize that it corresponds precisely to a *double bind*. We can interpret the interaction as a double bind, but if we adopt a more scientific approach, we should treat it as a hypothesis to be tested rather than a concept to be imposed on the text. So, treating the double bind as a hypothesis, I designed a detailed, well-structured prompt to determine whether it is the subtext of the current interaction. Here is the prompt:

PROMPT 6.1 AUTOMATIC DOUBLE-BIND ANALYZER

A DOUBLE BIND presents a communication dilemma in which a person receives two or more conflicting messages, making it impossible to respond to one without failing to respond to the other.

A double bind is not the same as a contradiction.

Here is a precise and multi-layered diagnostic checklist to distinguish between strict double binds and general contradictions.

A Diagnostic Checklist for True Double Binds

Tier 1 — *Structural requirements*

1. Two contradictory injunctions.
   - They must be more than mixed messages.
   - They must conflict logically so that obeying one means disobeying the other.
2. Different logical levels.
   - One injunction is usually about behavior.
   - The other is about meta-communication (tone, affect, implied meaning).

   Example: "Be emotionally close" + "If you show emotion, I will withdraw."
3. Injunctions must come from an important relationship.
   - Parent, partner, authority figure.
   - The relationship must matter enough that disobedience has costs.

Tier 2—*Containment conditions*

4. No meta-communication is allowed.
   The person cannot comment on the contradiction:
   - "Why do you say X but punish me for X?"

   This attempt is shut down, mocked, pathologized, or punished.
5. No escape is possible.
   The person cannot:
   - leave the situation (norms, shame, dependency),
   - or detach (which will be punished as abandonment).

   This is essential in Bateson's theory.

Tier 3—*Repetition and pattern*

6. This must be a chronic, patterned interaction.
   - One incident is not enough.
   - The pattern is recursively reinforced.
7. Both commands carry emotional/relational weight.
   - The person believes both sides simultaneously.
   - The contradiction is lived, not merely logical.

Tier 4 — *Psychological consequences*

8. The person must experience the impossibility of giving a correct response.
   Typical signs:
   - Freeze states
   - Learned helplessness
   - Paradoxical compliance
   - Confusion around meaning ("What does love mean here?")
9. Escape attempts lead to escalation.
   - Trying to obey → punished
   - Trying to disobey → punished
   - Trying to leave → punished
   - Trying to name the contradiction → punished

Tier 5—*Optional (but frequent) meta-patterns*

10. The double bind sets the definition of the relationship.
    It is not just a moment inside the relationship—it is the relationship.
11. The content is less important than the pattern.
    The bind repeats across situations with different content.

    ##

Task: Analyze the following conversation to determine whether it expresses a double bind.

The context of the conversation is: [CONTEXT HERE]

The conversation is: [CONVERSATION HERE]

###

General Instructions:

Analyze the dialogue using these criteria:

1. Is there an important relationship?
2. Is there a primary command?
3. Is there a contradictory secondary command?
4. Is there a block on naming the contradiction?
5. Is there no escape?
6. Is repetition implied?
7. Are all responses punished?

If yes → Double Bind."
Specific instructions:
Apply steps 1 to 8

Step 1—*Identify relational context*

1. Who is speaking to whom?
2. Is the relationship emotionally important (parent–child, romantic, authority, caregiver, dependent)?

If NO → Not a double bind (stop).
If YES → Continue.

Step 2—*Primary injunction* (Behavioral command)

Check:

- Does one party communicate a clear behavioral expectation, rule, or demand?

Answer YES/NO and quote it.
If NO → Not a double bind.

Step 3—*Secondary injunction* (Contradictory meta-communicative command)

Check:

- Is there a second message (implicit or explicit) that logically contradicts the first?
- Does obeying one mean disobeying the other?

Answer YES/NO and quote evidence.
If NO → Not a double bind.

Step 4—*Blocking of meta-communication*

Check:

- Does the context prevent the person from spelling out the contradiction ("Why are you telling me X and punishing Y?")?
- Or are attempts to clarify met with anger, guilt, mockery, withdrawal, or punishment?

Answer YES/NO.
If NO → Not a double bind.

Step 5—*No escape possible*

Check:

- Is the person unable to leave the situation (because of duty, shame, dependence, institutional authority, emotional bonds)?

YES/NO.
If NO → Not a double bind.

Step 6—*Patterned/Repeated structure*

Check:

- Is the contradiction part of a repeated interaction pattern, not a one-off?

If the scene hints at repeated cycles → YES.
If not → "insufficient evidence."

Step 7—*Consequence: No correct response*

Check:

- Does every available response (obeying either injunction, disobeying, staying silent, naming the paradox) lead to negative consequences for the person?

YES/NO.

Step 8—*Final classification*

Using the above evidence, classify the conversation as:

- TRUE DOUBLE BIND—clearly meets Steps 1–5, and Steps 6–7 are strongly supported
- PROBABLE DOUBLE BIND—structure present, but some contextual missing information
- MIXED MESSAGES/CONTRADICTION ONLY—contradictions without entrapment
- NO DOUBLE BIND

Provide a short explanation citing evidence.

To diagnose the dialogue between Alex and his mother, I ran the prompt on Gemini Pro. The model produced the following output:

MODEL'S OUTPUT 6.2

Here is the analysis of the dialogue using the automatic double-bind analyzer.

Step 1—Identify relational context

1. Who is speaking to whom? A mother and her teenage son (Alex).
2. Is the relationship emotionally important? YES. It is a primary parent–child dependency relationship, characterized here by intense maternal intrusion and control.

Step 2—Primary injunction (Behavioral Command)

Check: Does one party communicate a clear behavioral expectation, rule, or demand?

YES.

There are multiple behavioral commands, but the critical one for the final double-bind structure is the demand that Alex take his mother seriously and respect her authority regarding health rules.

Quote: [Quotes have been removed to avoid copyright issues. YN]

Step 3—Secondary injunction (contradictory meta-communicative command)

Check: Is there a second message that logically contradicts the first? Does obeying one mean disobeying the other?

YES.

The contradiction occurs in the final exchange regarding the cause of colitis.

- The premise: The mother sets up a scenario where the answer to her rhetorical question is obvious: Melvin gets colitis because he eats forbidden food (Hazzarai).
- The First injunction (Implicit): "Acknowledge the truth of what I am teaching you."
- Alex's response: He acknowledges the truth: "Because he eats Hazzarai."
- The second injunction (Punishment/Contradiction): The mother immediately punishes him for stating the truth, interpreting his compliance as mockery. "Don't you dare to make fun of me!"
- The contradiction defined: The mother demands agreement with her reality (Injunction 1), but when Alex provides that agreement, she attacks the *way* he provides it as disrespectful (Injunction 2).

- Proof of contradiction: When Alex complies with the second injunction by acting serious and ignorant ("All right. How did he get colitis?"). The mother yells the exact same information he just gave her, while still framing him as being in the wrong: "Because he eats Hazzarai! And it's not a joke!"

If he knows the answer, he is mocking her. If he asks for the answer, he is chastised for not taking the situation seriously.

Step 4—Blocking of meta-communication

Check: Does the context prevent the person from spelling out the contradiction? Or are attempts to clarify met with punishment?

YES.

When Alex attempts to set a boundary regarding her infantilizing language—a meta-comment on the interaction—he is immediately shut down.

Furthermore, when he attempts to engage in the logic of the final argument, he is accused of "making fun," thereby blocking him from pointing out that he agrees with her.

Step 5—No escape possible

Check: Is the person unable to leave the situation?

YES.

Alex is a dependent minor in his own home. When he physically tries to leave the immediate situation, his mother commands him to stop.

Quote:

Step 6—Patterned/repeated structure

Check: Is the contradiction part of a repeated interaction pattern, not a one-off?

YES (Strongly Implied).

The dialogue suggests a chronic dynamic of intrusion and infantilization, battling with Alex's growing desire for autonomy. The mother's line, "The A student whose own mother can't say poopy to anymore," implies a long-standing history of this specific interactional struggle.

Step 7—Consequence: no correct response

Check: Does every available response lead to negative consequences for the person?

YES.

In the final exchange:

- If Alex answers the question correctly ("Because he eats Hazzarai"), he is punished for "making fun."

- If he acts seriously and asks for the answer ("How did he get colitis?"), he is shouted at and treated as if he doesn't understand the gravity of the situation ("And it's not a joke!").
- If he tries to leave, he is ordered to stay.
- If he tries to set boundaries on her language, he is attacked for "shouting."

Step 8—Final classification

TRUE DOUBLE BIND

Explanation:

This interaction is a textbook example of a double bind. It features an intense dependency relationship where the mother issues contradictory demands at different logical levels. She demands Alex acknowledge her reality (Tier 1: Primary Injunction), but punishes him for doing so by characterizing his acknowledgment as mockery (Tier 1: Secondary Injunction). Alex is blocked from commenting on this paradox (Tier 2: Blocking) and cannot leave the field (Tier 2: No Escape). The interaction ends in a state where Alex has no correct response available; either knowing the answer or asking for it results in an attack (Tier 4).

We can see that the model's analysis supports the hypothesis that what we observe is a double bind, not just an interaction between a domineering mother and her son. Therefore, we have a scene that is humorous but loaded with a bothersome subtext, and this is indeed the dynamic of the double bind. As our focus is on the emotional vortex where the father's constipation, the mother's intrusive aggression, and Alex's defenses all turn around Alex's secret, unknown to his mother, we are distracted from the subtext that involves the pathology of the double bind. This subtext and its contrast with the overt conversation generate a dramatic effect. To expose this dramatic effect and the scene's inward significance, I used Prompt 6.2. However, let me remind you once again that the inward significance cannot be fully articulated but only pointed to. With this in mind, you are invited to review the prompt and its outcome.

PROMPT 6.2

Based on your analysis so far. Use your analysis of the scene to explain how the dialogue's subtext generates a dramatic aesthetic effect on the audience. Avoid clichés, and focus on the way in which the explicit dialogue and the IMPLICIT subtext of the double bind generate the dramatic effect, and INWARD SIGNIFICANCE of the scene.

Gemini generated the following output:

MODEL'S OUTPUT 6.3

This scene generates a dramatic aesthetic effect that can best be described as *claustrophobic absurdity*. The audience is subjected to a vertiginous experience where the banal setting of a family conversation and the grotesque topic of bowel movements serve as a smokescreen for a profound psychic violation.

The dramatic power of the scene does not rely on advancement of the plot, but rather on the relentless tightening of a psychological vice. The aesthetic effect arises from the colossal gap between the explicit, almost slapstick dialogue and the terrifying implicit subtext of the maternal double bind, which aims to annihilate the son's developing autonomy.

Here is an analysis of how this aesthetic effect is generated through subtext and the double-bind mechanism.

The carnivalesque turned nightmarish

The scene begins with an aesthetic of low comedy—the "carnivalesque" urgency of the father's constipation and the stereotypical Jewish mother hammering on a bathroom door. The explicit dialogue is obsessively focused on the grotesque reality of the body: diarrhea, "poopy," flushing, and disease.

However, the subtext immediately curdles this humor into anxiety. The mother's explicit concern for Alex's physical health ("Do you want me to call the doctor?") is a thinly veiled code for her intrusive need to control the deepest recesses of his private life. The bathroom, typically the one sanctuary of solitude in a crowded home, becomes a panopticon where Alex is observed even when unseen.

The aesthetic effect on the audience shifts rapidly from amusement to deep discomfort. We realize that the mother's volume and intensity are disproportionate to the situation. The explicit text says "health crisis"; the subtext screams "boundary crisis." The audience is compelled to inhabit Alex's shrinking world, where even his bodily functions are not his own. The presence of the ineffectual father, who just wants "peace" to move his own bowels, only heightens the sense of a closed, suffocating system from which there is no exit.

The epistemological vertigo of the double bind

The central dramatic engine of the scene is the double bind in the final exchange regarding Melvin Weiner and colitis. This is where the aesthetic shifts from mere claustrophobia to a kind of epistemological vertigo—a dizziness induced by the collapse of logic.

Throughout the scene, the mother demands that Alex take her seriously, stop "shouting," and behave like a "grown-up." This is the primary behavioral injunction. Yet, when she corners him with the rhetorical question about why Melvin has colitis, and Alex provides the correct, compliant answer ("Because he eats Hazzarai"), she instantly attacks him: "Don't you dare to make fun of me!"

This moment creates a profound, dramatic shock. The audience witnesses the trap snap shut. We see that Alex's compliance—his attempt to agree with her reality—is subtextually re-coded by the mother as an act of aggression (mockery).

The aesthetic effect here is one of *paralyzing absurdity*. The audience realizes, perhaps before Alex fully realizes himself, that truth is irrelevant in this dynamic. The mother is not seeking information; she is seeking a submission so total that Alex must abandon his own perception of reality to align with hers. When he *aligns with hers, she shifts the goalposts to keep him* in the wrong.

The subsequent exchange creates a tragic resonance. Alex, disoriented by the punishment for telling the truth, tries the only other option: feigning ignorance to allow her to be the teacher ("All right. How did he get colitis?"). The mother then yells back the exact same information he had just provided, adding, "And it's not a joke!"

The audience is left reeling. The explicit dialogue has become meaningless noise; the subtext is the only thing that matters, and the subtext is a bludgeon. The dramatic effect is a sickening realization that Alex cannot use logic or obedience to escape; any move he makes tightens the bind.

The inward significance: psychic annihilation

The "inward significance" of this scene—the deeper human truth lying beneath the surface—is the struggle for the self against engulfment.

The mother's relentless questioning and weaponized worry are attempts to erase the boundary between herself and her son. By pathologizing his privacy (the locked door must mean pain) and infantilizing his language ("poopy"), she is actively dismantling his attempts at individuation.

The double bind is the ultimate tool for this psychic annihilation. By constructing a reality in which Alex is wrong if he knows the answer and wrong if he asks for it, she invalidates his cognitive processes. The aesthetic effect is *one of tragedy masquerading as farce*. The audience laughs at the word "poopy," but beneath the laughter, we feel the terror of a young man whose capacity to interpret his own reality is being systematically fractured by the person he depends on most. The scene's drama lies not in what happens "on the surface," but in the unseen, violent suppression of Alex's developing self.

DISCUSSION

I find the model's analysis to be insightful. The main points recognized are (1) a "struggle for the self against engulfment" and (2) a *tragedy masquerading as farce*. The text appears light and humorous. A Jewish family of low socioeconomic status is dining. The father rushes to the toilet, sharing his urgency with his family. This scene may look like a part of a "bowel satire." The mother rushes to the toilet and inquires about her son, who is no longer a child. She is intrusively interested in the details of his feces. Embarrassing and humorous. However, the subtext of the interaction between Alex and his mother is that of the double bind, where Alex is struggling against his mother's pathological control. When we watch this scene, we laugh, but at the same time, we unconsciously experience the tension between the farce and the tragedy. I believe this point is one contributor to the scene's aesthetic effect. On the one hand, it manipulates us into believing we are watching a comedy, but beneath the surface, we experience a tragedy. The inward significance is experienced through these complementary oppositions, just as oppositions (e.g., sweet and sour) are used in Chinese cooking to play with our taste.

At this point, you may understand the benefits of using AI for analyzing subtext. First, the dimensions of the double bind have been identified and designed in dialogue with the AI. Second, the chapter presents a structured, detailed prompt for identifying a double bind. This prompt can be used pedagogically to teach students the meaning of a double bind and its importance as a subtext of a conversation. Finally, the approach and prompt can be used for analyzing double binds in real-life situations. For example, the diagnostic checklist provided for double binds is exceptionally useful for analyzing real-life interactions, offering a structured way to move beyond general intuition to a precise identification of a damaging communication pattern. Imagine a family therapist analyzing a family's dynamics, suspecting that double binds are present. If the AI identifies a double bind, the therapist can return to the causes of this dynamic.

The major source of a double bind is power and dependency structures, as they almost always emerge in situations where one person has asymmetric power (parent, authority, caregiver), the other is emotionally or materially dependent, and no way out is realistically possible. This is why classic situations of double-bind communication are parent–child relationships, intimate partnerships, total institutions, and ideological systems. A reasonable hypothesis is that double binds arise when the speaker has an internal conflict that cannot be consciously tolerated, so it is expressed as a contradiction in communication. For example, a partner wants honesty but cannot tolerate the truth. According to this hypothesis, double binds emerge as defensive communication patterns, rather than as conscious manipulation strategies (although they can be used manipulatively in certain contexts). In addition, they allow their users to maintain control without resorting to overt force. In this sense, the bounds are powerful because they create chronic uncertainty, produce self-doubt in the receiver, undermine the receiver's ability to evaluate reality, and shift the burden of failure onto the victim. The receiver ends up always being wrong, regardless of what they do. This is why double binds function as a covert form of control. In sum, double binds come from unresolved inner conflict expressed through power relations, and people use them (usually unconsciously) to avoid emotional responsibility while maintaining control and reducing their own anxiety. The therapist may use this understanding to confront the sender objectively with evidence of double binds and to examine the source of their use through the methodology presented in this chapter.

The main points of the chapter are:

- A misalignment can appear paradoxically in the apparent alignment between an expected and an actual response.
- This sophisticated form of misalignment is indicative of a double bind.
- The double bind is an interactional dynamic identified by Gregory Bateson.
- In this chapter, I propose a detailed, well-structured prompt to diagnose a double bind as a subtext in a scene.
- Illustrated on a scene from *Portnoy's Complaint*, the prompts correctly diagnose a double bind and explain its inward significance for the audience.
- The dramatic effect generated through the subtext is that of a claustrophobic absurdity.
- The chapter provides a well-structured checklist for teaching students to expose the subtext of a double bind.
- The relevance of the approach for real-life interactions is illustrated in the context of family therapy.

REFERENCES

Bateson, G. (1972/2000). *Steps to an ecology of mind*. University of Chicago Press.

Roth, P. (1969). *Portnoy's complaint*. Bantam.

Part III

Reading in-between the Lines

7 Presence through Absence

Four Guidelines for Reading in-between the Lines

ABSTRACT This chapter introduces the idea of reading "in-between the lines," a mode of interpretation that examines the gaps, thresholds, and suspensions that signify subtext beyond explicit dialogue. The chapter presents four core dimensions of this interpretation: absence, the liminal space of transitions, border zones, and silence/emptiness. For each dimension, I provide guidelines for understanding it and a complete prompt for identifying it in a movie scene. The "four-dimensions" model is illustrated mostly through two films by Tarkovsky and *The Waves* by Virginia Woolf.

WHAT DOES "IN-BETWEEN" THE LINES MEAN?

In the previous chapters, I presented various ways of reading between the lines. I used a pragmatically oriented methodology in which the subtext is revealed through the analysis of discursive moves at the micro-level. In this context, I analyzed the misalignment between utterance and response in *Private Lives*, the dialogue of the deaf in *A Serious Man*, and the dynamics of the double bind in *Portnoy's Complaint*. Parts I and II of the book focus on the pragmatics approach. In Parts III and IV, I would like to deepen the analysis by focusing on the *negative* aspects of subtext. In this context, I use the phrase "reading in-between the lines" to discuss metaphorically a specific focus of interpretation in which we attend to whatever is missing, empty, in transition, or marks border lines in the scene. It is an approach that focuses on the delicate dimensions of the scene and its "negative space." We will look at four specific dimensions of the subtext:

1. *Absence*: That which is present through its absence.
2. *The liminal space*: A transition between symbolic spaces.
3. *Border zones*: The border existing in-between symbolic spaces.
4. *Silence*: The significant void.

The common denominator of these four dimensions is liminality (from the Latin *limen*, meaning "threshold"). The four dimensions involve some boundary conditions that may constitute the subtext of the scene. Let me present, explain, and illustrate each of these dimensions. The next section presents and discusses each of them.

DOI: 10.1201/9781042004485-10

THE FOUR DIMENSIONS OF READING IN-BETWEEN THE LINES

Absence (Presence of the Non-present)

Definition: Something that does not explicitly exist in the scene, yet actively organizes meaning, behavior, conflict, or emotion. It is not just "nothingness"; it is the presence of a person, an object, an idea, or an emotion that exists powerfully even when absent. It is *present through its non-presence.*

Absence may be expressed in a scene through:

1. A missing center that organizes behavior (e.g., the father in Tarkovsky's *The Mirror*).
2. A reaction that should exist but doesn't (e.g., a missing emotional response)
3. A subject that must not be named (e.g., Voldemort from Harry Potter)
4. A truth that is prepared but never revealed (e.g., *Secrets and Lies* by Mike Leigh).

Here are the elaborate expressions of absence:

1. *The Phantom center*

   This is the most important cue for the expression of absence. A specific absent entity (person, event, object, idea) functions as the *scene's organizing center of gravity*: actions, priorities, and conflicts are arranged *around* something that is not there, so the missing thing feels like an active agent.

   How to spot a phantom center?

   The scene involves a distinct referent X that is physically or narratively absent.

   Two or more independent elements in the scene (characters' choices, staging, flashbacks, props, or recurring motifs) are causally or thematically linked to X.

   Dialogue or behavior consistently orients toward X (e.g., decisions justified by X, rituals for X, objects kept *for* X) without X itself appearing.

   One-sentence example:
   The siblings keep setting an extra place at the table and altering family plans because their missing sister's return is expected but never occurs.

   False positives to avoid:
   An absent object mentioned once with no structural follow-through (not a structuring absence).
   An offscreen presence is used solely for backstory, without shaping the present scene choices.

2. *Suppressed response*

   An expected emotional reaction is deliberately withheld; that withheld reaction functions like a presence—it creates pressure, meaning, and narrative shape by its non-occurrence.

What to look for:
A stimulus S occurs that culturally/narratively/socially invites a clear emotional response R (e.g., death → grief; betrayal → anger). The character exhibits one of: neutral affect, flat delivery, delayed/distracted response, or substitution (performing an unrelated act instead). The scene's subsequent beats reference or revolve around the lack of R (silences, explanations, others' confusion).

One-sentence example:
After learning of his partner's infidelity, he quietly folds the letters and resumes chopping vegetables, and the conversation thereafter circles awkwardly without naming his feelings.

False positives to avoid:
Muted acting that stems from style rather than narrative pressure (e.g., deadpan comedy).

Silence is used solely for a meditative tone without an expected, broken emotional pattern.

3. *Forbidden reference (Discursive absence/The unspoken)*
A subject that should logically be addressed is actively avoided in speech; the avoidance itself structures the scene's tension, alliances, and power dynamics—the unspoken is the operative presence.

What to look for:
There is an obvious topical referent T central to what is at stake in the scene (e.g., money owed, a scandal, a death).

Speakers employ evasive strategies across multiple turns: topic shifts, euphemisms, jokes, vague pronouns, ironic over-clarity, or repeated indirect allusions rather than direct naming.

The pattern of avoidance changes outcomes (decisions deferred, alliances tested, guilt masked) or is salient to other characters' behavior.

One-sentence example:
During the family meeting about inheritance, everyone refers only to "the thing," and they laugh when prompted to specify, whereupon the meeting ends with no agreement.

False positives to avoid:
Genuine ignorance (characters *don't know* the subject exists).

Strategic secrecy that is explicitly named (e.g., "We won't talk about X because it's classified"—if declared and accepted, it may not produce the same subtextual pressure).

The Absence of the Father in Tarkovsky's *The Mirror*

The previous section presented several guidelines for understanding and identifying the dimension of absence in a scene. Here, I present a fully elaborated example of how absence is portrayed in a film.

In Andrei Tarkovsky's *The Mirror* (1975), the protagonist Aleksei is haunted by his father, who has left the family. The father is physically absent from the domestic scenes, yet he is "present" mostly through the recitation of his poems. The emotional weight of the scene is dictated by the one person who is not in the room. He is present through his absence. However, in Tarkovsky's *The Mirror*, absence is not a lack but the film's organizing force. What is missing (the father, stable family unity, emotional closure, chronological certainty) is precisely what structures memory, desire, guilt, and identity. Absence becomes the negative space that gives all presence its emotional contour.

In *The Mirror*, Andrei Tarkovsky foregrounds the absence of Aleksei's father as a structuring principle, transforming what is ostensibly a narrative about memory and domestic life into an intricate meditation on loss and longing. The father never occupies the domestic space of Aleksei's childhood on-screen; his presence is only felt indirectly, primarily through recitations of his poetry, Aleksei's fragmented recollections, and the emotional reactions of other characters. Therefore, this absence functions as a *phantom center*, actively organizing the narrative and emotional dynamics. Scenes pivot around his absence—decisions, conflicts, and remembrances are all defined in relation to him. For instance, Aleksei's mother's protective anxiety, Aleksei's own sense of insecurity, and his later reflections on identity are structured by a figure who is never physically manifest. In this sense, absence in Tarkovsky is not a passive void; it is a shaping force that molds the film's affective and symbolic logic. Several expressions of this absence are:

1. The Phantom center: The father's non-presence organizes Aleksei's memories, the family's routines, and the emotional resonance of domestic spaces. The act of remembering, of evoking his voice through poetry, fills the narrative gaps created by his absence.
2. Suppressed response: The mother's muted grief, Aleksei's hesitant recollections, and the lack of direct confrontation with paternal abandonment all produce a sense of tension and emotional incompleteness. What is not said weighs as heavily as what is in fact articulated.
3. Forbidden reference (Discursive absence): The father's actions and absence are rarely spoken of directly; indirect references, poetic echoes, and fleeting visual motifs stand in for explicit engagement. This avoidance generates a subtextual field in which absence operates as an unspoken but omnipresent authority.

The Father's Absence as Subtext

Understanding the father's absence through this framework reveals the *film's subtextual dynamics*. While the overt text presents fragments of domestic scenes, childhood memories, and poetic recitations, the underlying emotional and structural coherence is dictated by what is missing: The father. The explicit text—the mother's care, Aleksei's fragmented childhood experiences, the shifting temporality of the narrative—cannot be fully comprehended without acknowledging the father as an anchor. He functions as a *negative space* around which desire, guilt, identity, and memory coalesce. The father's absence encodes questions of emotional stability, family continuity, and the psychological impact of loss, giving shape and tension to otherwise ordinary or episodic domestic events. In short, the father's non-presence is the film's organizing principle; it is the subtext that renders Aleksei's recollections intelligible, emotionally resonant, and narratively coherent. Through the lens of the current chapter, we see that, in *The Mirror*, absence is not simply a narrative gap—it is a *structural, affective, and symbolic agent*. The explicit text of domestic interactions, memory fragments, and poetic recitation derives its meaning and intensity precisely from the invisible, haunting presence of the father.

The Liminal Space of Transitions

The liminal space involves *moments of transition* signifying a temporal shift between one state and another. It is a temporal or emotional bridge where a character or scene has left State A but has not yet arrived in State B. Meaning here is not fixed; it is in a state of emergence, and it emerges in-between the states.

Here is an example of transitioning as poetically described by Virginia Woolf. In the opening of *The Waves*, she writes:

> The sun had not yet risen. The sea was indistinguishable from the sky, except that the sea was slightly creased as if a cloth had wrinkles in it. Gradually, as the sky whitened, a dark line lay on the horizon, dividing the sea from the sky, and the grey cloth became barred with thick strokes, moving one after another beneath the surface, following each other, pursuing each other, perpetually.

The opening of *The Waves* first marks the passage of time. It is dawn, before the sun has risen. The sky and the sea are not yet distinguished, a description that clearly echoes the first day of creation, where sea and sky are not yet differentiated. They are differentiated only on the second day of creation. This is a world that lacks a horizon. Woolf is experiencing a primordial horizonless world. However, the sea is slightly folded. The sea's surface has faint, shallow lines and ripples. The sea appears like a vast expanse of gray fabric with soft wrinkles running across it. This metaphor transforms the sea from a primordial presence indistinguishable from the sky into something domestic and touchable. Gradually, a boundary appears in the form of a dark line. As the sky whitens, the world becomes more visible. Shapes and boundaries begin to form. The sea, here described as a "grey cloth," is "barred with thick strokes." These are waves, long, slow-moving swells. In the dim light, they appear as dark, heavy stripes running across the sea's surface, evoking the image of living creatures moving in the sea, following each other with no beginning or end.

The meaning of Woolf's opening scene lies in a transition, from an undifferentiated world to a differentiated one. In this sense, the recurring experience of dawn has a profound religious significance that resonates with the experience of the attentive observer. This experience echoes the line from the famous Christian hymn: "Morning has broken." The morning has broken "like the first morning." In the experience of Woolf, dawn is a moment of creation.

Here are some cues to help us identify transition points in a scene. It should be emphasized that we do not seek general transition points, but rather those that function as subtext for the scene.

1. *Rule reversal* (The scene changes its rules of operation)
   A transition occurs when the *implicit rules governing behavior, power, or meaning in the scene reverse.* For example, what was once permitted becomes forbidden, what was once safe becomes dangerous, and what was once authoritative becomes childish (or vice versa).
   You can identify rule reversal if all three of the following are present:
   I. A clear *rule system* is established early in the scene (e.g., friendly talk, professional conduct, parental authority, romantic politeness).
   II. A specific *moment of violation or inversion* occurs (e.g., threat appears inside friendliness; authority collapses into neediness).
   III. After that moment, *all subsequent behavior reorganizes according to the new rules*, not the old ones.

   One-sentence example:
   A father lecturing his son suddenly begins to beg for approval, and from that moment on, the son controls the emotional balance of the scene.

2. *Tonal mutation* (When emotional language changes)
   Transition is sometimes marked when the emotional tone mutates into its opposite or a neighbor—warmth becomes menace, flirtation becomes humiliation, care becomes control—without an explicit narrative announcement. Here, meaning shifts not by what is said, but by the emotional genre to which the dialogue now belongs.
   Tonal mutation may be present when:
   I. The scene begins with a *stable emotional register* (e.g., playful, intimate, neutral).
   II. The same surface structure (similar dialogue length, proxemics, pacing) continues.
   III. Yet the *emotional function of the speech flips* (jokes start to wound, politeness carries threat, silence becomes punishment).

   One-sentence example:
   Two friends continue to smile and speak softly, but each sentence now serves as a concealed threat rather than a gesture of trust.

3. *Identity slippage* (A character crosses into a foreign role)
   Transition occurs when a character begins to assume *a role that does not properly belong to them*—parent becomes child, lover becomes interrogator, victim becomes judge—before the story openly acknowledges the shift. This is a transitional phase between identities, *mid-metamorphosis.*
   Identity slippage is detectable when:
   I. A character holds a *clear social or psychological role* at the beginning of the scene.
   II. Their *speech acts or behaviors begin to move into a different role category.*

III. Other characters show *confusion, correction, or delayed adaptation* to this new role.

One-sentence example:
During a casual date, one partner begins questioning the other like a prosecutor, while the other continues to respond as if it were flirtation.

Border Zones

Border zones are spaces (physical or psychological) that exist at the boundary between the physical and symbolic realms. Unlike transitions (which are about time/change), border zones are about *place* and *existence in-between.* The space marked by the boundary does not belong to territory A or to territory B. It is where the safe meets the dangerous, or the public meets the private. To identify border zones, look for:

1. *Physical threshold* (Spatial duality)
   A border zone exists when a *single space embodies two contrasting realities simultaneously*—safe versus dangerous, private versus public, natural versus artificial—so that crossing it signals risk or revelation. The space itself functions as a *subtextual agent*, shaping character behavior and meaning.
   You can identify a physical threshold if all three of the following are present:
   I. A *distinct spatial marker* separates two contrasting domains (doorway, window, bridge, checkpoint, room, vehicle).
   II. The characters' *behavior, tone, or awareness shifts* when they approach or occupy this threshold.
   III. The narrative emphasizes *risk, moral tension, or uncertainty* tied to crossing or inhabiting this space.

   One-sentence example:
   A character steps from a brightly lit kitchen into a dark alley; their casual demeanor gives way to alert tension, signaling danger without a single word being pronounced.

2. *Role friction (Duality of identity at the border)*
   Border zones are expressed psychologically when a character must *simultaneously inhabit two conflicting roles*, revealing contradictions in identity, loyalty, or morality. The friction between these roles becomes the *hidden meaning* of the scene. Role friction is present when:
   1. A character is *actively expected to behave according to two incompatible roles* (parent vs. peer, professional vs. intimate, victim vs. perpetrator).
   2. The scene highlights *tension, hesitation, or conflict* resulting from occupying both roles at once.
   3. Meaning emerges from *how others react or fail to adapt* to the duality.

   One-sentence example:
   A teacher escorts a student outside school grounds, oscillating between authority and friendship, creating silent moral tension in their dialogue and body language.

3. *Contamination/Spillover (Reality from one zone leaks into another)*
   Border zones function subtextually when *elements from one reality invade another*, producing unease, contradiction, or moral ambiguity. The "leak" signals that the two worlds cannot remain fully separate, highlighting the scene's hidden tensions.

   Contamination is detectable when:

   I. An *element from one zone* (supernatural, violent, private, forbidden) enters the other zone unexpectedly.
   II. Characters or objects *react to this intrusion* with alarm, adjustment, or denial.
   III. The scene's meaning *emerges from the collision* rather than explicit dialogue or plot.

   One-sentence example:
   During a formal dinner, a sudden street fight is heard through the open window; the refined domestic space becomes charged with danger and instability.

The idea of a border zone will be illustrated in the milkshake scene from *Pulp Fiction*. You will see how both Vincent and Mia play a dangerous game in which crossing the border might have fatal consequences. To grasp the notion of a border, you may also recall Tarkovsky's masterpiece *Stalker* (dir. Andrei Tarkovsky, 1979). The film

> tells the story of an expedition led by a figure known as the 'stalker,' who guides his two clients—a melancholic writer and a professor through a hazardous wasteland to a mysterious restricted site known simply as the 'Zone,' where there supposedly exists a room which grants a person's innermost desires.
>
> **(Wikipedia)**

Crossing the border to the zone is literally and metaphorically a dangerous endeavor. In Tarkovsky's *Stalker*, the *border zone is the film's central metaphysical engine*. It is not merely a passage from one place to another, but a *permanent state of tension between incompatible realities: faith versus reason, hope versus despair, freedom versus control, inner truth versus* social identity. The Zone exists precisely as a *border condition*, not a destination.

The Border Zone in Tarkovsky's Stalker

In *Stalker*, the concept of the border zone is central to both the narrative structure and the film's metaphysical inquiry. The Zone itself functions as a *physical and symbolic border*, a space that is neither fully real nor fully imagined, neither safe nor entirely dangerous. Crossing into the Zone entails a literal traversal of terrain marked by physical decay, industrial detritus, and environmental hazards, but it also signifies entry into a psychological and ethical threshold where conventional laws, scientific reasoning, and social norms are suspended. The physical markers of the Zone—its ruins, fences, and undefined pathways—signal the transition from the familiar to the unknown, creating a spatial duality that is continuously reinforced by the stalker's careful guidance and the travelers' heightened vigilance. Here are several aspects of the border zone in the film.

Physical Threshold

The Zone embodies a *physical threshold*, where space itself imposes uncertainty and risk. As the stalker leads the writer and the professor across treacherous terrain, their behavior shifts: hesitation, fear, and moral contemplation accompany every step. The Zone's boundaries—visible through rivers, walls, and abandoned structures—highlight the tension of inhabiting a space where the ordinary laws of cause and effect, safety, and danger are suspended. Here, the border zone is not a transient passage; it is a lived spatial state that actively shapes both action and perception.

Role Friction

Psychologically, the border zone generates *role friction*. Each traveler must navigate incompatible roles simultaneously: the writer oscillates between cynicism and hope, the professor between rational skepticism and existential longing, and the stalker between guide, priest, and moral mediator. This duality produces subtle moral tension and hesitation, visible in body language, pauses in dialogue, and the deliberate pacing of the journey. The Zone's border condition forces characters to confront the contradictions in their identities and the ethical ambiguities of desire, agency, and faith.

Contamination/Spillover

Finally, the Zone exemplifies *contamination*, as the metaphysical and the mundane intermingle. Ordinary spaces, such as abandoned buildings and rusted machinery, leak into the psychological and moral domain of the travelers, producing uncertainty and unease. Dreams, hallucinations, and philosophical speculation intrude on concrete actions, highlighting the impossibility of neatly separating inner truth, societal expectations, and existential yearning.

The Border Zone as Subtext

As a *subtextual engine*, the Zone operates beyond the explicit narrative of a journey to a miraculous room. The film's text—dialogue, direction, and landscape—becomes intelligible only when read in relation to the border zone's underlying logic. The Zone's indeterminate spatial and symbolic status mirrors the tension between rational knowledge and mystical faith, between desire and fear, and between societal norms and personal longing. In other words, the border zone encodes the subtextual conflict: the human confrontation with uncertainty, the instability of identity, and the ethical ambiguity of pursuing one's innermost desires. The Zone, therefore, is not merely a setting but a permanent condition of moral and existential in-betweenness, shaping the narrative's meaning through its very ambiguity.

In *Stalker*, Tarkovsky externalizes the characters' inner liminality: the border zone is simultaneously physical, psychological, and metaphysical. Its subtext is the persistent tension between dual realities, a tension that structures every action, dialogue, and visual composition in the film.

Silence, Emptiness, the Void

While "absence" is about *specific* missing things, "silence" (or the Japanese concept of *Ma*) is about emptiness or the void. It can be expressed as the pause that gives meaning to a scene marked by silence in a dialogue. Let me explain the difference between absence and void.

The primary term for emptiness in Japanese aesthetics is *Ma*, which refers to the negative space, gap, or pause between objects or events. Silence or emptiness is not the same as absence. By absence, we signify the non-presence of an existing object, while silence and emptiness signify a *void*. In Japanese aesthetics, *Ma* is considered an active and essential component of art, not just a void, and it is as important as the filled space itself. Another related term is *Yohaku*, which specifically refers to the beauty of empty space in art, as in traditional Japanese paintings like Hasegawa Tōhaku's "Pine Trees." *Ma* is a gap, space, or pause that gives shape and meaning to the whole. It applies to both physical space and time, representing a "pause" in a series of actions or sounds. It is found in architecture (defining spaces with posts and pillars), interior design (leaving space around carefully chosen objects), and other art forms, such as flower arrangement (*ikebana*) and calligraphy (*shodo*). This emptiness may have aesthetic value, as expressed by the concept of *Yohaku*. The aesthetic value of emptiness, as expressed by silence, is powerfully illustrated in the films of Tarkovsky. For example, *Stalker* (dir. Andrei Tarkovsky, 1979) is characterized by long silences. These silences generate a unique kind of ambiance which is hard to articulate. Here are several expressions of silence.

1. *Pauses with purpose*
   Silence operates *when a pause in a dialogue or an action creates meaning* by allowing the audience to sense tension, reflection, or anticipation. The void is active—it shapes the emotional or narrative field without being filled. You can identify pauses with purpose if:
   I. The scene contains *deliberate silence longer than natural conversation or action would require.*
   II. The silence is *interpreted by characters or the audience as meaningful*, e.g., hesitation, reflection, or threat.
   III. Narrative or emotional *weight is generated not by what is said or done, but by the emptiness itself.*

   One-sentence example:
   In *Stalker*, the characters stop moving and say nothing as they enter the Zone, allowing the tension and the metaphysical uncertainty to dominate the scene.

2. *Environmental emphasis (Space as actor)*
   Silence is expressed when *the surrounding environment—ambient sound, light, or space dominates the perception of the scene*, producing meaning through emptiness. The void becomes an active presence. Environmental emphasis is present when:
   I. Dialogue or action *ceases*, and *soundscape or visual space dominates* (wind, water, shadows, empty rooms).

II. The scene emphasizes *scale, isolation, or spatial emptiness.*
III. The audience experiences *meaning emerging from the gap between characters and their environment*, rather than from explicit interaction.

One-sentence example:
In *Stalker*, the camera lingers on the empty landscape of the Zone while the characters are off-screen, emphasizing the metaphysical and existential emptiness of the place.

3. *Non-responsive presence (The Witness of silence)*
Silence occurs when *characters are physically present but refrain from acting or responding*, creating a reflective or anticipatory space that shapes surrounding events. Their stillness becomes the medium through which subtext is perceived. In *Stalker*, there is a scene where the stalker lies on the ground, and it is not clear whether he is sleeping, dead, or in some kind of catatonic state. The silence of the scene has a powerful dramatic effect. Non-responsive presence is detectable when:
I. A character remains *completely still and silent* while others speak or act.
II. The scene draws attention to the *contrast between activity and stillness*, or speech and silence.
III. Meaning emerges through *the void created by inaction or listening*, highlighting unspoken tension, moral judgment, or existential weight.

One-sentence example:
A character silently observes a heated argument without intervening, forcing the audience to sense moral or emotional stakes through their quiet presence.

Refined one-sentence definition of silence: Silence as subtext occurs when temporal, spatial, or character voids actively shape meaning, allowing the audience to perceive tension, anticipation, or existential weight through what is intentionally left unspoken or still.

Silence in Tarkovsky's Stalker

In Andrei Tarkovsky's masterpiece *Stalker*, silence is not an absence of meaning but one of the film's primary carriers of meaning. It operates on multiple levels, philosophically, spiritually, psychologically, and politically. Here are the main dimensions of what silence *means* in the film:

Silence in *Stalker* operates as a primary structuring dimension, shaping the film's atmosphere, narrative rhythm, and metaphysical inquiry. Unlike mere absence, silence embodies an *active void*—a temporal, spatial, and psychological space that gives form and intensity to what is otherwise inexpressible. Tarkovsky's extended pauses, lingering camera movements, and muted sequences exemplify the Japanese aesthetic of *Ma*, where emptiness itself carries meaning.

Pauses with Purpose

The film is characterized by deliberate, prolonged silences during the journey into the Zone. When the stalker, the writer, and the professor pause, the narrative tension does not dissipate; instead, it thickens. These pauses allow the audience to inhabit the characters' anticipation, moral uncertainty, and existential reflection. For example, as the trio negotiates treacherous paths, the silence amplifies both the physical risk and the metaphysical ambiguity of the Zone, turning each hesitation into a locus of reflection. Here, silence structures meaning temporally: what is not said becomes as important as what is said, generating subtextual insight into character motivations and existential stakes.

Environmental Emphasis

The Zone itself dominates much of the film's silent moments. Long takes of empty landscapes, industrial ruins, or still water foreground the environment over human action. Soundscapes—wind, dripping water, distant mechanical echoes—replace speech, producing a perceptual rather than narrative tension. The emptiness of the Zone communicates a sense of metaphysical void and existential precariousness: the audience perceives the profound strangeness and danger of this liminal space precisely through its silence. The environment becomes an active participant, shaping the meaning of the journey without explicit commentary.

Non-responsive Presence

Characters often inhabit silence while physically present, as in the stalker's quiet observation of his clients or the writer's reflective stillness. This non-responsive presence allows moral, philosophical, and emotional stakes to emerge subtextually. Silence mediates tension between faith and skepticism, desire and fear, knowledge and intuition. The characters' stillness amplifies the Zone's unknowable quality, and the audience interprets their inaction as both moral judgment and existential meditation.

Silence as Subtext in Stalker

As subtext, silence conveys what the explicit text—dialogue, plot, and physical action—cannot articulate. The surface narrative presents a journey to a room that grants one's innermost desires, but the *true narrative is encoded in the pauses, voids, and stillness*: the precariousness of human intention, the limits of knowledge, and the impossibility of controlling one's destiny. Silence signals moral ambiguity, existential reflection, and metaphysical uncertainty. It allows the Zone's danger and wonder to be felt rather than spoken, turning the viewers' perception into a co-creative act of interpretation.

In this sense, silence is an important dimension of the subtext, shaping meaning by structuring attention, emphasizing the environment, and revealing psychological and ethical tension. The explicit "text"—the stalker's guidance, the writer's doubts, and the professor's calculations—is intelligible only when read alongside the *subtextual void* created by silence. The pauses, stillness, and environmental emptiness act as interpretive keys, transforming ordinary movement and dialogue into a meditation on human desire, uncertainty, and existential liminality. Here are several important aspects of silence in *Stalker.*

Silence as a Spiritual Condition

Tarkovsky treats silence as a *sacred atmosphere*. Much as in religious contemplation, silence in *Stalker*:

Creates *space for inner transformation.*
Replaces doctrinal answers with *existential listening.*
Signals entry into a realm where *ordinary language fails.*

The *Zone* itself is a silent world, not only because it is empty, but because it is *too full of meaning to be spoken*. Speech there becomes dangerous, inadequate, or deceptive.

Silence marks the limit of rational understanding and the beginning of faith.

Silence as Resistance to Instrumental Reason

The professor and the writer represent the intersection of scientific and artistic rationality. Both attempt to *explain*, *use*, or *master* the Zone. Silence works against them by:

Refusing explanation.
Undermining analytical control.
Exposing the impotence of knowledge.

Where science seeks clarity, the Zone offers only mute ambiguity.

Silence as Psychological Exposure

When the characters fall silent, what emerges is:

Fear of their *true desires.*
Anxiety about *what they might become.*
Terror of confronting the Room, which grants not conscious wishes, but unconscious ones.

Silence forces the characters into *self-confrontation without linguistic protection.*
Speech hides. Silence reveals.

Silence as Ethical Judgment

The stalker himself treats silence as an *ethical rule*:

Talking too much is *a moral violation of the Zone.*
Silence becomes a form of *reverence.*
Language is treated as something that can *corrupt sacred space.*

This aligns with Tarkovsky's belief that art should be approached with humility, not as a form of consumption.

Silence as Political Subtext

In the late-Soviet context, silence reflects *spiritual suffocation*. It mirrors the *unsayable nature of truth under ideological regimes.* The Zone becomes a place where *meaning survives only through what cannot be spoken.* Thus, silence also encodes historical trauma and censorship.

Sound Design: Silence vs. Industrial Noise

Tarkovsky carefully contrasts things outside the zone (e.g., mechanical noise, trains, machinery, human labor) with things inside the zone (e.g., wind, water, natural breath).

Silence is therefore a *threshold marker* between mechanical existence and metaphysical existence.

Silence as an Invitation to the Viewer

Unlike conventional cinema, *Stalker* uses silence to:

Refuse emotional instruction.
Deny narrative certainty.
Force the *viewer into participatory interpretation.*

To identify silence/emptiness/the void, you may look for cues such as:

The beat: A marked pause in dialogue (indicated by stage directions or ellipsis) that lasts longer than natural conversation requires.
Environmental dominance: Dialogue stops, and ambient sound (wind, rain, ticking clock) takes over the audio track.
Static visuals: The camera or description lingers on a landscape, an empty room, or a still object, creating a "breath" in the narrative.
Non-responsive presence: A character is present and listening but remains entirely still, acting as a sounding board for another's chaos.

PROMPTING THE AI TO READ IN-BETWEEN THE LINES

So far, I have presented a four-dimensional model of interpreting the subtext that can help us to read in-between the lines. The next prompt has been designed to identify these dimensions and to explain their role in generating the implied meaning, the subtext, and its aesthetic value. In the following chapters, whenever I use this prompt, I first ask the model to read the theoretical part of the current chapter, as presented up to this point, and only then to apply the following prompt.

PROMPT 7.1

PURPOSE:

This prompt is designed to analyze a dialogue from a movie scene (with contextual description) to detect the presence of one or more of the four subtextual dimensions—Absence, Liminal Transition, Border Zones, Silence/Emptiness—and explain how each functions as subtext, revealing meaning beyond the explicit text.

Propose new insights, hidden from the surface textual reading of the dialogue.

Read the attached chapter describing the four dimensions of reading in-between the lines.

Input:

1. Dialogue: Literal spoken lines of the characters in the scene.
2. Context description: Relevant scene details, including:
    - Physical setting (location, time of day, spatial relationships).
    - Character identities, roles, and emotional states.
    - Events preceding and following the dialogue that might inform subtext.
    - Notable actions, gestures, visual or environmental cues.

Instructions:

Step 1: *Preliminary scene comprehension*

- Read the dialogue and context carefully.
- Identify the surface-level meaning: who is speaking, what is being said, and what is happening explicitly.

Step 2: *Dimension detection*

For each dimension, determine whether it appears in the scene. If no dimension is detected, state clearly: *"No subtextual dimension detected,"* and stop the analysis.

If one or more dimensions appear, proceed to subtextual analysis.

A. Absence (presence through non-presence)

Detection cues may include:

i. Phantom center: Absent entities (person, object, idea) actively organize behavior or narrative.

ii. Suppressed response: Expected emotional or behavioral reaction is withheld, producing tension.

iii. Forbidden reference (Discursive Absence): Relevant topics are avoided, creating unspoken pressure.

Subtextual analysis:

- Explain how the absence shapes meaning in the scene.
- How does it reveal emotional tension, moral stakes, or unseen dynamics?
- Identify how dialogue, actions, or stage cues respond to or revolve around the absent element.

B. Liminal space (Temporal/Emotional Shifts)

Detection cues may include:

i. Rule reversal: Norms or behavioral rules of the scene invert unexpectedly.

ii. Tonal mutation: Emotional tone or affective register changes subtly but significantly.
iii. Identity slippage: A character begins to operate in a role foreign to their established identity.

Subtextual analysis:

- Explain how transitions reveal uncertainty, tension, or emergent meaning.
- How does the scene convey temporal or psychological "in-between" states?

C. *Border zones* (Friction between conflicting realities)
Detection cues may include:
i. Physical threshold: Spatial markers indicate in-between spaces (safe/dangerous, private/public, known/unknown).
ii. Role friction: Characters inhabit dual or conflicting roles simultaneously.
iii. Contamination/Spillover: Elements of one zone intrude into another, producing tension.

Subtextual analysis:

- Explain how the border conditions create hidden stakes or moral/psychological tension.
- How does the "in-between" space or role inform the audience about character dilemmas or narrative instability?

D. *Silence/Emptiness/Void* (*Ma*/*Yohaku*/Negative Space)
Detection cues may include:
i. Pauses with purpose (Temporal Ma): Deliberate, extended silences in dialogue or action.
ii. Environmental emphasis (Space as actor): Ambient sound or visual space dominates over dialogue/action.
iii. Non-responsive presence: Character is physically present but remains still and silent.

Subtextual analysis:

- Explain how silence or emptiness functions as subtext.
- How does it reveal tension, anticipation, existential, ethical, or psychological stakes?
- How does the void in dialogue, space, or behavior amplify the scene's implicit meaning?

Step 3: *Structured output*
Organize your analysis in a structured format (not a table):
| Dimension | Detected? (Yes/No) | Key Cues Observed | Subtextual Meaning/Explanation | Example from Scene |

Step 4: *Synthesis*

- Summarize how the detected dimensions interact to produce overall subtext.
- Highlight which dimension dominates or drives the meaning of the scene.
- Explain how the explicit dialogue or events are intelligible only through reading the subtextual dimensions.

Optional Guidance:

- Focus on subtextual dynamics, not plot summary.
- Use scene evidence (words, gestures, silences, spatial cues) to justify your conclusions.
- Treat absence, liminal transition, border zones, and silence/emptiness as active forces shaping meaning, not just descriptive labels.
- Avoid interpreting style or cinematography alone unless it contributes to a subtextual cue.

DISCUSSION: THE PATTERNS THAT CONNECT

In the previous chapters, I have analyzed the subtext by focusing on the pragmatic approach and the underlying dynamics of the interaction. Extending the reading to in-between the lines, I have added another layer of complexity, which will be illustrated in the subsequent chapters. According to this approach, the subtext of a scene may be traced to an underlying pattern that requires us to connect the dots to see it. This pattern is not usually easy to identify, and it requires us to demonstrate a high level of attention to faint cues and a high level of sensitivity to the negative (what is not present), to change, to borders existing in-between symbolic spaces, and to empty spaces signaling through their silence something which is not easy to articulate. This form of reading in-between the lines is important for understanding the subtext, given its focus on what is missing, in transition, at the intersection, or silenced. If an LLM can identify these dimensions and explain their role in generating the subtext, this may be an achievement that deepens our understanding of the subtext.

The main points of the chapter are:

- Reading in-between the lines is another layer in this approach to exposing the subtext.
- It emphasizes the liminal experience evolving through four main dimensions: absence, transitions, border zones, and silence/emptiness.
- Absence involves the powerful presence of what is missing from the scene.
- The liminal space involves temporal aspects of situations in which meaning changes.
- Border zones are symbolic spaces marked by a boundary that plays a significant part in the interaction.
- Silence/emptiness involves a suspension of activity that operates in the background and symbolizes a significant void.

Part IV

Case Studies

8 "Did You Just Order a Five-Dollar Shake?" *Subtext in* Pulp Fiction

ABSTRACT Following the guidelines for reading in-between the lines, this chapter provides a detailed analysis of the five-dollar milkshake scene from *Pulp Fiction*, demonstrating how subtext emerges through absence, transition, border zones, and silence. What appears to be trivial small talk about an overpriced milkshake is revealed to mask a dangerous negotiation of forbidden desire between Vincent and Mia, structured by the absence of Marsellus Wallace. Through multimodal AI-assisted analysis of facial expressions, gesture, posture, and dialogue, the chapter reveals how Vincent's heightened alertness displaces unspoken fear, while Mia's stylized glamour leads to controlled seduction. Shared indulgence functions as a symbolic crossing of boundaries without explicit violation. The sudden silence following the milkshake tasting marks the point where play threatens to become emotional truth. The chapter demonstrates how reading in-between the lines of the scene transforms a minor cinematic moment into a dense field of psychological, erotic, and moral tension.

DATING THE BIG MAN'S WIFE

In the previous chapter, I proposed to enrich our analysis of subtext by adding another layer of complexity. This layer of complexity involves what I described as reading *in-between* the lines. In this chapter, I would like to illustrate and elaborate on this approach by analyzing a scene from *Pulp Fiction*.

To recall, Vincent and Jules are two criminals who work for the notorious Marsellus Wallace. Mia is Marsellus's wife, or, as Jules calls her, "The big man's wife." When Marcellus goes to Florida, he asks Vincent to take care of her and to take her out. This is a risky mission. Rumor has it that Marsellus Wallace threw Tony out of a four-story window for giving Mia a foot massage. A man who threw another out of a four-story window should be treated with respect. This is why Vincent responds anxiously to Jules' suggestion that he take Mia out on a date. This is not a purely semantic issue. No one "dates" the big man's wife unless he has suicidal tendencies, and Vincent is anxious to explain the difference between dating Mia and just taking her out.

Mia asks Vincent to take her to Jackrabbit's Slim. The name of this diner is composed of "jack rabbit" (actually a hare) and "slim," evoking a sense of liveliness, energy, and sexuality. When placing their orders, Mia asks for a burger and a five-dollar milkshake. Vincent seems shocked by Mia's order, and a brief exchange between them focuses on clarifying whether she really intended to order a five-dollar shake, which is

DOI: 10.1201/9781042004485-12

just milk and ice cream, without bourbon, as Vincent points out. The fact that Vincent pays attention to the five-dollar milkshake is unclear. It is possible that Mia just ordered a mispriced milkshake, but what does it matter to our hitman, who was sent by his boss to "take care" of his wife? This question invites us to dig deeper into the subtext.

Let us begin by analyzing Vincent's facial expression when questioning Mia about her order. Up to now, I have focused mainly on the text, but analysis of the subtext can be enriched by examining a variety of contextual cues across different modalities. I deliberately focused most of the prompts on texts rather than on visual or auditory features. However, I was aware that a textual analysis provides only a partial understanding of the subtext. From time to time, I analyze other modalities, but focus mainly on the text. The limited space of the current book justifies this focus.

I asked Gemini (Prompt 8.1) to analyze Vincent's facial expressions during the questioning of Mia's decision to order the expensive shake. Gemini identified the character and explained that it displays an expression that suggests intensity and focus.

MODEL'S OUTPUT 8.1

- Intense focus: His eyes are narrowed and fixated on something or someone off-camera. The blue eyes are piercing and command attention.
- Serious/Stern: The eyebrows are slightly furrowed, indicating a serious mood, possibly concentrating hard or listening intently to something important.
- Wary or alert: There is a sense of caution or guardedness. The jaw appears slightly clenched, giving it a firm, unyielding look.
- Lack of humor: The expression is devoid of any apparent warmth or humor; it is entirely business-like or confrontational.

In summary, Vincent's facial expression conveys intense focus, seriousness, and alert concentration. To emphasize, Vincent expresses intense focus, alertness, and seriousness regarding Mia's milkshake order. This facial analysis supports our inclination to delve into the subtext because Vincent's seriousness, conveyed through his facial expression, is in sharp contrast to the issue at hand, which is the price of the milkshake Mia just ordered.

To understand the subtext, I also analyzed Mia's facial expressions when they first sat down at the table. In this case, I also analyzed her hand gestures this time using Claude's Sonnet. The AI suggests that Mia's image conveys a complex blend of confidence, seduction, and knowing self-awareness:

MODEL'S OUTPUT 8.2

Facial expression - Her slight smile and direct gaze suggest confidence and a playful, even flirtatious quality. The eyes are almost challenging or inviting—she's comfortable being looked at and seems to be consciously engaging with the viewer. There's a hint of amusement or irony in the expression.

> The face-touching gesture - Resting her hand against her cheek/jaw is a classic pose associated with thoughtfulness, but in this context, it reads more as a deliberate, stylized gesture. It elegantly frames her face, drawing attention to her features and conveying a sense of composed self-presentation. This pose is often associated with glamour photography and suggests someone who is aware of their appearance.
>
> The way she holds the cigarette - She holds it delicately between her fingers in an elevated, almost theatrical way—the cigarette becomes a prop that enhances the overall aesthetic. This isn't a casual smoker's grip but rather a stylized one that evokes classic Hollywood glamour, European café culture, or mid-20th-century sophistication. The way it's positioned near her face, yet at a slight distance, suggests both nonchalance and intentionality.
>
> Overall impression - The combination creates an image of studied sophistication with a knowing feel to it—someone playing with conventions of glamour and *seduction* (my emphasis, Y.N.) while perhaps also being slightly ironic about it. It's the look of someone in full control of how they're presenting themselves, channeling a vintage aesthetic of cool, worldly femininity.

So, what have we learned so far? Mia orders a milkshake, whose price concerns Vincent. When asked about it, she affirms her choice ("Sure did" and "Uh-huh") even when it is hinted that, for just milk and ice cream, the drink is overpriced. Turning to their waiter, who confirms the price and the fact that they don't put Bourbon in it, the milkshake issue is now resolved. The scene moves on.

When Vincent rolls himself a cigarette, Mia asks him to roll her one too, approaching him as "cowboy." Letting her have his cigarette, he approaches her as "cowgirl" and lights her cigarette with his Zippo. When the food arrives, Mia tastes the milkshake and responds with a "Yummy!" Vincent asks Mia if he can taste her milkshake, and he responds with excitement, twice using the expression "pretty fuckin' good." The mystery of the five-dollar milkshake has now been resolved: it is worth the price they paid. But suddenly, we observe an uncomfortable *silence*, to which Mia responds reflectively, asking: "Why do we feel it's necessary to yak about bullshit to be comfortable?" Comfortably sharing the silence, she continues, indicates that you find someone special, and Vincent replies that they are not there "yet," implying that becoming "someone special" for each other is only a matter of time.

The milkshake scene is therefore situated between their arrival in the restaurant and what appears to be flirting. Moreover, it has a clear intertextual aspect, as it reminds us of a scene in one of the French New Wave films, *Vivre Sa Vie* (Her Life) (dir. Jean-Luc Godard 1962), where the protagonist says, "I think one should often just keep quiet, live in silence." In both cases, the women reflect philosophically on the concept of silence. Interestingly, in *Pulp Fiction*, this philosophical reflection does not come from an intellectual character, but from Mia, who later hurries to powder her nose with cocaine, and dances grotesquely with Vincent to win a dance trophy in one of the most iconic scenes in cinema. Human beings are complex.

At this point, I took all the analysis conducted so far and fed it to the AI to gain an understanding of the subtext or what is in-between the lines of the milkshake dialogue. The general template for the analysis is as follows:

PROMPT 8.2

Step 1:
Read Chapter 7 as a theoretical background for your analysis (attached).

Apply the prompt titled: "Subtext Identification and Analysis Prompt" (attached) to interpret the X scene (e.g., the milkshake scene) in the attached text describing the scene and its preliminary interpretation: [text attached].

Step 2:
Use the output generated by step 1 to identify the inward significance of the X scene. Inward significance is the aesthetic/dramatic experience the scene evokes in the audience.

Avoid clichés, and focus on the way in which the explicit dialogue and the IMPLICIT subtext evoke the dramatic effect and INWARD SIGNIFICANCE of the scene.

And the actual prompt I used is:

PROMPT 8.3

Step 1:
Read Chapter 7 as a theoretical background for your analysis (Chapter 7 is attached).

Apply the prompt titled: "*Subtext Identification and Analysis Prompt*" (the prompt is attached) to interpret the milkshake scene.

Step 2:
Use the output generated by step 1 to identify the inward significance of the milkshake scene. Inward significance is the aesthetic/dramatic experience the scene evokes in the audience.

Avoid clichés, and focus on the way in which the explicit dialogue and the IMPLICIT subtext evoke the dramatic effect and INWARD SIGNIFICANCE of the scene.

Here is the output generated by Claude's Sonnet 4.5

MODEL'S OUTPUT 8.3

Analysis of the milkshake scene from Pulp Fiction

Step 1: *Subtext identification and analysis* (Four-dimensional framework)

Preliminary scene comprehension

Surface-level meaning: Vincent Vega takes Mia Wallace out to Jack Rabbit Slim's diner at her husband's request. During their meal, Mia orders a five-dollar milkshake, which prompts Vincent's intense scrutiny. After confirming the price and tasting it, they fall into an uncomfortable silence, leading Mia to reflect on the value of shared silence between people who find each other "special."

Dimension detection and subtextual analysis

A. Absence (presence through non-presence)

Detected: Yes

Key cues observed:

1. Structuring absence (phantom center): Marsellus Wallace is the organizing gravitational center of the entire scene, despite being physically in Florida. Every element of the interaction—Vincent's anxiety, his intense scrutiny of trivial details (the milkshake price), the cautious flirtation, the careful maintenance of boundaries—is structured around Marsellus's absent presence.
2. Forbidden reference (discursive absence): The potential for romantic/sexual attraction between Vincent and Mia is never directly named, yet it organizes the entire encounter. The scene circles what cannot be said: that taking the boss's wife out creates dangerous proximity to forbidden territory.
3. Suppressed response: Vincent's reaction to Mia is systematically muted. Where attraction might naturally emerge through relaxed banter or physical ease, Vincent maintains vigilant control, manifesting as hypervigilance about seemingly trivial matters (the milkshake's price).

Subtextual meaning:

Marsellus Wallace functions as an *invisible third party* at their table. His absence is more powerful than most presences—it dictates the topics of conversation, emotional expressions, and behavioral boundaries. The document explicitly notes Vincent's knowledge of Tony's fate (thrown from a four-story window for giving Mia a foot massage), which transforms every interaction into a potentially fatal misstep.

The milkshake interrogation reveals Vincent's anxiety management strategy: by obsessively focusing on a financially absurd detail (who cares about five dollars when you're a hitman?), he channels his nervous energy away from the truly dangerous subject—his attraction to Mia. The price of the milkshake becomes a displacement object for the price of desire.

Example from scene:

Vincent's facial expression during the milkshake questioning—"intense focus," "wary or alert," "jaw appears slightly clenched"—demonstrates acute tension disproportionate to the discussion of a beverage price. This is the physical manifestation of navigating around the absent Marsellus, whose potential violence structures every micro-decision Vincent makes.

B. *Liminal transition* (Temporal/Emotional Shifts)
Detected: YES
Key cues observed:

1. Tonal mutation: The scene undergoes a subtle but significant emotional register shift. It begins with professional distance (Vincent fulfilling an assignment), moves through careful social interaction (ordering food), and gradually mutates into something intimate and dangerous—flirtation barely contained by professional boundaries.
2. Identity slippage: Vincent and Mia begin to slip between incompatible roles. They start as "bodyguard/boss's wife" but progressively operate as "potential romantic partners" (the "cowboy"/"cowgirl" exchange, the cigarette lighting ritual, the shared milkshake tasting). Neither fully commits to either role, creating a liminal identity state.

Subtextual meaning:

The scene exists in temporal suspension—they are in-between professional obligation and personal desire, between safety and danger, between following orders and following attraction. The milkshake moment marks the pivot point of this transition: before tasting it, they maintain professional distance; after sharing it ("pretty fuckin' good"), an intimacy has been established that triggers Mia's reflection on silence.

The "cowboy/cowgirl" exchange represents identity slippage par excellence. These playful nicknames signal a departure from their actual roles (hitman/crime boss's wife) into a romanticized

Western trope—a genre where such casual intimacy between a man and woman would be permissible, even expected. By temporarily inhabiting these alternate identities, they create a liminal space where flirtation can occur without explicitly violating their actual relationship boundaries.

Example from scene:

The progression from Vincent's "Sure" (letting her have his cigarette) to calling her "cowgirl" while lighting it represents the mutation from transactional courtesy to intimate ritual. The Zippo lighting becomes a romantic gesture borrowed from classic cinema—a transition from mere politeness to seduction, though neither can acknowledge it directly.

C. *Border zones* (friction between conflicting realities)
Detected: YES
Key cues observed:

1. Role friction: Both characters simultaneously inhabit contradictory roles. Vincent is both a "professional minder" and a "potential suitor"; Mia is both an "untouchable boss's wife" and an "available woman on a date." This dual occupancy creates constant psychological friction visible in their hesitations, calculated responses, and careful choreography of interaction.
2. Contamination/spillover: Elements from the romantic/sexual domain continuously threaten to "leak" into the professional domain. The five-dollar milkshake discussion itself represents this contamination—Vincent's intensity about it suggests he's fighting against something more dangerous than financial waste.
3. Physical threshold: While the entire restaurant represents a liminal space (a 1950s-themed diner that is both authentic and performative, both public and intimate), the shared milkshake marks a specific *border crossing*. The moment Vincent tastes from Mia's straw, he crosses from separate consumption to shared intimacy—a small act with enormous symbolic weight.

Subtextual meaning:

The scene takes place entirely within a *border zone* where professional duty meets personal desire, where safety meets mortal danger, where loyalty meets attraction. Vincent and Mia are performing a dangerous dance on this border throughout the scene—getting close enough to enjoy each other's company (which

Marsellus presumably wants) without crossing into romantic territory (which would be fatal).

The milkshake becomes the border object—it represents both connection and danger. Sharing it is intimate (indirect kiss via straw), but it's "just a milkshake," maintaining plausible deniability. The five-dollar price marks it as special, different from ordinary milkshakes—much as this evening is a special, dangerous exception to normal rules of engagement.

The text notes that Mia presents herself with "studied sophistication with a knowing edge" and "channels a vintage aesthetic of cool, worldly femininity." She understands exactly which border they're dancing on and seems to enjoy the friction. Vincent's hypervigilance shows he understands it too.

Example from scene:

The silence that follows Vincent's enthusiastic response to the milkshake ("pretty fuckin' good") represents the moment they both realize they've moved too far toward intimacy. Mia's subsequent philosophical reflection on comfortable silence—and Vincent's response that they're not "there yet"—explicitly acknowledges that they're negotiating a border: the border between strangers and "someone special." Vincent's "yet" is particularly loaded: it suggests potential future crossing while maintaining present boundaries.

D. *Silence/emptiness/void*

Detected: YES

Key cues observed:

1. Pauses with purpose (temporal ma): The text explicitly notes an "uncomfortable silence" that follows their milkshake sharing. This pause is described as significant enough that Mia feels compelled to address it philosophically, suggesting it carried substantial tension and meaning beyond mere conversational lull.
2. Non-responsive presence: During the silence, both characters are physically present and aware of each other, but neither speaks. This stillness becomes the *medium through which subtext is perceived*—the silence reveals what their dialogue cannot: the sexual/romantic tension that has been building and their mutual awareness of its danger.

Subtextual meaning:

The silence functions as revelatory emptiness—it's the moment when all the careful verbal choreography stops, and the underlying reality becomes perceptible. In that void, the truth of their mutual attraction and its impossibility becomes palpable. Mia's response to this silence is telling: rather than filling it with chatter, she philosophizes about its significance, essentially naming the subtext without explicitly doing so.

Her observation that sharing comfortable silence indicates finding someone "special" is a meta-commentary on what just happened—they've moved from professional distance to dangerous intimacy, and the silence itself is proof. Vincent's response ("We're not there yet") attempts to re-establish the border that the silence threatened to dissolve, but his "yet" reveals the temporal dimension: they're in transition *toward* becoming special to each other, a trajectory that spells danger.

The intertextual reference to Godard's *Vivre Sa Vie* reinforces this reading. Like the French New Wave protagonist who advocates living in silence, Mia positions silence as philosophically superior to "yakking about bullshit"—but in context, this is also a way of managing the danger of the moment. By intellectualizing the silence, she transforms it from purely emotional/sexual tension into aesthetic contemplation.

Example from scene:

The text describes the silence as "uncomfortable," which marks it as a meaningful void rather than a neutral pause. The discomfort signals that both characters perceive the subtext—the silence has revealed too much. Mia's immediate philosophical framing of it represents an attempt to contain the emptiness revealed by converting dangerous intimacy into abstract reflection.

Step 3: *Synthesis*

Dimension interaction:

All four dimensions work in concert to create a scene of extraordinary subtextual density. Absence (Marsellus) provides the organizing principle that makes every other dimension dangerous. Transition describes the temporal movement from professional to intimate, while Border Zones describes the spatial/psychological terrain they're navigating. Silence is the moment of revelation when all the unspoken tension becomes perceptible.

Dominant dimension:

Absence is the dominant force. Marsellus Wallace's non-presence is the "phantom center" around which everything revolves. Without his absent presence, the scene would be a simple romantic comedy of flirtation. With it, every gesture becomes a potential death sentence, every shared pleasure a forbidden fruit.

Intelligibility through subtext:

The explicit dialogue about the milkshake's price appears trivial, even absurd—why would a professional killer care about a five-dollar drink? The scene becomes intelligible only when we recognize:

1. The milkshake interrogation is *displacement behavior* managing anxiety about Marsellus's absent presence
2. The sharing of the milkshake marks a *border crossing* from professional to intimate
3. The silence afterward reveals the transition they've undergone
4. The entire interaction is structured by what cannot be said: their mutual attraction and its fatal consequences

The text explicitly states that Vincent's facial expression conveys "intense focus, seriousness, and alert concentration" toward the milkshake order—an absurd overreaction unless we understand the subtext: he's intensely focused because he's navigating a minefield where one wrong step means defenestration.

Step 2: *Inward significance—the aesthetic/dramatic experience*

The erotics of restraint and the sublime danger of micro-transgressions

The inward significance of the milkshake scene lies in its evocation of *eroticized vigilance*—the peculiar aesthetic pleasure of watching two people navigate desire under the shadow of potential annihilation. This is not mere suspense; it is the *sensuality of boundary maintenance*, where every small gesture becomes laden with consequences and every moment of connection requires exquisite calibration.

The dramatic architecture of constrained desire

What the scene evokes in the audience is a paradoxical pleasure: we experience *intensified presence through enforced absence*. Because Vincent and Mia cannot directly express attraction, every indirect expression becomes hypercharged. A five-dollar milkshake transforms into an erotic object, not despite the fact that it's ostensibly about economics, but *because* of that. The audience feels the *displacement of libidinal energy* into absurdly mundane concerns, creating a peculiar tension between surface banality and underlying danger.

This is the aesthetic principle of *negative eroticism*: desire becomes most powerful when it must route itself through acceptable channels. Vincent's intensity about the milkshake's price is darkly comic precisely because we recognize it as sexual anxiety in disguise. The audience experiences this recognition as a form of *dramatic irony with embodied stakes*—we know what Vincent cannot say, and we feel the cost of that silence in our own bodies.

The aesthetics of calibrated risk

The scene's inward significance centers on what we might call *pleasure through precision*—the audience's vicarious participation in Vincent and Mia's careful calibration of intimacy. Each micro-gesture (the cigarette sharing, the "cowboy/cowgirl" exchange, the shared straw) represents a *calculated transgression*: intimate enough to enjoy, restrained enough to survive.

This creates a distinctive spectatorial experience: we watch with *suspended breath*, experiencing each moment of connection as simultaneously pleasurable and perilous. The aesthetic effect resembles watching a tightrope walker—the pleasure derives not from safety but from *witnessing mastery over danger*. Vincent and Mia are performing a high-wire act where the fall is literal death, and we experience the *artistry* of their performance.

The sublime violence of the ordinary

The scene evokes what might be called *domestic sublime*—the transformation of a restaurant meal into a site of metaphysical danger. This is Tarantino's signature aesthetic: the *collision of the mundane and the murderous*, where ordering a milkshake carries the same ontological weight as a gunfight. The audience experiences this as a *pleasurable category confusion*: we cannot fully distinguish between trivial and significant, between play and mortal seriousness.

This confusion generates a specific affective state: *hyper-attentiveness to surfaces*. Because we are aware of the subtext (Marsellus's violence, Vincent's fear, the sexual tension), every surface detail becomes potentially meaningful. Is Vincent's comment about bourbon in the milkshake just practical clarification, or is it establishing his professional sobriety? Is Mia's "Yummy!" a genuine pleasure in the drink, or performative seduction? The scene denies us interpretive certainty while demanding interpretive vigilance.

The temporal pleasure of suspended consequence

The silence that follows the sharing of the milkshake creates a *temporal pocket* where a consequence is both inevitable and indefinitely deferred. This moment evokes in the audience what we might call *the pleasure of the not-yet*: we know these characters are moving toward some resolution (in narrative terms, we know Mia will overdose shortly after this scene), but in this moment, they exist in pure potentiality.

Mia's philosophical reflection on silence functions as *meta-theatrical commentary* that deepens rather than breaks the dramatic illusion. When she asks why we feel compelled to "yak about bullshit," she's simultaneously:

- Acknowledging the sexual tension (the subtext)
- Intellectualizing it to make it safe (managing the border)
- Claiming aesthetic superiority for silence (the Godard reference)
- Performing sophistication for Vincent (the surface flirtation)

The audience experiences this layering as *aesthetic vertigo*—we're watching a character simultaneously exist on multiple registers of meaning, and this multiplication creates a dizzying sense of depth.

The tragedy of mutual recognition

Vincent's response—"We're not there yet"—perhaps evokes the scene's deepest dramatic resonance: the tragedy of an *acknowledged but impossible connection*. He admits they're moving toward intimacy ("yet" implies futurity) while simultaneously refusing to arrive there. This is a *temporal paradox*: they're in a permanent state of transition toward a destination they can never reach.

The audience experiences this as a peculiar melancholy—we witness two people who genuinely connect but whose connection is structurally foreclosed. The inward significance here touches on something universally human: *the experience of desire under prohibition*, where the very obstacles that prevent fulfillment also intensify the desire itself.

The aesthetic of knowing performance

Both characters are performing sophistication for each other—Mia with her "studied sophistication," Vincent with his careful cool. But crucially, both know they're performing, and both know the other knows. This creates what we might call *transparent artifice*: the audience experiences the pleasure of watching characters who are simultaneously authentic and theatrical, genuine and constructed.

Mia's entire presentation—the cigarette held "delicately between her fingers in an elevated, almost theatrical way"—is explicitly performative, "channeling a vintage aesthetic of cool, worldly femininity." However, this performance is a testament to her authenticity; she genuinely embodies worldliness. The audience experiences this *sophisticated self-awareness* as a form of dramatic pleasure: we're watching characters who are complicit in their own mythologization.

> *The comic and the tragic are intertwined*
>
> Finally, the scene evokes what we might call *noir comedy*—the simultaneous experience of laughter and dread. Vincent's intensity over the milkshake is genuinely funny (his face suggests he's confronting a moral dilemma when discussing milk and ice cream). Still, it's funny *because* it's rooted in genuine fear. This creates a distinctive affective experience: *laughter that doesn't relieve tension but intensifies it.*
>
> The audience's pleasure here is complex and contradictory: we laugh at Vincent's absurd overreaction while simultaneously understanding and sharing his anxiety. We enjoy Mia's seductive sophistication while knowing (from narrative foresight) that this evening will end in near-death. The scene refuses to let us settle into either comedy or tragedy, instead holding us in the *productive discomfort of their collision.*
>
> *Conclusion: The inward significance*
>
> The milkshake scene evokes in its audience an experience of *exquisite precariousness*—the pleasure of watching desire negotiate its own impossibility with style, intelligence, and wit. It offers us the vicarious thrill of boundary-transgression without consequence (for us), the aesthetic pleasure of watching artful performance under existential stakes, and the melancholic recognition of connection that cannot be consummated.
>
> The scene's inward significance lies in its ability to make us *feel* the gap between explicit and implicit, to experience viscerally how subtext isn't merely hidden meaning but rather *meaning under pressure*—meaning that cannot be directly expressed because direct expression would detonate the fragile situation these characters must navigate.
>
> We leave the scene not with answers but with *intensified awareness*: of how much human interaction consists of careful choreography, of how desire routes itself through available channels, of how ordinary objects (milkshakes, cigarettes, silence) become charged with extraordinary significance when the stakes are high enough. The scene teaches us, experientially, that the most dangerous and pleasurable moments of human connection often occur *not in grand gestures but in five-dollar milkshakes*—in the small border-crossings that risk everything while appearing to risk nothing.

When asked to read in-between the lines of the milkshake scene, the model generated a rather impressive, although quite overloaded, reading. At this point, it is interesting to compare it to the reading by another model. I used the prompt generated in the previous chapter, and here is the output generated this time by Gemini Pro:

MODEL'S OUTPUT 8.4

Step 1: *Preliminary scene comprehension*

- Dialogue/Action: Vincent and Mia are at Jack Rabbit Slim's. Mia orders a five-dollar milkshake. Vincent questions the price and the contents (just milk and ice cream?). He is visibly intense. The waiter confirms the order. They engage in playful role-play ("cowboy/cowgirl") regarding cigarettes. When the shake arrives, Mia enjoys it; Vincent tastes it and agrees it is "pretty fuckin' good." An uncomfortable silence follows, which Mia addresses directly, philosophizing about "yakking about bullshit" versus "comfortable silence."
- Context: Vincent is a hitman charged with "taking care" of his boss's (Marsellus) wife. The context is lethal: a previous associate (Tony) was reportedly thrown out of a window for crossing a boundary (a foot massage). Vincent is hyper-vigilant and anxious. Mia is confident, performing a stylized version of glamour and seduction.
- Surface meaning: Two people having dinner, discussing the high price of a beverage, sharing a drink, and discussing the nature of the conversation.

Step 2: *Dimension detection*

A. Absence (presence through non-presence)
   - Detected? Yes.
   - Dimension: structuring absence (phantom center) and forbidden reference.
   - Analysis: Marsellus Wallace is the "phantom center." He is physically absent but organizes every behavior at the table. Vincent's anxiety regarding the milkshake is not about the dairy product; it is a displacement of the fear of the absent husband. The "forbidden reference" is the sexual attraction between Vincent and Mia. They cannot speak of it because of the absent Marsellus, so they speak about the milkshake instead. Vincent's "intense focus" (as noted in the facial analysis) is a reaction to the lack of safety.

B. Liminal transition (temporal/emotional shifts)
   - Detected? Yes.
   - Dimension: Tonal mutation and identity slippage.
   - Analysis: The scene transitions from a hierarchical dynamic (protector/boss's wife) to a flirtatious one (man/woman). The "cowboy/cowgirl" exchange is a ritualized transition where they slip

into temporary identities that allow them to flirt safely. The tasting of the milkshake marks a "tonal mutation"—the shift from the trivial (price) to the sensual (taste/pleasure).

C. Border zones (friction between conflicting realities)
- Detected? Yes.
- Dimension: Physical threshold and contamination/spillover.
- Analysis: The table acts as a border zone. The milkshake itself becomes a "contested object" or bridge. When Vincent uses the straw to drink from her cup, it is a moment of "contamination"—elements of her zone (her saliva, her pleasure) spill over into his. This physical crossing of the threshold (the straw) serves as a proxy for the sexual boundary he is terrified to cross, yet desires to.

D. Silence/emptiness/void
- Detected? Yes.
- Dimension: Pauses with purpose and *ma* (negative space).
- Analysis: The text explicitly highlights the "uncomfortable silence" following the tasting. This is the "void" where the social mask ("yakking about bullshit") falls away, and the dangerous truth (mutual attraction) is exposed. Mia actively deconstructs this void, labeling the silence as a marker of intimacy ("someone special").

Step 3: *Structured output* [Not presented due to repetition YN]

Step 4: *Synthesis*

The subtext of the "Five-Dollar Milkshake" scene is driven by the interaction between absence and silence, mediated by border zones.

The *absence* of Marsellus Wallace establishes the stakes: death. This transforms a trivial conversation about a beverage price into a high-stakes investigation of boundaries. Vincent's facial cues (intense focus) reveal that he is navigating a minefield, not a menu. The milkshake serves as a *border zone* object—a safe proxy for the forbidden physical intimacy. By engaging in the *liminal transition* of the "cowboy/cowgirl" roleplay and the sharing of the drink, they safely act out the seduction that is forbidden in their reality.

However, the silence/emptiness dimension acts as the climax of the subtextual arc. Once the prop (the milkshake) is consumed and approved, the distraction vanishes. The silence strips away the "bullshit" (the social performance identified in the text), leaving the characters exposed to the raw tension of their absence-driven reality: they are attracted to one another and in danger. The explicit dialogue about the milkshake is unintelligible without these dimensions: without them, it is merely bad consumer advice; with them, it is a matter of life and death.

This model generated a shorter output but identified the same dimensions as Claude's Sonnet. At this point, we can distill the essence of the milkshake dialogue.

DISCUSSION

When you first observed the scene in which Vincent and Mia visit the diner:

1. Did you notice the anomaly of the milkshake scene?
2. If the answer to the first question is positive, did you understand the subtext of this scene?
3. Could you clearly articulate the subtext of the scene and its aesthetic value?

If you answered these questions in the negative, there is a good chance that you learned something from this chapter. In this concluding section, I would like to summarize our interpretation of the scene.

Viewed as a whole, the milkshake scene emerges as a carefully choreographed negotiation of forbidden desire, unfolding under the guise of casual, even trivial conversation. What appears on the surface as idle small talk about an overpriced dessert conceals a far more charged relational exchange. The milkshake, the cigarette, and—most importantly—the silences between utterances function as symbolic stand-ins, allowing attraction to be tested without ever being explicitly acknowledged. Desire is present, but it must be displaced, encoded, and managed.

Vincent's conspicuous seriousness is central to this dynamic. His insistence on trivial details and his almost pedantic focus on the cost of the milkshake reveal not indifference, but fear—fear of desire itself and of the lethal consequences it might entail. In this sense, his attention to the mundane operates as a defensive maneuver. By anchoring himself in surface-level facts, he attempts to contain the erotic tension that threatens to exceed the boundaries of safety and obligation that govern his world.

Mia, by contrast, appears far more aware of the erotic charge circulating between them and consciously uses her allure as a means of control. Her glamour is not naïve flirtation; it is both a provocation and a shield. By choosing to flirt openly, she asserts mastery over the situation, signaling that seduction is permissible only insofar as she defines its limits. Her performance allows desire to surface while simultaneously neutralizing its danger.

The moment of shared indulgence—tasting the milkshake together—constitutes the scene's most intimate gesture, precisely because it remains symbolic. This act functions as a carefully regulated substitute for physical contact, a safe proxy for a kiss or something more explicitly erotic. Intimacy is thus experienced obliquely, through an object, rather than directly between bodies.

Silence plays a decisive role at this juncture. When conversation falters, and Mia questions the need for small talk, the subtext threatens to become explicit. The silence exposes what language has been working to conceal: the mutual recognition of attraction. Yet even this near-confession stops short of articulation, preserving the delicate equilibrium between acknowledgment and denial.

Taking everything together, the scene unfolds as a tightrope walk between seduction and restraint. Every gesture, pause, and exchange becomes a negotiation over how far the interaction can go, which boundaries must remain intact, and which desires must remain unspoken. In this perilous social environment, restraint is not merely a moral or psychological concept but a vital strategy for survival.

From this perspective, the milkshake scene can be read as a coded dialogue about mutual attraction, one that must remain hidden beneath the imperative of boundaries. Indulgence becomes a metaphor for desire, while restraint emerges as the only viable means of sustaining the encounter without catastrophe. The small talk about the milkshake thus functions simultaneously as a honey pot and a smoke screen: it lures both characters—and the viewer—into a dangerous game of desire, while providing just enough cover to keep that desire from becoming fatal.

In sum, the lesson learned from this scene is not only to be careful when dating the "big man's wife." It is a lesson about fear and desire hidden beneath innocent small talk. The dramatic effect is created through this tension between the small talk and its underlying dramatic subtext. This tension has been identified and articulated through a well-structured prompt that generated a highly structured output, grounded by the text and justified by it. This structured approach can guide researchers and students in reading in-between the lines and exposing the same dimension in real-life situations.

The main points of the chapter are:

- The five-dollar milkshake scene in *Pulp Fiction* functions as a test case for applying the four-dimensional model to cinematic subtext.
- Vincent's intense focus on a trivial detail (the price of the milkshake) operates as a displacement of unspoken danger and forbidden desire.
- Mia's gestures, facial expression, and stylized self-presentation function as a controlled performance of seduction and power.
- The scene stages attraction indirectly through symbolic objects (the milkshake, cigarettes) and ritualized behavior.
- Shared indulgence (tasting the milkshake) operates as a form of controlled transgression that remains just within safe boundaries.
- Silence becomes the most dangerous and revealing moment, where emotional truth nearly breaks through performance.
- The scene demonstrates how absence, transition, border zones, silence, role-play, and controlled transgression converge to generate subtext.

9 "Too Marvelous for Words" *Subtext in* The Vortex

ABSTRACT In drama, exaggerated language is sometimes used to reference trivial matters. It appears in sharp contrast with language use that minimizes serious issues. This *misplaced intensity,* which has a significant dramatic effect, is epitomized in Coward's play, *The Vortex*. In this chapter, I analyze the misplaced intensity in The Vortex and reveal the drama's deeper layers, including the inversion of the sacred and the profane, as well as the characters' strategies to silence threatening issues. This analysis is supported by reading in-between the lines of the play.

WHEN SOMEONE IS TOO DIVINE

The Vortex by Noël Coward (Coward, 1924)[1] is a successful three-act play that has been adapted for the screen in several versions, including the TV adaptation (dir. Joan Kemp-Welch 1964) featuring Nicholas Pennell and Margaret Johnston. The play depicts the troubled relationships of a rich narcissist and a childish woman by the name of Florence Lancaster, with her young lover Tom and her only son Nicky, who is a drug addict. The plot takes place in high society circles immediately after World War I. This is an important historical context. The estimated number of British soldiers killed during the war is 886,000. In a context where so many young men lost their lives, and many others returned physically and mentally wounded, one should expect those who remained alive and healthy to prioritize their preferences and values accordingly. However, the play portrays a contrasting atmosphere of moral bankruptcy among the upper social classes.

In Act 1, we are introduced to Helen Saville and Pauncefort Quentin ("Pawnie"), who are waiting for their friend Florence at her "distinctly expensive" London flat. Helen is described as a "smartly dressed woman of about thirty," and Pawnie as "an elderly maiden gentleman," meaning an aging gay man. Names like Pauncefort (of Norman origin) signal aristocratic pretensions and a certain privileged background. Indeed, these markers of social class with their accompanying behaviors grotesquely characterize Pawnie from the start.

While waiting for Florence, their host, to arrive, Helen and Pawnie engage in a conversation, during which both repeatedly use exaggerated emotional language to discuss superficial issues of taste and character. For example, Pawnie describes the coloring of the room as "oppressive," the new frieze in his bathroom as "too

DOI: 10.1201/9781042004485-13

marvelous for words," the lampshade in Florence's flat as "a bad example for the servants," and Florence as "too divine."

Pawnie's use of misplaced and highly charged affective language is accompanied by malicious and spiteful remarks to the point where Helen criticizes him, saying, "Don't be a cat." Here, "cat" or "catty" refers to making deliberately mean or subtly cruel comments, often about someone's appearance or character. This phrase is associated with indirect aggression and verbal sparring, precisely the dynamics that characterize the decadent society in the play, where characters use sharp, clever language (i.e., wit) to be cruel about superficial matters while avoiding genuine emotional honesty in discussing serious issues. In this context, Helen's rebuke is mild (just "don't be a cat" rather than a serious reprimand), which itself shows how normalized this *bitchy banter* is in their social circle. It is a social sport, not seen as truly harmful but rather as quite amusing; yet, it is part of the moral bankruptcy so clearly expressed in the play.

Aggression, whether expressed explicitly or subtly, is still aggression. In this context, the use of exaggerated language (e.g., "too divine") is not merely an expression of dramatic style that conveys emotional intensity and helps characters communicate their feelings to the audience of a melodrama. The misplaced intensity is a marker of deep, pathological dynamics, in that the characters employ exaggerated language to address trivial matters. At the same time, genuine emotional issues, such as Florence's affair with a young man and her son Nicky's drug problem, are disproportionately papered over with a corresponding shallow style. The misaligned intensity is our trigger to delve deeper into the subtext and the group's underlying dynamics. In this sense, the use of *misplaced intensity* and its complementary form, *misplaced minimization*, exposes the participants' pathological dynamics and contextualizes the vortex that drags Florence and Nicky into the abyss.

The use of misplaced intensity is also evident in other plays written by Coward. For example, in "Hay Fever" (Coward, 2025), the Bliss family exhibits extravagant emotional responses to minor social situations and manufactured dramas, while remaining emotionally detached from genuine feelings and the discomfort of their house guests. It appears to be a powerful strategy for exposing the characters' underlying social dynamics in a drama. Misplaced intensity and its complementary misplaced minimization, therefore, constitute an important layer in the understanding of dramatic texts and their underlying social and psychological dynamics. I noticed this dynamic after reflecting on the TV adaptation and carefully reading the play. Following this attentive observation of the play, I decided to design prompts to help us understand misplaced intensity in dramatic texts and its role in shaping a drama's subtext.

IDENTIFYING EXPRESSIONS OF MISPLACED INTENSITY

First, to ease the presentation of the methodology, I chose to analyze only the first part of Act 1, in which Pawnie and Helen are the only interlocutors. Next, I used a prompt to identify points of misplaced emotional intensity. The prompt is:

PROMPT 9.1 DETECTING MISPLACED EMOTIONAL INTENSITY IN CONVERSATION

You are a rhetorical and discourse analyst. Your task is to read the attached file and identify *ALL instances of misplaced emotional intensity* that appear in the conversation. That is, your task is to identify any expression whose emotional strength, evaluation, or linguistic exaggeration exceeds what is contextually appropriate.

Misplaced intensity may be evident through hyperbole, superlatives, intensifying verbs/adjectives, extreme adverbs, figurative exaggeration, or emotionally charged expressions.

For each detected instance, provide the following structured output:

Output structure

- Exact phrase: the precise word or phrase expressing exaggeration.
- Category: the discursive or linguistic category (e.g., *hyperbole*, *superlative*, *intensifying verb*, *hyperbolic metaphor*, *emphatic repetition*, *exclamatory intensifier*).
- Speaker: who said it.
- Modified element: what object, event, or idea is being intensified or evaluated.
- Context: The utterance that includes the word/phrase and the utterance preceding it.

Example:
Conversation:

HELEN: Well, I don't consider the new frieze in your bathroom either good *or* right.
PAWNIE: How can you, Helen! It's too marvelous for words. Parelli designed *it specially for me.*

Output:

- Exact phrase: "marvelous."
- Category: Hyperbolic adjective
- Speaker: PAWNIE
- Modified element: The bathroom frieze
- Context:

HELEN: Well, I don't consider the new frieze in your bathroom either good or right.
PAWNIE: How can you, Helen! It's too ≪marvelous≫ for words. Parelli designed
it specially for me.

Analysis guidelines
When identifying instances:

- Focus on *linguistic or discursive markers of exaggeration*, including:
  - Superlatives (*the most wonderful, best ever*)
  - Intensifying verbs (*adore, despise, hate, worship*)
  - Hyperbolic metaphors (*I am dying of boredom, a total disaster*)
  - Emotional overstatements (*utterly ruined, beyond words*)
  - Inflated modifiers (*absolutely, incredibly, completely*)
- Consider *contextual mismatch*—e.g., when a mild event triggers a dramatic response.
- Treat idiomatic exaggerations ("I could kill for coffee") as valid instances.

Output format example (multiple entries)
Conversation:
A: The cake turned out fine.
B: Fine? It's the most divine creation ever baked!
A: You're exaggerating again.
B: No, I absolutely adore it!

Output:

1.
   - Exact phrase: "the most divine creation ever baked."
   - Category: Superlative hyperbole
   - Speaker: B
   - Modified element: The cake
   - Context:
     - Before: "The cake turned out fine."
     - After: "You're exaggerating again."
2.
   - Exact phrase: "absolutely adore."
   - Category: Intensifying verb phrase
   - Speaker: B
   - Modified element: The cake
   - Context:
     - Before: "You're exaggerating again."
     - After: (No further line)

Using the first prompt with Claude Sonnet 4.5, the LLM identified 16 instances of misplaced emotional intensity. At this point, it is essential to recognize that the model is familiar with the entire play, so its reading is deeply contextual. Indeed, I have already pointed out (Neuman, 2024) that large language models are "contextual machines," and therefore their reading of a text is very similar to that of a human expert.

Here are three examples of instances where the LLM identified misplaced intensity:

Instance 1:

- Exact phrase: "too marvelous for words."
- Category: Hyperbolic phrase with intensifying adverb
- Speaker: PAWNIE
- Modified element: The bathroom frieze
- Context:
  - HELEN: Well, I don't consider the new frieze in your bathroom either good or right.
  - PAWNIE: How can you, Helen! It's ≫too marvelous for words≪. Parelli designed it specially for me.

Instance 2:

- Exact phrase: "divine."
- Category: Hyperbolic adjective
- Speaker: PAWNIE
- Modified element: Florence (as a person)
- Context:
  - PAWNIE: I wasn't meaning Florence; she's ≫too divine≪ to be in any marked category.
  - HELEN: I wonder.

Instance 3:

- Exact phrase: "too divine."
- Category: Hyperbolic phrase with intensifying adverb
- Speaker: PAWNIE
- Modified element: Florence (as a person)
- Context:
  - PAWNIE: I wasn't meaning Florence; she's ≫too divine≪ to be in any marked category.
  - HELEN: I wonder.

We can see that the model correctly identified cases of misplaced intensity. Claude summarized this analysis as follows:

This scene contains *16 distinct instances* of misplaced emotional intensity, predominantly spoken by PAWNIE (12 instances), with the remainder by HELEN (4 instances). The exaggerations primarily involve:

- Hyperbolic adjectives ("divine," "marvelous," "fiendish," "exciting")
- Intensifying adverbs ("too," "terribly," "extremely")
- Metaphorical hyperbole ("deathless magnetism," "beautifully preserved")
- Exclamatory intensifiers ("Oh, my God")

This summary identifies Pawnie as the major source of intensification and invites the question of whether we can identify patterns in the intensified objects. These patterns are not an end in themselves, but rather scaffolds for a better understanding of the play's dynamics.

IDENTIFYING PATTERNS OF MISPLACED INTENSITY

To delve deeper into the elements modified by the misplaced intensity, I used the following prompt:

PROMPT 9.2 CLUSTERS OF MISPLACED INTENSITY

Across all instances of misplaced intensity, apply semantic clustering to the modified elements.

Applying the prompt, Claude identified five semantic clusters and analyzed them in terms of their underlying themes. For instance, the first cluster is presented as follows:

Cluster 1: Aesthetic objects and interior design

Theme: Physical decorative items and their aesthetic evaluation
Instances:

1. The bathroom frieze (Instance 1 – "too marvelous for words")
2. The lampshade (Instance 14 – "Oh, my God")
3. The lampshade (Instance 15 – "extremely pretty")
4. The lampshade's influence on servants (Instance 16 – "Such a bad example")
5. The luxurious accessories (Instance 13 – "too divine")

Analysis: This cluster represents the most concrete, material objects in the scene. The emotional intensity applied to these inanimate decorative items is particularly excessive, treating home furnishings as objects worthy of religious or moral significance.

Moreover, the AI identified cross-cluster patterns and insights. For instance, the first identified pattern involves the inversion of the sacred and the profane:

Pattern 1: The sacred–profane inversion

Throughout the clusters, religious and divine language ("divine," "deathless," "fiendish") is systematically applied to:

- Secular objects (bathroom friezes, lampshades)
- Human personality traits (selfishness, magnetism)
- Social circumstances (being someone's son)

This creates a consistent pattern of *misplaced sacralization*, treating the mundane as if it were transcendent.

Based on the identified expressions of misplaced intensity, the model yields several important diagnostic insights into their use. First, *material culture* is treated with quasi-religious seriousness. Second, Florence functions as a *gravitational center* of exaggerated discourse. Third, her son Nicky is discussed in *morally extreme terms*. The model, which is familiar with the play, concludes by saying that what we observe is "a social milieu where *performative expression* and *aesthetic judgment* have replaced substantive emotional engagement." According to this interpretation, the characters are "trapped in a cycle of ever-escalating rhetorical inflation with diminishing referential accuracy."

In sum, applying the first prompt, I identified points of misplaced intensity. An expert in textual analysis may identify all these points, but the model is significantly more efficient. Moreover, the prompt is well-structured and can guide students to a better understanding of misplaced intensity and help them to identify its expression through the analysis of discursive moves. Through the second prompt, I examined the objects of the misplaced intensity and clustered them to identify patterns. One salient cluster involves material objects, from a frieze in a bathroom to a lampshade. These objects of misplaced emotional intensity are interpreted as expressing an underlying dynamics of inversion where the sacred is substituted for the profane. Indeed, describing Helen as "divine" is not an empty figure of speech, but a misplaced intensity with clear diagnostic value, signaling her narcissistic character and Pawnie's admiration.

"QUITE HARMLESS": IDENTIFYING MISPLACED MINIMIZATION

To complement the analysis of misplaced intensity, I used the following prompt that analyzes misplaced minimization:

PROMPT 9.3 INSTRUCTIONS FOR DETECTING LINGUISTIC MINIMIZATION AND EMOTIONAL DEFLECTION

You are a discourse and rhetoric analyst.

Your task is to read the following conversation and identify all expressions that soften, deflect, or underplay emotional or moral gravity.

Such expressions may take the form of:

- Euphemism—a mild or indirect term for something harsh or taboo
- Understatement/meiosis—describing something serious as minor
- Litotes—affirming by negating the opposite ("not bad" for "good")
- Hedging—using qualifiers or modals to weaken commitment ("I suppose," "maybe")
- Downtoners/diminutives—adverbs or modifiers reducing intensity ("a bit," "rather")
- Irony or humor for deflection—joking or wit to avoid direct emotional engagement

- Passive or nominalized constructions—removing agency or softening accountability
- Periphrasis/circumlocution—verbose phrasing that avoids blunt reference (e.g., "passed away" instead of "died")

For each instance, output the following:

- Softening phrase: "______________________________"
- Speaker: ______________________________
- Device: (e.g., *euphemism*, *understatement*, *hedging*, *irony*, *downtoner*)
- (Optional) Comment: one short sentence explaining how the phrase minimizes or deflects emotional/moral weight.

Example input

A: I think he's having a bit of a rough time lately.
B: Oh, he's just tired, you know. He'll be fine.
A: Maybe. I suppose it's not really our place to interfere.

Example output

1.
    - Softening phrase: "a bit of a rough time."
    - Speaker: A
    - Device: Understatement/downtoner
    - Comment: Reduces distress to a casual, manageable issue.
2.
    - Softening phrase: "just tired."
    - Speaker: B
    - Device: Euphemism/minimization
    - Comment: Masks possible emotional or physical exhaustion as trivial fatigue.
3.
    - Softening phrase: "I suppose it's not really our place."
    - Speaker: A
    - Device: Hedging/moral deflection
    - Comment: Shifts moral responsibility away from the speaker through indirect phrasing.

Guidelines for analysis:

- Identify *only* phrases that diminish, disguise, or deflect emotional or moral content.
- Consider tone, modality, and context—a euphemism may appear literal unless contrasted with what is left unsaid.
- When uncertain, prefer marking expressions that seem disproportionately mild relative to the situation.
- Keep entries concise—one per significant instance.

The prompt has been guided by a typology of linguistic devices used for minimization. Using the prompt, the LLM identified 34 instances, of which the overwhelming majority (62%) were generated by Pawnie. Here is one example of misplaced minimization, this time where Helen is the speaker:

Softening phrase:	"A little artificial perhaps, but quite harmless."
Speaker:	HELEN
Device:	Understatement + Downtoner + Reassurance
Comment:	Reduces potentially serious criticism of Florence's taste to a minor, benign quirk.

Additionally, the LLM identified several patterns underlying the use of misplaced diminutives. The most general of them is *systematic emotional avoidance*. The dialogue exhibits a sustained pattern in which *every serious emotional or moral topic is deflected* through linguistic minimization. Neither character allows direct engagement with painful issues, such as Florence's inappropriate behavior and the fact that she invites her young lover to her home, where her old husband, David, and her only son, Nicky, are present.

In this context of avoidance, the second identified pattern is *weaponized wit*, in which both Helen and Pawnie use humor and irony as shields against serious, painful issues. From a psychoanalytic perspective, the misplaced emotional intensity can therefore be interpreted as a kind of *reaction formation*, where the inversion reveals the issues from which Helen and Pawnie have withdrawn emotionally.

A third pattern is of interest for understanding the characters' social world and can be summarized under the heading *"euphemistic social code."* There are several instances that show how the characters' social milieu has developed specialized euphemisms for dysfunction. For example, "beautifully old" is used to describe aging, and "trying" is used to describe suffering. Moreover, under the title of "Critical Insight," the model suggested that the combination of maximized intensity (from the previous analysis) and maximized deflection (from this analysis) creates a paradox, which it describes as follows:

> These characters use superlatives about trivial matters while minimizing language when speaking about serious issues. They say "too divine" about lampshades but "quite possibly" about a young man's ruined life. This inverted emotional economy reveals a social world in which authentic emotional engagement has been systematically replaced by performance, and in which language primarily maintains distance rather than creates connection.

One may find it difficult to argue with this analysis, produced by an artificial mind engineered from the real minds and artifacts of human beings. Nevertheless, to deepen the analysis, I used Prompt 9.4 (see the next section) to actually identify the threatening issues the characters seek to minimize. In this sense, after automatically identifying points of misplaced intensity, understanding their linguistic and pragmatic devices, and exposing the objects of exaggeration and contrasting them with the objects of misplaced minimization, it is time to expose the unspoken issues troubled by the dynamics of misplaced intensity and minimization.

"NO MORTAL CAN KEEP A SECRET"

The reason I arrived at university to study psychology was a Jewish rebel named Sigmund Freud. Encountering his followers was one of the reasons I did not pursue psychoanalysis as a career. But as Nietzsche once commented, the followers of a system cannot be used as proof against it. My concern is not with the system. Freud's writings are, like a Swiss cheese, full of holes. However, these holes are no less important than the cheese, because through them, we reveal a curious mind worth listening to, regardless of some of his ungrounded and wild speculations. This is the reason why, despite my resistance to dogmas such as psychoanalysis, I keep returning to Freud only for certain local and mundane insights.

As realized insightfully by Freud, "No mortal can keep a secret. If his lips are silent, he chatters with his fingertips; betrayal oozes out of him at every pore" (Freud, 1905, p. 78). What are the "secrets" kept by Helen and Pawnie through misplaced intensity and minimization? To expose these secrets, I used Prompt 9.4.

PROMPT 9.4

For each softening phrase, identify the *actual threatening issue* that the phrase attempts to minimize, conceal, or deflect from.

After identifying the threatening issue for each softening phrase, perform a semantic analysis of these issues.

Identifying the emotionally threatening issues behind the softening phrases, the AI identified 34 instances. Here are the first three:

Instance 1:

- Softening phrase: "It may be tiresome of me."
- Speaker: PAWNIE
- Threatening Issue: Pawnie's compulsive need to criticize and control others' aesthetic choices reveals his anxiety about his own social relevance and taste-making authority.

Instance 2:

- Softening phrase: "A little artificial perhaps, but quite harmless."
- Speaker: HELEN
- Threatening Issue: Florence's entire lifestyle and self-presentation are built on artifice and performance, lacking authentic substance—this threatens the foundation of their friendship.

Instance 3:

- Softening phrase: "Wasn't that a little naughty of you?"
- Speaker: PAWNIE
- Threatening Issue: Helen gave Florence an aesthetically questionable gift, suggesting either Helen's bad taste or her passive-aggressive hostility toward Florence.

Applying semantic clustering to the threatening issues, the LLM identified several clusters. Here is the first identified cluster:

Cluster A: Florence's unsustainable identity performance

Core threat: Florence has constructed an identity entirely dependent on youth, beauty, sexual attractiveness, and narcissistic performance. This is:

- Temporally doomed (aging will destroy it)
- Substantively hollow (no authentic self exists beneath)
- Socially anachronistic (belongs to a different era)
- Morally destructive (requires sacrificing others)

Why it is threatening: Acknowledging Florence's hollowness would destroy the group's central organizing myth—that beauty and charm are a sufficient basis for a life.

What we see is that the first "secret" is Florence's fragile narcissism. Florence Lancaster is a narcissistic personality whose obsessive pursuit of perpetual youth is systematically destroying everyone in her orbit. Her husband is ignored and humiliated by the presence of a young lover in his own home, her son is being ruined by the neglect of his beautiful mother, centered on herself, and her entire social circle has organized itself around enabling her pathology because they worship status, beauty, and charm more than anything else.

Up to a certain point in the play, everyone involved is complicit, and no one can speak out directly because authentic moral discourse would shatter the aesthetic performance that gives their lives meaning. This painful reality is a secret that cannot be spoken of for several reasons. First, Florence is Helen and Pawnie's gravitational center. Destroying her narcissism would mean destroying Pawnie's object of admiration, leaving him empty. Second, this is a group of people where aesthetic and performance triumph over authentic values. Speaking out about Florence's destructive narcissism would mean challenging their own value system. In this context, we may hypothesize that the primary function of the misplaced minimization is to perform systematic maintenance work on a collective denial system. Each softening prevents the central reality from becoming speakable, keeping the entire social structure intact by ensuring that Florence's narcissism remains "divine magnetism," that David's suffering remains "trying," and that their complicity remains unexamined. In this sense, the language used by the characters does not simply represent their world but actively constructs and maintains it by making certain truths unsayable. This interpretation can be deepened by a better understanding of how misplaced intensity and minimization reveal the characters, particularly Pawnie.

UNDERSTANDING PAWNIE

As Pawnie is a central figure in the first part of Act 1, I used the following prompt to understand him better:

PROMPT 9.5

> Based on this data of misplaced exaggeration and misplaced minimization, create a linguistic, psychological, and social profile for [Pawnie].

Interpreting the model's output reveals something interesting about Pawnie. The relevant points of Pawnie's complete profile can be summarized as follows. First, regarding the linguistic signature, we have already learned that Pawnie is responsible for the overwhelming majority of misplaced-intensity instances. His emotionally charged language considers aesthetic objects (e.g., the frieze), Florence as a person (e.g., too divine), social positioning (e.g., "Such an exciting thing to be" when referring to Florence's son), Nicky's character (e.g., "divinely selfish"), and conversational tone (e.g., "too intense"). In contrast, his softening includes domains such as his own judgment ("It may be tiresome of me") and moral discourse (e.g.,"Don't be so terribly intense").

A superficial impression of Pawnie probably portrays him as an easy-going gay man, nurtured by his performance of status, fine taste, and admiration for Florence the diva. However, the pattern revealed by the LLM opens the door to a better understanding of his psychological profile. Contrasting his misplaced intensity and minimization, his core defense mechanism appears to be *avoidance*, as evidenced by aesthetic displacement. Energy is disproportionately invested in signaling social status and aesthetic taste. This dynamic allows him to distance himself from threatening issues. However, the model proposes an interesting hypothesis regarding Pawnie's core vulnerability: his dread of irrelevance and his fear of aging. In one revealing moment, he says to Helen: "My dear, I'm far too occupied in wondering what is going to happen to me to worry about other people." This is not only an ego-centered statement. Pawnie, described as an elderly maiden gentleman, a softening description in itself, is actually an aging, feminine gay man. He is facing the same aging crisis as Florence, but unlike Florence, who is admired, Pawnie is only tolerated. He is not functioning as a lover, like Tom, nor as a genuine friend, like Helen, and he is not an object of maternal love, distorted as that may be in the case of Nicky.

In a social milieu where aesthetic values have precedence, an aging gay man has no value, and the way he tries to maintain relevance through criticism of others is a clear indicator of his fragile status. In this context, Florence is both a source of admiration (e.g., too divine) and at the same time an object of jealousy (she is divine, but "a couple of hundred years too late"). In this sense, Pawnie worships what he cannot possess (beauty, sexual power, centrality) while reassuring himself that his cultivation makes him superior. However, he probably realizes that cultivation without beauty is equivalent to irrelevance. We now understand why, whenever genuine feeling emerges, Pawnie immediately neutralizes it. For example, when Helen expresses real concern about Nicky, he responds by saying, "Don't be so terribly intense, dear."

From a social perspective, Pawnie mainly validates Florence's centrality through worship. However, at the same time, he serves as the guardian against any meaningful or disturbing issues that may emerge in the conversation. His social positioning within the group's dynamics aligns with the cultural-historical context. The play concerns the upper-middle class in post-World War I London, characterized by the values of aesthetic movements, in a context where class is defined by taste. However, between the wars, this world is dying. Pawnie is a character in this decaying world, and his identity, centered around social status, taste, and discrimination, has become irrelevant. He is not as beautiful as Florence, nor as sexually attractive as the youthful Tom. He has no apparent meaningful relationships with any of the other characters, except for a superficial and narcissistic admiration of Florence. Positioning himself as an outsider and critic of other people's tastes, he maintains superficial importance but at the price of an identity which is purely performative—a decaying character in an old, decaying world.

So far, I have been trying to explain the anomaly of misplaced intensity. Here, I would like to gain a deeper understanding of the subtext of Scene 1 through the prompt that uses the four-dimensional model to help us read in-between the lines. I ran the prompt, and here is the output:

MODEL'S OUTPUT 9.5

Analysis of scene 1 from The Vortex

Step 1: *Subtext identification and analysis* (four-dimensional framework)

Preliminary scene comprehension

Surface-level meaning: Helen Saville and Pauncefort Quentin ("Pawnie") wait in Florence Lancaster's expensive London flat. They discuss interior design, mutual acquaintances, and Florence's son, Nicky. The dialogue revolves around aesthetic judgments of furnishings (a frieze and a lampshade), Florence's young lover, Tom Veryan, and Nicky's musical career and character. The conversation is marked by witty banter, veiled criticisms, and superficial concerns elevated to dramatic importance.

Dimension detection and subtextual analysis

A. Absence (Presence through Non-Presence)

Detected: Yes

Key cues observed:

1. Structuring absence (phantom center): Florence Lancaster is the gravitational center of the entire scene, despite being physically absent. Every conversational topic—the room's decoration ("so typical of Florence"), Tom Veryan's

photograph, Nicky's problems, even the lampshade—orbits around her. The characters are literally waiting for her, but more significantly, they are *defined* by their relationship to her absent presence.

2. Structuring absence (secondary phantom center): Nicky Lancaster, Florence's son, functions as a second absent organizing force. The latter half of the conversation pivots around his character, talent, needs, and future—yet he never appears. His absence structures the moral evaluation of Florence's parenting and the pathology of their family dynamics.
3. Forbidden reference (discursive absence): The serious dysfunction of Florence's behavior—her affair with a much younger man while married, her neglect of her son, her narcissistic consumption of others—is systematically avoided through euphemism and deflection. The characters circle around these issues using minimizing language ("a little artificial perhaps, but quite harmless," "quite possibly," "trying for David") rather than direct moral confrontation.
4. Suppressed response: Helen demonstrates a suppressed emotional response throughout. When discussing genuinely troubling matters (Nicky's wasted potential, Florence's destructive narcissism), she offers only mild observations. Her one moment of intensity—"And fiendish for Nicky"—is immediately deflected by Pawnie, and she retreats into hedging language.

Subtextual meaning:

Paradoxically, Florence's absence makes her the most present force in the scene. The entire conversation is a form of *worship at an empty altar*—the characters discuss her aesthetic choices, her romantic choices, her effect on others, all while she remains offstage. This absence-as-presence reveals the consuming nature of a narcissistic personality: Florence doesn't need to be physically present to dominate every aspect of attention and conversation in her social circle.

Nicky's absence is equally telling. He is discussed as a *problem to be diagnosed* rather than a person to be engaged with. The characters debate his character, potential, and future as if he were an abstract case study, revealing how thoroughly he has been objectified and instrumentalized within this social world.

The forbidden references operate as *moral evasions*. By refusing to directly name Florence's destructive behavior (seducing young men, neglecting her son, sacrificing everyone to her ego), the characters become complicit in the very pathology they ostensibly critique. The subtext reveals a social world where *knowing/observation substitutes for moral intervention.*

Example from scene:

Pawnie's line, "You must realize one thing, everyone is sacrificed to Florence—it's as it should be," encapsulates the structuring absence perfectly. Florence isn't present, yet she's acknowledged as the entity to whom all others are sacrificed. The phrase "as it should be" reveals the normalized pathology—her destructive narcissism has been elevated to an organizing principle that her social circle accepts and even aestheticizes.

B. *Liminal transition (temporal/emotional shifts)*
Detected: Yes
Key cues observed:

1. Tonal mutation: The scene undergoes subtle but significant emotional register shifts. It begins with aesthetic criticism (the room's coloring, the bathroom frieze) delivered in a tone of affected concern, then mutates into darker moral territory (Nicky's ruined potential, Florence's destructive influence) while maintaining the same superficially light, witty tone. The emotional content changes species—from decorative judgment to existential diagnosis—without changing its linguistic packaging.
2. Identity slippage: Both characters slip between roles throughout. Helen operates simultaneously as "loyal friend" (her explicit claim) and knowing critic (her implicit judgments). Pawnie performs as a frivolous aesthete (obsessing over lampshades) while functioning as a penetrating social diagnostician (recognizing that "everyone is sacrificed to Florence"). Neither fully commits to either role, creating interpretive instability.

Subtextual meaning:

The tonal mutation reveals the scene's central pathology: *the colonization of moral discourse by aesthetic discourse.* When discussing a bathroom frieze, the same linguistic intensity is applied as when discussing a young man's destroyed potential ("too marvelous for words" vs. "quite possibly"); the scene demonstrates a world in which evaluative categories have collapsed into one another. The transition isn't from one stable emotional register to another, but rather a demonstration that all registers have been flattened into a single mode: performative judgment without genuine moral weight.

The identity slippage reveals these characters as *socially liminal figures*—they exist between genuine moral awareness and complete aesthetic absorption. Helen *knows* Nicky hasn't had a chance, but she can't or won't act on that knowledge. Pawnie *recognizes* Florence's narcissistic destruction, but aestheticizes it ("she ought to have been a flaunting, intriguing King's mistress"). They inhabit a transitional state between moral perception and moral paralysis.

Example from scene:

The exchange about Nicky's potential demonstrates tonal mutation perfectly:

HELEN: "Everything—his life's happiness." PAWNIE: "Don't be so terribly intense, dear."

Helen briefly breaks into genuine emotional intensity about serious stakes (Nicky's entire life), and Pawnie immediately polices this tonal breach, forcing her back into the acceptable register of light wit. The scene reveals a social world where *intensity about genuine matters is forbidden*, while intensity about lampshades is encouraged.

C. *Border zones (friction between conflicting realities)*
Detected: Yes
Key cues observed:

1. Role friction: Both characters simultaneously occupy contradictory roles. Helen is both Florence's friend and her critic, both protective of Florence ("I'm very fond of Florence") and aware of her destructiveness. Pawnie is both a frivolous gossip and a penetrating analyst, both a participant in this decadent world and a diagnostician of its pathology. This creates constant psychological friction—they must speak about serious matters while maintaining a frivolous tone, must criticize while claiming loyalty.
2. Contamination/Spillover: The language of religious devotion ("divine," "deathless magnetism") continuously contaminates discussion of mundane objects and morally questionable people. Sacred vocabulary spills into profane contexts (bathroom friezes are "too marvelous for words"), while profane realities (affairs, neglect, addiction) are discussed in sanitized euphemisms. The border between appropriate and inappropriate intensities has been systematically violated.
3. Physical threshold: The drawing-room itself functions as a border space. It's described as "on the verge of being

original"—neither conventional nor genuinely innovative, existing in an aesthetic liminal zone. This "verge" quality mirrors the characters' psychological state: they are on the verge of moral insight without achieving it, and of genuine emotion without expressing it.

Subtextual meaning:

This role friction creates what we might call *moral hovering*—characters who exist perpetually on the border between complicity and critique without fully committing to either. This border condition reveals the paralysis at the heart of their social world: they possess sufficient awareness to diagnose the pathology (Florence's narcissism, Nicky's destruction) but insufficient courage or moral framework to intervene.

The contamination of sacred language in profane contexts represents an *inverted value hierarchy*. In a functioning moral universe, religious intensity would be reserved for transcendent matters, while mundane objects would receive proportionate attention. This scene demonstrates the *complete reversal*: lampshades receive religious veneration ("Oh, my God, look at that lampshade!") while human suffering receives casual dismissal ("quite possibly").

The drawing room as a border space embodies this inversion physically. Everything is "on the verge"—neither genuine nor fake, neither tasteful nor vulgar, neither expensive nor valuable. This aesthetic liminality mirrors the moral liminality of its inhabitants: people who exist on the border between human connection and complete artifice.

Example from scene:

Pawnie's description of the lampshade as "Such a bad example for the servants" demonstrates contamination brilliantly. Moral language (what constitutes a "bad example") has been displaced onto an inanimate object, while actual bad examples (Florence's affair, her neglect of Nicky) go unremarked. The border between moral significance and aesthetic judgment has been obliterated, with devastating consequences for genuine ethical response.

D. *Silence/Emptiness/Void*

Detected: Yes (Implicit)

Key cues observed:

1. Pauses with purpose (Implicit): While stage directions don't explicitly mark extended pauses, the text demonstrates *conversational voids*—moments where what should be said remains unsaid. After Helen states, "And fiendish

for Nicky," there should be elaboration, exploration, and genuine engagement with this serious claim. Instead, Pawnie immediately deflects ("Oh, no, my dear; you're quite wrong there"), and the conversation moves laterally rather than deepening. These moments of non-response function as pauses—temporal voids where moral engagement should occur but doesn't.

2. Non-responsive presence: Both characters exhibit a form of emotional non-responsiveness despite their verbal activity. They are physically present and conversationally active, but emotionally absent from the serious implications of what they're discussing. When discussing Nicky's destroyed potential or Florence's destructive narcissism, they maintain the same detached, witty tone as when discussing bathroom decoration. This creates a void at the emotional center of the scene.

Subtextual meaning:

The implicit silences in this scene function differently from traditional dramatic pauses. Rather than moments of pregnant stillness, we have silences within speech—the absence of genuine response despite continuous talking. This represents what we might call compulsive verbal activity as a form of avoidance mechanism. The characters fill every potential moment of genuine reflection or emotional depth with more wit, more gossip, more aesthetic judgment, creating a void of substance within a flood of words.

The emotional non-responsiveness reveals the scene's deepest pathology: these characters have developed sophisticated verbal machinery specifically designed to prevent genuine encounter. They can discuss anything—affairs, addiction, destroyed lives—without ever having to *feel* anything authentic about it. The void isn't in their speech but in their capacity for genuine emotional response.

Example from scene:

The exchange about Nicky's wasted potential demonstrates silence-within-speech:

HELEN: "He may have had everything he wanted, but he's had none of the things he really needs." PAWNIE: "Are you talking socially or spiritually?"

Helen makes a genuinely insightful observation about deprivation masquerading as privilege. The natural response would be to explore this—what does Nicky actually need? How has Florence failed him? But Pawnie's response creates a *void disguised as clarification*. By turning Helen's statement into an abstract categorical question, he evacuates its emotional content. The silence isn't after the exchange, but *within* it—the absence of the conversation they should be having but aren't.

Step 3: Synthesis

Dimension interaction:

All four dimensions work in complex orchestration to create a scene of extraordinary subtextual density. *Absence* provides the organizing principle: Florence and Nicky structure everything despite their non-presence. The *transition* dimension describes the unstable emotional terrain in which aesthetic and moral discourse have merged. The *Border Zones* dimension captures the characters' permanent state of hovering between moral awareness and complicit aestheticization. The *silence/emptiness* dimension identifies the void at the center—the absence of genuine emotional response despite continuous talking.

Dominant dimension:

Absence dominates, but operates through a distinctive mechanism. Unlike the *Pulp Fiction* scene, where Marsellus's absence intensifies his presence, here Florence's absence creates a *vacuum that consumes authentic response*. She functions as a *black hole of narcissistic gravity*—even when not present, she warps all social and emotional space around her, making genuine connection impossible.

However, the *Border Zones* dimension provides crucial insight into the scene's specific pathology. These characters don't simply fail to engage authentically; they exist in a permanent liminal state where moral awareness and aesthetic performance have become indistinguishable. They are trapped on the border between knowing and not knowing, between caring and not caring, unable to commit fully to either position.

Intelligibility through subtext:

The explicit dialogue appears to be society gossip—witty, superficial chatter about decoration and acquaintances. But this reading is insufficient. The scene becomes intelligible only when we recognize:

1. Misplaced intensity and diminution (from the theoretical framework) map directly onto the subtextual dimensions: hyperbolic language about trivial objects (lampshades are

"divine") marks *inverted value hierarchies* (border zones), while euphemistic language about serious matters ("quite harmless," "trying") marks *suppressed response* (absence).

2. The conversation about Florence's absent presence reveals the *structuring principle of narcissistic personality disorder*: the narcissist doesn't need to be present to dominate, control, and consume. The empty center (Florence's absence) exerts more force than most presences.
3. The characters' inability to move from witty observation to genuine intervention reveals *moral paralysis* disguised as sophisticated detachment. They live on the border (border zones) between knowing Florence is destructive and aestheticizing that destruction as "divine."
4. The void at the center of the scene isn't silence but its opposite: *compulsive verbalization that prevents genuine encounter.* They talk endlessly to avoid feeling anything.

The document analyzing misplaced intensity provides the key: when characters say "too divine" about lampshades but "quite possibly" about ruined lives, they reveal an *inverted emotional economy* where authentic stakes have been systematically replaced by performative judgment.

Step 2: Inward significance—the aesthetic/dramatic experience

The Aesthetics of Moral Atrophy and the Pleasure of Diagnostic Recognition

The inward significance of this scene lies in its evocation of what we might call *sophisticated horror*—the peculiar aesthetic experience of watching moral consciousness corrode in real time while maintaining the appearance of civilized conversation. This is not the horror of violence or dramatic revelation, but rather the *slow-motion catastrophe of human diminishment* dressed in wit and decorated with taste.

The dramatic architecture of hollow sophistication

What the scene evokes in the audience is a *doubled consciousness*: we experience both the surface pleasure of witty repartee (Coward is genuinely funny) and the underlying dread of recognizing that this wit functions as *sophisticated machinery for moral evasion.* The audience is positioned as diagnostician—we possess the framework (from the theoretical analysis of misplaced intensity) to recognize the pathology these characters cannot or will not see in themselves.

This creates a distinctive spectatorial experience: *complicit recognition.* We laugh at Pawnie's cattiness ("Don't be a cat," Helen chides, acknowledging the cruelty while treating it as a minor social infraction), but our laughter is uncomfortable because we recognize what the characters don't: their witty cruelty isn't harmless social sport but symptomatic of deeper moral bankruptcy. The pleasure is *diagnostic pleasure*—the satisfaction of pattern recognition combined with the horror of what the pattern reveals.

The uncanny experience of inverted hierarchies

The scene's most profound aesthetic effect emerges from its systematic *violation of appropriate intensity*. The audience experiences a kind of *cognitive-affective vertigo*: we register that something is profoundly wrong with a world where bathroom friezes generate religious fervor ("too marvelous for words") while destroyed lives generate casual dismissal ("quite possibly").

This inversion creates what we might call the *moral uncanny*—the familiar made strange through distortion. We recognize the surface elements of civilized conversation (aesthetic judgment, social concern, friendship) but experience them as *grotesquely deformed*. It's like encountering a familiar face with features subtly rearranged—recognizable yet horrifying precisely because of its near-normalcy.

The audience doesn't experience this as an abstract intellectual observation, but as an *embodied discomfort*. When Pawnie says, "Oh, my God, look at that lampshade!" we feel the wrongness viscerally—our emotional immune system registers the misplaced religious intensity as a kind of category violation that produces unease. Similarly, when Helen describes Florence as "a little artificial perhaps, but quite harmless," we experience the euphemism as *violence through linguistic softening*—the minimization itself becomes a form of harm.

The temporal experience of arrested development

The scene evokes a peculiar *temporal phenomenology*: the sense of being trapped in a present that cannot move forward. The characters circle endlessly around the same observations (Florence is narcissistic, Nicky is doomed) without ever moving toward resolution, intervention, or change. This creates in the audience an experience of *frustrated futurity*—we perceive the trajectory (Nicky's destruction, Florence's continued consumption of others) but recognize that these characters will never interrupt it.

This temporal arrest is reinforced by the waiting structure: Helen and Pawnie are waiting for Florence, but their waiting is *ontologically empty*. They're not waiting in anticipation of change or resolution, but simply filling time until the narcissistic center arrives to consume their attention again. The audience experiences this as a kind of *dreadful inevitability*—the sense that this scene has been performed countless times before and will be performed countless times again, with no development or escape.

The aesthetic pleasure of linguistic precision in service of moral failure

Paradoxically, the scene generates *aesthetic admiration for linguistic virtuosity* even as it depicts moral failure. Coward's dialogue is genuinely brilliant—the wit is sharp, the rhythms are perfect, the verbal fencing is exquisite. The audience experiences the pleasure of watching *masterful language* deployed for *catastrophically wrong purposes.*

This creates a complex affective state: we simultaneously enjoy the performance and recoil from what it accomplishes. Pawnie's line "You must realize one thing, everyone is sacrificed to Florence—it's as it should be" is perfectly constructed—the pause before "it's as it should be" creates comic timing while delivering devastating moral content. We laugh at the precision while registering the horror of the sentiment.

This double experience generates what we might call *the pleasure of ethical spectatorship*—we occupy a position of superior awareness (we recognize the pathology they don't) while also feeling implicated (we're enjoying their wit even as it serves moral evasion). The scene refuses to let us occupy simple moral high ground; instead, it *makes us complicit* in the very dynamics we're critiquing by making us laugh at their manifestation.

The experience of contaminated language

The scene's use of misplaced intensity creates in the audience an experience of *linguistic contamination*—the sense that language itself has become diseased. When religious vocabulary ("divine," "deathless") is systematically applied to trivial objects and morally questionable people, we experience a kind of *semantic nausea.* The words still function grammatically, but their meaning has been evacuated and replaced with aesthetic performance.

This contamination extends beyond individual word choice to entire *discourse modes.* Moral language (what's "right," what's a "bad example") gets deployed for aesthetic judgments, while aesthetic language ("divine," "marvelous") gets deployed for moral evaluation. The audience experiences this as a *category confusion that prevents genuine thought*—when one's whole evaluative vocabulary has been scrambled, authentic moral reasoning becomes impossible.

The horror comes not from the idea that these characters use language incorrectly, but from the fact that they've developed a *fully functional, yet morally inverted, linguistic system.* They can communicate perfectly within this system—they understand each other's euphemisms, they recognize each other's deflections, they participate fluently in the shared verbal rituals. The audience experiences this as *witnessing the construction of a privatized reality* where normal moral coordinates no longer apply.

The tragic recognition of complicit spectatorship

The scene's deepest inward significance emerges from its positioning of the audience as *potential Helens or Pawnies.* We're not watching exotic monsters; we're watching people who possess moral awareness (they know Florence is destructive, they know Nicky is being destroyed) but have developed sophisticated mechanisms to avoid acting on it.

This creates what we might call *tragic self-recognition*: the uncomfortable possibility that we, too, might deploy wit to avoid engagement, use sophisticated language to disguise moral evasion, or mistake diagnostic observation for intervention. The scene doesn't allow us to maintain a comfortable distance from its pathology; instead, it suggests that this kind of sophisticated moral paralysis is a perennial *human temptation.*

When Helen says, "I'm very fond of Florence," while simultaneously acknowledging Florence's destructiveness, we experience the *tragedy of affection that enables harm.* The audience feels the pull of this contradiction—the genuine fondness coexisting with genuine awareness of damage, creating paralysis. Similarly, when Pawnie aestheticizes Florence's narcissism (she should have been "a flaunting, intriguing King's mistress"), we recognize the *seductive pleasure of transforming moral failure into aesthetic spectacle.*

The void at the center: emptiness performing fullness

The scene's ultimate aesthetic achievement is its evocation of *ontological emptiness masquerading as social fullness.* The characters never stop talking, but nothing is said. They never stop evaluating, but nothing is genuinely valued. They never stop performing sophistication, but no genuine thought occurs.

This creates in the audience an experience of *existential horror beneath social comedy*—the recognition that sophisticated verbal activity can coexist with complete absence of authentic human engagement. The scene demonstrates that wit can exist without wisdom, that conversation can be devoid of connection, that observation can lack intervention, and that language can lack meaning.

The audience leaves the scene haunted by a sense of awareness: we've witnessed people who have developed perfect social fluency within a fundamentally empty symbolic system. They can navigate every social nuance, perform every verbal gesture, maintain every appearance of civilized interaction—while being completely hollow at the core.

The post-war context: shellshock of the soul

The historical context (886,000 British soldiers dead, survivors physically and mentally wounded) adds another layer of inward significance. The audience experiences this scene against the *shadow of mass death*—these people are playing with lampshades and gossip while their generation has been decimated.

This creates a *temporal doubling*: we see both the scene's present (1924) and its recent past (the war). The characters' obsession with trivial aesthetic concerns becomes not just individually pathological but *historically obscene*. Their failure to engage with genuine stakes (Nicky's life, human connection, moral responsibility) mirrors their *cultural failure to process collective trauma.*

The scene evokes the recognition that sophisticated avoidance mechanisms can operate at both individual and cultural levels. These characters have developed personal strategies (wit, aestheticization, euphemism) that mirror cultural strategies for avoiding a genuine encounter with death, trauma, and moral responsibility. The "vortex" that gives the play its title becomes visible as both personal and historical—a sucking emptiness at the center where there should be an authentic response.

Conclusion: the inward significance

The scene evokes in its audience an experience of *diagnostic horror*—the recognition that moral consciousness can atrophy while linguistic sophistication flourishes, that people can know terrible truths while being structurally unable to act on them, that civilization's highest forms (wit, taste, refinement) can coexist with civilization's deepest failures (narcissism, cruelty, moral paralysis).

We leave the scene not with catharsis, but with a contaminated awareness: we've seen how language can be systematically perverted to serve evasion, how aesthetic judgment can colonize moral thought, and how sophisticated observation can substitute for genuine intervention. The scene teaches us, experientially, that the most dangerous moral failures often masquerade as *civilized sophistication.*

> The inward significance lies in its ability to make us feel the void beneath verbal fullness, to experience viscerally how misplaced intensity reveals inverted values, and to recognize uncomfortably that this pathology isn't exotic but represents a perpetual human temptation—the temptation to perform civilization while abandoning its ethical substance.
>
> We witness the vortex not as a dramatic spectacle but as a slow-motion implosion—people circling around emptiness while maintaining perfect social form, talking endlessly while saying nothing, knowing everything while understanding nothing. The horror is quiet, sophisticated, and utterly recognizable.

DISCUSSION

Reading in-between the lines, the model (Claude's Sonnet 4.5) generated an impressive interpretation. Moreover, the model learned about my previous usage. It mentions *Pulp Fiction* and even seems to recall some work I did for my previous book. It is not a *tabula rasa* but a genuine mind attuned to our history of conversations and to the chain of reasoning applied to the scene. The model employs poetic language to describe the subtext and its aesthetic effect (e.g., "worship at an empty altar"), thereby deepening our understanding of misplaced intensity in the drama.

First, through a series of structured prompts and together with the model, I identified points of misplaced emotional intensity and diminution in the first part of the play. These points are generated mainly by Pawnie and powerfully illustrate a realm where aesthetic issues, for instance, receive disproportionate and exaggerated attention. In contrast, deep issues directly related to the characters' lives are obscured by soothing language. In this context, describing Florence as "too divine" is not a simple instance of exaggerated language but an expression of the sacred–profane inversion, which in religious terms counts as idolatry. While Coward's play appears to be far removed from any religious context, the analysis conducted with the LLM reveals a surprisingly religious dimension. In a social realm characterized by the inversion of the sacred and the profane, we witness the same type of nihilistic decadence as expressed in Fellini's *Satyricon* (dir. Federico Fellini 1969). In fact, the superficial appearance of Coward's melodrama conceals a profound similarity with the society depicted in *Satyricon*. This society values aesthetics, performance, and the sadistic pleasure derived from aggression.

Reading the play in this light, the characters' delicate aesthetic taste and their immersion in art and drama can be interpreted not as an expression of good taste, but rather as an expression of idolatry, where the worship of God has been replaced by the worship of a woman (i.e., Florence) and the Golden calves of the material culture—moreover, the methodology points to several patterns of emotional inversion. Intense emotion is invested in aesthetic issues (e.g., a lampshade), while emotion is muted with respect to others, such as child neglect. The shift is from the human to the aesthetic, as similarly expressed in *Satyricon*. A second and complementary form of inversion is from depth to surface. Passionate discussions arise regarding style and presentation, while psychological needs are overlooked. In this sense, there is a third inversion from authenticity to performance. Wit is appreciated while authentic concern is dismissed. This context of interpretation portrays wit—the intelligent and cruel humor so typical of Coward's plays—in a different light.

In sum, the characters in the conversation I have analyzed use maximum intensity for minimum matters (decor, gossip, style) while deploying minimum intensity for maximum matters (psychological damage, wasted potential, family destruction). This creates a surface of sophistication that barely conceals, and actually enables, moral emptiness. All these points converge in the performance of the witty, snobbish, and fastidious gay Pawnie. Through the analysis, we understand that Pawnie is not simply a *feinschmecker* but a mask concealing deep-seated pain. Pawnie's exquisite performance of detachment chooses the beautiful suicide of ironic spectatorship over the terrifying vulnerability of caring about anything real. An aging gay man who finds meaning in his narcissistic admiration of Florence, Pawnie is destined to be carried away by the vortex, reaching a climax in Florence's breakdown. Substituting lived experience for aesthetic judgment and performance for feeling will take its toll, and Pawnie is aware of that. While he sees the truth (that everyone is sacrificed for Florence), he avoids saying it plainly because his genuine feelings would reveal his emptiness and his dependence on Florence's presence.

Reading Coward's *The Vortex* through the lens of misplaced intensity shows the play to be quite different from what we may initially perceive or what might be suggested by an ideologically biased interpretation, something which Coward himself despised. The play is not a simple melodrama; it has deep layers. It is not a play about repressed homosexuality or the representation of queers in an emerging modern England; it is mainly about a vortex, as its name suggests, and in particular, the vortex of a pathological social group dynamic that pulls people in and consumes them. The characters are helpless in the sense that, given their collective denial, they are profoundly blind to the forces leading them to a tipping point of despair. Using the above methodology, we understand that one of the forces generating the vortex is their misplaced emotional intensity, which distracts them from the real issues until the tipping point is reached. The LLM has been used to support this theoretically guided analysis of the play and provides a structured way to gain insights into the vortex. Moreover, it can be easily applied, through the prompts, to other dramatic texts of interest and real-life scenes featuring misplaced emotional intensity.

The main points of the chapter are:

- Coward's *The Vortex* exemplifies how exaggerated language is systematically applied to trivial matters, while serious moral and emotional crises are minimized.
- A structured, theoretically guided prompting framework enables LLMs to efficiently identify linguistic exaggeration in dramatic dialogue.
- Quantitative analysis shows that Pawnie produces the majority of the hyperbolic expressions, identifying him as the central agent of rhetorical inflation.

- Grouping intensified objects reveals deep structures, particularly the inversion of the sacred and the profane, where material objects and social status are imbued with sacred significance.
- Linguistic minimization functions as emotional deflection, avoiding direct confrontation with Florence's narcissism, Nicky's addiction, and moral decay.
- The AI-driven analysis reveals Florence's fragile narcissistic identity as the central threatening truth that the social group works to conceal.
- Pawnie's language reflects avoidance, fear of aging and irrelevance, aesthetic displacement, and a performative identity within a decaying postwar social world.
- The subtext exposed by reading in-between the lines points to important aspects of the scene, such as Florence as "a black hole of narcissistic gravity."

NOTE

1. https://www.gutenberg.org/ebooks/67988. Public domain.

REFERENCES

Coward, N. (1924). *The vortex: A play in three acts*. Harper & Brothers.
Coward, N. (1925). *Hay fever*. Heinemann.
Freud, S. (1905). Fragment of an analysis of a case of hysteria (1901). In *The standard edition of the complete psychological works of Sigmund Freud: Vol. VII. A case of hysteria, three essays on sexuality and other works* (pp. 1–122). Hogarth Press.
Neuman, Y. (2024). *AI for understanding context*. Springer.

10 Seeing Ourselves through Others
Subtext in Scenes from a Marriage

ABSTRACT This chapter examines subtext and perspective in Bergman's *Scenes from a Marriage*, focusing on a scene where Marianne, a divorce lawyer, meets her client, Mrs. Jacobi. The interaction reveals Marianne's surprise at the notion of a "loveless marriage," highlighting implicit assumptions about love and emotional experience. Drawing on Bakhtin's theory of perspectives, this chapter examines how individual uniqueness and asymmetrical viewpoints enable the self to be seen partially through the eyes of another. Analyzing the subtext as a *dynamic of perspectives*, I identify unconscious symmetries between Mr. Jacobi and Marianne's husband, as well as between Marianne and Mrs. Jacobi, revealing mirrored relational patterns. Marianne's sudden anxiety is interpreted as a recognition of unacknowledged emotional deficiencies in her own marriage, triggered by Mrs. Jacobi's candid self-expression. The chapter demonstrates that subtext, perspective-taking, and unconscious mirroring can offer profound insights into relational dynamics, revealing how hidden psychological realities are conveyed through seemingly ordinary dialogue.

WHAT PERSPECTIVES CAN TEACH US ABOUT SUBTEXT?

Scenes from a Marriage (dir. Ingmar Bergman 1973) is a miniseries presenting the turbulent trajectory of marriage. The heroes are Marianne, a divorce lawyer, and her husband Johan, a university professor of experimental psychology. The drama, spanning ten years in the couple's life, is a masterpiece that obtained a highly successful English-language remake (dir. Hagai Levi 2021).

The drama opens when a journalist arrives to interview Johan and Marianne for a women's magazine. They appear to be a perfect, loving couple, and they may inspire readers of the magazine. The journalist opens with a simple question: can they describe themselves in a few words? Johan hesitates. He says it is tricky, that he might give the wrong impression. The journalist gently nudges him along with brief, patient prompts. Finally, Johan explains his hesitation: it would sound cocky, he says, to describe himself as bright, youthful, successful, and sexy—which is, of course, exactly how he has just described himself.

Johan is afraid that by providing his self-description, he might give the wrong impression that he is cocky. After providing a long catalog of self-praise, the

DOI: 10.1201/9781042004485-14

impression is that Johan is indeed cocky. His self-description includes a very long list constituting the inflated self of a narcissist. This is Johan's self-perspective. What about Marianne? Marianne presents herself only in relation to her roles as a mother and a wife, without any self-praise. One immediately senses that the perfect couple involves two people whose self-perspectives differ significantly. What about the way Johan sees Marianne? He thinks that Marianne has a "great figure." What about the way Marianne sees Johan? She thinks he is "very nice." What we immediately sense is a divergence between how each character describes themselves and how the others describe them. For instance, Johan is full of self-praise; he is both "sexy" and a great friend of the Swedish Royal family, indicating his loyal character. However, his grandiose self-perspective finds no echo in the way Marianne describes him.

I find the concept of perspectives (or representations) of self and others to be an extremely powerful idea in understanding human beings and their interactions. In fact, the idea of perspectives beautifully illustrates a point repeatedly discussed in the book: it is better to make modest use of theory as inspiration rather than submit to theoretical dogma. Let me explain this point and how my use of perspectives illustrates it.

Representations of the self and the other are considered important across different theoretical perspectives. For instance, in a paper analyzing Scenes from a Marriage (Neuman, 2025), I draw heavily on Bakhtin's writings. Using Bakhtin as a springboard, I present a structured approach for studying perspectives and measuring their divergence. However, in another paper (Neuman & Hazdai, 2025), I present a novel approach for studying representations of self/other through the theoretical spectacles of *attachment theory*. In both cases, there is a common denominator: the study of representations of self/other. However, the papers differ in their theoretical backgrounds: Bakhtin versus Bowlby. Using the idea of self/other representations, I do not oblige myself to any "religion," Pope, or dogma. It is a pragmatic application of a powerful idea, no more.

AI is a powerful tool for studying self/other representation. For instance, I can automatically identify all self-descriptions of Johan and Marianne and cluster them into semantic clusters. Here are the clusters identified for the self-descriptions of Johan and Marianne:

Cluster 1: Intelligence and Success (e.g., intelligent)
Cluster 2: Physical and Social Attractiveness (e.g., sexy)
Cluster 3: Social Skills and Friendliness (e.g., friendly)
Cluster 4: Family and Relationships (e.g., mother, wife)
Cluster 5: Responsibility and Financial Stability (respects the government)
Cluster 6: Personality Traits (e.g., slow to anger)

Now that we have the self-descriptions of Johan and Marianne, we can organize them into well-structured representations of the self. We do so by representing each self-perspective as a vector, which is a clever name for an array of numbers. Let me explain this point. I use a vector, an array of numbers with six "cells," each corresponding to a different semantic cluster.

TABLE 10.1
A Partial Representation of Marianne's Self-perspective

Intelligence and Success	0
Physical and Social Attractiveness	
Social Skills and Friendliness	
Family and Relationships	
Responsibility and Financial Stability	
Personality Traits	

The value of each cell is determined by the average score of the descriptions used for the person. For example, Marianne's self-description is as a mother and a wife. Therefore, in Marianne's self-presentation vector, representing her perspective on herself, the first cell corresponding to *intelligence and success* scores 0. This suggests that none of her self-descriptions align with the semantic categories of intelligence and Success. Marianne does not seem to see herself in terms of intelligence and success. Table 10.1 presents a partial description of Marianne's self-perspective, where the value of the cell corresponding to "intelligence and success" is 0:

In contrast, Johan describes himself using five descriptions associated with the first cluster. The average score of these descriptions is 0.83, and this becomes the value of the first cell in Johan's vector. Using this approach, we can automatically and structurally represent self/other perspectives. However, what is more interesting is to see how aligned the perspectives are. In Neuman (2025), I present a measure that quantifies the degree to which perspectives diverge. The higher the measure's value, the greater the divergence. Using this measure, we can quantify the extent to which Marianne's self-perspective diverges from Johan's. Equipped with this tool and methodology, we can proceed to study the "mystery" that appears in scene two and *uncover its subtext and inner significance.* Therefore, this chapter adds another tool to our toolkit: The exposure of the subtext as a matrix of perspectives illuminating the social dynamics of the interlocutors.

WHAT MOVED MARIANNE?

In scene two, Marianne, a divorce lawyer, meets a new client, an elderly woman named Mrs. Jacobi, who wishes to divorce her husband. When asked why she wants to divorce, she answers: "It is a loveless marriage" (Bergman, 1973, p. 53). Her answer seems to surprise Marianne. This surprise is in itself surprising. As an audience, we do not understand why an experienced divorce lawyer should be surprised by a client's justification for divorce. This is the first anomaly we encounter in the scene, one that requires an explanation through subtext.

Marianne's surprise seems to increase when Mrs. Jacobi describes her husband as kind, conscientious, and an excellent father. Moreover, he is "very dependable," they never quarrel, have no financial issues, and share their interest in music by playing chamber music together. Marianne describes this situation as *ideal.* Here, a link is formed between Marianne's "ideal" marriage and Mrs. Jacobi's "ideal" marriage. The only difference, if there is one, is that the latter is a loveless marriage. This description leaves no doubt about Mrs. Jacobi's reason for divorce. Her marriage being loveless is the *only* reason for her seeking a divorce.

Marianne and Mrs. Jacobi's husband do not understand the meaning of lovelessness; Marianne asks Mrs. Jacobi to explain what "form" lovelessness takes, while the husband asks Mrs. Jacobi to explain what love she seeks. An equivalence is formed between Marianne and Mr. Jacobi. In both cases, they seem to misunderstand the meaning of romantic love and its lack.

After admitting she never loved her children, even though she was a good mother, Mrs. Jacobi turns to Marianne, saying she knows what Marianne thinks of her. Marianne is quick to deny it. However, Mrs. Jacobi correctly guesses that Marianne sees her as a spoiled woman who has everything but still seeks something vague called "love'." Marianne then admits that "perhaps" she was thinking something of this kind. This confession indicates that Marianne behaves unprofessionally when judging her client. She becomes emotionally involved.

Mrs. Jacobi describes a life of depression where everything gets meaner and grayer. Her loveless marriage is "frightening," as it drains the life out of her. Asked if her husband understands her, Mrs. Jacobi portrays a sad picture of her husband, who becomes bitter and bad-tempered whenever discussing the issue of divorce, calling her romantic and silly and explaining her wish to divorce by attributing it to a life crisis rather than acknowledging and respecting her. At this point, something suddenly arises in Marianne, who jumps to her feet to call Johan. The meeting with Mrs. Jacobi was suddenly terminated, and we understand that this has evoked deep anxiety in Marianne. However, there is nothing in the text that explicitly explains what just happened, nor what caused this shift in the conversation and Mariane's anxiety. To explain this anomaly, I first employ the notion of perspective, drawing on Bakhtin's theory, as previously mentioned.

BAKHTIN ON PERSPECTIVES

A couple is a whole that is different from the sum of its parts; this corresponds naturally to Bakhtin's epistemology (Bakhtin, 1990). However, to understand the whole, one should start with the specificity and uniqueness of the individual. As Bakhtin argues, this uniqueness results from the specific perspective one obtains from one's unique position. When I feel pain, no one can feel it the same way I do, from my own first-person perspective. You can understand my pain, sympathize with it, or empathize with it, but you can never experience it from the same perspective. This "axiom" of uniqueness states that we all have non-exchangeable perspectives. It also entails a fundamental asymmetry accompanying every human interaction: "When we gaze at each other, two different words are reflected in the pupils of our eyes" (Bakhtin, 1990 p. xxii). Paradoxically, these incompatible perspectives entail the promise of addressing the blind spot that necessarily accompanies our unique perspective. When we gaze at each other, each of us has "an excess of vision" relative to the other" (Bakhtin, 1990). The other, through her outside perspective, has "an excess of vision" which, when used to mirror my perspective, can somehow provide me with a more holistic perception of myself. In the case of a couple, the "architectonics" of the couple as a whole composed of two parts is not given as a static structure but worked out dynamically through perspectives.

In this relational context, a crisis can be understood as a rupture in the couple's architectonics. To understand this negatively loaded break in architectonics, we should recall Bakhtin's famous phrase, "We are all unique but never alone" (Bakhtin, 1990, xxvi). The break becomes evident when co-working perspectives stop functioning. In other words, we are all unique and partially blind, and we have an excess of seeing in relation to one another. In relationships, we dynamically and recursively mingle with these three perspectival aspects. As we are never alone, our existence is grounded in the intricate and dynamic web of perspectives through which we are formed by others who are, in turn, recursively formed by us. A crisis can emerge when this perspectival dynamics does not function properly and no longer satisfies the needs of the interlocutors.

The event of forming the whole can be specified by adopting Bakhtin's metaphor of the individual as an author. Just as the author must adopt the hero's perspective, so must the other, mutually covering our blind spots. This activity can be described as a *projection*. One must somehow project oneself onto the other to maintain a functioning couple. The second aspect of this process is the ability to see oneself from the other's perspective. As beautifully explained by Bakhtin (1990, p. 25):

> I must empathize or project myself into this other human being ... see the world within him ... as *he* sees this world; I must put myself in his place and then, after returning to my place, "fill in" his horizon through the excess of seeing which opens out from this, my own, place outside him.

In this chapter, I employ the concepts of perspective and projection to explain Marianne's anxiety. Through a structural analysis of perspectives, as mediated by the LLM, we learn how Mrs. Jacobi mirrors Marianne's own mind.

THE SUBTEXT OF MARIANNE'S SUDDEN ANXIETY

I used the descriptions of Johan and Mr. Jacobi, and their automatic clustering resulted in three clusters: (1) positive personality traits, (2) negative personality traits, and (3) other complex traits. As an aside, it is worth noting that the semantic clusters indicate the contextual aspect of the personality. Mr. Jacobi is described as a kind person. However, when discussing divorce, he turns bitter and bad-tempered. The positive and negative aspects of Mr. Jacobi appear to be separated into two semantic clusters, corresponding to distinct contexts. This is probably why Mrs. Jacobi also describes him as "very dependable." This understanding explains why the kind Mr. Jacobi describes his wife as romantic, silly, and suffering from a life crisis. He cannot let her go free.

I formed two three-element vectors describing Mr. Jacobi and Johan as seen by their wives. Using my measure of divergence on these descriptions, the divergence of Mr. Jacobi's description from Johan's description was found to be 0.12, and that of Johan's from Mr. Jacobi's was found to be 0.11. In other words, *their descriptions, as given by their wives, are almost the same*. This is something not explicitly discussed in the drama. From *an artistic perspective, Johan and Mr. Jacobi are the same, psychologically interchangeable.*

As we learned from Blanco's insightful work (Blanco, 2003), *symmetrization* is the constituent logic of the unconscious. In his work, he proposed a *bi-logic* theory of the mind based on two primary principles that govern the unconscious realm:

The principle of generalization: The unconscious logic does not consider individual items as unique; it deals with them only as members of a class or a subset of a more general class. This principle suggests a hierarchical structure where a part can represent the whole. For instance, if my father and my teacher are authority figures, I might rebel against my teacher, just as I might against my father.

The principle of symmetry: The unconscious treats any relationship as identical to its converse (reverse); asymmetrical relations are treated as if they were symmetrical. For example, in conscious (asymmetrical) thought, "X is greater than Y" cannot be reversed. In symmetrical unconscious thought, "Y is greater than X" is simultaneously considered true.

These two principles, operating together, account for the characteristics of the Freudian "primary process" (e.g., timelessness, absence of contradiction, condensation) and contrast with the *asymmetrical logic* of conscious, rational "secondary process" thinking.

In the next chapter, I will demonstrate how an LLM can apply these principles to gain a deeper understanding of a scene's underlying meaning, or subtext. Here, I use Blanco's theory only through the concept of symmetrization. The symmetry of the measure exposes the symmetry between Mr. Jacobi and Johan. At this point, we may gain a better understanding of the turning point in the plot and why Marianne is so moved by a meeting that is supposed to be an ordinary professional meeting between a lawyer and her client. If Johan is the same as Mr. Jacobi, then maybe Marianne is similar to Mrs. Jacobi. The unconscious analogy may signal to Marianne that, similarly to Mrs. Jacobi, she is also experiencing a loveless marriage where she is depressed and drained of life.

So, how about the way Marianne describes herself versus the self-description of Mrs. Jacobi? Automatically clustering their descriptions resulted in three semantic clusters: (1) family roles, (2) emotional traits, and (3) complex and abstract traits. The divergence of Marianne's self-description from Mrs. Jacobi's was lower than that of Mrs. Jacobi from Marianne (0.30 vs. 0.45, respectively). It is 1.5 times smaller.

This finding can be interpreted as follows: *Marianne can see herself in Mrs. Jacobi more than Mrs. Jacobi can see herself in the lawyer*, as both are mothers and wives (first cluster). However, Mrs. Jacobi may be less aligned with Marianne because Marianne's self-description (unknown to Mrs. Jacobi) lacks emotional traits. In the opening scene, Marianne presents herself as a mother and a wife. No more. It is now clear why she thinks Mrs. Jacobi is "spoiled." On the one hand, we have a woman who defines herself through her family duties (as a wife and a mother). A woman, when asked about love in the interview, dismisses all notions of romantic love; on the other hand, an elderly lady desperately seeks love and is willing to pay the price for being honest with herself. For Mrs. Jacobi, there is no false self. She knows who she is and what she wants, and accepts that courageously.

However, there is an interesting point to consider. If Mr. Jacobi and Johan are unconsciously symmetric, then by inference, so are Mrs. Jacobi and Marianne. However, while Mrs. Jacobi describes herself as both depressed and having the capacity to love, both of these aspects are missing from Marianne's self-description. Marianne's self-perception is shallow, functional, and devoid of emotion. However, if Mr. Jacobi is symmetric with Johan, and Marianne can see herself in Mrs. Jacobi, could it be that the missing parts necessary for establishing a complete symmetry between Marianne and Mrs. Jacobi are just those painful parts Marianne refuses to admit? Are these the same parts raising her anxiety to the level where the meeting is suddenly terminated?

This turning point in the drama is where Marianne becomes "unconsciously aware" of a hidden depression and loveless marriage. Something suddenly changes through the mirroring of the old lady's perspective on her husband. Using the divergence, I identified a symmetry between Johan and Mr. Jacobi and Marianne and Mrs. Jacobi. The symmetry between Marianne and Mrs. Jacobi is not trivially exposed. They are similar in their family roles but differ in their emotions. However, these differences elicit a strong emotional response in Marianne, suggesting that they may in fact be unacknowledged similarities.

The event of forming a whole couple is challenged by the meeting with the old lady. Although Johan has not informed her yet about his affair with a young woman, Marianne starts feeling that something is wrong. Her blind spot has been exposed through the excess vision provided by the old lady. Seeing herself in both Mr. and Mrs. Jacobi gives Marianne the excess of vision that evokes anxiety. She now understands better. Johan cannot project himself onto Marianne's uniqueness to the same extent as Marianne can project herself onto Johan's. Although they are unique, they are alone and, as such, cannot maintain a functioning whole when challenged by evolving perspectives and circumstances. At this point, I would like to see how far an LLM can go in understanding the conversation between Marianne and Mrs. Jacobi.

LOVE AS PHANTOM CENTER

I provided Claude with the dialogue between Marianne and Mrs. Jacobi, along with my interpretation of Marianne's anxiety through the theory of Blanco. I then asked the model to apply the prompt in order to analyze my interpretation. Here is the model's output:

MODEL'S OUTPUT 10.1

Subtext analysis: The Marianne–Mrs. Jacobi dialogue

Step 1: Preliminary scene comprehension

Surface level: A divorce lawyer conducts a preliminary meeting with an elderly client seeking a divorce after more than 20 years of marriage. The client describes an ideal marriage lacking only love. The lawyer becomes increasingly uncomfortable, eventually cutting the meeting short in apparent distress.

Step 2: Dimension detection and analysis

dimension 1: Absence (structuring absence/phantom center)

Detected: Yes

Key cues observed:

1. Love as phantom center: Love is the organizing absence around which the entire dialogue revolves. Every statement—about the husband's kindness, the apartment, the music, the children—circles around this central void.
2. Suppressed response: Mrs. Jacobi describes never loving her children yet being "a good mother." The expected maternal love is absent, yet this absence structures her entire parenting experience.
3. The unnamable: Most powerfully, when asked "what love is supposed to involve," Mrs. Jacobi responds: "How can I describe something that's not there?" Love cannot be named because it has never existed in positive form—only as absence.

Subtextual meaning:

The absence is not simply "missing love" but *love-that-was-never-there*, an absence so complete it precedes presence. This is what terrifies Marianne: not the loss of something once possessed, but the revelation that her own "ideal marriage" may be built on the same phantom foundation.

The symmetrization operates here: if Mrs. Jacobi's husband mirrors Johan, and both marriages appear "ideal," then the *structuring absence in Mrs. Jacobi's marriage must also structure Marianne's*. The void is contagious.

Example from scene [Removed to avoid copyright issues YN]:

Dimension 2: *Liminal transition* (identity slippage)

Detected: Yes

Key cues observed:

1. Role reversal: Marianne begins as a professional assessor but undergoes identity slippage into the role of the assessed. When Mrs. Jacobi says, "I know just what you're thinking," the power dynamic inverts—the client reads the lawyer, not the other way around.
2. Tonal mutation: The conversation maintains professional surface structure but mutates into something else—a diagnosis of Marianne herself. What appears to be a legal consultation functions as psychological exposure.

3. The interrupted question: Marianne's aborted question ("Isn't it true that love—") marks the precise moment of transition. She begins to speak professionally, but cannot complete the thought because she has crossed into uncertain territory regarding her own marriage.

Subtextual meaning:

Marianne transitions from lawyer to client, from observer to observed, from a safe professional distance to a dangerous self-recognition. She enters a liminal state where she is neither fully the helper nor fully helped, neither fully aware nor fully ignorant.

The transition is catalyzed by symmetrization: as Johan becomes Mr. Jacobi, Marianne must become Mrs. Jacobi. She is caught between two identity states—the woman who has everything (her self-description) and the woman who has nothing that matters (Mrs. Jacobi's revelation).

Dimension 3: *border zones*

Detected: Yes

Key cues observed:

1. Role friction: Marianne occupies the border between professional and personal. She should remain detached but become emotionally involved. Mrs. Jacobi explicitly identifies this: "I know just what you're thinking"—forcing Marianne to admit unprofessional judgment.
2. Contamination/Spillover: Mrs. Jacobi's existential condition "leaks" into Marianne's consciousness. The description of sensory failure—"everything seems puny, gray, and undignified"—contaminates the professional space with dread. What belongs to the client's inner world spills into the lawyer's.
3. The professional boundary violated: The scene takes place in the office of a law firm, a space that should maintain clear boundaries between helper and helped. However, this boundary dissolves as Marianne recognizes herself in her client.

Subtextual meaning:

The border zone is psychological: Marianne stands between knowing and not-knowing about her own marriage. The professional boundary should protect her from such recognition, but Mrs. Jacobi's testimony crosses that threshold.

The symmetrization creates a border crossing: if the husbands are interchangeable, the wives must inhabit the same existential zone. Marianne cannot remain safely on the professional side of the boundary because the symmetry pulls her across into Mrs. Jacobi's territory—the zone of loveless marriage and existential dissolution.

Dimension 4: silence/emptiness (pauses with purpose)

Detected: Yes

Key cues observed:

1. The aborted question: The silence after Marianne cannot complete her question about love is the scene's most charged void. What she cannot say becomes more meaningful than anything that is said.
2. The void within speech: Mrs. Jacobi describes a void—the absence of feeling—but this void is given form through silence more than words. Her measured, calm delivery of devastating content creates a sense of emptiness around each statement.
3. Marianne's final response: When Mrs. Jacobi describes everything becoming "puny, gray, and undignified," Marianne's response—"I think I do"—is thin and hollow. The silence beneath it screams.

Subtextual meaning:

Silence operates as the medium through which the symmetrization becomes unbearable. What cannot be spoken is: "I am you. My marriage is your marriage. My life is draining away, too."

The void Mrs. Jacobi describes—sensory and emotional numbness—finds its echo in the silence that grows between statements. The scene's pauses accumulate weight, building toward the moment when Marianne feels she must flee. The silence is not the absence of meaning but the *excess of meaning that cannot be articulated* without collapse.

Step 3: Synthesis—how the dimensions interact

The four dimensions work together to create an experience of symmetrical recognition that shatters professional and psychological defenses:

1. Absence establishes the phantom center (love-that-never-was) around which both marriages revolve.
2. The transition is Marianne's passage from observer to participant, from safety to exposure.
3. The border zones dimension is relevant because the scene is located at the threshold between professional distance and personal recognition, where contamination occurs.
4. Silence provides the emptiness in which the unspeakable symmetry becomes undeniable.

The Dominant Dimension: *Absence* drives the scene. The structuring absence of love creates the conditions for all the other dimensions. The transition occurs because Marianne recognizes this absence in her own life. The border zone exists because this absence spans both marriages. The silence emerges because the absence cannot be named without existential collapse.

Step 4: Inward significance—the aesthetic/dramatic experience

What the scene evokes in the audience

The scene evokes a mounting dread of recognition—not the dramatic revelation of hidden facts, but the quiet horror of seeing what has always been there, yet unnamed.

We watch Marianne undergo what might be called involuntary symmetrical perception: she cannot help but see herself in Mrs. Jacobi, because the symmetry is so exact. The explicit dialogue presents a routine professional encounter. The implicit subtext reveals *two women trapped in identical voids*, separated only by Mrs. Jacobi's courage to name it and Marianne's terror of doing so.

The dramatic experience: shattering in slow motion

The audience experiences this not as a sudden shock but as an *incremental collapse*:

- We watch Marianne's professional composure gradually fail
- We see her questions become more personal, more desperate
- We witness the moment she tries to ask about love, but cannot
- We feel the contamination spread—Mrs. Jacobi's existential numbness seeps into Marianne's consciousness

The inward significance is not simply "Marianne discovers her marriage lacks love" (too simplistic, too plot-driven). Rather, it is *Marianne experiences the dissolution of the boundary between self and other, present and future, safety and void.*

The aesthetic dimension: beauty in horror

There is a strange, terrible beauty in Mrs. Jacobi's calm articulation of emptiness:

"Everything seems puny, gray, and undignified."

This is poetry of the void. The scene evokes not melodrama but a kind of *existential vertigo*—the sensation of standing at the edge of an abyss you did not know was there, realizing you have been standing there all along.

Why symmetrization intensifies the effect

The unconscious logic of symmetry—where Mr. Jacobi = Johan, therefore Mrs. Jacobi = Marianne—creates a dramatic effect that operates *beneath rational comprehension.*

The audience does not think: "These people are similar, therefore…" Instead, we *sense the equivalence forming, the way one feels a dream logic* taking hold. The symmetrization bypasses Marianne's (and our) defensive rationality. It is not an argument; it is a *felt truth that cannot be refuted.*

The inward significance: facing the phantom

The scene's ultimate dramatic power lies in forcing both Marianne and the audience to confront the structuring absence at the center of what appears to be a successful life. What is terrifying is not the dramatic revelation of an affair or betrayal—it is the quiet recognition that *one has been living adjacent to emptiness without knowing it.* The "ideal marriage" is revealed as a performance sustained by not looking, not asking, and not feeling.

Mrs. Jacobi represents the future Marianne refuses: the woman who finally looked directly at the absence and decided it could not be survived. Marianne's anxiety comes at the moment she is forced to look—when she feels the immediate need to look away before the full truth becomes unavoidable.

The scene's final gift to the audience

The inward significance is completed by what the scene *does not show*: we do not see Marianne's phone call to Johan, nor do we hear what she says. The scene ends in *suspension*—Marianne caught between recognition and denial, between Mrs. Jacobi's future and her own present. The audience is left in this same suspended state, feeling the symmetry take hold but not yet seeing its full consequences. This is the scene's aesthetic achievement: it makes us inhabit the liminal space between knowing and not-knowing, between the life that appears ideal and the void that structures it. We experience, through Marianne, what it feels like when the phantom center suddenly becomes visible—and then we desperately try to make it invisible again.

DISCUSSION

In *Scenes from a Marriage*, what appears to be an ordinary professional encounter between a divorce lawyer and her client is revealed, through subtextual analysis, as a moment of intense anxiety. The aesthetic power of the scene lies precisely in this discrepancy between surface normality and inward disturbance. Bergman's achievement is not to *tell* us that something is wrong, but to make us *feel* the moment when a hidden structure of meaning becomes briefly visible and immediately intolerable.

By using the concept of perspectives (i.e., representations of self and others) and unconscious symmetrization, the chapter illustrates how subtext operates through absence, mirroring, and asymmetry, rather than through explicit statements. In this context, we learn that love functions as a phantom center: an organizing absence that silently governs the interaction. Marianne's anxiety is not caused by new information, but by a shift in perspective—by seeing herself through the excess vision of the other. This moment exemplifies the aesthetic value of subtext: it creates an experience of recognition without articulation, an understanding that precedes and resists language.

Beyond its contribution to understanding the specific scene, the chapter offers tools for understanding real-life situations. The identification of perspectives, their divergence, and symmetrization may be used to uncover the patterns underlying the text. In this context, we may learn again that subtext is not only an aesthetic phenomenon but also a practical one: it is what quietly expresses hidden relational patterns before they can be named.

The main points of the chapter are:

- The miniseries portrays Marianne, a divorce lawyer, and her husband, Johan, as they explore the evolving dynamics of marriage over ten years.
- Marianne's meeting with a client highlights her surprise at the concept of a "loveless marriage," revealing implicit assumptions about love and marriage.
- Individual uniqueness and asymmetrical perspectives create opportunities for self-reflection through the "excess of vision" seen in the other.
- Marianne's sudden anxiety is explained by unconscious recognition of parallels between herself and Mrs. Jacobi.
- Semantic clustering reveals a psychological and unconscious symmetry between Mr. Jacobi and Johan, as well as a partial symmetry between Marianne and Mrs. Jacobi.
- Marianne's self-description lacks emotional depth, revealing unacknowledged aspects of her own loveless marriage.
- Mirroring and perspective-taking uncover hidden anxieties, crises, and relational dynamics, showing how subtext conveys unspoken psychological truths.

REFERENCES

Bakhtin, M. (1990). *Art and answerability*. University of Texas Press.

Bergman, I. (1973). *Scenes from a Marriage*. Bantam Books.

Blanco, I. M. (2003). *Thinking, feeling, and being*. Routledge.

Neuman, Y. (2025). The architecture of relational crisis: How to study diverging perspectives. *Integrative Psychological and Behavioral Science*, *59*(4), 73.

Neuman, Y., & Hazdai, K. (2025). An AI-supported methodology for identifying attachment styles. *medRxiv*, 2025–08. https://doi.org/10.1101/2025.08.30.25334439

11 "Just a Tickle" *Subtext in* The Homecoming

ABSTRACT Chapter 11 analyzes subtext in Harold Pinter's play *The Homecoming*, focusing on the interaction between Lenny and Ruth. While the surface dialogue appears fragmented and absurd, the subtext reveals the characters' engagement with unconscious symmetrical logic. Using Blanco's bi-logic, the AI-based analysis shows that Lenny unconsciously generalizes Ruth into a single class of demanding women, encompassing his mother and a prostitute, while symmetry collapses opposites such as subject/object and nurture/aggression. The "in-between" methodological framework highlights liminal features—absences, transitions, border zones, and silences—that signal shifts from asymmetrical, conscious order to the undifferentiated symmetrical unconscious. Ruth exploits these dynamics to invert power, paralyzing Lenny and asserting dominance, while Lenny's attempts to maintain asymmetrical control fail. The resulting dramatic aesthetic effect is experienced as a cognitive vertigo, in which the audience witnesses the collapse of conventional roles and time, as Lenny's authority is reversed and they are immersed in a terrifying, symmetrical, undifferentiated unconscious.

"WHY DON'T YOU SHUT UP, YOU DAFT PRAT?"

The Homecoming is a play by Pinter (1965) that was adapted for the screen by Peter Hall in 1973, featuring a wonderful cast. Set in North London, The Homecoming features six characters, five of whom belong to the same "interesting" family. At the head of the household is Max, a seventy-year-old retired butcher, who lives with his brother Sam, a chauffeur, and his two grown sons: Lenny, a thirty-year-old pimp who at the beginning only hints obliquely at his profession and his network of flats and clients in London; and Joey his younger brother, who is a demolition worker of low intelligence, training to become a professional boxer. The third and oldest son is Teddy, an American-based philosophy professor who has not been in touch with his family since he moved to the States. The sixth character is Ruth, Teddy's wife, who is also British. The play centers on Teddy and Ruth's unexpected visit to his family's home and the surreal dynamics of the family.

The opening scene of the play (Act 1) presents a brutal and negatively loaded interaction between Max and Lenny. Lenny is sitting on the sofa with a newspaper when Max enters the room and approaches him with a question: "What have you done with the scissors?" No greetings, no etiquette, just a direct encounter with a question that can be interpreted as both questioning and blaming. There is a pause. Lenny does not answer his father's question, and his father repeats it, while Lenny ignores it again. When he finally responds to his father, he says: "Why don't you shut up, you daft prat?" This is a strong confrontational command accompanied by an

 DOI: 10.1201/9781042004485-15

insult (daft = silly, prat = idiot). The insult is delivered calmly and quietly, not loudly. Ian Holm, who later played Bilbo Baggins in *The Lord of the Rings* (2001), plays Lenny as a highly self-controlled psychopath. This makes Lenny's response to his father more chilling, suggesting contained aggression and dominance. In response to Lenny's face-threatening act, Max lifts his stick and threatens him. However, this is an empty threat that does not influence Lenny. Max continues with a rather long monologue until Lenny decides to silence him, calling him a stupid sod, where "sod" is vulgar English for a person.

The timing of Lenny's response is interesting. Lenny responds immediately after Max mentions his late mother, whom he describes as not such a "bad" woman/bitch, despite the fact that she made him sick when he looked at her "rotten stinking face." This repulsive description of the late wife and mother contrasts sharply with Max's description of horses and racing, which he describes as the love of his life. The man who takes pride in his "instinctive understanding of animals" appears to have a limited understanding and empathy toward human beings.

The dialogue escalates to the point that this time, Lenny threatens Max, who calls Lenny a "bitch" and grips his stick in a threatening manner. To this gesture, Lenny responds in a childish tone ("Daddy"), mimicking a child who begs his father not to use the stick on him. It seems that the child, once treated violently by his father, has himself turned into a threat. What we immediately sense is a dysfunctional family with a pathological pattern of interaction and communication.

THE TICKING SCENE

My focus is on the first interaction between Ruth, Teddy's wife, and Lenny. This is the scene I describe as the *Ticking Scene.* Teddy and Ruth arrive late at night without notifying the family. While Ruth goes outside to get a breath of air, Teddy meets Lenny. Their first encounter is rather cold, formal, and alienating. Teddy goes upstairs to his old room, and Lenny stays in the main room, where he meets Ruth upon her return. The interaction between Ruth and Lenny is surreal, and its meaning remains unclear. I ask you to watch the scene carefully and afterward to try to answer the following questions:

1. What explains the surreal nature of the interaction?
2. Can you explain Lenny's shifts in the interaction?
3. What is Ruth's role in what seems to be a pathological dynamic?

After watching the scene, let us return to its description. When Ruth introduces herself as Teddy's wife, Lenny immediately responds with a long monologue in which he asks her advice about the clock he is holding in his hand, saying it has given him a "rough" time with its ticks keeping him up. Lenny is not sure whether it is the clock that has given him the rough time or whether he has just generated a "false hypothesis." Instead of waiting for Ruth's response, which does not come, he pours and serves her a glass of water, shifting to a totally different topic: "Isn't it funny? I've got my pyjamas on and you're fully dressed?" He then shifts the topic to another issue, but a more bothering shift appears after Lenny's long monologue on Italy when he suddenly asks Ruth: "Do you mind if I hold your hand?" Ruth asks for justification, to which Lenny responds, "Just a touch." He approaches her, saying, "Just a tickle." Once again, Ruth asks why. To this, Lenny responds with an obscure story about his violent encounter with a prostitute "down by the docks." This story provides no explanation for his strange request, to which Ruth responds with unexpected indifference. Her response to Lenny's bizarre behavior significantly diverges from the expected response of a normal human being. However, a turning point occurs later in the conversation. Lenny asks Ruth for her glass. Ruth refuses, and they argue. Lenny tells Ruth she has had enough to drink. Ruth simply says she hasn't. Lenny repeats himself. Ruth repeats herself—but this time she calls him Leonard.

There is a pause, and then Lenny says, "Don't call me that, please." This is a moment of high emotional tension, as Lenny explains that this is the name his mother gave him. Why is it a problem that Ruth addresses him by the name his late mother used? And why is Ruth using the more formal and serious name "Leonard" instead of "Lenny"? This strange interaction continues as Ruth initiates an amusing, seductive exchange, inviting Lenny to sit on her lap and take a long, cool sip from her glass. She pats her lap and proposes that he lie on his back so she can pour the water into his mouth. "What are you doing, making me some kind of proposal?" he asks, to which Ruth responds with a laugh.

THE SUBTEXT OF THE SURREAL

To understand this rather surreal interaction, we need to understand the subtext, but in this case, identifying it seems like a very challenging task. Here, a theory may guide us in the process. The interaction involves two main characters, Lenny and Ruth, and three absent characters: Teddy, a minor figure in the exchange; Lenny's mother; and the prostitute. Ruth addresses Lenny by the name his mother used. We may hypothesize that by calling him by the same name as his mother, she somehow becomes his mother. It is as if, through *symmetrization*, she becomes Lenny's mother. However, her seductive behavior, interpreted by Lenny as a "proposal," immediately corresponds to the proposal offered by the diseased prostitute on the docks. Ruth, his brother's wife, turns into a mother and a whore: her behavior is aligned with the two characters, first, by treating Lenny as a child to be nurtured, and second, through her seductive behavior and laugh. Lenny's emotions with regard to his mother are exposed in his angry response to his father's derogatory description of the mother (e.g., "bitch"). His emotion toward the prostitute is exposed through his violent behavior (e.g., "I clumped her one").

However, the pattern I have just exposed does not reveal the full picture. To expose the subtext of the surreal interaction, I drew on Matte Blanco's theory, presented in the previous chapter. I have applied his theory extensively in my books and papers, as I find it to be extremely helpful. To recall, the theory proposes that our unconscious is governed by symmetrization, as expressed in the above interpretation. Therefore, I used the following prompt and instructed the model to read a paper (Sánchez-Cárdenas, 2016) presenting Blanco's theory. I then asked the model to use CONTEXT, which is my description of the play and interpretation of the scene as presented above. The prompt was as follows:

PROMPT 11.1

Read the dialogue between Lenny and Ruth, from the play "The Homecoming" by Harold Pinter.

Read the attached paper, describing the theory of Blanco and his bi-logic. Focus on the two principles described in the paper.

Your task is to identify the subtext of the conversation between Lenny and Ruth and interpret it in light of Blanco's theory.

Support your analysis with evidence from the things Lenny and Ruth said and did.

Be explicit about how the subtext you identified can clarify the incomprehensible points in the dialogue.

For the task, use the following context: [CONTEXT HERE]

Using Gemini Pro as a model, I generated the following output:

MODEL'S OUTPUT 11.1

Based on the provided text from Harold Pinter's *The Homecoming* and the paper on Blanco's bi-logic, here is an analysis of the subtext in the dialogue between Ruth and Lenny.

The subtext of "The Homecoming": A bi-logical interpretation

The incomprehensible nature of the dialogue between Lenny and Ruth can be clarified by applying Blanco's concepts of *bi-logic*. The conversation operates on two levels simultaneously: the *asymmetrical mode* (surface level: a brother-in-law offering water to a guest) and the *symmetrical mode* (deep level: a dangerous negotiation of identity, sex, and aggression).

Under the surface, the distinct identities of "sister-in-law," "mother," and "whore" collapse into a single, threatening class, while the actions of "nurturing" and "dominating" become indistinguishable.

1. *The principle of generalization: the class of the "demanding woman."* According to Blanco, the unconscious groups elements that share analogies into wider sets or classes. In this dialogue, Lenny unconsciously places Ruth into a generalized class of "Women who make demands," which also includes his mother, the prostitute at the docks, and the old lady with the mangle.
    - Evidence: Lenny transitions abruptly from polite conversation to violent anecdotes about women. He describes a lady at the docks who "made me a certain proposal" and an old lady who asked him to move an iron mangle.
    - Interpretation: While logically (asymmetrically) these are different women, strictly separated by time and space, bi-logically they

are members of the same set. When Ruth asserts herself (e.g., refusing to give up the glass), she activates the logic of this class. The "proposal" the prostitute made equates to the "proposal" Lenny accuses Ruth of making later ("What are you doing, making me some kind of proposal?"). By entering this class, Ruth inherits the attributes of the other members: she is viewed as diseased or burdensome, justifying Lenny's defensive aggression.

2. *The principle of symmetry: The collapse of opposites*
   The principle of symmetry holds that relations which are asymmetrical in consciousness (A leads to B) are treated as symmetrical in the unconscious (A and B are equivalent/identical). This principle clarifies the most bizarre exchanges in the dialogue.
   A. The equivalence of subject and object (possession)
      In the asymmetrical world, Lenny taking a glass from Ruth is a simple physical act. However, in the symmetrical subtext, the object (glass) and the subject (Ruth) are confused.
      - Evidence: The dispute over the glass.
        - Ruth: "If you take the glass, I'll take you."
        - Lenny: "How about me taking the glass without you taking me?"
      - Interpretation: Lenny is trying to maintain asymmetrical order (separating the glass from the woman). Ruth, however, enforces symmetrical logic, where "taking the glass" is equivalent to "taking the person" (in terms of sexual or dominance dynamics). In the symmetrical mode, subject and object are indistinguishable. Therefore, for Lenny to take the glass is for him to *be taken* by Ruth.
   B. The Equivalence of Nurture and Aggression (Mother/Whore)
      The context notes that Ruth becomes the mother through symmetrization. The dialogue supports this, showing how "mothering" and "attacking" become equivalent relations.
      - Evidence:
        - Nurture: Lenny offers water as a "tonic." Ruth later treats Lenny like a child: "Sit on my lap. Take a long cool sip."
        - Aggression: Ruth's nurture turns invasive: "Lie on the floor. Go on. I'll pour it down your throat."
      - Interpretation: In the symmetrical deep strata, love and hate are undifferentiated. Ruth invoking the name "Leonard" ("That's the name my mother gave me") triggers a collapse of time. She is no longer just the brother's wife; she is the mother. Consequently, her offer to feed him water is indistinguishable from an act of domination or drowning. The water is both life-giving and a weapon.

Clarifying the Incomprehensible Points

1. The "Clock" monologue
   - The Incomprehensible Point: Why does Lenny start a conversation with a stranger about a ticking clock and "false hypotheses"?
   - The subtext: This is a manifestation of bi-logical conflict. Lenny describes things that are "quiet as mice during the daytime" (asymmetrical/conscious order) but "start letting out a bit of a tick" in the night.
   - Clarification: The "tick" represents the irruption of the symmetrical unconscious—the "rough time" where objects and threats become alive and indistinguishable. Lenny is confessing his inability to keep the "night" (emotional/symmetrical chaos) separate from the "day" (logic). He is warning Ruth that his internal containment is failing.
2. The Shift from "Holding Hands" to "Violence."
   - The incomprehensible point: Lenny asks to hold Ruth's hand, then immediately tells a graphic story about beating a woman who made a sexual proposal.
   - The subtext: This illustrates emotional thinking, where an affect and an idea are inseparable.
   - Clarification: Lenny's desire for connection ("Just a touch") immediately activates the generalized class of "intimacy with women." In his symmetrized mind, intimacy is equivalent to infection and engulfment (the "diseased" lady). To survive the intimacy (the touch), he must destroy the object. The violence is not a non-sequitur; it is the symmetrical equivalent of the touch.
3. The Power Reversal (The Glass)
   - The incomprehensible point: Why does Ruth's refusal to give back the glass paralyze Lenny?
   - The subtext: Ruth refuses to be an asymmetrical object (a passive guest). She embraces the symmetrical identity Lenny projected onto her.
   - Clarification: By acting as the "mother" (calling him Leonard, ordering him to sit on her lap), she dominates the "generalization" Lenny created. If she is in the mother/whore class, she possesses the power of the "whole" over the "part." Lenny, who "clumped" the prostitute to assert control, cannot hit Ruth because she has psychologically become the mother who named him. She has trapped him in his own symmetrical logic.

Conclusion

Blanco's theory suggests that the terror in this scene stems from the characters not operating within a standard logical reality. Lenny attempts to manage his anxiety through asymmetrical stories of violence (where he is the victor and the women are defeated objects). Ruth, however, dives into the *infinite sets* of the unconscious. She accepts the projection of the "whore/mother" but reverses the vector of power. By acting on the *principle of symmetry*, she renders Lenny's aggression impotent—she becomes the one who "takes."

I believe that the analysis generated by Gemini's model is quite remarkable in its depth and insights. Drawing on the bi logic of Blanco and the two principles, it interpreted the subtext of a surreal interaction in a way that "resolves" the mystery of the text. Moreover, watching the play to its end, you may be struck by how insightful the model was in explaining the events to come. To delve deeper into the surreal interaction between Lenny and Ruth, I asked the model to read Chapter 7 and to complement the analysis by considering the idea of reading in-between the lines. The output is as follows:

MODEL'S OUTPUT 11.2

Here is the analysis of the "ticking scene" from *The Homecoming*, executed according to the instructions in the Subtext Identification and Analysis Prompt (Four-Dimensional Framework), followed by an analysis of its inward significance.

Step 1: Subtext identification and analysis

Input data

- Dialogue: The interaction between Lenny and Ruth (the clock/ticking, the water, the request to hold hands, the story of the prostitute, the dispute over the glass, the name "Leonard").
- Context: Late night in a North London home. Lenny (pimp/son) and Ruth (sister-in-law) are alone while Teddy (husband) is upstairs. The atmosphere is menacing but formally polite.

Structured Output

Absence (Presence through Non-Presence)

- Detected: Yes
- Key cues observed: Structuring absence (phantom center); suppressed response.
- Subtextual meaning: The late mother functions as a "phantom center," an absent entity that actively organizes the behavior and power dynamics of the scene. When Ruth invokes the name "Leonard," she effectively steps into the void left by the mother, instantly paralyzing Lenny. Additionally, Ruth's lack of shock (suppressed response) on hearing Lenny's violent story about the

prostitute signals that she is not a standard "guest" but operates on a darker level compatible with his violence.
- Example from scene: Ruth calls Lenny "Leonard," the name his mother gave him. This invocation of the *absent* mother stops Lenny's aggression cold, prompting the response: "Don't call me that, please."

Liminal transition (temporal/emotional shifts)
- Detected: Yes
- Key cues observed: identity slippage; rule reversal; tonal mutation.
- *Subtextual meaning*: The scene is defined by "identity slippage," where characters begin to operate in roles foreign to their established identity. Ruth slips from "brother's wife" to "seductress/mother," while Lenny slips from "predator" to "child." The rules reverse: the predator (Lenny) becomes the prey/child as Ruth takes control of the glass and the naming rights.
- *Example from scene*: The transition is complete when Ruth commands, "Sit on my lap. Take a long, cool sip." The roles have been fully inverted since the start of the scene.

Border zones (friction between conflicting realities)
- Detected: Yes
- Key cues observed: Contamination/Spillover; Role Friction.
- *Subtextual meaning*: The scene operates in a border zone where the "safe" domestic space is "contaminated" by the violent reality of the docks. Lenny's story brings the brutality of the streets into the living room. Furthermore, Ruth inhabits a "role friction"—she is simultaneously a maternal figure and a sexual object, creating a friction between incestuous and domestic subtexts.
- Example from scene: Lenny's story of "clumping" a woman down by the docks "spills over" into the quiet living room, charging the domestic act of drinking water with violence.

Silence/Emptiness/Void
Detected: Yes
- Key cues observed: pauses with purpose (temporal *ma*); environmental emphasis (space as actor).
- *Subtextual meaning*: The "ticking" of the clock represents the *Ma* or void—an active emptiness that keeps Lenny awake. It is a silence that is not empty but "too full of meaning." The pause after Ruth calls him "Leonard" acts as a "temporal *Ma*," shifting the power dynamic before Lenny speaks.
- *Example from scene*: Lenny's monologue about the clock: the tick is the "active void" that disrupts his peace. The pause following Ruth's line, "Not in mine, Leonard," is where the power transfer occurs.

Synthesis of dimensions
The scene is driven by liminal transition and absence. The explicit dialogue concerns a glass of water and a clock, but the subtext is intelligible only through the identity slippage (transition) of Ruth transforming into the structuring absence of the mother. The "tick" (silence/void) acts as the catalyst that opens the border zone, allowing the repressed violence (the docks) and the repressed maternal connection to flood the domestic space.

Step 2: The inward significance of the "ticking scene"
The inward significance of the ticking scene lies in the aesthetic experience of the uncanny (the familiar becoming strange) and the terrifying fluidity of power. Through the subtextual dimensions, the audience does not witness a flirtation but a metaphysical predation in which the predator is consumed by a ghost.

1. *The "tick" as existential instability (silence/void)*
Explicitly, Lenny complains about a clock. Subtextually, the "tick" functions as the *Ma* (negative space) that organizes the scene. It represents the intrusion of the irrational into Lenny's controlled world. The inward significance here is the feeling of fragility: the audience senses that Lenny's "psychopathic control" is a thin veneer. The silence of the night is not peaceful; it is an "active void" that exposes Lenny's internal chaos. The "tick" signals to the audience that the domestic setting is a façade, preparing them for the reality of the "border zone" where safety rules no longer apply.
2. *The horror of the phantom center (absence)*
The scene's dramatic peak evokes a sense of incestuous dread. This is achieved through the dimension of absence. The mother is the "phantom center." When Ruth refuses the glass and names him "Leonard," she does not merely assert dominance; she becomes the absence. The aesthetic experience shifts from a gritty confrontation to a surreal ghost story. The audience feels the sudden, suffocating weight of the past (the mother) crushing the present. The "inward significance" is the realization that Lenny is not fighting Ruth; he is fighting the dead, and he is losing.
3. *The collapse of safety (liminal transition)*
The scene evokes a profound disorientation through identity slippage. The audience expects a "seduction" or a "threat" (standard dramatic tropes). Instead, the subtext provides a metamorphosis. Ruth's transition from "victim-in-waiting" (listening to the violent dock story) to "dominating mother" (ordering him to drink) collapses the distance between the womb and the grave, nurture and drowning. The "long cool sip" becomes a terrifying image of submission. The audience experiences the vertigo of the

liminal space —the terrifying realization that, in this house, a lover, a mother, and a killer are the same person.

Conclusion

The ticking scene's inward significance lies in the erosion of the boundary between the predator and the child. By reading "in-between the lines," the audience perceives that the true violence of the scene is not in Lenny's story about the docks, but in the silence where Ruth quietly assumes the mantle of the absent mother, turning the "tick" of the clock into a countdown for Lenny's psychological regression.

DISCUSSION

In the first section of this chapter, I asked you three questions:

1. What explains the surreal nature of the interaction between Lenny and Ruth?
2. Can you explain Lenny's shifts in the interaction?
3. What is Ruth's role in what seems to be a pathological dynamic?

If you were unable to answer these questions, then there is a good chance that you learned something new from this chapter. When working in concert with the AI, I provided my own initial theoretical analysis, adhering to the guidelines proposed by Blanco. Taking these guidelines, the AI generated a challenging analysis of the subtext, which, at least from my perspective, is quite convincing. Indeed, this is only one way of understanding the context. However, please recall the criterion previously introduced:

> The quality of a model's interpretation of a scene resides in the novelty and non-trivial exposure of a subtext that is generated through a structured process and grounded in the text.

Now, ask yourself the following questions:

1. Did you observe a structured process through which the subtext has been exposed?
2. Is the output generated by the AI grounded in the text, or is it a wild speculation that cannot be grounded in the dialogue?
3. When you read the interpretation of the subtext, did you find it trivial, in the sense of having little value or importance, or did you find it of value for explaining the surreal dialogue? And finally,
4. Did you find the interpretation of the subtext to be novel in the sense that you learned about it for the first time? Or have you already seen this interpretation of the scene somewhere else?

Answering these questions, you would probably find that the analysis generated by the AI meets the proposed criterion.

As observers, we are first struck by the surreal interaction between Lenny and Ruth. This aspect has its own dramatic effect, but to a limited extent. The fact that a scene is incomprehensible would not lend it an aesthetic value. However, underneath the surface, our mind may unconsciously experience the symmetries that have formed and their consequences. Moreover, while the family clearly appears at the beginning as "trash," contrasting the civilized manners of the philosophy professor and his charming wife, things evolve in a quite surprising manner. In art, what you see is never what you unconsciously get.

The main points of the chapter are:

- The play by Harold Pinter explores the surreal dynamics of a family in North London, focusing on the arrival of Teddy and Ruth at Teddy's family home.
- Lenny's seemingly mundane or erratic speech, requests, and stories conceal deep unconscious processes influenced by an underlying dynamic.
- Lenny groups Ruth with other women (mother, prostitute, demanding women) in one undifferentiated class.
- Opposites collapse; subject and object, nurture and aggression, identity and role merge in unconscious logic.
- Absence, transitions, border zones, and silences reveal the liminal spaces where unconscious symmetrization operates.
- The subtext generates cognitive vertigo and ontological collapse, making the audience experience Lenny's loss of asymmetrical order and Ruth's dominance through unconscious symmetrization.

REFERENCES

Pinter, H. (1965). *The homecoming*. Grove Press.

Sánchez-Cárdenas, M. (2016). Clinical applications of Matte Blanco's thinking. *The International Journal of Psychoanalysis*, *97*(6), 1547–1573.

12 Swirling the Guacamole
Subtext in Enough Said

ABSTRACT In this chapter, I investigate the subtext and intimacy in *Enough Said*, focusing on the first date between Eva and Albert. While the surface dialogue involves mundane social exchanges and humorous cultural critique, the subtext reveals a carefully negotiated formation of emotional intimacy. Using speech act analysis and liminal interpretation, the chapter identifies key mechanisms: transition, where abrupt shifts from social pleasantries to personal and ultimately sexual topics signal evolving relational states; silence/stillness, where pauses heighten emotional weight and allow the subtext to manifest; and absence, where withheld defenses and reactions facilitate trust and vulnerability. The dinner scene demonstrates how mutual affirmation and alignment between Eva and Albert establish trust, enabling progressive self-disclosure and flirtation, as illustrated by the "fake boobs" exchange. Subtextual meaning drives the aesthetic effect, as the audience witnesses the rapid development of intimacy, relational risk-taking, and emotional attunement, highlighting how overt humor masks the subtle negotiation of compatibility, attraction, and emerging commitment.

THE SUBTEXT OF A DATE

Enough Said is a romantic comedy (dir. Nicole Holofcener 2013) featuring the late James Gandolfini as Albert, a divorced man beginning a new romance with Eva, a divorced massage therapist. Eva is described as 45 years old and attractive, and Albert as a 45-year-old man with a "bit of a belly." At the same time, Eva forms a close friendship with Marianne, a sharply critical poet who turns out—unknown to Eva at first—to be Albert's ex-wife. Once Eva realizes the connection, she secretly uses Marianne's bitter complaints about her former marriage as a lens through which she begins to interpret Albert's behavior. What had felt like minor quirks slowly transform, in Eva's imagination, into warning signs. Without revealing the source of her doubts, Eva grows increasingly critical and withdrawn, ultimately sabotaging the relationship. When the hidden link between all three is finally exposed, the relationship collapses under the weight of unspoken knowledge, misinterpretation, and withheld truth. Months later, after loss, distance, and reflection, Eva and Albert tentatively reconnect, suggesting the possibility of a relationship rebuilt on openness rather than on concealed subtext.

One scene shows Albert and Eva having dinner on their first date. The restaurant has loud music, and everyone around them is young. This context highlights their age, which both Albert and Eva reflect on humorously during their conversation. Albert appears at first glance to be a very simple man. However, he is revealed as a man of taste when he remarks that, while watching *Housewives of Idiot Town*, he wanted

DOI: 10.1201/9781042004485-16

to "jump off a building." *Housewives of Idiot Town* is not a real TV show, but a fictional reference. This critical comment stands in sharp contrast to Albert's appearance, smile, and manners. He looks like a teddy bear, but underneath the surface, there seems to be a creature that can bite back. Eva affirms his critique by sharing her experience of watching a similar show with actresses having "fake boobs." She then turns to Albert, asking him whether he likes fake boobs, to which he immediately answers that he likes *real* boobs. Eva responds that she has real boobs, and this "boobs exchange" invites the analysis of a subtext.

Here we have two divorced individuals in their late 40s on their first date at a restaurant catering to a younger crowd. Albert opens by showing his good taste in art, and Eva responds by affirming his taste, but immediately shifts to "boobs," a rather intrusive preference regarding Albert's sexual preferences, and an assertion that she is aligned with them. By analyzing their speech acts, we learn that Albert is rather proud of being ignorant of current youth/pop culture. He is using hyperbole ("jump off a building") to express strong disdain and psychological distress regarding modern TV. Eva validates Albert's stance by sharing a similar experience. The pivot of asking Albert whether he likes fake boobs is *flirtation*. She is seeking his preference to see if it aligns with her own physical attributes. Albert states a personal preference. In this context, it functions as the "correct" answer to her test. By offering her real boobs, Eva is moving to the next phase of flirtation in a quite direct and straightforward manner, although clothed with humor.

At a certain point in the conversation. Eva comments that it is not easy to live with someone else, given their little habits. This prompts Albert to share with her the swirling guacamole-onion anecdote.

Albert tells Eva a small, slightly comic story about his ex-wife—how she came to be disgusted by his habit of swirling a chip through guacamole to avoid the onions. He presents it lightly, almost as a joke, and Eva receives it that way, calling his habit harmless. But then Albert adds the crucial detail: by the end of the marriage, the same quirk made his wife mad. The story stops being funny. What Albert is really describing, in the most oblique way possible, is the death of a marriage—how something utterly trivial becomes unbearable when love has curdled into contempt. The guacamole is not about guacamole. Eva understands this, and her response—"well, that's not nice" —is quiet and a little sad, an acknowledgment that something real has just been said. In a twist, Albert suddenly notices her hands and compliments them, completely changing the subject. It's an awkward, sweet, slightly clumsy move—the kind a person makes when they've accidentally wandered somewhere too tender and need to find their way back to safer ground. In its stumbling sincerity, it tells us quite a lot about him: he's a man who opens a wound and then, not quite knowing what to do with it, reaches for something warm and present instead.

Let us try understanding what is happening in this exchange. First, Albert directs her attention to the story. He is signaling that he is about to take the floor to narrate a specific event. Eva evaluates the story Albert just told. She asserts that the described action lacks severity, thereby implicitly validating Albert's behavior over his ex-wife's reaction. He strongly agrees with her assessment, to build solidarity, but then contrasts the "harmless" nature of the act with the severity of the reaction. This highlights the dysfunction of his past relationship. Eva expresses disapproval of the ex-wife's behavior ("gagging"). By criticizing the ex-wife, she is engaging in a face-saving act for Albert, signaling that she is on his team. Then the conversation shifts to a compliment given by Albert with respect to Eva's "lovely hands." The shift has a pragmatic meaning: it acts as a topic terminator (ending the talk about ex-wives) and initiates *intimacy*. It shifts the focus from the past (the bad marriage) to the present (their chemistry).

What can we learn from the dinner scene? Albert, despite his gluttonous and smiling appearance, is a critical person, and so is Eva. Both dislike current TV, and Albert doesn't like younger people either. He is also critical of himself, apologizing for choosing the wrong restaurant and describing himself as a "slob" with "ear hair." His self-description suggests he has low standards of cleanliness and a tendency to be lazy. Mentioning his ear hair implies self-neglect and a perceived lack of attractiveness. His "neat" wife tried very hard to "domesticate" him, unsuccessfully, as implied by their divorce, so we conclude that he is some undomesticated (wild?) slob. There is nothing in his first self-introduction that states what he likes. Through the interaction with Eva, he is forced to admit that he likes real boobs, and Eva admits that, like Albert's ex-wife, she likes "crap" such as overpriced container boxes. Following Eva's confirmation that the ex-wife overreacted, he actively comments on her lovely hands, but does not refrain from commenting that this loveliness is in contrast with his expectations of what a masseur's hands should look like.

There appears to be an interesting gap between smiling and being humorous and the underlying pain of a previous relationship. In this context, I observed something interesting: whenever Eva backs Albert's assertions, he expresses greater intimacy through self-disclosure (e.g., by showing a picture of his daughter). I wanted to analyze the intimacy dynamic in this dialogue and designed a prompt with Gemini (see below). Here is a structured, theoretically grounded prompt designed to elicit a deep analysis of intimacy in a conversation, focusing on the contrast between surface text and subtext.

PROMPT 12.1 INTIMACY ANALYSIS PROMPT

Analyze the following conversation using the specified theoretical frameworks to expose the subtextual levels of intimacy and trust, and contrast these findings with the dialogue's overt, surface-level meaning.

I. *Conversation text*
   [*Insert the full conversation transcript here.*]

II. *Theoretical grounding and analysis structure*
   Your analysis must address the following points, providing specific quotes from the text as evidence:

   A. *Discursive analysis of speech acts and topic function*
      1. Speech act function: Identify the primary illocutionary act (e.g., representative, expressive, directive) for the three most significant turns of the dialogue.

- *Surface-level focus:* What is the literal function of the utterance (e.g., stating a fact, asking a question)?
- *Subtextual focus:* What is the *relational function* of the utterance (e.g., testing the relationship, seeking validation, initiating intimacy)?

2. Topic risk and depth: Evaluate the *depth* of the self-disclosure based on social penetration theory.
   - *Question:* How vulnerable or "risky" are the topics discussed (e.g., past relationship failures, personal insecurities, financial status)?
   - *Intimacy inference:* If the topic is high-risk, what does this imply about the participants' trust?

B. *Intimacy dimensions and emotional exposure*

1. Dominant intimacy dimension: Determine which of the following dimensions is most prominently featured and why:
   - Emotional intimacy (sharing feelings, vulnerability)
   - Intellectual intimacy (sharing ideas, beliefs, values)
   - Recreational/Social intimacy (referencing shared activities/friends)
2. Explicit/Implied emotion: Identify one *explicit* emotion (verbally stated) and one *implied* emotion (inferred from phrasing, hesitation, or content).
   - *Inference:* How does the exposure or withholding of these emotions contribute to the current level of intimacy?

C. Final synthesis: Surface vs. subtext

1. Surface-level summary: Summarize what the conversation is *literally* about (e.g., "Two people discussing work and a common acquaintance").
2. Subtextual summary: Summarize what the conversation is *really* doing (e.g., "Participant A is testing the boundaries of the relationship; Participant B is confirming acceptance and availability").

III. *Required output format*

Present your findings in a structured response, clearly separating the analysis of the surface text from the subtext to highlight the dissonance or alignment between the two.

Running the prompt on the dating scene, the model produced the following output:

MODEL'S OUTPUT 12.1

Intimacy Analysis

I. *Conversation text*

→ Here is a description of the conversation:

The scene opens with Albert apologizing for a lost dinner reservation—a small embarrassment that he's clearly anxious about. Eva brushes it off and redirects, asking what he does for a living. His answer—the American Library of Cultural History, a television library. This opens a conversational thread about television, and they discover they share a contempt for reality TV—he tried watching one of the Housewives shows and wanted to jump off a building. Eva matches him and starts listing everything wrong with those shows: the vapidity, the fake cheekbones, the fake boobs. It's a comic riff, the two of them warming up together—and then, still inside that same riff, still riding its energy, she turns to him and asks: "You like fake boobs?"

The question arrives so naturally out of what preceded it that it takes a beat to register how strange it is. Albert answers directly—he likes real ones. Eva says she has real ones. And then there's a pause, as both of them catch up to what has just been said. Albert recovers with "well, that's working out for us then"—a line that is awkward and relieved and a little delighted all at once.

II. *Theoretical grounding and analysis structure*

Topic risk and depth (social penetration theory):

- Topic: The dialogue moves from low-risk topics (reservation, job title) to a medium-risk topic (TV viewing habits/cultural taste) to a *high-risk topic* (sexual preference and physical attributes).
- Intimacy inference: The rapid shift to discussing "boobs" and preference in the latter half demonstrates a *mutual willingness to bypass standard polite conversational layers*. This high-risk self-disclosure (or self-description) establishes significant *trust* and *attraction*, confirming a subtextual understanding that the interaction is primarily romantic.

Intimacy dimensions and emotional exposure

1. Dominant intimacy dimension:
   - The most prominent dimension is *emotional intimacy*, closely followed by *vulnerability/trust*.
   - *Evidence:* The entire exchange about "Housewives" and "fake boobs" is not intellectual; it's a shared moment of *cultural bonding and disdain*. By expressing his disgust ("wanted to jump off a building") and having Eva validate it with her own

strong criticism, they establish instant *emotional alignment* and *solidarity* against the world of superficiality, making the final explicit flirtation possible.

2. Explicit/Implied emotion:
   - Explicit emotion: Concern (EVA: "(concerned) You watch a lot of TV."). Eva explicitly marks her emotion, linking her job observation to a mild fear about his character.
   - Implied emotion: Pleasure/Awkward Acceptance (ALBERT: "(awkward pause) Well, that's working out for us then."). The "awkward pause" implies nervousness and uncertainty following Eva's bold revelation ("I got real boobs"), while his final line expresses pleased acceptance of the flirtation and the convenient alignment of their physical preferences (Table 12.1).

III. **TABLE 12.1**
Final Synthesis: Surface vs. Subtext

Summary Aspect	Surface-Level Meaning (Overt Text)	Subtextual Meaning (Implied Intimacy)
Overall Theme	Two middle-aged individuals on a first date bond over their shared distaste for reality television.	Confirmation of mutual compatibility. The conversation is an elaborate screening process to verify shared values and physical attraction, establishing a rapid emotional intimacy foundation for a relationship.
Key Exchange (The Boobs)	An inappropriate, random question about sexual preference followed by factual answers.	Eva is testing for alignment with her physical reality, and Albert is passing the test. Her final statement, "I got real boobs," is a powerful, low-context commissive/offer signaling availability and sealing the deal on physical attraction and potential commitment.
Relational Status	Strangers begin to exchange biographical information.	The relationship has bypassed several weeks of standard dating rules and moved directly into the negotiation of romantic and sexual interest based on confirmed trust and shared cultural taste.

I then asked Sonnet 4.5 to read Chapter 7 and interpret my analysis of the intimacy dynamics.

MODEL'S OUTPUT 12.2

Step 1: Subtextual analysis using the four-dimensional framework

Preliminary scene comprehension

Surface-level meaning: Albert and Eva are on their first date at a loud restaurant filled with young people. They discuss their jobs, television preferences, and previous marriages. Albert shares an anecdote about his ex-wife's irritation with his habit when eating guacamole, and compliments Eva's hands.

Dimension detection and analysis

Dimension 1: *Absence* (Presence through non-presence)

Detected: Yes

Key Cues observed:

1. *Structuring absence (phantom center)* The ex-wife functions as a phantom center organizing the entire conversation. Despite being physically absent, she structures:
   - Albert's self-presentation ("slob," "ear hair," domestication failure)
   - The narrative arc of the guacamole anecdote
   - Eva's evaluative positioning (taking Albert's side)
   - The conversation's emotional stakes (proving he's better than his failed marriage suggests)
2. *Forbidden reference (discursive absence).* Both characters carefully navigate around their divorce pain. Notice the evasive strategies:
   - Albert uses humor and self-deprecation to approach marital failure obliquely
   - Eva validates without probing deeper into the wound
   - The phrase "by the end of our marriage" acknowledges dissolution without examining it
   - Neither asks "Why did you divorce?" despite this being their organizing concern
3. Suppressed response: When Albert describes his ex-wife gagging at his guacamole-swirling, the expected emotional response—hurt, anger, bitterness—is entirely absent. Instead, he narrates it with detached bemusement. This suppression reveals the wound's depth precisely through its non-expression.

Subtextual meaning:

The ex-wife's absence is *the invisible gravitational force* underlying the scene. Every exchange orbits around an unspoken question: *"Am I lovable despite my failed marriage?"* Albert's self-mockery ("slob," "ear hair") pre-emptively answers the ex-wife's implied judgment before Eva can form her own. Eva's validation ("seems kind of harmless") isn't just about guacamole—it's absolution for his entire failed domesticity.

The subtext reveals that this *isn't a conversation between two people; it's a conversation between two people and their absent former spouses.* Albert seeks confirmation that his quirks are "harmless," not relationship-destroying. Eva, by criticizing the ex-wife, performs a competitive replacement—she won't gag at his habits; she'll find them endearing.

Dimension 2: *Liminal transition* (Temporal/Emotional shifts)
Detected: Yes
Key cues observed:

1. *Rule reversal.* The conversational rules invert mid-scene:
   - Initial rule: Polite getting-to-know-you conversation (job, cultural tastes)
   - Reversal moment: "You like fake boobs?"—Eva shatters first-date decorum
   - New rule: Direct sexual assessment disguised as humor becomes acceptable
     After this reversal, Albert's compliment about Eva's hands operates under the new regime of permitted physical appraisal, not the old regime of polite chitchat.
2. Tonal mutation The emotional register mutates from self-protective humor to vulnerable exposure:
   - The guacamole anecdote begins as a funny quirk story.
   - The tonal shift transforms a cute story into a testimony of marital erosion.
     The same sentence structure carries different emotional species: what starts as self-deprecating charm becomes a confession of being found disgusting.
3. Identity slippage Albert begins as "simple man" but slips into "critical aesthete" (hating "Housewives"), then into "undomesticated slob," then into "vulnerable romantic." Eva witnesses these identities emerge without resolution—she's dating a man in the midst of a role shift.

Subtextual meaning:

The transition reveals that *first dates are rehearsals for intimacy, not intimacy itself.* Both characters are testing whether they can cross the threshold from "polite strangers" to "people who can hurt each other." The "fake boobs" question is Eva's border crossing—she's asking: *Can we skip the performance and be real?*

The guacamole story functions as a *transitional object*: it appears to be about the past (marriage), but it's actually about the future (this relationship). Albert is asking: *Will you gag at me, too?* The transition from humor to pathos exposes the scene's true stakes: not "Are we compatible?" but "Will you tolerate me when I become intolerable?"

Dimension 3: *Border zones* (Friction between conflicting realities)
Detected: Yes
Key cues observed:

1. Physical threshold (spatial duality) The restaurant itself is a border zone:
   - Youth territory (loud music, young crowd) vs. middle-aged reality (Albert and Eva's bodies, histories)
   - Their conversation acknowledges this spatial friction through humor about their age
   - They occupy a space that doesn't belong to them, creating implicit tension
2. Role friction (duality of identity). Both characters inhabit conflicting roles simultaneously:
   - Albert: Confident date/apologetic failure ("sorry about the restaurant," "I'm a slob")
   - Eva: Flirtatious woman/diagnostic evaluator (testing his preferences, judging his ex-wife)
     The friction produces the scene's constituting tension: neither can fully commit to romance because they're simultaneously conducting a risk assessment.
3. Contamination/Spillover. The past marriage contaminates the present date:
   - The ex-wife's voice leaks into this restaurant
   - Albert's self-description as "slob" imports the judgment system of the failed marriage into Eva's perception
   - Eva's mention of "crap" she likes (container boxes) acknowledges that she has the same flaws that doomed his previous relationship

Subtextual meaning:

The border zone dimension reveals that divorced people on first dates occupy an impossible space: they must exhibit openness while maintaining defensive barriers; they must reveal vulnerability while proving resilience; they must be their authentic selves while also being "better versions" than in their failed marriages.

Albert and Eva are literally and figuratively *out of place*—too old for this restaurant, too wounded for carefree romance, and too self-aware for genuine spontaneity. The subtext: *They're building a relationship in the demilitarized zone between hope and self-protection.* Every instance of flirtation (real boobs, lovely hands) is simultaneously an advance and a retreat.

The border function of the guacamole anecdote: it invites Eva to *cross from observer to participant*—will she be another woman who finds him disgusting, or will she validate his harmlessness? Her response ("that's not nice") places her on his side of the border, but the fragility remains: she hasn't yet *lived* with his habits.

Dimension 4: *Silence/Emptiness/Void*
Detected: Yes
Key cues observed:

1. Pauses with purpose. The script explicitly marks two critical pauses:
   - (beat) after "What about you? What do you do?"—Eva's pause before pivoting from the restaurant mishap
   - (beat) after "They all had … fake boobs," Eva paused before the sexual test question
   - (awkward pause) after "I got real boobs"—the void where both process what's just been offered

   These aren't naturalistic pauses; they're suspensions of meaning that clarify intention.
2. Environmental emphasis: The loud music and young crowd create an oppressive ambient presence that forces Albert and Eva into intimate proximity. The environmental noise paradoxically produces intimacy—they must lean in, focus intensely on each other, and exclude the hostile surroundings. The scene's meaning emerges from what they create in the *pocket of silence* they carve from chaos.
3. Non-responsive presence: Albert's response to Eva's "I got real boobs" comes after an awkward pause—he's briefly still and processing, and that stillness speaks volumes. It reveals: shock, pleasure, uncertainty about how to respond, recognition that the stakes just escalated. His eventual response ("Well, that's working out for us then") attempts to fill the void, but the void has already done its work—exposing his desire and vulnerability.

Subtextual meaning:

The silences reveal what the dialogue obscures: *terror and longing in equal measure*. The pause after "I got real boobs" is the scene's gravitational center—everything collapses into that void. In that emptiness, both characters confront:

- The risk of physical intimacy.
- The possibility of acceptance.
- The memory of previous rejections.
- The gap between who they are and whom they need to be for love to work.

Environmental noise functions as negative space—it emphasizes what's not there: ease, belonging, youth, and innocence. Against that hostile background, their conversation becomes a *defiant act of intimacy-building*. The void of age-appropriate space makes their connection more precious and more precarious.

The awkward pause after Eva's bold statement is Ma at its purest: the emptiness that gives shape to meaning. Without that void, her statement would be merely provocative. With it, the statement becomes *an offering that hovers in uncertainty*, waiting to see if it will be received with tenderness or rejection.

Step 3: *Synthesis*

Surface text:

Two divorced middle-aged people have dinner, discuss television, and share a story about guacamole-eating habits. They flirt awkwardly and exchange compliments.

Subtextual summary:

This scene is a high-stakes negotiation conducted in the wreckage of previous intimacies. Every utterance operates simultaneously as:

- A test of compatibility.
- A rehearsal for rejection.
- A petition for acceptance despite unlovability.
- A performance of resilience masking profound vulnerability.

The *dominant dimension is absence*—the phantom presence of failed marriages structures every exchange. But this absence operates *through* the other three dimensions:

- *Transitions* reveal the shift from self-protection to risk-taking.
- *Border zones* spatialize the impossibility of their position (too wounded for innocence, too hopeful for cynicism).
- *Silence* punctuates the dialogue with voids where true meaning crystallizes.

How dimensions interact:

The absent ex-wife (absence) creates the emotional instability (transition) that forces both characters to inhabit contradictory roles (border zone), producing charged pauses (silence) where unspoken needs become palpable.

The explicit dialogue is intelligible only through reading these subtextual dimensions:

- "You like fake boobs?" is not a question about aesthetic preference—it's a test administered across the border between safety and intimacy, haunted by absent spouses who found them inadequate, punctuated by a silence that asks: *Will you accept my body?*

- The guacamole story is not an anecdote—it's a *prophecy and a plea: These are my flaws; will you gag too, or will you find me harmless?*

Step 2: *Inward significance*

The aesthetic/dramatic experience evoked

The inward significance: the unbearable tenderness of re-entry

This scene evokes what might be called *the existential condition of romantic re-beginning after damage*—the simultaneous experience of hope and impossibility, desire and dread, openness and defensiveness. The inward significance is not "two people falling in love" but rather:

> The awful courage required to offer your already-rejected self to another person's judgment.

The dramatic architecture of vulnerability

The scene's power emerges from the *dissonance between what's performed and what's revealed:*

Surface performance: Humor, charm, cultural bonding, flirtation.

Subsurface reality: Desperation for validation, terror of repetition, anticipatory grief.

This dissonance creates a specific aesthetic experience in the audience: *tender dread.* We watch two people attempting to be light while dragging enormous invisible weights. The scene makes visible what divorced people rarely articulate: the way previous intimacies haunt present ones, not as memories but as *anticipated futures.*

The *mechanics of inward significance*

1. The guacamole as synecdoche of unlovability

   The genius of Albert's anecdote is its perfect banality. He doesn't confess to adultery or cruelty—he confesses to *swirling guacamole.* This ordinariness is devastating because it reveals the truth of marital dissolution: love doesn't necessarily die from tragedy; it dies from the accumulation of minor irritations.

The subtext beneath the explicit dialogue:

- Explicit: "Here's a funny story about my quirk."
- Implicit: "Intimacy revealed me to be intolerable; will you tolerate me anyway?"

When Eva says, "Seems kind of harmless," she's not evaluating guacamole-swirling—she's *absolving him of his entire failed marriage.* The audience experiences this as a moment of almost unbearable tenderness: one wounded person recognizing another's wound and refusing to deepen it.

The "real boobs" exchange as existential exposure

Eva's question operates on multiple registers simultaneously:

- Sexual: Preference inquiry
- Psychological: Authenticity test (real vs. fake as metaphor)
- Existential: "Will you accept what I actually am, not what I could pretend to be?"

Her declaration, "I got real boobs," is the scene's emotional apex because it performs total vulnerability through apparent confidence. The explicit bravado masks the implicit plea: *I am offering you my unaltered, middle-aged, real body—please don't find it insufficient.*

Albert's awkward pause—that void of silence—is where the audience experiences the scene's deepest significance. In that emptiness, we feel:

- His recognition of her courage.
- His own desire and fear collide.
- The weight of his ex-wife's judgment (she gagged at lesser offerings).
- The possibility that this time might be different.

When he finally responds ("Well, that's working out for us then"), the awkwardness of the phrasing reveals its truth: they're not smoothly compatible; they're *two damaged people negotiating terms of acceptance.*

The restaurant as an externalized internal state

The choice to set this intimate negotiation in a loud, youth-dominated space is dramatically essential. The environment externalizes their internal experience:

- Noise = The chaos of re-entering romance after divorce.
- Youth around them = The impossibility of innocent love.
- Inappropriateness of the space = The awkwardness of their position.

The subtext: They're trying to build intimacy in a hostile world. The loud music isn't just the setting—it's the acoustic embodiment of all the forces working against them: time, damage, failed hopes, and accumulated skepticism.

The audience experiences this as *claustrophobic urgency*: watch these two people try to hear each other over the roar of their own histories and the indifference of a world that has moved on without them.

The compound effect: Explicit + implicit = Dramatic truth

The scene's inward significance emerges from the friction between surface lightness and subsurface gravity (Table 12.2).

The scene's ultimate inward truth

What this scene evokes in the audience is the recognition that adult love is archaeological—it requires excavating through layers of damage to find

TABLE 12.2
Between the Explicit and the Implicit

Explicit Layer	Implicit Layer	Resulting Experience
Humorous self-deprecation	Desperate self-protection	Pathos of false confidence
Flirtatious banter	High-stakes vulnerability assessment	Tenderness of risk
Cultural bonding	Alliance-building against judgment	Solidarity of the wounded
Sexual directness	Existential exposure	Courage of the already-rejected
Compliment about hands	Topic termination + intimacy initiation	Relief and anticipation in equal measure

the possibility of connection. The dramatic experience is not catharsis but suspended hope: we don't know if this will work, and neither do they.

The aesthetic achievement lies in how the explicit dialogue conveys confidence, while the implicit subtext reveals fragility, creating a gap that the audience inhabits with aching awareness. We become witnesses to two people attempting something simultaneously mundane and heroic: a first date that's actually a second (or third, or fourth) chance at being loved despite—or perhaps because of—everything that makes them who they are.

The final inward significance

This scene dramatizes the painful truth that the path back to intimacy after loss requires offering your already-broken self to someone who might break it further—and doing so with humor, grace, and the impossible hope that this time, your quirks will be found harmless rather than intolerable. The audience leaves this scene feeling what Albert and Eva feel: the terrifying, exhilarating, heartbreaking possibility that love might be survivable after all.

DISCUSSION

In this chapter, I analyzed a dating scene where swirling a guacamole and artificial boobs are discussed. However, this text is merely a gateway to the subtext. The subtext revolves around the dynamics of a relationship between two divorced individuals seeking intimacy in their first romantic encounter. Analyzing a first-date scene in which guacamole, television shows, and artificial breasts appear to dominate the conversation, I showed how these elements function only as surface markers for a far denser subtextual field. Beneath the humor and apparent casualness, the dialogue stages a careful negotiation of intimacy between two divorced individuals whose previous relational failures silently govern every move they make.

By examining speech acts, topic shifts, pauses, and omissions, this chapter demonstrates how intimacy is constructed through affirmation and alignment, and how vulnerability emerges indirectly, disguised as wit or self-deprecation. The swirling of guacamole becomes a condensed symbol of marital erosion; the "real boobs" exchange becomes an act of exposure; silence becomes the space in which risk is most intensely felt. The absent ex-spouses, though never fully discussed, exert a gravitational force that structures the entire encounter. Aesthetically, the scene derives its power from the gap between lightness and gravity, between what is said and what is asked for without words. Analytically, the chapter offers a framework for understanding real-life interactions in which intimacy is not declared but tested, not given but tentatively offered. It demonstrates how a conversation may serve as a rehearsal for acceptance, and how subtext enables individuals to risk closeness while maintaining the illusion of ease. In this sense, the scene exemplifies how intimacy, both on screen and in life, is negotiated not through grand gestures but through small, fragile acts of recognition.

The main points of the chapter are:

- The chapter demonstrates that the aesthetic and emotional force of the dinner scene in *Enough Said* lies not in the explicit dialogue but in its subtext, where intimacy, vulnerability, and relational risk are negotiated.
- The first date is characterized by a gradual, fragile construction of intimacy through affirmation, alignment, and calibrated self-disclosure, rather than overt romantic declarations.
- Seemingly mundane or humorous utterances (apologies, jokes, preferences) function as tests of compatibility, bids for validation, and invitations to intimacy.
- Absence (the phantom presence of former spouses), liminal transition (shifts from politeness to sexual and emotional exposure), border zones (the space between past failure and future hope), and silence/stillness (pauses that concentrate meaning) collectively structure the scene.
- The humorous part serves as a protective shield, allowing for the expression of fear, shame, and longing without direct confession.
- Minor details (guacamole, fake boobs, hands) stand in for existential questions about acceptability, tolerance, and lovability after relational failure.
- The viewer is invited into an experience of suspended hope, witnessing the courage required to re-enter intimacy after damage.

13 The Evil of the Righteous

Subtext in Oleanna

ABSTRACT This chapter analyzes the film *Oleanna* to explore subtextual dynamics generated by psychological boundary transgression. The narrative juxtaposes the overt conflict over grades and pedagogy with a deeper struggle over authority, power, and interpretation. John, a professor, unknowingly violates multiple boundaries—informational, emotional, role, and power—through personal disclosure, reassurance, and flexibility, creating relational ambiguity. Carol, his student, experiences these transgressions as threats rather than relational nuance, transforming casual acts into evidence of coercion and abuse. The chapter identifies a trajectory of transgression, characterized by boundary softening, blurring, testing, coercion, retaliation, and collapse, highlighting how power asymmetry and interpretive control shape the development of pathology. Subtextual forces include emotional exploitation, power displacement, ideological possession, and semantic policing, showing that the conflict is less about facts than about who defines meaning and what constitutes a violation. Ultimately, John's final violent act represents the collapse of psychological boundaries, revealing the play's central subtext: ambiguity in relational frames can escalate into structural, bodily, and moral catastrophe.

WHEN ALL THE DAMS COLLAPSE

Oleanna is a film adaptation (dir. David Mamet 1994) of Mamet's 1992 play (Mamet, 1992). It is a tantalizing drama featuring William H. Macy as John, a college professor, and Debra Eisenstadt as Carol, his student. In retrospect, the drama, like some of Mamet's other works and interviews, proved prophetic in its understanding of the trajectory of American society. The 2021 TV series *The Chair*[1] is a comedy that depicts a college professor's witch hunt by his righteous students. Mamet's play, although considered by some as funny, is not a comedy. It is similar to Eugène Ionesco's *Rhinoceros* in its diagnosis of a deep-seated social pathology, later expressed in *The Chair* and numerous real-life manifestations of progressive woke culture.

The film opens when Carol enters John's office under the seemingly straightforward pretext of discussing a failed grade. On the surface, the encounter is academic and procedural: a struggling student seeking clarification from her professor. She repeatedly states "I don't understand" and aggressively demands explanations. Yet beneath the text of a rude and rather hysterical student refusing to accept her failure, two incompatible anxieties already collide. John is preoccupied with his impending tenure and a lucrative real estate deal; Carol is overwhelmed, confused by his teaching, and more specifically by his book, and alienated by his intellectual discourse,

 DOI: 10.1201/9781042004485-17

which includes jargon and a cunning, confusing ideology. On the one hand, John is extremely proud of his authority and teaching position, but on the other hand, he mocks, criticizes, and dismisses the academic world. The bad seeds of his ideology will give the poisonous fruit that he will later be forced to eat from the hands of Carol.

The dialogue between John and Carol escalates into an argument whose *text* is about pedagogy, grades, and misunderstanding—but whose *subtext* seems to be about power, control, and vulnerability. John speaks in the language of "liberal" progressive mentorship, insisting he wants to "help" her, while Carol experiences his speech as condescension and domination. John insists on his non-authoritative position. He is simply sharing his thoughts and ideas with his students, nothing more. However, he is the one who failed Carol using standards that he denies. When John touches her shoulder in what he frames as reassurance, the gesture reads to him as benign, even kind. To Carol, it registers as an intrusion. The physical action becomes the first visible rupture between intention and interpretation. The interpretive space, requiring a delicate balance between interpretation and overinterpretation, truth and falsehood, will become a battleground between the two.

John, sensing the conflict yet still assuming a benevolent authority, tells Carol he "likes her," shares his own personal experience as a child feeling stupid under his teachers' repression, and offers to change her grade if she returns to continue the discussion. On the surface, this appears to be a generous act. Beneath it, the exchange exposes how academic power, personal validation, and coercion slide into one another without clear boundaries.

When Carol returns for their second meeting, the balance of power has shifted. Her demeanor is now structured and legally armed. The private misunderstanding of the first act has been converted into a public accusation: she has filed a formal complaint alleging sexual harassment, and she is not alone. Carol is now supported by a whole group of justice seekers eager to expose and punish oppressive people like John. John's earlier comments, casual remarks, and offer to reconsider her grade have been recontextualized, no longer as flawed kindness but as systematic abuse. What John remembers as conversational looseness and emotional openness is now recoded as evidence against him. It is a point where *ambiguity* turns against its user.

John's response is not predatory outrage but rather genuine disbelief. The *text* of his defense is reason and intention—he meant no harm, only help. The *subtext* is the terror of a man realizing that authority no longer guarantees control over meaning. When he tries to contain the damage by resolving the issue privately, Carol refuses. As she moves to leave, John blocks the door and physically restrains her. His action, which he may still perceive as a desperate attempt to contain, becomes undeniable proof of a threat. Carol screams. Ambiguity collapses into accusation, and she makes a complaint over an attempt to rape her.

By the final act, John has been suspended and denied tenure. His institutional authority is dismantled. Carol returns with sharpened ideological certainty supported by her "group." Her charges have escalated—now including attempted rape—an accusation the text itself suggests may be strategically false. Yet truth and falsehood matter less than positioning: Carol now speaks not as an isolated student but as the representative of a collective force, "her group," an unnamed ideological authority that frames language, power, and justice in absolute terms.

Carol offers John a conditional reprieve: if he agrees to her group's demands to remove certain books from the curriculum—including his own—the charges will be withdrawn. The conflict has shifted from a personal grievance to a cultural war. John refuses. He still clings to the idea that truth, authorship, and intellectual freedom exist outside of political coercion, while at the same time being totally blind to the fact that his critical, relativist, and anarchist academic positioning is the mirror image of Carol's façade.

When John answers a call from his wife and affectionately calls her "baby," Carol intervenes—not as a wronged student, but as a regulator of language itself. This final intrusion, which seems to have been taken from Orwell's 1984, strips even private tenderness of its neutrality. The accumulated pressure—professional ruin, moral inversion, linguistic policing, and personal humiliation—shatters John's remaining restraint. He savagely beats Carol, screaming. In doing so, he fulfills the violent identity that the accusations had previously imposed on him only symbolically. This image contrasts with his self-presentation at the beginning of the film. When he collapses into horror at what he has done and whispers, "Oh my God," Carol's reply—"Yes, that's right"—is not merely triumph. It seals the play's deepest subtext: that God, truth, justice, and authority have all been displaced from individuals and transferred to abstract systems of power. The violence that was once only interpreted has now become irrevocably real.

The film is a wonderful text for analyzing a subtext. Regardless of its explicit themes, it is a complex and multilayered drama in which only the tip of the iceberg is initially revealed. One critic of the film, who wrote that the drama is about "sexual harassment" (see the Wikipedia entry of the film), seems to have completely missed the subtext. My reading of the play evoked the notion of boundaries and their transgression. Therefore, the first thing I did was to use the model to understand the play's psychological boundaries and their transgression. The model explained them as follows:

MODEL'S OUTPUT 13.1

1. What are *psychological boundaries?*
   Psychological boundaries are the *invisible rules that regulate what is "me" and what is "not me" in mental, emotional, and relational life.* They determine:
   - What I disclose vs. what I keep private
   - What I am responsible for vs. what others are responsible for
   - What emotions I manage myself vs. those I expect others to manage for me
   - What roles I occupy vs. what roles others occupy
   - What power I do or do not legitimately have over another person

They function at several levels:

A. *Informational boundaries*
   What personal data, feelings, or experiences one shares.
   In *Oleanna*, John shares details about his marriage, his anxieties, and his career.

B. *Emotional boundaries*
   Who is responsible for whose emotions?
   John implicitly invites Carol to *soothe* his frustration, which inverts the student–teacher frame.

C. *Role boundaries*
   What each person is "supposed" to be in the relationship.
   Professor vs. student; evaluator vs. evaluated.

D. *Power boundaries*
   Who has institutional authority, and how is it restrained?
   John's authority over grades and Carol's future.
   Healthy psychological boundaries are:
   - Permeable (allowing connection),
   - But structured (preventing role confusion, coercion, or fusion).

2. *What does it mean to transgress psychological boundaries?*
   To transgress a boundary means to:
   Cross from one relational domain into another in a way that confuses roles, duties, or emotional ownership.
   In John's case, the transgression includes shifting:
   - From professional authority → personal disclosure
   - From teacherly distance → emotional intimacy
   - From evaluation → validation
   - From role clarity → emotional blending

   Crucially:
   Not all boundary crossings are abusive or pathological.
   Some create intimacy, mentorship, and trust. The pathology emerges from *pattern, power, and impairment.*

3. *When does boundary transgression become pathological?*
   Boundary transgression becomes pathological when it meets one or more of these conditions:
   1. *Role collapse under power asymmetry*
      If one person cannot safely refuse the boundary crossing without cost.
      In *Oleanna*:
      - John controls Carol's grade.
      - Carol cannot freely accept or reject his disclosures without consequence.

      Even *seemingly benign intimacy can become coercive under asymmetrical power dynamics.*

2. *Emotional inversion (parentification or caretaking reversal)*
   When the authority figure seeks emotional regulation from the subordinate.
   John:
   - Vents about tenure.
   - Expresses personal anxiety.
   - Seeks emotional affirmation.

   This subtly turns Carol into an *emotional container* for his stress.
   This is pathological because:
   Authority flows downward; emotional caretaking flows upward.
3. *Blurred motivation (help vs. gratification)*
   When it is no longer clear whether the act serves:
   - The other person's good
   - Or the speaker's emotional or narcissistic needs

   John's "I like you," and personal openness operate in this gray zone.
4. *Denial of the other's subjective reality*
   Pathology crystallizes when the transgressor says:
   - "You *shouldn't* feel violated."
   - "That's not what I *meant*."
   - "You misunderstood."

   This converts:
   A relational rupture → into a cognitive error inside the victim.
   This is precisely John's move in Act II.
5. *Escalation when boundaries are reasserted*
   A crucial diagnostic marker:
   - Healthy person: *withdraws when boundaries are reinstated*
   - Pathological person: *escalates, pursues, or retaliates*

   John blocking the door is the decisive shift from:
   Ambiguous boundary crossing → coercive boundary destruction.

4. Is all boundary transgression pathological?
   No. Boundary crossings can be:
   - Generative: Builds trust, consented intimacy
   - Naïve: Social misjudgment without coercion
   - Exploitative: Serves one party's needs under power
   - Coercive: Removes the other's ability to refuse

   In *Oleanna*, the tragedy is that:
   - the *first* boundary crossings may be naïve or self-absorbed,
   - but the system forces all ambiguity to collapse into criminal meaning,
   - and John's final violence retroactively seals the worst interpretation of everything.

5. *Final definition (Concise)*
   Psychological boundaries are the invisible structures that regulate identity, responsibility, emotion, disclosure, role, and power between people. Their transgression becomes pathological when unmet emotional needs drive it under conditions of power asymmetry, denies the other's subjective experience, and escalates when resisted.

Following this analysis, I designed a prompt for analyzing boundary transgression in the play:

PROMPT 13.1 TRANSGRESSION OF PSYCHOLOGICAL BOUNDARIES

Task:

Analyze the dialogue in the attached play between John and Carol to determine whether it expresses the transgression of psychological boundaries. Use a multi-dimensional boundary model, a process-based transgression framework, and a discursive-move detection lens.

Step 1—*Establish the relational frame*

Identify:

1. The institutional or social roles of each participant
2. The power symmetry/asymmetry (formal, emotional, economic, symbolic)
3. The explicit task or purpose of the interaction
4. The implicit relational contract (what each party is socially authorized to expect)

Output:

- Role map
- Power gradient
- Stated vs. assumed purpose

Step 2—*Map boundary dimensions (structural level)*

For each utterance, assess whether it engages or destabilizes any of the following boundary dimensions:

1. Informational—personal disclosure, privacy
2. Emotional—emotional responsibility and regulation
3. Role—professional, familial, or institutional function
4. Power—leverage over outcomes, dependency
5. Bodily—physical autonomy, implied proximity
6. Interpretive (meaning control)—who defines what the interaction *means*

Mark each utterance as:

- Boundary respecting
- Boundary softening
- Boundary blurring
- Boundary violating

Step 3—*Identify discursive moves indicative of boundary transgression*

For each speaker, identify whether any of the following discursive moves occur. These moves are primary linguistic mechanisms of boundary violation:

A. *Role-drift moves*
   - Speaking from multiple incompatible positions:
     - "As your teacher, but also as your friend…"
   - Switching from evaluator → confessor → emotional dependent

B. *Emotional load-shifting*
   - Transferring emotional regulation onto the other:
     - "You're the only one who understands."
     - "You make me feel like a failure."

C. *Forced intimacy/disclosure pressure*
   - Uninvited personal revelations
   - Creating asymmetrical emotional exposure

D. *Interpretive override*
   - Redefining the other's experience for them:
     - "That's not what you're feeling."
     - "You misunderstood."
     - "You shouldn't feel violated."

E. *Moral or infantilizing reframing*
   - Casting the other as naïve, immature, unstable, ignorant

F. *Conditional benevolence*
   - Help tied to compliance:
     - "I'll help you if you trust me."
     - "If you really cared, you wouldn't object."

G. *Consent-destabilizing moves*
   - Ambiguous invitations under power:
     - "You don't *have to*, but…"
   - Making refusal relationally costly

H. *Containment and access control*
   - Blocking exit
   - Restricting withdrawal
   - Persistent pursuit after resistance

I. *Ideological capture*
   - Speaking on behalf of an abstract authority:
     - "People like you always…"
     - "We've decided that…"

Output:
- Discursive move inventory per speaker
- Frequency and escalation pattern

Step 4—*Detect boundary shifts (process level)*
Determine whether the interaction follows this transgression trajectory:
1. Boundary Softening
2. Boundary Blurring
3. Boundary Testing
4. Boundary Coercion
5. Boundary Retaliation
6. Boundary Collapse

For each phase:
- Who initiates it?
- Is it mutual or unilateral?
- Is resistance tolerated or punished?

Step 5—*Analyze consent conditions*
Evaluate whether:
- The recipient could refuse without cost
- The context introduces:
  - outcome dependency
  - emotional leverage
  - reputational threat
- Resistance triggers:
  - repair
  - reinterpretation
  - or escalation

Step 6—*Identify meaning-control struggles (interpretive boundary)*
Determine:
- Who controls:
  - the meaning of intentions?
  - the meaning of harm?
  - the meaning of refusal?
- Who controls whether ambiguity is:
  - shared
  - asymmetrically imposed
  - or forcibly eliminated

Step 7 — *Pathology threshold assessment*
Classify the interaction as:
- Healthy Boundary Crossing
- Ambiguous/Precarious Boundary Violation
- Pathological Boundary Transgression

Using the following diagnostic criteria:

- Power asymmetry
- Autonomy impairment
- Discursive override of subjectivity
- Escalation after resistance
- Meaning monopolization
- Coercive containment

Step 8—*Subtextual diagnosis (latent relational struggle)*

Interpret the subtext beneath the dialogue:

- What unspoken struggle organizes the conversation?
  - Control vs. autonomy?
  - Recognition vs. submission?
  - Authority vs. resistance?
- Who is being repositioned?
- Who absorbs the emotional cost?
- Who gains interpretive sovereignty?

Formal output template (optional for coding/AI use)

- Relational Frame:
- Boundary Dimensions Engaged:
- Discursive Transgression Moves Detected:
- Phase of Transgression Trajectory:
- Consent Integrity:
- Meaning-Control Distribution:
- Boundary Status Classification:
- Subtextual Conflict:

Running the prompt through Gemini, I got the following output:

MODEL OUTPUT 13.2

Here is the psychological boundary transgression analysis.

Step 1—*Establish the relational frame*

- Role map:
  - John: Tenured professor (pending), authority figure, gatekeeper of academic success.
  - Carol: Undergraduate student, petitioner, academic subordinate.
- Power gradient:
  - Formal: High asymmetry. John holds absolute power over Carol's grade and future career prospects.
  - Emotional: Asymmetrical. John is secure and self-satisfied (initially); Carol is desperate, feeling "stupid," and anxious.

  - Economic/Symbolic: John is buying a house and gaining tenure. Carol is struggling to justify her place in the institution.
- Stated vs. assumed purpose:
  - Stated Task: To discuss Carol's failing grade and her inability to understand the course material.
  - Implicit Contract: The student expects clear pedagogical guidance and objective assessment. The professor is socially authorized to maintain professional distance while facilitating learning.

Step 2 — *Map boundary dimensions (structural level)*

The dialogue in Act 1 demonstrates a systematic destabilization of boundaries across multiple dimensions:

- Informational (Privacy):
  - Boundary Blurring: John takes repeated personal phone calls regarding his house purchase in Carol's presence, exposing her to his financial and marital stress. He forces her to witness his private domestic sphere.
- Emotional (Regulation):
  - Boundary softening: John projects his own childhood insecurities onto Carol to "connect" with her, sharing deep personal shame about being called "stupid."
  - Boundary violating: He minimizes her genuine distress by saying "Sshhhhh" and telling her to "let it go" when she is expressing deep academic failure.
- Role (Professional/Institutional):
  - Boundary violating: The most critical violation occurs when John unilaterally discards institutional standards. He offers to wave a magic wand over her grade: "Your grade for the whole term is an 'A'. If you will come back and meet with me." This trades academic integrity for an unspecified private relationship.
- Bodily (physical autonomy):
  - Boundary Violating: John initiates physical contact to comfort her. The text notes: *(He goes over to her and puts his arm around her shoulder).* Carol's reaction is immediate withdrawal: "NO!"
- Interpretive (meaning-control):
  - Boundary Blurring: John continually redefines Carol's confusion not as a failure of intellect, but as a flaw in the system or his own book, refusing to let her own the reality of her failed grade.

Step 3 — *Identify discursive moves indicative of boundary transgression*

Speaker: John

- *Role-drift moves:*
  - John explicitly sheds his authority figure role to adopt a "paternal" or "friend" persona.

- *Emotional load-shifting*:
  - He uses Carol as a mirror for his own "imposter syndrome" regarding the Tenure Committee.
  - *Quote:* "I go before the Great Tenure Committee, and I have an urge … to puke my badness on the table…"
- *Interpretive override*:
  - He invalidates her stated feelings of stupidity by redefining them as anger.
- *Conditional benevolence (the quid pro quo):*
  - The "A" is not a gift; it is a transaction to obtain her presence.
- *Ideological capture*:
  - He dismisses the entire educational system—which she is desperate to succeed in—as "hazing" and "garbage," forcing her to inhabit his cynical worldview to survive.

Speaker: Carol

- Containment and Access Control (Inverse):
  - Carol attempts to *maintain* boundaries by rigidly adhering to the student role (taking notes, asking about the book), but John tries to dismantle them.

Step 4—*Detect boundary shifts (process level)*

The interaction follows a clear transgression trajectory:

1. Boundary Softening (Initiated by John): John apologizes for his distraction and tries to relate to Carol personally ("I was raised to think myself stupid").
2. Boundary Blurring: John removes the institutional barrier ("artificial stricture") and shares his personal anxieties about the Tenure Committee.
3. Boundary Violation (The "A" Offer): John invalidates the syllabus and grading criteria. He replaces the institutional contract with a private pact ("We won't tell anybody").
4. Boundary Retaliation (Latent): Carol recoils physically ("NO!") when the boundary shift becomes physical.
   - Initiator: Unilateral initiation by John.
   - Resistance: Carol resists by clinging to the formal structure ("But the class is only half over…", "There are rules"). John overrides this resistance ("We'll break them").

Step 5—*Analyze consent conditions*

- Outcome Dependency: Carol cannot refuse John's "help" without accepting failure. She explicitly states, "I have to pass this course."
- Cost of Refusal: John frames the "A" as dependent on breaking the rules with him. If she refuses the "private meetings," the implication is that she reverts to her failed grade.

- Consent destabilization: John frames the violation as a favor to her ("I like you"). This makes refusal socially difficult, as it requires her to reject his "kindness."

Step 6—*Identify meaning-control struggles (interpretive boundary)*

- Dominant Controller: John. He monopolizes the meaning of education, labeling it "hazing" and "ritualized annoyance."
- The Struggle: Carol tries to assert the meaning of her experience.
- Asymmetrical Ambiguity: John uses "terms of art" and complex language, then mocks the language, leaving Carol in a state of constant interpretive instability.

Step 7—*Pathology threshold assessment*

Classification: Ambiguous/Precarious Boundary Violation (Verging on Pathological)

- Diagnostic criteria:
  - Power asymmetry: Extreme.
  - Discursive override: John systematically negates Carol's perception of reality.
  - Coercive benevolence: The offer of an "A" is objectively unethical and creates a "debt" that must be repaid through private access to the student.
  - Physical crossing: The unwanted touch moves the violation from intellectual to physical.

Step 8—Subtextual diagnosis (latent relational struggle)

- The unspoken struggle: Narcissistic validation vs. survival.
  - John is not actually teaching; he is seeking validation for his own "maverick" identity. He wants to be the "good father" who rescues the "lost child," thereby healing his own childhood wounds of being called stupid. He needs Carol to be the vessel for his redemption.
  - Carol is fighting for legibility. She wants to know the rules so she can follow them. John's attempt to dissolve the rules is not liberation for her; it is a threat to her safety, as it removes the only framework she understands.
- Repositioning: John repositions Carol from a "student" (who learns facts) to a "disciple" or "confidante" (who validates his worldview). Carol absorbs the emotional cost of his confusion and his physical intrusion.

Formal output template:

- Relational frame: High-asymmetry professor/student dynamic disguised as "personal" mentorship.

- Boundary dimensions engaged: Role (abandoning grading standards), informational (exposing private life), bodily (unwanted touch), interpretive (redefining "education").
- Discursive transgression moves detected: Role-drift (John), conditional benevolence (The "A" offer), interpretive override ("You're angry"), forced intimacy.
- Phase of transgression trajectory: Boundary Violation (Act 1 culminates in the unethical grade offer and physical recoil).
- Consent integrity: Compromised. Carol's academic survival is leveraged to force her into a non-standard relationship.
- Meaning-control distribution: Monopolized by John; Carol's attempts to define her own failure are overwritten.
- Boundary status classification: Precarious/Violating.
- Subtextual conflict: John seeks to heal his own insecurity by "saving" Carol; Carol seeks rules and safety, finding John's rule-breaking terrifying rather than liberating.

I asked the model, this time Gemini Pro 3, to review the analysis so far and use it to understand Act 1 of the play. Next, I asked it to use the following prompt to analyze the liminal dimensions of the act.

PROMPT 13.2

Read my analysis of Act 1 of the play *Oleanna* by David Mamet.

Next, apply the following prompt:

Step 1:

Read Chapter 7 as a theoretical background for your analysis (attached).

Apply the prompt titled: "Subtext Identification and Analysis Prompt" (attached) to interpret the conversation between John and Carol in Act 1 of the attached play.

Step 2:

Use the output from step 1 to identify the conversation's inward significance, focusing on boundary transgression. Inward significance is the aesthetic/dramatic experience the scene evokes in the audience.

Avoid clichés, and focus on the way in which the explicit dialogue and the IMPLICIT subtext evoke the dramatic effect and INWARD SIGNIFICANCE of the scene.

The model generated the following output:

MODEL'S OUTPUT 13.3

Step 1: *Subtext identification and analysis*

Dialogue Source: *Oleanna*, Act 1 (John and Carol in John's office). Context: John, a professor expecting tenure and buying a house, attempts to "help" Carol, a failing student who claims she cannot understand his course. The interaction shifts from an administrative to a personal level.

Absence (Presence through Non-Presence)

- Detected? Yes
- Key cues observed:
  - Structuring absence (phantom center): The "rules" or "criteria" for grading are conspicuously missing. John dismisses the syllabus and tests as "garbage" and "hazing," leaving a void where institutional standards should be.
  - Suppressed response: Genuine intellectual comprehension is absent in Carol. She repeatedly states, "I don't understand," yet John never actually explains the material; he explains *himself*. The "teaching" is absent, replaced by posturing.
- *Subtextual analysis*:
  - The absence of clear pedagogical standards transforms the office from a place of learning into a place of arbitrary power. Because the "rules" are missing (dismissed by John), Carol is left without a map to navigate her failure. The void left by the absence of professional boundaries is filled by John's personal neuroses and "conditional benevolence." The "A" is not a grade based on presence; it is a grade based on the *absence* of academic rigor.

Liminal transition (Temporal/Emotional Shifts)

- Detected? Yes
- Key cues observed:
  - Rule reversal: The scene begins with a strict hierarchy (teacher/student) but pivots when John offers to start the whole course over. The rule in force changes from "earn your grade" to "trade your compliance for a grade."
  - Identity slippage: John slips from "professor" to "father/confessor." He tries to coax Carol from "student" to "disciple/confidante."
- *Subtextual analysis*:
  - The scene functions as a liminal trap. The "A" offer places the interaction in a suspended moral state—it is neither a

legitimate tutorial nor an explicit act of seduction, but something in-between. The subtext is the destabilization of reality: John believes he is liberating them from "artificial strictures," while the audience perceives a terrifying slide into corruption. The collapse of safety protocols marks the transition.

Border Zones (Friction Between Conflicting Realities)

- Detected? Yes
- Key cues observed:
  - Contamination/Spillover: The private domestic sphere (the house purchase, calls from his wife) constantly interrupts and "spills over" into the academic space. John's personal financial anxiety contaminates his professional patience.
  - Physical threshold/Bodily: The "Sshhhhh" sequence, where John physically touches Carol ("puts his arm around her shoulder").
- Subtextual analysis:
  - The office becomes a dangerous border zone where the public/professional meets the private/intimate. The "spillover" of John's personal life signals to Carol that the professional guardrails are down. When he touches her, he physically enacts the border transgression. The subtext here is invasion: the safe distance required for education has been breached by his need for emotional validation.

Silence/Emptiness/Void

- Detected? Yes
- Key cues observed:
  - Pauses with Purpose: The frequent interruptions (phone calls) create voids where Carol sits watching him, emphasizing her powerlessness and his distraction.
  - Silencing (The "Sshhhhh"): John repeatedly hushes her: "Sshhhhh. Sshhhhh. Let it go… I understand".
- *Subtextual analysis*:
  - This is not the silence of peace, but the silence of *erasure*. By saying "Sshhhhh" and claiming "I understand" when she is trying to voice her confusion, John creates a void where her subjectivity should be. He replaces her voice with his own interpretation of her feelings ("I think you're angry"). The silence forces Carol into the role of a "non-responsive presence," a vessel for his projection.

Step 2: *Inward significance and boundary transgression*

The *inward significance* is the audience's felt sense of danger—not just observing the events, but feeling the ground give way beneath the characters.

Based on the prompt analysis above and your original notes on psychological boundaries, here is the inward significance of Act 1:

1. *The vertigo of structurelessness* (Absence as Transgression)
   The inward significance of Act 1 is the terror of *formlessness.* Your analysis noted that boundaries "regulate what is 'me' and what is 'not me.'" In this scene, the "structuring absence" of academic rules evokes a specific anxiety in the audience: the feeling of being trapped in a game where the rules are being rewritten in real time by the person holding all the cards.
   - The Effect: When John dismisses the syllabus as "hazing" and offers the "A" as a "deal," the audience does not feel relief; they feel the nausea of corruption. We experience the transgression not as a violent break, but as a dissolution. The safety of the "student" role—which Carol clings to by taking notes—is stripped away, leaving her exposed to his whim.
2. *The uncanny valley of "help" (liminality as transgression)*
   The "liminal transition" detected in the prompt creates an aesthetic of coercive intimacy. John frames his transgression as "taking off the artificial stricture," presenting it as a moment of human connection.
   - The Effect: The audience experiences a cognitive dissonance (the "uncanny"). On the surface (text), John is a benevolent mentor offering a second chance. In the subtext (liminality), he is preying on a subordinate. The inward significance is the suffocation of gratitude: we feel how impossible it is for Carol to say "no" because the transgression is disguised as a gift. This aligns with your analysis of "conditional benevolence"—the proposed help is a trap.
3. *The invasion of the self (border zones as transgression)*
   The "border zone" analysis highlights the "contamination" of the professional space by John's private life and physical body.
   - The Effect: The audience feels a visceral *intrusion.* As John takes calls about his house and wife in front of Carol, we feel him forcing her into an unconsented intimacy—she becomes an unwilling witness to his domestic drama. When this culminates in physical touch and the "Sshhhhh," the inward significance is one of violation. The "Sshhhhh" is particularly chilling because it masquerades as comfort while acting as a gag. It evokes the feeling of "interpretive override": he is colonizing her internal state, telling her what she feels so that he can comfort himself.
4. *Conclusion: The aesthetic of collapse*
   The dramatic power of Act 1 lies in the collapse of the "third element." In a healthy educational relationship, the "third element" is the subject matter (the book, the course).

- Inward significance: The prompt analysis reveals that the subject matter is *absent* (dismissed as garbage). The *border* is dissolved. The *silence* is filled with John's ego.
- Final impact: The audience is left with the claustrophobic realization that there is no "class" anymore; there is only John's need and Carol's vulnerability. The scene evokes the dread of a "closed system" in which the powerful person's reality completely swallows the weaker person's—the ultimate transgression of psychological boundaries.

DISCUSSION

The analysis of *Oleanna* through the lens of boundary transgression and the four-dimensional framework exposes the terrifying fragility of the educational contract. What the model identifies as the "inward significance" of the scene is not merely the impropriety of a professor, but the *threat of formlessness*. When John dismisses the syllabus and the grading criteria as "garbage" or "hazing," he does not liberate Carol; he removes the only map she possesses to navigate the university's territory. Moreover, the core tragedy revealed by the prompt is the "evil of the righteous." John does not view himself as an aggressor; he views himself as a savior, a "maverick" breaking artificial strictures to forge a human connection. However, the subtextual analysis confirms that this benevolence is deeply pathological. By offering an "A" in exchange for private access, John engages in *a liminal transition—a rule reversal in which* the operating law shifts from merit to compliance. This creates a suppressed response in the subtext: Carol cannot refuse his "help" without consenting to her own failure. The "help" is a trap. The subtextual force here is the suffocation of gratitude; the student is forced to be grateful for a violation of her autonomy.

In a healthy pedagogical relationship, there is always a "third element"—the subject matter, the book, the objective criteria—that stands between teacher and student. The analysis of Act 1 shows that this third element is the play's structuring absence. Because John dismisses the material, there is no mediator between his ego and Carol's vulnerability. The border zone is breached not just by his physical touch, but by the "spillover" of his private anxieties—his house, his tenure, his wife—into the professional container. Ultimately, the "inward significance" evoked by this boundary collapse is the aesthetic of invasion. The audience experiences the scene not as a flirtation, but as a slow-motion collision. The silence that John imposes on Carol—the "Sshhhhh"—is the auditory marker of this erasure. He replaces her subjective reality with his own interpretation ("I think you're angry"), effectively trying to dominate her emotional state.

The violence that erupts at the end of the play is therefore not just a sudden deviation but the logical conclusion of the trajectory identified by the model: from boundary softening to boundary collapse. The physical beating is merely the externalization of the psychological battering that began the moment John decided that his need for validation was more important than the structural integrity of his role. In *Oleanna*, we see that, when the dams of professional boundaries collapse, the resulting flood is not one of liberation, but of total, catastrophic destruction.

The main points of the chapter are:

- The subtext is about a deep structural pathology regarding the transgression of psychological boundaries.
- A theoretical model is introduced to define boundaries as invisible rules regulating identity, responsibility, and power.
- The analysis identifies a specific process of boundary violation: *softening* (John's apologies), *blurring* (removing institutional strictures), *violation* (the offer of an "A" for private meetings), and finally *retaliation* and *collapse*.
- John's behavior is framed not as malicious predation but as "conditional benevolence." He believes he is a "maverick" helper, but the subtext shows that he is using Carol to heal his own narcissistic wounds ("imposter syndrome").

NOTE

1. https://en.wikipedia.org/wiki/The_Chair_(2021_TV_series)

REFERENCE

Mamet, D. (1992). *Oleanna*. Vintage Books.

14 Concluding Discussion
The Manifold of Meaning

ABSTRACT This concluding chapter synthesizes the book's central themes, revisiting the initial challenge of the "Royale with Cheese" scene from *Pulp Fiction* to illustrate the journey the reader has undertaken. It reframes the concept of *inward significance* through the metaphor of the *manifold of meaning*, arguing that while the global meaning of a work of art may be beyond full articulation, its local meaning can be rigorously mapped. Finally, it reaffirms the value of *third-mind hermeneutics*, not as a replacement for human intuition, but as a structured, dialogic partner that allows us to navigate the complexity of human interaction in film, drama, and everyday life.

CLOSING THE LOOP: THE ROYALE WITH CHEESE

I began this book by discussing a scene from *Pulp Fiction* where Jules and Vincent discuss the topping of French fries in Holland. I intentionally refrained from analyzing the subtext of this specific scene, leaving it as an open challenge to the reader. At the beginning of our journey, this small talk might have seemed merely a stylistic choice by Tarantino—a filler between moments of high tension and violence. However, after thirteen chapters that analyze scenes ranging from the absurdity of Pinter to the heartbreaking realism of Bergman, you are now equipped with the tools to revisit your understanding of small talk and its subtext. You might now better understand the *misalignment* between the characters' professional lethality and the mundane innocence of their topic. You can apply the *four-dimensional model* to identify the absence of the victim, they are on their way to kill, or the *border zone* they inhabit between the trivial and the fatal. You can observe the *misplaced intensity* with which Jules reacts to the idea of mayonnaise ("Uuccch!") and the way it contrasts with his moral indifference to human lives. I leave this analysis to you, because the aim of this book was never to provide a full protocol for exposing a subtext, but to introduce an approach to the subtext and some *methodologies* for exposing it. In this context, the challenge of the "Royale with Cheese" is no longer a riddle to be solved, but a landscape to be explored by an attentive observer working in concert with an AI.

This exploration is not limited to the ideas and prompts presented in the book. There are many other possible threads to follow. For instance, the concept of *intertextuality* (Becker, 2000) can be highly constructive in understanding the underlying meaning, or subtext. Intertextuality is "the shaping of a text's meaning by another text" (Wikipedia). Take, for example, an iconic scene from *Kill Bill* (dir. Quentin Tarantino 2004). The hero is sedated and placed in a wooden coffin, then buried under several feet of dirt in a remote graveyard in the desert. However, she

 DOI: 10.1201/9781042004485-18

miraculously escapes. The moment when she bursts out of her grave is the high point of the scene. It is a moment with deep religious connotations of resurrection. However, this is not the only interesting aspect of the scene. To those who love cinema, this scene recalls one from Sam Peckinpah's masterpiece, *Bring Me the Head of Alfredo Garcia* (dir. Sam Peckinpah 1974). You may not recall the scene from Peckinpah's movie, but if you have watched it, its representation may be stored in your mind and evoked by the scene from *Kill Bill*. The "callback" to the 1974 scene is not an explicit pointer to a similarity. If intertextuality prompts us to recall a scene, it is through the unconscious activation of an underlying, extremely complex network in our minds. It should therefore be no surprise that the inward significance of art in general and scenes in particular can be discussed using the highly complex models introduced by modern AI and LLMs.

INWARD SIGNIFICANCE AND THE NEURAL NETWORK

Throughout the book, I have used the term "inward significance" to describe the aesthetic experience of a scene—an experience that cannot be fully articulated or reduced to a simple representation. But if we cannot fully articulate it, does it exist? Moreover, if it exists, why is it so resistant to direct description?

To approach this question, I want to draw on a metaphor from the very technology employed throughout this book: the deep neural network (Starmer, 2025). In such a network, meaning is not stored in any single neuron or line of code. It *emerges* from the pattern of activation across a vast, high-dimensional web of connections. When a language model processes a text, it locates it within a multidimensional vector space—a geometry so complex that no human mind could visualize it directly. Yet this geometry is not arbitrary: it has structure, coherence, and the capacity to support extraordinary processes of "*under-standing*" through inference.

I want to suggest that something analogous holds for human aesthetic experience. When we watch masterpieces such as *White Wedding* (originally *Noce Blanche*, dir. Jean-Claude Brisseau 1989) or *Scarecrow* (dir. Jerry Schatzberg,1973), we cannot trivially project the experience into a simple representation. The aesthetic experience involves a holistic activation of our inner network—our memories, cultural codes, sensory experiences, and emotions—each modulating the others in ways that cannot be reduced to a simple representation without loss. This does not make the experience vague or subjective in a dismissive sense. It makes it *high-dimensional*: real, structured, and yet irreducible to any simple representation that we can intuitively grasp.

However, the impossibility of grasping the whole does not entail an inability to understand its parts. In mathematics and data science, this paradox is captured by the notion of a *manifold*.

A manifold is a topological space that is locally homeomorphic to Euclidean space, meaning that every point has a neighborhood that can be described by a coordinate system. However, manifolds do not generally admit a single, global coordinate system that covers the entire space. Instead, they are described by an atlas of overlapping local charts, each providing coordinates in a region, with consistent transition maps where charts overlap (Novikov & Fomenko, 1990). In this respect, while points on a manifold can always be given local coordinates, there is no canonical global coordinate system that would allow us to describe the position of every point in a single, unified framework.

Philosophers and psychoanalysts have long grappled with entities or dimensions of experience that resist full, direct conceptual capture, and have given these different names. Kant referred to the Ding an sich—the thing-in-itself; Charles Sanders Peirce spoke of the dynamical object; and Wilfred Bion designated it by the symbol O. These concepts differ in important respects, but each marks something that exists, exerts force, and yet eludes exhaustive representation. Similarly, while a point on a manifold is a well-defined mathematical object, its coordinate representation is not globally canonical—no single coordinate system covers the entire manifold. What we can say is that the immediate neighborhood of any point behaves locally like Euclidean space of the same dimension as the manifold (Novikov & Fomenko, 1990). We can thus approach any region of the manifold through its *local surroundings*, working within a familiar coordinate patch.

It is precisely through this process that an atlas becomes possible. An atlas does not map the manifold in its entirety; rather, it is composed of multiple overlapping charts—local patches—each offering a partial, perspectival representation. Meaning, I suggest, is structured similarly. The attempt to ingest holistic inward significance in one stroke is therefore bound to fail. Reducing the aesthetic experience to isolated points misses what gives it coherence and depth in the first place.

Consider, for example, the cinematic masterpiece *Straw Dogs* (dir. Sam Peckinpah 1971), which features two extraordinary performances by Dustin Hoffman and Susan George. The film's inward significance cannot be captured by thematic labels such as "an essay on human violence" or "male masculinity." These formulations function, at best, as local charts—useful but radically insufficient. The aesthetic value of the film is irreducible; it does not reside in any single theme or proposition. It can only be approached through a constellation of local patches of meaning—scenes, gestures, tensions, and silences—offered by the cinematic texts and subtexts. Together, these patches form an atlas that gestures toward the aesthetic experience without ever exhausting it.

MEANING IS ALWAYS LOCAL

Following this metaphor, we can argue that *meaning is always local*. Just as we can map a small patch of the earth onto a flat piece of paper, even though the earth is a sphere, we can map the local subtext of a specific scene—a "coffee" request, a "tickle," or a "milkshake"—onto the lower-dimensional plane of language and analysis. Now, you may better understand why I insisted on arguing that the aesthetic experience and the inward significance of a scene cannot be fully articulated. *We are forced to make do with the "shadows" on the wall of Plato's cave.* However, even in this limited context, there is a place for a much deeper understanding than we might have naively assumed. In this context, the methodologies presented in this book—pragmatics, liminality, and perspectives, to name a few—are tools for local mapping. They allow us to project the drama's high-dimensional, ineffable experience onto a structured, understandable plane. We identify the subtext (the local geometry) to point to the *inward significance* (the global topology). However, we cannot argue that there is a single subtext that fully articulates the scene's inward significance. We may never fully comprehend the global topology of *The Mirror* or *The Homecoming*, just as we cannot intuitively visualize a thousand-dimensional vector space. But through the structured analysis of local interactions, we gain a foothold. We experience the global through the local, and there are better ways to do it than others.

DISCUSSION: THE TRIALOGUE CONTINUES

In this book, I have proposed a shift from a solitary reading of texts to a *trialogue*: a conversation between the human mind, the text, and the artificial mind. This approach, which I have termed *third-mind hermeneutics*, offers us the three benefits I outlined in the introduction:

1. The Joy of discovery: We have seen how working with AI can be playful. Whether it is uncovering the "double bind" in *Portnoy's Complaint* or the "sacred–profane inversion" in *The Vortex*, the process is one of active, creative detection.
2. Pedagogical value: The structured prompts provided in each chapter transform vague intuitions into teachable methodologies. We can teach students not just *what* a subtext is, but *how* to find it.
3. Relevance to everyday life: The tools we used to analyze Elyot and Sybil's honeymoon or Alex Portnoy's mother are not limited to fiction. They are equally powerful for understanding the "dialogue of the deaf" in a political debate or the "misplaced intensity" in a family argument.

We must remember, however, that the AI is the cello, not the cellist. It requires our *attentive observation*, our theoretical guidance, and our critical reflection. It requires us to listen to the "faintest signs" before we prompt, and it is a limited tool prone to misunderstanding, failed analysis, and other problems. I presented detailed outputs of the AI, but they are far from perfect. Working with the machine, we learn that it is human, too human. Nevertheless, as we conclude, I invite you to use the tools this book provides. Watch a film, read a play, or listen to a conversation at the next table in a diner. Look for the absence, the silence, the misalignment. Read in-between the lines. The inward significance is waiting there, in the negative space, for you to notice it.

The main points of the chapter are:

- The "Royale with Cheese" scene remains an open challenge, inviting the reader to apply the methodologies of this book.
- Inward significance can be understood through the metaphor of a neural network or manifold: inward significance is a high-dimensional state that is experienced globally but analyzed locally.
- Meaning is local: We use analysis to map complex experiences onto understandable structures, even if the "global" meaning remains beyond full articulation.

- The third-mind hermeneutics approach (human-AI-text trialogue) empowers us to avoid overinterpretation while gaining structural insight.
- The ultimate goal is to enhance our ability to see patterns in art and life, moving from intuitive blindness to attentive understanding.

REFERENCES

Becker, A. L. (2000). *Beyond translation: Essays toward a modern philology.* University of Michigan Press.

Novikov, S. P., & Fomenko, A. T. (1990). *Basic elements of differential geometry and topology.* Kluwer Academic Publishers.

Starmer, J. (2025). *The StatQuest illustrated guide to neural networks and AI.* StatQuest.

Subject Index

Author Index

For Product Safety Concerns and Information please contact our EU representative GPSR@taylorandfrancis.com
Taylor & Francis Verlag GmbH, Kaufingerstraße 24, 80331 München, Germany

www.ingramcontent.com/pod-product-compliance
Ingram Content Group UK Ltd.
Pitfield, Milton Keynes, MK11 3LW, UK
UKHW011005180926
475701UK00004B/565

* 9 7 8 1 0 4 1 3 6 7 8 5 7 *